WHEREOF
ONE
CANNOT
SPEAK

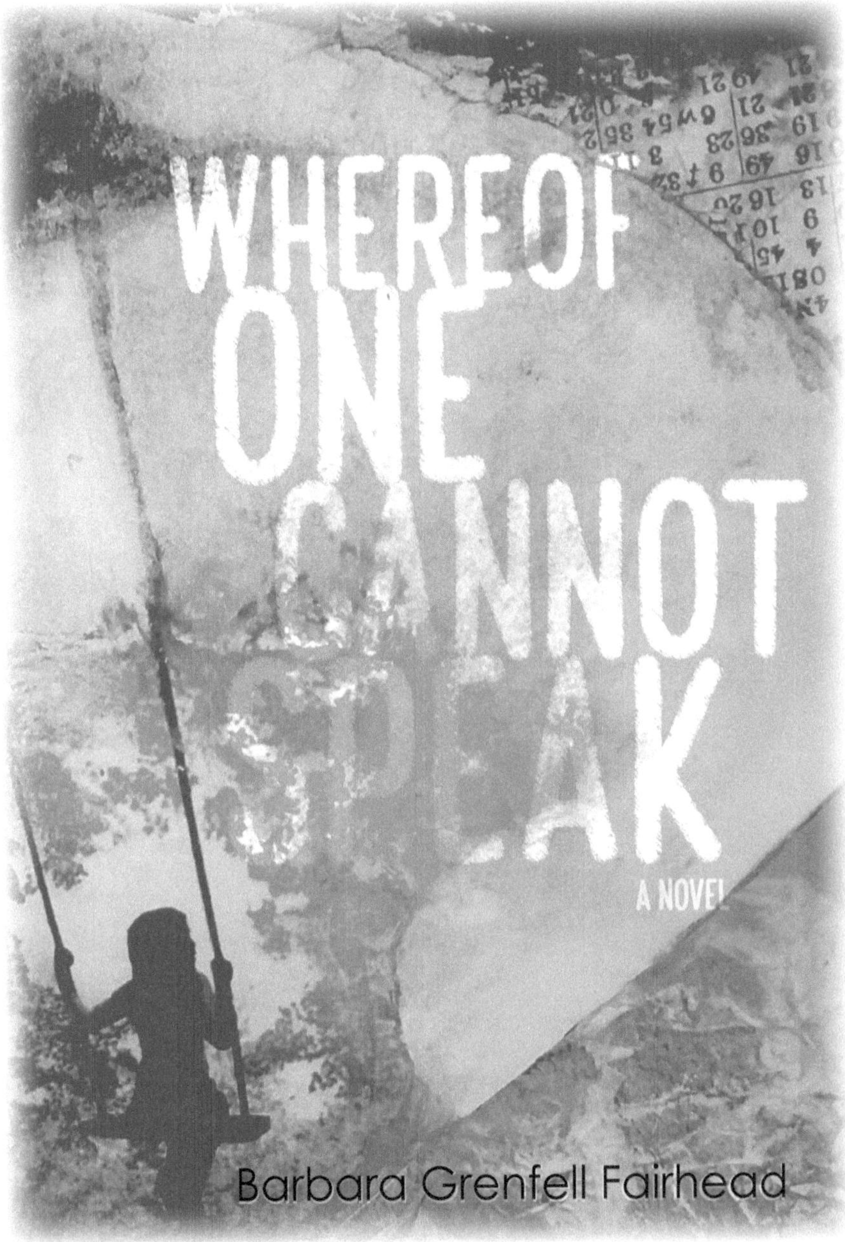

WHEREOF ONE CANNOT SPEAK

A NOVEL

Barbara Grenfell Fairhead

SUNSTONE
PRESS

SANTA FE

Sunstone books may be purchased for educational, business, or sales promotional use.
For information please write: Special Markets Department, Sunstone Press,
P.O. Box 2321, Santa Fe, New Mexico 87504-2321.
Printed on acid-free paper
∞
eBook 978-1-61139-527-3

Library of Congress Cataloging-in-Publication Data

Names: Fairhead, Barbara Grenfell, 1939- author.
Title: Whereof one cannot speak : a novel / by Barbara Grenfell Fairhead.
Description: Santa Fe : Sunstone Press, 2017.
Identifiers: LCCN 2017037043 (print) | LCCN 2017050976 (ebook) | ISBN
  9781611395273 | ISBN 9781632932013 (softcover : acid-free paper)
Subjects: LCSH: Self-actualization (Psychology) in women--Fiction. |
  Self-realization in women--Fiction. | Women artists--Fiction.
Classification: LCC PR9369.4.F35 (ebook) | LCC PR9369.4.F35 W48 2017
(print)
  | DDC 823/.92--dc23
LC record available at https://lccn.loc.gov/2017037043

SUNSTONE PRESS IS COMMITTED TO MINIMIZING OUR ENVIRONMENTAL IMPACT ON THE PLANET. THE PAPER USED IN THIS BOOK IS FROM RESPONSIBLY MANAGED FORESTS. OUR PRINTER HAS RECEIVED CHAIN OF CUSTODY (COC) CERTIFICATION FROM: THE FOREST STEWARDSHIP COUNCIL™ (FSC®), PROGRAMME FOR THE ENDORSEMENT OF FOREST CERTIFICATION™ (PEFC™), AND THE SUSTAINABLE FORESTRY INITIATIVE® (SFI®). THE FSC® COUNCIL IS A NON-PROFIT ORGANIZATION, PROMOTING THE ENVIRONMENTALLY APPROPRIATE, SOCIALLY BENEFICIAL AND ECONOMICALLY VIABLE MANAGEMENT OF THE WORLD'S FORESTS. FSC® CERTIFICATION IS RECOGNIZED INTERNATIONALLY AS A RIGOROUS ENVIRONMENTAL AND SOCIAL STANDARD FOR RESPONSIBLE FOREST MANAGEMENT.

WWW.SUNSTONEPRESS.COM
SUNSTONE PRESS / POST OFFICE BOX 2321 / SANTA FE, NM 87504-2321 /USA
(505) 988-4418 / ORDERS ONLY (800) 243-5644 / FAX (505) 988-1025

FOR JACQUES

Whereof one cannot speak, thereof one must be silent.

—Ludwig Wittgenstein

CONTENTS

ACKNOWLEDGEMENTS / 8

PART ONE
THE BLACK ROOM / 9

PART TWO
THE WHITE ROOM / 127

PART THREE
THE YELLOWING / 151

PART FOUR
THE RED ROOM / 319

EPILOGUE / 378

READERS GUIDE / 380

ACKNOWLEDGEMENTS

This book is the product of so many voices; so many people who have dedicated their lives—in whatever discipline they follow—to the fearless scrutiny of their own thoughts, words and deeds. It takes moral courage to examine the hidden motives behind the things we say and do; to expose our reluctance to admit to mistakes, our lies, our downright dishonesty and unkindness; and so arrive at more inclusive levels of conscious awareness.

I want to thank my husband, Jacques Coetzee, for the many late-night discussions we have enjoyed, unraveling the web of self-deception that protects us from knowing both the best and the worst of ourselves. I also want to thank him for his extraordinary editing skills. He has brought coherence to a book that was difficult to write. I feel incredibly fortunate to have such an impeccable editor.

I want to thank Trilby Krepelka for giving me permission to use a portion of her haunting artwork for the cover.

To Tamzon Woodley—my deep appreciation, as always, for the impeccable cover layout, and for the mysterious quality she has brought to the image.

My sincere thanks go to Sherry Woods who corrected all the errant formatting.

My thanks go to Mandy Dix-Peek, Robyn Cowie and Rodney Dart for all their support and encouragement in this enterprise.

My very sincere thanks to Tracey-Lee Shuttleworth, as well as Glenda and Thompson Katsande for picking up so many of the day-to-day demands, thus making it possible for me to close my study door and get on with it.

My gratitude goes to all at Sunstone Press in Santa Fe, New Mexico, USA, for publishing this book.

And, finally, to the unforgettable New Mexico landscape, the cultural richness of its people, and to all the generous and warm-hearted New Mexican friends I have made during my many visits—my heart-felt thanks.

—Barbara Grenfell Coetzee
2017

PART ONE
THE BLACK ROOM

Image I

The woman stands naked, regarding her image in the long mirror.

Her body glistens with the oil that she has just applied to it—sweet almond oil.

Her right hand moves across her breast. Touches her nipple. Draws a finger around the pink aureole.

Leaves it aroused.

She reaches up to adjust the angle of the overhead lamp. The bright, white light distorts the definition of her body, highlighting the breast, the curve of her waist and thigh; throws the rest into shadow.

She arches her back. Turns to the right; reaches for the pencil next to the easel. Begins to sketch the outline of the form; marks the areas of light and shade.

She crosses the room. Removes a mask from the wall. Holds it at arm's length and studies it: brushes the long, blonde hair off the face and watches as it slowly falls forward. She fastens it over her face, tucking away all of her long, black hair.

Slips into an over-size man's shirt. Leaves it unbuttoned.

Crosses the room. Stares at the image in the mirror. Traces the line of the brow with a finger. Kisses her fingers, and touches the mask's half-closed eyes. Makes a gesture as if to push the mass of corn-colored hair behind her ears.

She readjusts the light, and turns as if to embrace the figure that was standing in the space previously. Again checks the image in the mirror. Studies it minutely.

She leans forward. Her lips move into the mouth-space in the mask, and part as if to take the nipple into her mouth. Her right arm reaches down into shadow. The light enhances the long curve of her throat. In the mirror she studies every angle of the form; every place where the brightness of the light has written out the detail or cast it into shadow.

Turns back to the easel. Takes the pencil, and with deft strokes sketches in the second figure. Shades the dark areas. Thick, black pencil. Cross-hatched lines. Until the figures appear to emerge out of black shadow into startling brightness.

The image on the easel shows the erotic embrace of two figures, two lovers; half-exposed, half-hidden. One half of the man's face and his throat are in full light; his mouth open, reaching forward. The woman's head is thrown back and to the side. Her long hair falls away from her face, and hangs down straight, black and silent. An image made more striking by the sharp contrast of light and shadow; black and white.

She removes the mask. Takes a towel. Rubs the oil off her body. Reaches for a black silk gown. Slips it on. Ties the belt. Stands examining the two figures.

She crosses the room. Lights a cigarette.

Selects a record from the shelf: Puccini. Tosca. Moves to the record player. Selects the track: E Lucevan le Stele. Presses the repeat button.

"Lucien."

It is a whisper.

She turns off the lamp. Sits in the dark, allowing the music to enfold her.

Pages from Childhood

The small procession on the pink hill makes its slow way up the steep, zigzag path.

The pony, led by a young girl of about eleven, carries a boy who is tall for his fifteen years. On a cushion in front of him he holds a small child, olive-skinned with sleek black hair. Her face, with its high cheek-bones and black, almost oriental eyes, is distinctly different—foreign—when compared to those of the other two, who are both blue-eyed and very fair. The boy's hair, the color of ripe corn and cut long, falls over his eyes and face for all that he pushes it back and tries to fix it behind his ears. The young girl has the fair alabaster skin that goes with red hair, hair which today is dark with perspiration and tied back for the heat.

"We're nearly at the top, Lucien."

The young girl gives the pony a tug, and trudges up the final stretch of the narrow path to the place where the yuccas grow—just below the white cross.

The boy does not look up, but bends to whisper something to the child. She in turn claps her small, brown hands, and leans her body back against his chest—laughing.

The pony comes to a halt close to a large slab of basalt.

"Here we are, Octavia. Let me lift you down."

Two little brown arms reach out, and the small child is swung down to the ground.

"Luc'en!" The little girl pulls at the boy's jeans. "Luc'en come too! 'Fia! 'Tavi' want Luc'en. Luc'en must come sit!"

The boy is helped off the pony, and led to a smooth seat on the warm rock. The small child clambers up to sit beside him.

12

Sofia brushes her long red curls off her forehead, and reties the loose ribbon. Her face is flushed from the exertion of the climb.

"Tell me what you see, Octavia."

The boy waves a wide-sweeping hand.

While the small child chatters excitedly, pointing to all the things she has names for in the valley below them, Sofia loosens the girth, and ties the pony to a bush. She fastens the nose-bag to the bridle, and gives him a pat.

"Who is ready for tea? We have your favorite sandwiches, Octavia."

From the saddle-bag Sofia removes the small basket that Georgia—Lucien and Octavia's mother—has packed for them; fruit juice and sandwiches for their tea. She brings this over to the rock, and sits down next to Lucien.

He reaches out to find her, and puts an arm around her shoulders.

"Thanks for bringing us all this way."

She gives his hand a squeeze.

□□□

It was a warm spring morning, and Lucien was home for the Easter break. Because of the distance, he was a weekly boarder at the school for the visually hand-icapped in Alamogordo, where he would graduate in three years' time and proceed to college. He was a brilliant pupil and, in spite of his blindness, he would easily adapt to a mainstream curriculum. He wanted to study piano and music theory. He had been writing songs since the age of eight. Music was his passion—and song-writing in particular.

"They're back! Lucien and Sebastián are back!"

Sofia came running to where Georgia was working in her studio.

"Thanks for calling me, Sofia. I'll just tidy up and join you at the house."

The Adobe, where they lived, was a small-holding in the country, outside Las Madres. It was run by the owner, Sebastián Chavez, his wife, Georgia, and a group of nuns. Originally it offered a small school for local children, and a clinic. Over the years, as more people came to live and work in the area, it evolved to include an art and music center.

Salvador, Sofia's father, was teaching Lucien to play both the piano and the violin. Lucien had already written several songs for Sofia, whose voice, for all her youth, was legendary. They had given a few small concerts in Las Madres, the nearby town, where they were well received.

□□□

The journey up the zigzag path of the pink hill was Octavia's first pony ride, and it was the first time she would see the whole valley from such a height.

"'Tavi' want juice!"

Sofia rummaged in the basket for the small cup, while the young child kicked her legs with impatience.

"Juice! 'Tavi' want—"

The child took the cup in both hands, and drank noisily.

□□□

Sofia sat looking down at the valley. She had known this place all her life, and yet it never failed to fill her with joy. She remembered the first day when Lucien arrived with his mother and au pair, Matilde, from Paris.

She had never met anyone who was blind, and she wasn't sure how he would manage the rough paths.

"How do you walk around when you can't see?" she asked. "And I must warn you, these paths are all bumpy."

"I take someone's arm, and I can feel where they are going; and I don't worry about bumps. I just pick my feet up a bit and step over them."

So Lucien had taken her arm with confidence, and she had shown him around The Adobe, telling him all the things that she saw: the pink hills, the cottonwoods—which were getting their new foliage now—the fields of lavender and chili, the herb garden, the ponies, and of course the aviary and the white doves.

"Now it's your turn, Lucien. What do you see if you can't see?"

She gave a smile, remembering his reply; remembering so clearly the way he stood—so still—his hands reaching out and making little movements, as if he was feeling the landscape through the tips of his fingers.

"I see happiness," he said.

And happiness was what filled the valley then. Sofia had never seen Sebastián so full of joy—and in love: so full of love for Georgia, as if someone had lit a lamp inside him. And of course someone had!

The days flew by. Sebastián and Georgia were married by Father Rafael in the chapel, which had been built many decades earlier by the Penitente Brotherhood.

They had a small reception in the concert hall, where Lucien gave the speech for the bride and groom.

"...and when I listen to my beautiful maman, I think it is no surprise that Sebastián has fallen in love with her. I want everyone to raise their glasses and drink a toast to Sebastián and Georgia, and to wish them happiness!"

The musicians played La Vie en Rose for the bride and groom's first dance, and then Lucien asked Matilde if she would join him on the dance-floor where, accompanied by much applause, they gave a demonstration of the dance steps they had learned together in Paris; one of the many skills Matilde had introduced into the young boy's life.

Sofia remembered it as a day of joy and laughter; a day of happiness. The next day the couple left for a honeymoon in Mexico.

It was such a short time ago. How things had changed.

Shadows from the Past

Sofia remembered such an exciting month; days spent in the Adobe concert hall with Lucien and Matilde; with her father and grandfather, Santiago; and with Reuben Mendoza, her father's music partner from years ago.

"How did you and my father meet?"

They were having tea under the cottonwood when Sofia asked Reuben the question.

"Purely by chance. I was in a huge transport vehicle, playing the bandoneon for the driver. Salvador happened to hear it, and he followed the music. The rest is history."

"Whatever were you doing in a transport vehicle, and why were you playing a bandoneon?"

Reuben told her the story.

"I heard some tango music when I was young, and I knew instantly that I would be a musician and learn how to play the bandoneon. My parents died when I was eighteen, so I decided to make my way to Buenos Aires and find a teacher. I spent three years there. I came back by cargo ship and train, and by catching lifts with the huge transport vans. I paid my way by playing tango to the drivers."

"Did you play tango music all the way from Buenos Aires to Santa Fe?"

"Yes—only it was Albuquerque."

Sofia looked at Reuben with admiration.

"Your father and I began performing tango evenings for audiences in Albuquerque. It was only later that we heard the truth about your mother—and you."

"I never saw my mother, but Sister Piadosa has told me all about her. She was very beautiful."

"And Salvador tells me that you look just like her."

It was some days later that Sofia asked if she could go with her father into Santa Fe. Salvador was going to buy new violin strings, and pick up some goods for Sister Piadosa's clinic.

They were passing through Española when Sofia turned to face Salvador with her eyes full of tears.

"Salvador," she said, "please will you tell me all about my mother—how you met; how old you were then; how you fell in love? I want to know everything. When I think of her, I want to have pictures in my mind; pictures of the two of you together. I know you loved her very much, but I want to feel that I was there with both of you; that we were—are a family."

Salvador looked at his daughter. For just a second he could have sworn that this was María sitting with him in the car; María with her extraordinary composure; María with the blue fire in her hair; he and María together, in love, and with everything ahead of them.

And yet he remembered writing a song for her; writing so feverishly that his father asked him what the hurry was.

"Look at you! You look a wreck. You don't eat; you don't sleep. Slow down."
"I can't, father. There is very little time."
"Little time? You are young. Your whole life is ahead of you."
"I can't explain it, father. I only know that there is very little time."

"What do you say we pull over and find somewhere to have coffee and cool drink?"

They pulled into the dirt yard of a little shop that had three tables and umbrellas under a tree. They ordered coffee and a milkshake and cookies.

"I met your mother when I was thirteen and she was nine. Her mother, Catherine, brought her to the church where my father taught the Sunday school choir. I used to play the organ for him. María was to join the choir, and as such she would be asked to sing a solo so that Santiago could know where to place her voice in the group."

"How did you feel when you first saw her?"

"I can't remember what I felt right then. It was when she began to sing the pigeons out of the eaves; sing with the same full, glorious voice that you have, that I fell head over heels in love with her. Whatever it was I felt, even then I knew it would be for all time."

Sofia looked down at her fingers.

"Did she feel the same way?"

"Well, we didn't talk about it then. I don't think we even put the feelings into those words. But when we were a few years older—yes; then we both knew that we would be together always."

"What happened?"

"Well, when María was almost sixteen and I was twenty, my father suggested I present a Las Madres Church Choir concert in Santa Fe. I wrote several choral works for it, and for the final item on the program I wrote a love duet where María and I— dressed as Romeo and Juliet—would sing the solos, with the choir singing a slow chant beneath our voices."

"It sounds magic! What happened next?"

"Everything! And it happened very fast. Her father was furious. He had some weird obsession about women—even young women—wearing their hair loose. Your mother's hair was just like yours, full of the same fire; the same blue sparks, and she was wearing it full and long for the concert. She was in a white, flowing dress. She looked so beautiful, I could hardly breathe."

It was Salvador's turn to look down.

Sofia touched her father's hand.

"We don't have to talk about this now."

"But I would like to. I too would like to hold us all as a family." He gave her hand a squeeze. "Shall I go on?"

Sofia nodded.

"I must tell you a bit about her father, Lorenzo de la Cruz. He was a man who had to be right—all the time. And he insisted on being obeyed in all things. And he was a cruel man; cruel to people who were, to his way of thinking, inferior to him. Cruel to his wife—and cruel to animals. I only met him a few times, but that was enough to see that he thought about others only as far as they were useful to him. It is possible that he worshipped María—or rather, his idea of her—but he certainly did not love her. He thought only of himself.

"María said that the day after the concert he stormed about the house, yelling at his wife—what did she think she was doing? He referred to me as a young man with no means, and the son of a common little piano teacher; he said that María would not go back to choir lessons. She would not meet me or my father again. She could forget about the singing.

"He thought it was common for his daughter, a well-bred young woman, to sing in public."

"What does common mean?"

"The way he meant it—she was making herself cheap: nice people didn't do such things."

"But this was a church. Everyone sings in church."

Salvador looked at his daughter.

"That wasn't the real reason for his anger. It wasn't really about hair or singing. He was jealous—perhaps of her singing; most probably because he saw that his daughter had a boyfriend. He wanted to have María all to himself. He wanted to have control over everything she did."

Sofia frowned.

"Did you know that your grandmother, Catherine, had the same exceptional voice?"

Sofia shook her head.

"And the same hair," he added.

"He stopped her singing as well. He was jealous of her success and the attention it brought her, so he stopped it. He demanded absolute obedience. When he married her she was very young, and he was a bully. She did what he told her to. What else could she do? She too was never allowed in public with her hair loose. He said only cheap women wore their hair that way."

17

"What a horrible man. What happened next?"

"Lorenzo, without consulting María, chose the man that she would marry—a young man who would live and work at the rancho in a house that he, Lorenzo, would have built for them, and do what he was told. This way he would be able to control María. He organized an engagement party, a huge affair to coincide with her sixteenth birthday—a band, dance-floor, special supper, champagne, the works—and hundreds of influential guests."

"What did you do?"

"We made plans to elope—and we did! Everyone was so busy doing this and that, that nobody missed María. They all thought she was getting dressed. I came to her window to call her. I was dressed like one of the band members so no one would pay any attention to me. We moved unseen down an arroyo close to the house, which led to the road where I had parked the car. I borrowed it from a friend for our departure—a bright, lime-green lowrider. It was painted with garlands of roses, Jesus on the hood, and the Virgin of Guadaloupe bringing up the rear—not exactly a discreet car for the purpose!"

Sofia chuckled.

"And where did you get married?"

"We drove to Alejandro's house—he is a justice of the peace; that means he can marry people—and he married us in two services; a civil service—which means that we were legally married—and then in a religious service that people of the Catholic faith used in the old days, when they lived far out and had a priest visit them only once a year."

"What did mama look like? Was she beautiful?"

"She took my breath away."

Sofia saw his eyes moisten.

"She looked so lovely; like some fairy princess who stepped out of a picture book. She wore the wedding dress that she had been stitching and embroidering for her trousseau, and the most beautiful veil with tiny beads that shone, stitched onto it."

Salvador smiled at the memory.

"I, of course, was wearing a very dashing mariachi band costume and a large sombrero. We were quite a sight. It was full moon—so romantic. As we drove through all the little villages, people came out and waved and called out blessings. I will always be grateful that we had the wonder of that evening."

Salvador was quiet.

Sofia waited.

"Her father caught up with us on the Interstate. We were going slowly because of the limitations of the car. He ran us off the road, grabbed María and was gone."

"Did you go after her?"

"Not then. She was under age. He might have tried to annul—cancel the marriage if he found out."

Salvador shook his head.

"No, I didn't see her again until the evening before her twenty-first birthday—just before midnight. The house was quiet. She knew I would come for her, and she was waiting. We fell into each other's arms. It was like a delayed honeymoon."

"And did you both leave then? Did you run away together?"

"No. Her father was still awake, and we hadn't seen the light in his study. He came charging in, holding a hunting-knife. He said if I didn't leave he would kill María.

"There was a fight. I tried to argue. I asked María to come with me, but she shook her head.

"'He means what he says, Salvador. Go! Go!'

"That was the last time I saw her. I think you know the rest."

"She was sent to The Adobe?"

"Yes. But I didn't know that then. I tried all the ways I knew how to find her, but I couldn't. No one was talking. I think they were too afraid of what he might do to them. I did hear that de la Cruz was looking for me, so I changed my name and moved to a small house outside Albuquerque."

"What did you do while you were there?"

"I made violins and sold them."

"You made them?"

"Yes. I was taught how to do this by Alejandro when I was a boy. It was from there, while I was sitting outside one evening, that I heard this amazing music. It was coming from the cab of a huge transport vehicle. I jumped into my car and followed it. That is how I met Reuben."

"So how did you finally learn where my mother was taken?"

Salvador looked away. He remembered the evening so vividly.

"It was during a concert we were giving in Santa Fe. I was concerned about performing so close to home, so for the show I wore a clown mask with one tear on the cheek. As it happened, my father was in the audience. He had been unable to find me because of my changed name—Angelo María Mestas—and was surprised to learn that this name in the program was me."

"How did he know it was you if you had the mask?"

"He and Alejandro, who was with him, both knew as soon as I began to play. They recognized the violin."

"Did you make that one too?"

"Yes, I did. Anyway, during the interval he came backstage. It was an emotional meeting. You can imagine. He told me that María had died, and that I had a daughter. That I would find you—Sofia—at the place called The Adobe.

"After the interval, and before the second half of the performance, I came on stage in front of the curtain, my mask and violin in my hand. It would not matter who recognized me now.

19

"I dedicated the concert to my wife: María Teresa de la Cruz Fuentes."

Sofia had tears in her eyes.

"That was my mother's full name?"

"Yes."

She repeated it softly.

He waited before continuing.

"When the final curtain came down on the performance, I left all the packing-up arrangements to Reuben. I drove as fast as my car would go straight to The Adobe, where I woke Sister Piadosa by ringing the chapel bell.

"We sat up most of the night; she telling me the story from the time María arrived at The Adobe."

Sofia listened in silence. Her hands were clutched together. Her face was very white.

"It was a few weeks after her arrival at The Adobe that Sister Piadosa discovered that María was pregnant, and the whole story came out."

"I'm pregnant?"

Sister Piadosa nodded.

"How do you know?"

"You have all the signs, my dear. But surely you knew this. Wasn't this the reason your father brought you here?"

María took hold of the nun's arm.

"No. He brought me here because I refused to marry a man he chose for me. I didn't know I was pregnant, and there was no way he could have known either. Oh, sister, my father must never know of this."

María clung to the nun's arm.

"Please say you will keep this secret. If he comes here, you won't have to tell him, will you? He will take the child away from me."

María's face was deathly white, and she was shaking.

"He will take the baby away from me! He will ruin another life!"

Tears ran down her cheeks.

"Please, sister—promise me he will never take this baby away."

"There, hush, María. He need never know about this. We will find a way to manage everything, never fear."

"Manuel and Refugio were delighted to say that you were one of their twins. Refugio loves children—as you know—and you would be very close to The Adobe. The one slight problem was that you and Pedro-Manuel could not have looked more different."

"They don't look like twins to me," remarked a woman from the community.

20

"Where do those blue eyes come from—and that red hair?"

"Manuel has a great-grandmother who is Italian," stuttered his blushing wife.

"The little girl looks just like her."

"Italian! Red hair! How very strange."

"I heard how your mother defied the bigoted French priest, Father Jean-Luc Sel. She refused to make her confession to him. Sister Piadosa said he was beside himself with anger. He was very full of himself, she said. He was arrogant. No one liked him; in fact, she told me that many people stopped going to church because of it."

"I watched the furious priest stamp his way along the infirmary corridor, hitting his prayer-book vehemently against his hand, and I hurried to María's room.

"'He says I will burn in hell,' María said through her tears. 'He says I am wicked, and that God will turn away from me, and my soul will be lost for all time because I would not let him hear my confession.'

"'My dear, he is a foolish man. What does he know? You are not going to hell; that is evil talk from a man who knows nothing about the love of God.'"

"So in the end she heard your mother's confession and blessed her. But there was nothing she could do to prevent the priest from branding María as a heretic. He refused to allow her to be buried in the small graveyard. She was buried a short distance away, close to the old cottonwood tree."

"I know the place. My swing is there. It is where I go to talk to mama sometimes."

Salvador smiled.

"Maybe—but only if you would like it—we could go together sometimes, and tell her how she is always with us; tell her how much we love her."

"Would it be our secret?"

"Our very special secret."

Sofia was silent for a while.

"Is that when you met me?"

"Yes. And I will never, ever forget that moment. You came walking to meet me, holding Sister Piadosa's hand. You were so beautiful; I couldn't take my eyes off you. I couldn't quite believe that you were my daughter. It seemed like a dream. I remember asking you if I could give you a hug. It must have been very strange for you to meet this man, who suddenly arrived out of the blue."

"Oh, no. Sister Piadosa told me when she dressed me that morning that I was a very lucky girl, because I had two fathers. Most people only have one. So I did sort of know something. And then when she said that you loved my mother, then I knew you were very special."

Sofia ran to her father and hugged him.

"I am so glad you found me," she said.

A Special Present

"Salvador," Sofia asked one morning while the honeymoon couple was still away, "do you think you and Reuben could compose a piece of music that would give Lucien an idea of what the white doves look like when they fly? Something like a picture in sound?"

"What were you thinking of exactly?"

"You know how they fly up high and then swoop down over the fields. And the way they turn, and almost disappear, until the light catches their wings again."

Sofia was dancing the flight pattern as she spoke.

"I have an idea for a celebration, and the doves would be part of it."

"And what is the celebration about?" he asked.

"You know, when Georgia and Lucien first came here it was around his tenth birthday, and somehow it got missed. So much was going on then. I think we should have a party and give him the music—the flight of the white doves—as a birthday present."

She looked up at her father.

"Can you make the music do that? I know Gregorio hasn't released them yet this morning. Perhaps we could all go and watch them fly—and listen."

They sat on a log, watching the doves push through the open door and lift themselves into the air in a rush of flapping wings.

Sofia took Lucien's hand.

"They always start like that, like an untidy crowd, but once they are all in the air it seems as if they have one mind."

"One mind?"

"Yes. It is as if they are all thinking the same flight pattern."

She thought for a bit.

"I suppose it would be like a band, all playing different parts of a song out of time with each other, and then they all come together in harmony in the same piece of music, and then you hear the song. That is what I mean by one mind."

The doves were flying over the fields, a fluid wave, about to turn to clear the cottonwoods.

"There," whispered Sofia, "do you see that, Salvador? They are there, and then they aren't. And then the light catches up with them and we see them again. Lucien cannot see or hear that."

Her cheeks were pink with excitement and the beauty of the white doves, and the vast blue sky. And then the doves flew down low over their heads again.

Sofia touched Lucien's arm.

"And here they are back again. Listen to that rushing sound. Do you hear that, Lucien?"

"Yes," he said, "it is like the wind in the trees."

"Will everyone find a seat? Lucien, would you sit here?" Salvador showed him to a chair. "And pull it forward a bit so that you are close to the platform. We will be playing almost above you. We are, of course, the white doves this morning."

Sister Piadosa and Sister Ana, who had been invited by Sofia to attend A Concert for the White Doves, sat quietly, waiting to learn what the concert was all about. They knew about the tea party, and had prepared it in readiness for the birthday. It was to be a surprise.

"So, would everyone put on a mask and make sure you cannot see anything."

There were small eye-masks made of black cloth on all the chairs; one for each person except Lucien.

Santiago, Salvador's father, had come to listen to the music. He sat quietly on the stage, his eyes on Lucien.

That night, when Alejandro, his friend since their school days, came to visit him, he described the short concert, and in particular Lucien's face.

"It would have brought tears to your eyes, Alejandro. It did to mine. I have never seen such a sensitive, wistful play of emotion—so deeply felt—move over a face before; not like this.

"The music was very lovely. It did justice to the flight of the doves. But then, we knew what the music was saying. But what did it convey to Lucien?"

Alejandro shook his head.

"Have you ever thought about what it must be like to be blind? Blind from birth?"

"I can't begin to imagine it."

"I asked him what he felt about the music. He was obviously very moved by it. He told me that he doesn't think in images."

"So how does he relate to an image?"

"Well, unless someone speaks about it, or it makes some kind of sound that suggests the image, or he can touch it—for him, it has no meaning; no reality; it doesn't exist."

"You mean he has to take it on faith that it is there at all?"

"Exactly," Santiago said. "You should suggest that to Father Rafael. He might put it into a sermon."

Santiago laughed.

"So what did he say about the sound of the doves—and the music?"

"He said he would compose something, and play his response."

"How very remarkable."

"Indeed."

□□□

Sofia gathered her thoughts. Octavia was getting restless. She packed the small picnic basket back into the saddle-bag together with the pony's nosebag, in preparation for their return trip down the hill; then paused to gaze one last time, out over the valley she loved.

What had happened to change everything?

She cast her mind back, trying to remember when she first felt that something had changed: that life was not quite as happy as it had been. It was the first time she realized that things were not as simple as she imagined them to be. She felt—uneasy? About what, she was unable to say.

The Birth of Octavia

"Sister! Sister Piadosa!"

Sebastián came running down the path to the clinic where the sister worked during the week-day mornings.

A nun's head looked out of the doorway of the small adobe building.

"It's Georgia! I think the labor has started."

The sister turned to the nun who was assisting her.

"Sister Ana, I'm sure you can manage the rest of the morning. When you are finished here, come and help me in the birthing-room."

With these words she followed the anxious Sebastián to his casita.

Georgia sat in a chair in the bedroom, bent over a cramp. The sister put a comforting hand on her shoulder.

"There we are," she said. "We'll soon have you comfortable. How far apart are the pains?"

"I think about half an hour." Georgia's lips were white.

Sister Piadosa turned to Sebastián.

24

"Can you arrange for Lucien to spend the night with Salvador? I will take Georgia across to the ward, and you can come when you are ready."

Sebastián bent to kiss his wife. "I won't be a minute. I will be there soon. Soon!"

Georgia managed to flash him a smile before the next pain had her bending forward again.

The late afternoon sun was shining through the west window into the little room where Georgia lay, breathing her way through the pains. All the windows were open, for the day had been hot and the heat still hung in the valley. The overhead fan made a soft click and whirr as it turned, bringing a little relief to her labor.

Sebastián sat beside her, rubbing her back and talking encouragingly.

"Nearly there. Nearly there." His voice was calm, but he gave Sister Piadosa an anxious glance. The waters had not broken. He wasn't sure of the significance of this; only that it had to happen. If only it would happen soon.

Sister Piadosa offered Georgia a sip of some herbal drink. "This will help." She gave Sebastián the cup to hold, and bent to sponge Georgia's face.

An hour passed. Sebastián looked at Sister Piadosa's calm face, and felt reassured.

He bent again to continue rubbing her back.

"You are wonderful," he said as he massaged her back, over and over. "Am I doing this right?"

For an answer, Georgia gave a sudden, heaving groan as the waters broke.

While Sister Ana busied herself with making the bed fresh, Sister Piadosa prepared for the delivery.

He sat beside his wife, talking to her while the nuns were busy. His face was very white. He had never witnessed a birth before, and he was shocked by the physicality of it. Why did women ever have more than one child?

His thoughts were interrupted as a sudden contraction gripped Georgia.

"Now—there we go," said Sister Piadosa. "Push!"

Georgia pushed.

When the contraction passed, the nuns sponged her face and arms. But there was little respite.

"Let your body guide you, Georgia. Wait for the contraction. There now! Push!"

Georgia heaved and strained and pushed.

The contractions were coming fast now. Sebastián was amazed by the sheer exertion that was required. He felt exhausted just watching, as Georgia strained with all her might.

"Nearly there," said Sister Piadosa. "One more—push! Good girl. You're doing fine."

Georgia pushed.

Another hour passed.

Sebastián was surprised when Sister Ana switched on the light. He looked at his watch. Georgia had been in labor for almost ten hours. He looked anxiously at Sister Piadosa, but she was focused on Georgia, giving her constant encouragement.

"Nearly there—very nearly there."

The tiny head had crowned perfectly. The nun was guiding it carefully.

"Wait, Georgia: don't push now. Let your body do the work. I'll tell you when to push."

Sebastián watched anxiously.

"Now. One more push will do it."

He could see the dark head. And then a shoulder. And then, with a rush, the baby slid out into Sister Piadosa's hands.

She lifted the little form, and placed a soft birthing-blanket loosely around it for warmth. Gently she placed the infant on Georgia's belly.

Sebastián felt a rush of tears. This little being was his child—their child. He looked in wonder at this tiny miracle—the perfection of each feature; the tiny, shell-like ears, the little fingers. He marveled at the peace in the face of this small being who had just come through such an arduous transition.

"She is so beautiful," he whispered. He bent to kiss his wife. "She is beautiful," he whispered again.

"You have a little girl, Georgia," said Sister Piadosa.

Georgia was too exhausted to raise her head, but she gave a smile.

Sister Piadosa waited until the pulse in the umbilical cord had completely stopped before tying and cutting it.

A loud wail filled the room as Sister Piadosa wrapped the baby up again and placed her in the crook of Georgia's left arm. She rearranged the pillows so that Georgia could look at her daughter.

ooo

"Octavia is crying, maman!"

Lucien bent over the crib and felt for a small hand. Held it gently. He sang a little French nursery rhyme, very softly. The baby stopped crying and looked at him.

Georgia came into the room, carrying a sun-warmed towel.

"It is time for her bath and a feed. Matilde has gone into Las Madres with Sebastián. Do you want to stay and help?"

Lucien nodded. He crossed the small nursery and found the baby's bath, which he took down the passage. In the bathroom he ran some warm water, testing the temperature with his elbow the way Sister Piadosa had shown him.

Octavia was crying again. Loud wails. Georgia helped Lucien to place the bath correctly. The infant was wrapped in the towel, and kicking. Her wails grew louder.

Georgia washed and dried the furious little face. How strange and flat it looked. She washed the black hair, and held the baby sideways over the bath to rinse off the shampoo; dried the hair with the corner of the towel, and placed Octavia back on the work-table. She opened the towel and soaped the frantic infant. Octavia was yelling now. Her eyes were screwed up. Her face was scarlet.

"Can I hold her in the bath, maman?"

"Yes, of course." Georgia's voice was tight.

Lucien lifted his little sister the way Sister Piadosa had shown him: a firm grip on one soapy leg and his wrist under her head and neck, his hand grasping one arm close to the armpit. Slowly he lowered her into the warm water.

Octavia stopped crying. Her lips were quivering, and she gulped some tremulous indrawn breaths. She squinted up at the face bending over her. Lucien let go of her leg and swished water over the small, brown body. Octavia gurgled. Her legs kicked and splashed.

"You like the water, don't you, Octavia?" He moved the infant up and down the bath so that the water could rinse off all the soap. He let her kick some more until she relaxed in the warm water, enjoying the feel of it washing over her.

"Is the towel ready, maman?"

"Right here, Lucien."

Georgia helped to guide his hand to the towel. She wrapped the baby in the towel, and picked her up to cuddle her for a moment.

Octavia began to wail again.

"If you like, maman, I will finish drying and dressing her if you just put the clothes out and the nappy ready."

Lucien did not see the tears in his mother's eyes, but he could feel her distress.

"That would be nice," she managed to say. "I'll go and warm her bottle."

Lucien wrapped the towel warmly around the infant, and held her up close to his left shoulder. Sister Piadosa had shown him how to do this so that the infant would hear his heartbeat.

"She has been listening to that sound for nine months, Lucien. Most babies are soothed by that beat. You'll see how it settles her."

Octavia had flatly refused to be breastfed. Sister Piadosa consoled a frantic Georgia, telling her that it was not unusual; some babies were just like that. She helped Georgia prepare the feed, showing her how much the small infant would probably need at first.

"When she is a little settled, we will try her with the breast again."

But it was quite clear that Octavia would not accept the breast.

"I don't think she likes me," Georgia said with a sob.

"Nonsense, my dear. She will settle soon. You'll see. All babies are different."

But as time went on, nothing improved between Georgia and her daughter. Sebastián was distressed to see his wife growing more and more withdrawn. He spoke to Sister Piadosa, who suggested that Georgia might be suffering from post-partum depression. A doctor was consulted and medication was recommended. It helped a little for Georgia to cope with Octavia, but it made no difference to Octavia's rages whenever her mother handled her.

Finally, in tears, Georgia confided in Sister Piadosa.

"She doesn't like me. And when I look at that ugly, flat little face, those slanting eyes and that dark skin, that black hair, I don't know where she came from. It feels as if she doesn't belong to me."

"Georgia, my dear, your daughter is going to be a beauty one day. You'll see. I think she will take after her grandmother, Magdalena. I never met Sebastián's mother, but by all accounts she was the most beautiful woman Las Madres has ever seen. Her father's family came originally from South America, so it is not surprising to see these genes making an appearance once more. But I can understand what it must feel like to have given birth to two such very different children."

She paused to consider.

"But just look at Lucien. I think he would die for her. Such a bond they have. Something wonderful has happened in him."

"Yes, sister. They have bonded so easily. Why can't I? I must be a terrible person. I want to love her, but I can't feel it. She won't let me near her."

"Give it time, my dear. You are going to be so proud of her one day. And she is going to love you."

A Parting

"Have you got your passport?"

"Oui. Ici." Matilde nodded.

"And you know you must claim and re-check your baggage for your final flight?"

"Oui."

"I am going to miss you, Matilde!—so much. I miss you already. You have done so much for me. In Paris, you were the one person who stood by me through all those difficult and painful years. How can I ever thank you? How am I ever going to get used to your being gone?"

Georgia flung her arms around the young woman, and burst into tears.

Georgia and Matilde met in Paris. Georgia had won a scholarship to go there and study under the well-known art teacher, Professor Henri le Noire. In Paris she became his protégée. He promoted her work; organized what turned out to be a well-attended and financially rewarding exhibition. He wined and dined her, and introduced her to influential luminaries of the art world. She was hugely flattered by the attentions of the great man.

Matilde was an artist's model. She earned money by posing for life-drawing classes, and she often had difficulty making her rent payments, especially during college vacations.

It was when Georgia became pregnant, and was subsequently dropped from the professor's classes, that she woke up, too late, to the realities of the world she was living in. She did on one occasion meet the new girl—the professor's latest conquest—a beautiful and extremely gifted artist from Jamaica. Georgia warned her of the pitfalls, but it appeared that the young woman was far more worldly and able to look after herself than she had ever been.

Matilde moved in to share the tiny flat that Georgia was renting. In return for not having to pay rent, she helped her through the pregnancy, the birth, the traumatic discovery of Lucien's blindness, and the years that followed. Daily she attended a special clinic for sight-impaired and blind infants. It was Matilde who taught the young boy how to find his way around the apartment, first crawling on his hands and knees and later walking. She took him to a special pre-school where he learned how to clap a rhythm, how to move to music, make pictures, fit blocks into especially shaped spaces. She took him for riding lessons to a place that had retired ponies, selected for their even temperament. Finally he attended a school for the blind where, in addition to his other lessons, he learned to read and type Braille and walk with a cane.

Without Matilde, Georgia would not have managed those ten difficult years. Her parents, disappointed, and feeling that she had thrown away all the opportunities that had been given to her, sent some money and told her to get on with it.

At the end of ten years, by working hard and selling her work, Georgia managed to save enough money for the three fares back to the US. She had no idea what she would do when she got there, but at least she would be on home ground. Matilde said that she would stay and help her until Georgia was settled.

On arrival in Albuquerque, Georgia swallowed her pride and sent Sebastián a telegram with her phone number, saying that if he didn't want to see her she would understand. She was well aware that he might still be angry, especially after the way she had upped and gone off, leaving him just as they were on their way, with two friends, to Mexico. They had just become lovers, which had been a big step for both of them, so her abrupt departure had left him devastated. Now she didn't even know if he was single—or married. All she knew was that she wanted to see him.

In response to her telegram he had come immediately to Albuquerque, and they all went back with him to The Adobe. She and Sebastián were married a few months later.

Matilde stayed until after Octavia's birth, and then, homesick for her country, decided to return to France.

"If you ever get tired of Paris, you have only to say—'I'm coming back', and we will have your room ready."

Georgia wiped away her tears.

"What will you do when you get back? Do you have any plans?"

Matilde shook her head.

Georgia took a note out of her bag.

"Sebastián has put some funds into your Paris account. It is a hopelessly inadequate thank you for all that you have given us. This is a copy of the money transfer in case you need to offer proof. And if there is any problem at all, they must contact us. You have all our details."

"You do not 'ave to—"

"It has nothing to do with have to. You have been mother, sister and friend to me, and possibly the most significant person Lucien will ever have in his life. It is all thanks to you that he is where he is today. And I where I am too. And remember, if you are ever in difficulty—of any kind—we will come to Paris, if necessary, to do whatever needs to be done."

Matilde was struggling not to cry.

"I will remember what you say, Georgia. And I will write and tell you 'ow I am doing. I am going to miss you too—et mon bébé aussi. Maybe too much! Maybe I will 'ave to come back."

She bent down to hug Lucien.

"You won't forget me? Non?"

"Never. And I have a present for you. Santiago helped me to write it down."

Matilde opened the large folder. Inside was music manuscript paper with music printed on it.

"When you get to Paris, you must find a musician to play this for you. This is a song I have written for you. It is only for you!"

Lucien clung to her.

"When I am big, Matilde, I will come to Paris. And I will take you shopping in the Champs Elysées. And—and I will buy you beautiful dresses. And I will hire a boat. And we will go down the Seine. And I will take you out to dinner and give you roses."

He hugged her tightly.

"And I will play you this song, and sing it to you."

He wiped away his tears.

"Oh, Matilde. I won't ever forget you. Jamais!"

Matilde's flight was announced. She gave Georgia and Lucien one last embrace. Picked up her hand luggage and walked to the security check. Once through, she turned and blew a kiss. Then she was gone.

Lucien was trying his best not to cry.

"Maman. Will we see Matilde again?"

"I think we will. Maybe for a holiday. Maybe she will come and live here. We must wait and see."

Together they walked to their car. At the check-out, Lucien handed in the ticket and five dollars. And then they were on their way.

Neither of them spoke on the drive home.

What's in a Name?

Lucien's schooling had finally been arranged. He was to be a weekly boarder at the school for the blind in Alamogordo. Sebastián would take him through to the airport at Albuquerque early on Monday mornings, where he would put him on a plane for the short trip to Alamogordo. Although this meant that Lucien would have to get up very early, it also meant that Sebastián could then buy all the necessary weekly provisions, medical supplies, and feed for livestock in Albuquerque before going back to The Adobe. Lucien would fly back to Santa Fe on Friday afternoons, and he would fetch him from there. This arrangement provided an opportunity for the two of them to get to know each other.

"What did you do when you were a boy, Sebastián? Where did you grow up? What did your parents do—your mother; your father?"

Sebastián hesitated. Only then did he realize that neither of them had ever known their father.

"I grew up with my mother—Magdalena. She was a wonderful—an extraordinary woman. When I was small and still in school, we lived in a little town—not far from Las Madres—and she did dress-making. I had a dog called Amigo."

He didn't mention his other dog—an imaginary friend that only he was able to see.

"Then, when I finished school, we went to live in Las Madres where, of all things, she opened a salon."

"What kind of a salon?"

"It was a place where people—men, as it turned out—could come in the evening after work, and have a drink and relax. There was a piano, and sometimes Santiago would play, and some of the men would sing."

He gave a chuckle.

"I became a barman."

"A barman!"

"Yes. I became quite good at it."

"And your mother—?"

"Oh, she was wonderful and outrageous. She bought the property; an old house that had belonged to an eccentric santero—that is a carver and painter of religious works. It was full of paintings of the saints—on all the walls and on the ceilings. The women of Las Madres were appalled that she served drinks under the noses of the saints, but the men loved it. She was famous for her story-telling. The men worshipped her, I think. Only when I was older did I realize how exceptional she was."

"And your father? What did he think of this?"

"I never knew my father."

Sebastián was relieved that he could at last feel compassion for the man he had never met.

Lucien made a strange gesture with his hands.

"I also do not know my father," he said.

Sebastián waited.

"I believe he is an artist. He lives in Paris. But he never came to see me or my mother when we lived there."

Still Sebastián said nothing.

"I think—perhaps he was ashamed to have a blind son."

Sebastián stared at him. Of course he would think that. He remembered how ashamed and angry he had felt as a boy. And here he was, on the other side of the experience, and yet searching for the right words; searching for words that might be helpful.

"Did he ever ask about you?"

"I don't know. I don't think he ever saw my mother after I was born. I don't know when he left her."

"So maybe he knows nothing about you."

Lucien considered this.

"Maybe he doesn't know you are blind. Doesn't even know if you are a boy or a girl."

Lucien chewed a knuckle.

"Maybe his leaving has nothing to do with you."

"All the other boys and girls at my school had fathers—all of them."

Sebastián reached out and took Lucien's hand. He could feel the child's self-blame; that all of it was his fault. And he could feel that lonely emptiness. How well he knew it.

"Maybe we can share what we feel about our fathers—with each other. Just the two of us. I think we will understand each other very well."

He paused.

"And when—or if—you think you might like it, I would very much like to be

32

your father. I would love to have you as my son. I always hoped I would have a son one day."

Lucien's eyes brimmed with tears.

"Would I be your real son?"

"Yes. Absolutely!"

"Will I have your surname?"

Sebastián paused, remembering the account of his grandfather's obsession with horses, blood-lines and breeding—and of course the famous family name that, in the end, he had been offered on his grandfather's death-bed. When it was discovered that Magdalena was pregnant, his son, Antonio, had not been permitted to marry her, the daughter of his foreman, because she was of mixed blood; mestizo—and a servant girl into the bargain. It was the final concession the old man had made, in the face of having no other heir to carry on the Merejildo name, that it should go to his illegitimate grandson.

Sebastián still hadn't made any formal change to his documents. He didn't think he would. He was his mother's son. There was nothing to connect him to his father's family or the famous name—and certainly not to the famous tradition that had so impressed his paternal grandfather. No. Chavez was his name, and he would stick with it. He smiled when he considered how people, looking at the very fair, blonde, blue-eyed boy, would wonder at the name—Chavez.

"We will sit down with your mother and arrange everything."

Passion

Georgia stood in the large studio room that Sebastián had built for her. Through the skylight she could see the blue New Mexican sky that she loved. She was back in the place she had grown to love in her student days. It was only now that she was back, she thought, that she realized how much this landscape meant to her.

There was something tangible in the quality of light, and the sense of space and emptiness, that made it easier to breathe.

The room was full of this light—from the skylight, the large north-facing windows, and reflected from the high, white walls.

Two large landscape paintings hung on the wall, and an unfinished portrait of Lucien and Sofia stood on the easel.

It had been decided that while Lucien was away at school, Sister Ana would take Octavia, and bring her to Georgia at feed-times; that this was in everyone's best interest. It was hoped that when she grew a little older, Octavia's rages in her mother's presence would stop.

So Octavia spent her days, sleeping in her pram close to the herb garden when Sister Ana worked there, or awake and kicking her legs when the white doves, released from the aviary, flew over her pram and up and out over the valley.

The evenings remained a difficult time for both Georgia and Octavia. Initially, Georgia left the door to the nursery open at bed-time so that Octavia would be able to see the light—hear the small evening sounds of activity and conversation—but she cried inconsolably. Georgia tried everything she could think of, with no success. Months went by, and Georgia came to dread the evenings—Octavia's rages, the crying that would only end when, utterly exhausted, she fell asleep.

And then one evening, quite by accident, Georgia left the nursery curtains open. Octavia was put into her cot and tucked up for sleep, and then the usual battle began: kicking and crying—fighting the blankets. Georgia, watching helplessly, wondered what demon Octavia was fighting. Was she the demon? She turned the baby onto her back, and it was at this moment that Octavia, looking up, saw the night sky—and the stars.

There was a sudden silence in the room. Octavia lay quite still, staring out of the window. Georgia tiptoed out of the room to tell a surprised Sebastián what had happened.

The very next day, while Octavia was out with Sister Ana, Georgia brought her paints into the nursery and painted the whole ceiling full of bright, silver stars in a midnight-blue sky. Thereafter the curtains were never drawn, and there were no more evening tantrums.

Sister Piadosa, when she was told about it, commented that it never failed to impress her how individual babies were.

"People forget that babies are people. They do not enter the world like little empty jugs, waiting for the world to fill them up. Babies are not machines. And just look at this! Where does this come from? She is certainly the first baby I have known to love to look at stars. And, I must say, I am surprised she can see them at all. But there you are. We know so little about such things. Perhaps we should ask Alejandro what he thinks about it."

Alejandro Jaramillo was a carver of angels. He came to The Adobe once a week to give instruction in wood-carving.

When he was a boy of ten, he had a visitation by an angel who commanded him to carve all the angels that were in The Heavenly Host. When he asked how many that might be, the answer was: "As many as stars."

"I will do it," was his reply.

He had to overcome opposition from his parents, and from teachers who thought it was just a rather strange phase he was going through. But from that day, with very few interruptions, he had stood out under the night sky, counting and plot-

34

ting the stars—for what was to be his life's work—on a special map he had made, and carving a unique angel for each star.

The following week Alejandro was introduced to Octavia.

He had come with a gift for the infant; a delicately carved angel, very different from the angels he customarily carved.

"A red angel! Why have you painted this particular angel red? Surely they must be white—or unpainted?"

Georgia and Sebastián stared at the little figure. It was the color of red earth.

"It is very lovely—but red?"

Alejandro looked bemused.

"After I finished carving it I began to wrap it in tissue, but something stopped me. I had the gift-box ready, and the ribbon—but something told me that the angel wasn't finished. I spent a whole morning considering what might be missing. An image of the pink hill kept appearing in my mind; the pink hill in the rain, and how it turns just this tone of red after a storm."

"What did that say to you?"

"It didn't say anything. I just found myself painting the angel red."

He handed the gift to Georgia with a smile.

"This might not be a good time to give it to her."

It was known that Octavia did not take well to strange faces, so there had been some hesitation about this meeting. But Alejandro strode over to the pram, bent down and lifted the chubby infant up and into his arms.

"So, my fine lady, what is all this fuss about—and what do you know about stars?"

Octavia stared at him.

And Alejandro stared back at her small, dark face.

No one said a word.

Alejandro walked away a little distance with the child. He appeared to be listening to her, for from time to time he nodded. Then he pointed up at the blue sky. He pointed everywhere, all around, turning to point behind as well. The child looked up—and then back at his face. Alejandro bent toward her, as if listening. Did he hear something? Something beyond words—a silent cry? For what? He hugged the baby close to his heart and held her there, a look of compassion on his face. Slowly he walked back to the pram, where Sister Piadosa stood waiting to receive the child.

He crossed to where Georgia and Sebastián were standing. His face looked grave.

"She is in love with passion," was all he said. "In love with passion."

A Tea Party

Octavia was yelling.

Georgia was washing her hair over a basin, and attempting to rinse off all the shampoo. She was trying—barely managing—to hold onto her temper. She was struggling with a mixture of anger and guilt; struggling not to let her frustration be felt by the six-year-old child.

"Hush, Octavia. When we are done, we will all go and have tea and cake with Sister Piadosa. Lucien says she has a chocolate cake, baked by Refugio."

Refugio Montaño and her husband Manuel were Sofia's foster-parents. She had lived with them and their son, Pedro-Manuel, who was a few days older than her, from the time of her birth until her father came to The Adobe. She was only told of her mother's death much later, some time after Salvador arrived. Even then, she was told only as much as it was thought she could understand.

Georgia wrapped the towel around Octavia's head, and rubbed it dry.

"There. All done!"

She began to comb out the long, black hair, taking care not to pull on any knots.

"Is Lucien having cake as well?"

"Yes. And Sofia and Pedro-Manuel. We will have a tea party."

Octavia jumped up and down with delight.

"We're going to have a tea party!" she sang.

The hair was combed. The little girl ran out into the sun.

"Come, mama!"

Georgia hung the wet towel over a chair, and joined her daughter.

Octavia, dark-skinned and dusky, had grown into her features. Her face no longer looked flat. Her high cheek-bones enhanced her slanted eyes, which were large and dark—and hypnotic. Her nose, like her father's, was slim, with clean lines and slightly flaring nostrils. Her lips were full and already—inviting? Georgia was shocked to acknowledge this. In a six-year-old!

She took Octavia's hand, and together they walked down to the old cottonwood, just beyond the camposanto where Sofia's mother was buried. The others were already there. On a large table, tea and cake had been set out on a white cloth. Sofia was sitting on a bench close to Lucien. He was bending down toward her, intent on what she was saying.

Octavia ran up to them and squeezed herself between them. She was laughing.

"Hello, Luc'en." She pulled his head down and gave him a kiss.

"Hello, Sofia. Hello, Pedro-Manuel. We are having a tea party. Hello, Sister Piadosa. Hello, Refugio."

She chattered on.

"I'll tell you later." Sofia abandoned the conversation that she and Lucien were having. Octavia had taken center stage, and was directing the course of the party.

"I will give everyone their cake. Pedro-Manuel—you can give everyone their iced tea. Sister Piadosa and mama must sit together—over there with Refugio! Now everything is perfect."

The little girl ran about, passing plates of cake to everyone.

"And Luc'en must play for us on the violin."

"Maybe later," said Georgia.

"No! Now! Now!"

Sofia glanced at Georgia, who gave a nod.

"I will go and fetch the violin if you feel like playing, Lucien."

"Certainly. I will play."

Sofia ran off to fetch the instrument.

"What would everyone like to hear?"

"I know! I know!" shouted Octavia before anyone else could speak. "The song of the stars!"

Sofia returned with the violin. Lucien plucked the strings—tightening some. When he was satisfied with the tuning he bowed a few notes, then waited for everyone to be quiet.

"Come, Octavia, move a little toward me; we must give Lucien more room."

Sofia patted the place next to her, and Octavia moved reluctantly closer to her, but she sat facing Lucien, her legs crossed, her eyes fixed on him.

"What is the song of the stars?" asked Refugio.

"It is from a Puccini opera—Tosca," Sofia said. "E Lucevan le Stelle—it means the stars were brightly shining."

With the first notes, everything about Octavia changed. She sat motionless. Her face grew soft. And then tears began to slide down her cheeks. She put her hands together, almost in the position of prayer.

Sister Piadosa, watching her, recalled Alejandro's words. "She is in love with passion," he said. What exactly did he mean—what would it mean in the child's life? Certainly, with the beauty of the clear notes, she had become transformed.

She remembered the early days, after she entered the convent. It was only then that she had come to know the full meaning of the Passion of Christ. From her own life she knew that passion would inevitably involve suffering. She knew that today it also meant to feel intensely—but wasn't this the same thing in the end? Passion, she thought, often demanded a heavy price. How well she knew this.

Octavia had not taken her eyes off Lucien. Sister Piadosa was shocked to see— was it adoration?—on her face. But it was more than that: it was something almost sensual. No! Surely it couldn't be that in a six-year-old child?

She was relieved when the playing stopped and everyone clapped.

Octavia got up, ran to Lucien and hugged him.

"That was so beautiful," she whispered. "Thank you, Luc'en." She took his hand. "Tonight, when I listen to the stars, I will think of you—and your music."

Sofia came up to take the violin.

"Shall I take it back to the music-room?"

"That would be good. I will need it tomorrow for my lesson with Salvador."

He turned back to Octavia.

"What do you mean—listen to the stars?"

"Don't you listen to them? I thought that was where you heard your music."

"I think I feel them."

"It's the same thing."

A Place That Has No Name

Octavia was crying again.

Georgia tried everything she knew to pacify her, but with no success. Nothing, it seemed, would stem the flood of tears, the huge sobs that shook her small body. She appeared to be utterly inconsolable.

"What happened?" asked Lucien, coming into the room.

"It's the usual thing; this sudden flood of tears when, as far as I can tell, nothing has happened to trigger it. It is as if she suddenly feels something that is overwhelming."

"Let me take her to the rocking-chair for a while, until she calms down."

He held out a hand and the child took hold of it, still sobbing. He led the way to his room, and sat in the wooden rocking-chair that Gregorio had made for him. He lifted Octavia up onto his lap and began to rock, back and forward, over and over again, humming a little French song Matilde had taught him when he was small.

Gradually the sobbing stopped, and was replaced by deep, shuddering breaths. Finally Octavia put her head on Lucien's chest and became quiet. He continued to rock her until her breathing was normal.

"Shall we go and have tea and some cookies?" he suggested.

Octavia nodded.

"We are at our wits' end!"

Georgia was sitting with Sister Piadosa in the admin office, telling her about Octavia's unfathomable behavior.

"I don't think it is right that Lucien should have to pick this up. He can't spend so much time rocking her; besides, it's getting to be a habit. There must be something that she cannot tell us. Maybe she herself doesn't know what it is."

Sister Piadosa was thoughtful.

"You know, there is something I have read about; how some children—babies, even—feel very insecure when everything is still. When there is no movement. That is why fretful babies go to sleep if they are taken for a drive in a car. Maybe, in some deep way, the movement reminds them of feeling safe while the mother was carrying them for all those months."

"But we can't start driving around with her when she gets like this. It would be just as bad as the rocking-chair."

"Let me think about this for a while. I'm sure we will come up with some solution."

It was on repeating this conversation to Sister Ana that she was reminded of how Sofia, when she was a little girl, would occasionally grow sad if she had a dream about her mother.

"She was not able to speak to me," she would sob. "Not ever."

At the time it was Gregorio who came up with a wise and simple solution.

"Why don't we give her something, or maybe a place to go to when she feels sad, which is only hers? Maybe she will be able to take her sadness there, stay for a while and leave it there."

"Do you have an idea for this?" Sister Piadosa asked.

"I think so."

And so it was that Gregorio set about making a beautiful swing seat. He suspended it from a high branch of the old cottonwood on two long ropes. This was a tree that stood some little way beyond the camposanto. He kept the seat low to the ground to accommodate her little-girl legs.

It became a refuge for Sofia. There, while enjoying the slow swings, out and back, she would have long conversations with her mother about all that was happening at The Adobe.

"Sister Piadosa helped me pick some flowers for you. We chose some of the red roses, and a few yucca blooms that look like bells—and, of course, lavender. I have put them close to the statue of Jesus with the blue eyes and the rays of gold on his heart. He watches over you. The old cottonwood's leaves are beginning to turn yellow and the ground is all covered with them, like a carpet."

Sofia took time to swing in silence for a while, kicking her feet in the leaves and making them rustle and fly about.

"Sister Piadosa showed me how your doves still fly up to your window, every morning and evening. They haven't forgotten you. And I know you are right here with me. Don't tell anyone, but this is The Place that Has No Name—so nobody will ever know where to find it. Just you and me, mama."

Sofia was consulted on how she would feel about Octavia inheriting her place and the swing.

She gave a laugh. "Of course she may. What a good idea. It is such a peaceful place."

"And you never, ever told us," said Sister Piadosa, "anything about it—what you thought or felt; what the place meant to you."

"How could I ever tell it?" she said. "It was beyond words."

Georgia and Lucien walked with Octavia down the path, past the camposanto to the old cottonwood that had seen so many comings and goings over the decades. The swing had been tied back to the tree for safety. Georgia untied the rope, brushed away some dust and leaves and let it hang, moving slightly.

"Would you like to feel it, Lucien?" she asked.

Lucien walked through the rustle of dry leaves. His hands felt the strong ropes and the smooth wooden seat.

"I wish I was small again and had a swing like this," he said. "Come, Octavia." He held out a hand. "Let me lift you onto the seat."

Octavia ran to him, and was lifted onto the smooth wooden plank. He showed her how to make sure she was seated correctly, and how to keep a tight hold on the ropes.

"Are you ready?"

Octavia nodded.

Lucien repeated the question.

"I'm ready, Luc'en."

Lucien gave a gentle push. The swing moved a little.

"Do you like that, Octavia?"

Octavia nodded.

"Push more, Luc'en. More."

He stood, hands out in front of him, waiting to feel the swing's return; waiting to give another gentle push.

Octavia laughed with delight.

Finally he allowed the swing to grow still.

"Now, show us how you get off and then on again."

It was a game Octavia was enjoying.

"And now, Octavia," said Georgia, "let me show you how to make the swing go if there is no one around to push it for you."

In no time Octavia had mastered that. Her face shone with pleasure.

"Is this swing for me?" she asked.

"Yes. This is your swing."

"Any time I want to swing?"

"Yes. Just tell me or someone that you are going to swing, so we needn't worry. Will you do that?"

"I can swing now. You and Luc'en can go!"

Lucien laughed.

"She can learn diplomacy another day," he said. "I think we have just been dismissed."

Image II

The woman lies on the white linen sheet. Her sleek black hair, coiled behind her head—a heavy mass. A bright overhead lamp throws her body into sharp contrasts of light and shade.

Her body is naked. Glistens with oil—oil with the fragrance of neroli—which she has applied. A ritual act. She arches her back. One knee is raised, and falls out to the right. One hand arouses her left nipple. Her arms reach over her head to lift the heavy mass of hair. Her head turns to the right to gaze in the mirror. A long gaze.

Her lips part slightly. The tip of her tongue moistens first the upper lip, then the lower. They glisten with wetness. The dark, heavy-lidded eyes take in every detail.

She gets up and moves to the easel. Begins to sketch from memory the rough outline of the image.

She crosses the room. Removes a mask from its hook on the wall. Fixes it over her face. Tucks away all traces of her black hair. Pushes back the long, blonde hair. Tucks it behind her ears. Watches it slip free and fall forward again. Moves to gaze in the mirror. Traces with a finger the line of the brow. Kisses a finger, and touches the mask's half-closed eyes.

She slips into the over-size man's shirt. Leaves it unbuttoned. Adjusts the overhead lamp. Light floods the white sheet which lies over the table.

He climbs onto the white sheet. Kneels between the open legs of the woman below. Places his hands on either side of her. Arms straight. The long, blonde hair swings over the breasts—falls on her aroused nipples. He leans forward, as if to take her nipple into his mouth. Turns his head to the left to study the image in the mirror. The outline. The areas of light and shade. Holds this position until the image is printed into memory.

On the easel, a sketch. Two figures—a man and a woman. Dramatic contrasts of light and shade add to the feeling of tension: tension that longs to break—and not to break.

She removes the mask. Takes a towel. Rubs the oil off her body. Reaches for a black silk gown. Slips it on. Ties the belt. Stands, examining the two figures.

She crosses the room and lights a cigarette. Selects a record from the shelf: Puccini. Tosca. Moves to the record player. Selects the track: E Lucevan le Stelle—presses the repeat button.

"Lucien."

It is a whisper.

She puts the lamp out. Sits in the dark, allowing the music to enfold her.

Music

Sebastián was uneasy.

He observed, with concern, the way Octavia behaved when she was with Lucien. He did not speak to Georgia about it. She was having a difficult enough time with her daughter, without any extra worry being added to it. But he did take his uneasiness to Sister Piadosa.

"Am I imagining it, sister? I never had any siblings. I have no idea how they behave. Do you think her adoration is just normal admiration for a much older brother—a kind of crush?"

"I think it may just be a stage. She is very young. I would find it hard to believe any unnatural feelings could be present in such a young child. But I do think it would be good for her, generally, to go to the school in Las Madres. I know she could attend the Adobe School, but I think it would benefit her to mix with other children, some of whom may be as strong-willed as she is."

"I hope you are right, sister. It is not only Georgia who is having a rough time. I think Lucien is feeling awkward. When Octavia was born I felt such love for her—still feel it. But it seems she has eyes only for Lucien. It is not jealousy—although, maybe that too—but she seems to have grown so distant. I know this happens with teenagers. But in a child so young? She is not even seven. Surely not."

"She does have a passionate soul. The change in her when Lucien played the violin at the tea party was beautiful to see. It was not just him: I think his music unlocks something that may otherwise be trapped inside her."

Sister Piadosa was thoughtful.

"You saw Alejandro's face when he held her as a baby—when he said she was in love with passion. So grave. In a religious context, one might say she thirsted for

42

the Holy Spirit—I know that is not how you would put it. But sometimes we need to give things a far broader context. Perhaps we might say a longing for something—and we need not name it. Just that there is something that calls us."

"I will settle for beauty. Perhaps we should introduce her to music: to art—to beauty. Maybe she is thirsty for this, without knowing it."

Sebastián stood in the music shop, discussing the various features of three record players with the assistant.

"It is for a young girl," he said. "It needs to be good, but simple to operate."

"This one, sir. My young son has this model. I would recommend it. It is sturdy. Has a good tone. Simple and basic."

Sebastián made the purchase. His next stop was a record shop. He bought two long-playing records—both of favorite opera arias. He made sure that Octavia's star song was on one of them.

On the drive home he wondered what Octavia would make of his gift. Would it fill some space in her hungry soul? He remembered the day he wrote his first poem. How it had filled him with joy; the thrill when he knew he had found something that he could never lose. Would music be this for Octavia?

With surprise he realized that he was nearly home. At the old cottonwood he made the sharp turn into The Adobe, and bumped his way up the track. He parked in the shade at the side of their casita.

"What is it? What is it?"

Octavia jumped up and down.

"Open it and see."

Octavia sat on the floor with the parcel in front of her.

"It's not my birthday!"

"No—this is an un-birthday present."

Octavia pulled back the brown paper wrapping and stared at the box.

"What is it?"

"Here—let me help you take it out."

Octavia stared at the record player in wonder. "Is it mine?"

"All yours. And so is this."

Sebastián gave her the packet with the two records.

"Oh, Sebastián!"—Octavia refused to call him papa—"Can we play one now?"

"I am going to set this up in your room. Come. You can help me. I will show you how it works, and then we can play something and sit and listen together."

"Can I choose?"

"Of course. This is yours."

"Oh, Sebastián!"

Sebastián and Georgia decided that, when Octavia turned seven, she would attend the school in Las Madres. There, hopefully, she would learn a bit of give and take: how to fit in with children in a larger class than the Adobe School could offer. Sofia still had a year there before she went to high school, so Octavia would not feel too cast out and alone.

Lucien would soon graduate and go to college as a resident student. How quickly they grew up, Georgia thought. She had no worries where he was concerned. He was so confident; so steady. It helped that he knew exactly what he wanted to do with his life.

But now the long summer vacation was ahead of them. Lucien was practicing for a concert that he and Sofia were invited to give in Las Madres, and the two of them spent hours with Salvador and Reuben, rehearsing in the music-room: words and music, written by Lucien. He would play the piano, Salvador the violin and Reuben the bandoneon. Sofia was the vocalist. Since he first heard her sing, Lucien had fallen in love with her voice.

"Your voice makes me feel that I can see—maybe not the way sighted people see, but when you sing I know what it feels like to see the sky, the moon—even Octavia's stars!"

He was fascinated by the sound of the bandoneon.

"Reuben, I don't know how to write for bandoneon. It has no keyboard; only buttons. Will you teach me?"

So Reuben spent the summer showing Lucien how the bandoneon worked.

"It is like Braille," said Lucien with a laugh. "Only, there are many more than six dots. How did you learn to play?"

"I have loved the sound of the bandoneon since I first heard it, when I was fifteen, at a dance club. They were playing some early tango dance music. When my parents died, I was only eighteen. I had nothing—and nothing to lose. The world was wide open and waiting for me."

Reuben paused to consider this; then he added: "It is surprising how having nothing brings such rich freedom!"

Lucien looked incredulous.

"Freedom?"

"Yes—sounds like a contradiction, doesn't it? Anyway, I decided to go to Buenos Aires and find someone who would teach me how to play it."

There were many activities planned for that summer at The Adobe. Georgia hoped that this might free up some time for her work. She wanted to have enough canvases for an exhibition in Santa Fe early in the fall. The owner of a gallery there remembered her paintings from her master's exhibition, and was very keen to be the first to exhibit her new work. It was a wonderful opportunity, and she was determined to have her very best canvases ready for him.

Sebastián thought the holiday would provide an opportunity to enlarge the casita, which had suddenly become very small.

"While you are at it, can you give Octavia a play-room—preferably sound-proof—on the other side of the house? If I have to listen to that star song one more time, I think I will go crazy."

And so it was that Octavia was to have her own play-room—outside, a little away from the family house—on the one condition that the record player was kept there.

Octavia was thrilled.

"I want it to have high walls like mama's. And I want a skylight too. And I want to paint it black."

"Black?"

"Yes. Black."

"But why black?"

"I want it to look like night. And I want to be able to see the stars."

"But this is your play-room, Octavia. Black will make it very dark and gloomy."

"I want black!"

A familiar note had crept into Octavia's voice. It was the preface to a rage.

"Well, let's build it first," said Georgia diplomatically. "Then we can decide on the color."

But it was not good enough.

"Promise me I can have a black room—promise me!"

Sebastián glanced at Georgia.

"I think your mother is right. We will build it first."

"I want a black room!"

"Octavia—we will build it first, or we will not build it at all."

Georgia gave him a grateful glance.

Octavia got up and went to her room. Slammed the door. Soon E lucevan le Stelle could be heard, at full volume and—as they soon discovered—on repeat.

Image III

The woman is naked. Her body gleams with the oil she has applied— musk-scented oil. She kneels on the white linen sheet. Her back is arched. Her head is thrown back and to one side. Her right side. Her hair hangs in a twisted coil between neck and shoulder. Hangs down between her breasts. Her mouth opens slightly. Her lips are moist.

She looks at the image in the long mirror.

Reaches up to adjust the overhead lamp.

Slowly her left hand slips up out of shadow to trace the outline of her left breast. In the mirror she watches as her nipple becomes aroused.

She stares at the image. Commits the details to memory.

She steps down from the raised bed and moves to the easel. With eyes half-shut, she sketches the outline of the form. Neck, throat and breast are in white light. The nipple. And the moist lips.

She crosses the room. Pours herself a glass of wine. Red wine. Drinks deeply. Puts the glass on the table. She returns to the easel. Examines the drawing critically. She reaches forward, and with a finger traces the line of the throat. The shoulder.

She walks to where the mask hangs on the wall. Removes it, and brings it back to the mirror. She holds it close to her cheek, and studies the two reflected faces. Turns to face the mask. Kisses the half-closed eyes. A long kiss.

She ties the mask over her face, tucking away her black hair. Tilts her head until the long strands of blonde hair hang forward to cover her left eye. Makes a move to tuck the hair back behind an ear. Watches as it slowly falls forward again.

She stares at the face.

Her hand reaches up. A finger traces the line of the brow. Touches the half-closed eyes.

She reaches for the large shirt. Slips it on. Leaves it unbuttoned.

He stands behind the kneeling woman. His head bends forward to kiss the small of her back. Hair falling forward. His left hand reaches for her breast. One finger just touches the raised nipple.

A hand adjusts the angle of the light. The white glare erases certain details, throwing others into deep shadow.

He turns his head to look at the image in the long mirror. Studies it closely.

He removes the mask.

With eyes half-closed, she outlines the form of the man. Bending forward. Hair falling over his eyes. His hand on her breast.

She shades the image dramatically, emphasizing the face, the form of the breast and the hand just touching the nipple. Her slender white throat. And the kiss.

She crosses the room. Replaces the mask on its hook on the wall. Lifts the glass and finishes the wine.

She picks up the towel. With eyes shut, she slowly rubs the oil off her body. Reaches for a black silk gown. Slips it on. Before tying it, she walks to the mirror and stares at her body—her breasts, the dark triangle. The perfection of her long slim legs.

She ties the belt.

Stands, examining the two figures.

She crosses the room and lights a cigarette. Selects a record from the shelf: Puccini. Tosca. Moves to the record player. Selects the track: E Lucevan le Stelle—presses the repeat button.

"Lucien."

It is a whisper.

She puts the lamp out. Sits in the dark, allowing the music to enfold her.

The Sky Is Round

The renovations to the casita were almost complete. Georgia was thrilled with the extra space and light, and Sebastián was enjoying the pleasures of a small personal office.

"Now, at last, I will be able to see what I am cooking—and you will know what you are eating. And you won't have fried beans and chili all over your papers."

Lucien was given his own study so that the sound of his Braille typewriter would not disturb the rest of the family. He also had a built-in sound system with headphones, and shelves from floor to ceiling for his music collection. Sebastián spent hours with him, organizing things into an order that would make it easy for Lucien to find everything: his collection of records and his CDs, new on the market then, all marked with Braille tape; his Braille books, and the folders holding the songs he had written. He had a desk that was covered with Braille papers, and his tapes: audio cassettes of novels, poetry and plays, and educational tapes; and a collection of small objects that Sofia had given him from their walks together in a nearby arroyo.

Sebastián purchased a number of small bells, all with different tones, which he hung in particular places around Lucien's room to help him locate his books and music.

"Sebastián," said Octavia, "why don't we make some paths with bells, so that Lucien can walk with his cane to the office and the chapel and down to the clinic? He is very good with his cane now. And then he won't have to wait for someone to come with him. Gregorio can make the paths, and I will hang the bells."

"That's a great idea, Octavia. We can plan it together and surprise Lucien when it is finished."

He looked at his young daughter approvingly.

Octavia took charge of the project, choosing the routes, making sure that there were places along the way where a bell could hang and a log seat or a stone could be placed, in shade to sit on.

"And Gregorio,"—Octavia's voice, as she addressed the elderly man, had the note of one used to having her demands met promptly—"I think we should make a long path down to the cottonwoods, near the stream. It is such a lovely place to sit when it is hot."

So Gregorio engaged the help of the men who worked at The Adobe, and the paths were duly laid—the bells placed at strategic intervals along the routes.

Lucien was delighted.

"It was my idea, Luc'en," said Octavia with pride. "I hung all the bells."

"Come over here and let me give you a hug," said Lucien.

Octavia flung herself into his arms.

"Oh, Luc'en—I am so glad you like it."

She hugged him.

"I did it for you, Luc'en," she whispered.

Octavia's play-room was the last project on the list.

"I want to have it over here, Sebastián."

Octavia swept her hands outward, indicating an area some distance from the house.

"And I want a round room. And I want a skylight."

He took a seat on a juniper stump.

"Come and sit here for a minute, Octavia."

Octavia ran over to join him.

"It would be very nice if you asked if you could have it here, please—and if it could be round. 'I want' will not get you very far in life. 'Please' is a word you must practice a little. It will take you places where 'I want' will not get good results. So! Let's begin again."

Octavia jumped up.

"Please, Sebastián, can I have my room here?"

She pointed to the area again.

"And, please can we make it a round room, with a skylight like mama's? And please can I show you how big I would like it to be?"

Octavia walked a large circle.

"I think you will get lost in such a big room."

"Please, Sebastián."

She gave him her seductive, slant-eyed look.

"With high walls like mama's—please?"

"I will have to speak to the builders. It all depends on the length of the beams. A long room is easier to build. Why do you want a round room?"

"Because the sky is round."

Octavia divided her time between supervising the building of the play-room, and the swing. Both held a fascination for her. It was thrilling to see the foundations rising, and the builders laying the adobe bricks in the time-honored tradition.

"Is it really mud?" she asked one of the men.

"Mud and straw, and a few million years," he replied.

"What is a million?"

"A very long time," he laughed.

"Oh," she said.

But the swing was a different kind of discovery for her.

If she swung early in the morning, she felt the sun on her face when she moved forward. She was surprised to discover that the shade moved over her when the swing went the other way. Why was that? In the afternoon it changed again. Surely trees can't move?

Eventually she came to realize that it was the sun that moved. Did stars move? They seemed to stay very still. It was when she first climbed onto the seat in the morning that she noticed that her toes were in the sun, and her back was in the shade. There was a kind of line, then, that you couldn't see, that she kept breaking through as she swung. Light and shade. Light and shade. Was this the same as black and white; night and day? Or yes and no? When you turned a light on, it was on—and off was off. Was there a line between them as well, that you couldn't see?

It fascinated her.

She didn't want to ask anyone about it.

Summer Vacation

"I'm back! I'm back!"

Octavia, clutching her school books, her long hair streaming out behind her like a black wind, came rushing into the house.

She threw her books on the table and ran to the kitchen, where Georgia was preparing lunch.

"I'm home, mama. Has Lucien come back from college yet—is he home?"

Octavia was a stunningly beautiful young woman. Although she was only thirteen, she had developed early, and would pass for eighteen anywhere. She was tall and slim. Her sleek, black hair hung straight and heavy down her back. Her eyes, black and slanting above pronounced, high cheek-bones, were haunting: lazy and seductive when she wanted to charm someone; dark and inscrutable when she was thinking.

It was the beginning of the long summer vacation. Sofia had one more year at her music college, and Octavia would be going to senior school. But for Lucien—who had graduated cum laude—it meant he would be back at The Adobe. He had received a request from the Society for the Blind to compose words and music for a fund-raising concert. His theme was to be light, searching for a path through darkness. Salvador and Reuben would perform with him, and Sofia would be the vocalist.

"Sometimes when I hear you sing, Sofia, I almost believe I can see."

"I think I saw Lucien walking with Sofia in the direction of the large cottonwood. Perhaps you would like—"

But Octavia was gone.

She ran past the chapel and down the path that led to the camposanto, and on to the cottonwood. As she came round the last bend, she stopped abruptly.

In front of her she saw Lucien, standing in the gold-dappled light, his arms around Sofia—and kissing her.

Octavia froze. A small, dark wind blew a shadow across the path.

A moment of indecision—and then she was running down the path, as carefree as if she hadn't seen them.

"Lucien! I'm back! I'm back!—Oh! There you are."

Lucien and Sofia sprang apart. Both were looking flushed.

"Hello, Lucien! Isn't it wonderful? We have the whole summer ahead of us!"

She danced around gaily, keeping up a flow of chatter.

"Lucien! You have finished your studies, lucky dog. Aren't you glad? I would be. Are you going to work this summer? What are your plans?—Oh! Hello, Sofia."

Sofia stood in a shaft of sunlight. Her reddish-gold hair sparkled with little blue flashes each time she moved. With her gentian-blue eyes and flushed cheeks, she looked like a madonna. Octavia was glad that Lucien could not see her. Things were bad enough without that.

"I think mama has lunch ready for us, Lucien. We'd better go back and wash hands. See you later, Sofia," she said artfully, and led her brother back up the path.

She was still chatting about this and that and nothing when they entered the house.

"Where is Sofia? I thought she was going to have lunch with us," said Georgia.

"Oh, she went back home, I think," said Octavia. "Maybe she changed her mind."

"I'll go back and fetch her," said Lucien. "I won't be a minute."

"I'll go," said Octavia—and she was out the door like a flash.

Lucien sat down.

"Sometimes I wish people weren't so eager to help me. I invited Sofia. She will think it very strange when Octavia shows up."

Georgia looked at her son.

"Is there something the matter?"

"Oh—not really. Only that Octavia always wants to take charge. Of everything."

At this point Octavia came back, her face flushed from running.

"Sofia is having lunch with Salvador, and then they are going to Las Madres to visit Alejandro. They won't be back till late afternoon."

She took her seat at the table.

"Where is Sebastián?" she asked.

"He is down in the stable. One of the ponies is lame, and the vet is coming to take a look. He said not to wait for him."

Georgia began to dish up the food.

"Oh, Lucien! It's so good to have you back—and for the whole summer. I have so many plans for things we can do."

Octavia seemed not to notice Lucien's frown and tight lips.

"I want to take you swimming in the hot springs. You haven't been there, I think. The hot water comes gushing out of the earth, and it smells all funny. People say it is very good for you. Would you like that? We can do it tomorrow."

"Tomorrow I have a music rehearsal with Salvador and Reuben—and Sofia. Sorry. I think I am going to be quite busy with the show this summer."

Lucien kept his head down.

Octavia's eyes narrowed.

"We could go this afternoon. Mama, will you take us? Please?"

Lucien raised his head. His face was flushed. The fingers and thumb of his left hand made swift, fluttering movements—like the wings of a trapped bird.

"I don't want to go swimming, Octavia. I don't want to go anywhere. I've just got home. I want to chill out—listen to some music; dream into the story for the show."

Octavia was silent.

Georgia looked at her two children. What had happened, she wondered, to make Lucien—always so attentive to his sister—rebuke her so sharply? She said nothing.

When the meal was finished, she cleared away the dishes and asked Octavia to help her wash and dry them.

"I think you will have to find things to do with friends or on your own this summer. This is not just a holiday for Lucien—not any more. He has to work hard with Salvador and Reuben. They have not invited him to be part of the music just to have him run around and play. He has a career ahead of him, and he must prove himself. No favors, Octavia."

Octavia looked sulky. She did not make any reply, but dried the dishes in silence. When they were done, she left without saying anything.

"Please, Sebastián, may I have my allowance early? And can I come with you into Las Madres today? I have some shopping to do."

Octavia gave Sebastián her most beguiling smile. They were having breakfast, and Octavia was still in her night-dress.

"If you can be ready in ten minutes."

Sebastián was making a list of all the stops he had to make to collect everything for The Adobe.

"And don't forget the washers for the tap. I couldn't find them when I went in on Tuesday," Georgia called from the kitchen. "And Lucien forgot his Braille paper at the college. I called and asked them to send it up to the bookstore. It should be there by now."

Las Madres was their closest town, but it was small and often ran out of items, just—it seemed—when you needed them. Sebastián hoped he wouldn't have to make the considerably longer trip to Santa Fe for the washers.

"How urgent are the washers?"

"Urgent."

Georgia popped her head around the door.

"And if you want to be an absolute dear, I have run low on the antique-white oil paint. The art shop will have it—number 001 D—but only if you have time."

"I'm ready, Sebastián."

Octavia emerged, stunning in a pair of jeans and a green T-shirt.

"Anything else?"

"No. That's it."

They got into the pick-up, and rumbled off down the bumpy track.

Octavia stood in the center of her play-room. How silly to call it a play-room. She would find another name for it. She was wearing a pair of old overalls and work-gloves. Her hair was tied back into an untidy knot. A step-ladder stood next to the wall. On the table beside her was a large tin of paint. The paint was black. Next to this was a roller and a paint tray. The door was locked.

She had removed the red angel, given to her by Alejandro, from its hook on the wall, and for safety she wrapped it in protective tissue-paper. All other drawings and artwork lay on her table, covered with a large sheet of brown paper. She was prepared.

Octavia gazed up through the skylight. There was not a cloud visible in the blue that hung above her. The stars were there, she knew, even though you couldn't see them. She felt happy just knowing this. Even through the windows—which she had asked to have set high in the walls—all she could see was blue sky. She gave a sigh of pleasure.

Octavia walked over to the record player and chose Puccini in Love. She moved to the old wicker chair and sat, eyes closed, listening to the music. She let the whole record play to the end before she got up.

She stirred the paint, and poured some into the tray.

Two thirds of the room was painted. Black. Floor to ceiling.

Above the sound of the music, Octavia heard a knocking on the door.

She climbed down the ladder. Wiped the paint off her hands and went to open it.

"Octavia! I've been knocking for ages. Lunch is ready."

Lucien started to walk in with his cane, but Octavia quickly slipped out and locked the door behind her.

"What's all the secrecy? I can't see what you are doing anyway."

"It's not that, Lucien. I have to keep the place safe."

"You what?"

"I have to keep the space safe. It's for the stars. I want there to be a place where they will feel safe."

"I still don't understand—what do you mean?"

"I want there to be a place where I can listen to the stars, and no one will laugh at me—us. People don't understand stars—well, maybe Alejandro does. But people don't listen to them."

"You still listen to stars?"

"Yes."

"Oh!—well anyway, lunch is ready. You'd better clean up a bit. You smell of paint."

"She's painting her room black—inside and out. She doesn't want anyone to go in. Lucien says she told him that she has to have a place where it's safe to listen to the stars."

Sebastián put a dry dish onto the growing pile. It was part of their midday ritual to discuss the events of the morning over dish-washing.

"Listen to the stars!"

"Yes."

"So why can't anyone go in?"

"Apparently she doesn't want anyone to laugh at her, or the stars."

Georgia dried her hands on a dish-cloth.

"Isn't this all a bit weird?"

"Yes. But something happened on the day they started their vacation. I don't know what it was, and neither of them has said anything. But Lucien was upset. Very short with her. Not like him at all. And almost immediately she went and bought that paint."

"Well, now she wants a load of black river stones to make a spiral around the outside of her room—she calls it the Black Room. And do you know, the odd thing is that my mother ordered a load of black river stones for the labyrinth path in the herb garden. I laid them the summer you went to Paris."

"What do you think it is all about?"

"I don't know, but I am going to speak to Alejandro. He's the only person I know who might understand what she's on about."

He gave a shrug.

"You know, the more I learn about Octavia, the more compassion I feel for my mother. I was a very complicated child. I had an invisible dog that used to keep me safe from the place where the light isn't. I too had some strange darkness in me. People said I was touched by the duende when I was born—that a dark wind blew down my throat just as I drew my first breath."

"The what?"

"The duende. It is an ancient earth energy. The poet Lorca described it as dionysian. It is a mysterious force that can be felt but cannot be explained. Do you remember that we spoke about it?"

"Vaguely. I think I had other priorities at the time. So, how do you mean it can be felt? And how do you know it is this duende thing?"

"Lorca wrote a lot about it. He wrote a poem about a famous bull-fighter who was killed by the bull. Just reading it makes you shiver down your spine. You cannot mistake that touch."

"And you say that you too were touched by this?"

"It is what I was told. I never spoke about it as a child. Everyone thought I was a bit weird, anyway. I just didn't fit in. I think I deliberately kept quiet. I just knew that I was different from the other kids."

"So where did it come from? You say it blew down your throat."

"That was the only language the people knew. They were simple but very knowing, I was told. But it doesn't come from outside us. Lorca said it is a struggle that makes its way up the body, from the ancient spirit of the dark earth."

"You are giving me goose-bumps."

"Well, that is exactly what the duende does. It's not a gentle muse."

"Is it possible that I could have been touched by something like this when I was working toward my master's? I often look back to that time, to see what I was doing then that made the works so powerful. I seem to have lost something."

"You must answer that."

Georgia was thoughtful.

"In Paris, Henri said that my new work was good, but not as exceptional as the work he saw here. He said I should study the work of van Gogh. But the more I tried to analyze his painting style, the more I became confused; uncertain."

"You probably wouldn't have discovered anything by doing that."

"Oh? Why not?"

"The duende isn't reasonable. In fact, you have to let go of intellect. It is said that the duende only shows up when death is possible."

"Whose death?"

"Your own. Or maybe it is something you think you are—and that has to die."

"How do you know all this?"

"I told you. I read up on it—all I could find. Lorca speaks very eloquently about it."

"And where is the duende in your life now?"

"That's just it. I think I betrayed it. Now I see it in Octavia."

"And are you telling me that Octavia has been touched by this—this duende energy?"

"I think so. Her difficulty may be that she is still too young to contain all that energy."

"And what about you now?"

Sebastián was quiet for some time.

"I see that I have only flirted with it. A dangerous thing to do. I think—maybe I fear—that it will not return. Or perhaps my real time to shudder is still ahead of me. You cannot learn this; rather, it is the reverse. You have to let all the skill you have ever learned be torn out of you."

Georgia listened, wide-eyed.

"But there is even more to it than this; especially for artists, writers, musicians—any form of art. It is what comes when the true artist allows himself, metaphorically speaking, to die."

"I don't follow you."

"Well. Think of Piaf. She sang with duende. You can feel your hair stand on end at that something other in her voice. It speaks of her triumph over all the pain and losses in her life. But she didn't fight it. She was willing to let go of any idea of control. She allowed the dark earth to take her. Few of us have the heart for this. But that's duende."

An Image in a Round Jug

Octavia sat in the shade outside the Black Room. Beside her, on a makeshift table, stood a jug of spring water and a glass. She filled the glass and drank thirstily. There wasn't a breath of wind; not a leaf stirred, and the valley baked in the hot sun.

She moved her chair back a little to keep it in the adobe's shade; wiped some perspiration from her face, and sat back.

She sat, eyes half-closed against the glare, looking at nothing in particular. She was thinking of Lucien and Sofia; the kiss she had witnessed. She could still feel the shock of it in her chest, and something between fear and rage beginning to move low down in her stomach. She would have to do something to make things right again. Yes.

Turning her head slightly, she saw a reflection in the jug of water; saw something pale—and a large, black shadow. What was it? It looked like a gigantic, black wave, about to break. The pale shape seemed to be a part of it.

She remembered watching a program about the havoc wrought by a tsunami that had wiped out an entire island somewhere in the Pacific; this unbelievable power that turned houses into match-sticks; that took down everything in its path. She had watched the terrible devastation in awe. People fleeing; drowning. Cars floating down muddy, raging rivers, surrounded by a mass of random bits of debris and unlikely objects, all floating away: small boats, suitcases, tables, a doll; a dog, standing on a floating plank; a pink, upside-down sun-umbrella. And all the time the water-level rising, inexorably, destroying more and more in its wake.

She remembered thinking that it was like some Biblical punishment, sent by God for disobedience. Now the word—wrath—came into her mind.

She looked deeper into the image in the jug. The pale image had the strange whiteness of those worms and centipedes that live under big rocks; that never see the light. This entity had risen up inside the black wave. It was a huge serpent, its mouth open wide as a cave, and about to swallow a dark, red orb—a sun—that was drowning in the dark water. She could not see, but she could feel the scaly coils of the serpent slithering through each other as it woke up after a great sleep. What had called it up?

When she looked again, the light had shifted. The image was gone. But not the image that was now imprinted in her brain.

Octavia rose, picked up the jug and glass, went back into her black room and put them into the small sink. Next, she pulled her easel into a position under the skylight, and began to draw the image.

She made four small sketches, each time remembering another detail from the image in the jug.

She had a sense that the eyes were yellow and evil, and at the same time oddly dull, almost sightless—as if the serpent's wrath was directed at the light that was being brought into its dark world; a light it could not and would not tolerate.

She had kept to the round shape of the image, which had been established by the shape of the water-jug. It pleased her; the sense of something so powerful and contained, that was about to shatter the fragile walls that held it, and to show the world of light the power of the rejected creature that lay in the unseen depths.

Octavia stood back, considering the four images. She would paint the last one.

It was late afternoon when she finished the painting. She viewed it with pleasure. It was, understandably, and—for her, very satisfactorily—disturbing.

She went over to the record player, selected the track for the star song, and sat looking at the finished work.

She sat there until the light faded.

She left the room, locked the door behind her, and went back for supper.

Alejandro Comes For Lunch

Alejandro was at The Adobe to give his weekly wood-carving class. His pupils were learning the art of making bultos—painted carvings of the saints. There was one young boy who had a most eccentric understanding of style and color—for most bultos were painted in colors that, depending on the saint, were prescribed by tradition. This young boy fascinated Alejandro, for he had broken with all tradition, saying that he looked inside for the truth.

"We are not living hundreds of years ago. This is today. Why aren't my ideas of color just as good as those of artists long dead?"

Alejandro smiled, but he encouraged the boy to follow his truth. He was young. He did not have to justify his ideas to anyone—yet. If he did become a gifted santero, he might have an interesting time with traditionalists. But that was later.

"This carving of Saint Sebastián, with a shield catching the arrows—tell me about it."

"The way I see it, sir, maybe long ago there was a virtue in allowing painful arrows to pierce you. Maybe it proved something—how devout you were—a martyr—something like that.

"The way I see it, today there is no virtue in being so passively accepting. People may shoot the arrows—we can't make them stop if that is what they do—but we don't have to allow them to pierce us. The arrows will only harm us if we allow it."

"I see," said Alejandro. "Interesting. Maybe you would like to make some notes for me about the other carvings as well. Would you do that?"

"Yes. Of course, sir," the boy said, blushing at the compliment.

Alejandro arrived for lunch with Georgia and Octavia half an hour early. Georgia greeted him, and told him that Octavia was in the Black Room. Alejandro had already been told about its new color scheme.

"Shall I take you there?—it is behind the house, and a path leads up to it. You can't miss it."

"I think I would rather stroll up there on my own. What time will lunch be ready?"

"About one o'clock, but it won't spoil if you need to be there longer. Just come when you are ready."

Alejandro set off, wondering what kind of reception he would receive. He remembered the difficulties he experienced in his youth, when he said he wanted to spend his life carving angels. His parents were devastated. He had been sent to a priest and a psychiatrist—both of whom were slightly baffled. His parents were told by the psychiatrist that it might do harm to interfere in what he thought might be genius—a condition, he said, that was very hard to cure.

Alejandro stood outside the door. On the ground to his left, protected by a low wall made from pieces of basalt, was a circular design, about twenty-four inches in diameter. It consisted of what he supposed to be a base of mud or clay, into which small pebbles of varying colors and sizes had been pressed to form a spiral pattern. Between the lines of the spiral were indented footprints filled with fine black sand, walking toward the center. They grew smaller and smaller as the path narrowed. Alejandro stared at it, hypnotized by the power and the simplicity of the design.

He knocked at the door.

Octavia peeped out. Seeing Alejandro, she came out, closing the door quickly behind her.

"Hello, Octavia. I have been invited for lunch, as I have an extra class this afternoon, but your mother is still cooking. I thought I'd come and say hello."

Octavia looked flustered.

"Oh—hello, Alejandro. How are you?"

"I'm well, thank you."

He gave her a smile, and pointed to the artwork.

"I have been admiring this design. Did you make it?"

Octavia blushed at the compliment.

"Yes. It's just things that I picked up around here."

"Aren't you worried that the rain will wash it away?"

"No. If the rain comes, it must do what it does—and then I will make it good again. It is like a conversation. Don't you think?"

He did think so. But what an extraordinary view in one so young.

"Yes. Yes, it is."

"And have you been working on your angels, Alejandro?"

"Well—I've been my usual busy self. The stars around Orion are keeping me occupied. So many stars. So many angels. But I love my work. I am busy carving the Angel of Prophecy, and she is giving me a hard time. Shall we take a walk?"

"Yes, that would be lovely. I'll just quickly lock up."

Octavia disappeared inside. She returned with a key, and locked the door. Alejandro made no comment.

"How do you know she is the Angel of Prophecy—and why do you call her 'she'? I thought angels were not like humans—were neither he nor she."

"You're right, of course. But I like to have a very personal relationship with each and every angel I carve. Otherwise I would begin to feel like a factory, you know, just churning out pieces of wood in the shape of angels."

"And so—?"

"Well, I talk to them a little. Mostly I listen. I think that is why people love my angels. Of course, they think I am a little touched—and maybe I am. People say they don't hear the angels talk to them. That is because they don't know how to listen, even to themselves. But they are drawn to them, nevertheless."

Octavia looked at him quizzically.

"When did you start carving angels?"

"When I was ten. Santiago and I were at school together. It was our first wood-working class, and we were all given a piece of cottonwood. I don't quite know what happened, but I carved an angel, and was finished long before the class was over. All the other boys were still sweating over their stumps of wood—only just beginning to make some progress.

"Then suddenly my angel seemed to come alive. It started hovering."

"Hovering?"

"Yes. I got the fright of my life. I hid it under my shirt and slipped outside. I could feel the angel, hot against my chest."

"Hot? Like it was burning?"

"Well, sort of—like it was full of energy. I found a place under a tree, at the far end of the playground. There it told me it had come to give me a message from The Heavenly Host. All the time it was hovering in the air. I know it must sound crazy to you."

"Oh no! Not at all!"

"It said I had to carve an angel for each member of The Heavenly Host. When I asked how many, it said—as many as stars. I knew right then that I would do it."

He gave Octavia another smile.

"I remember telling Santiago on the way home. He was doubtful then that I would be able to keep it up. I remember he said to me: 'We are only boys, Alejandro: we are only ten. We can't know yet what we will do.' But I did know. It was my calling, you see. I never doubted it."

"And what did your parents think?"

"Oh, they thought I was crazy. They took me to various people who didn't really know what to say. And so eventually my parents came to see that I was serious about what they thought of as my angel fantasy. Sometimes the world makes it very hard to follow our truth. But we dare not give in to it. Too many people do that—some very early in life. It is such a loss of what might be a very unique life."

"And, in what way is this angel giving you a hard time?"

"She is telling me something—I know that much. I can feel her urgency. But for some reason I am unable to hear her message."

"How extraordinary."

Alejandro thought he had said enough, and changed the subject.

"And what is your plan for the summer vacation?"

"I don't really know yet. I have just finished painting my room. I am so happy with it. And Sebastián is going to order a load of black river stones. I want to make a path—a spiral path that goes around and around the outside, and leads to the door. I am so excited about this. It will probably keep me busy for quite a while."

"I see that you like the spiral."

"Yes. I like the way you can go in—and come out again."

"Have you ever looked closely at the herb garden?"

"Not really."

"Next time you are there, take a good look. I think it will surprise you."

"Well, it must be nearly time for lunch. Shall we go and look at it on our way back?"

□□□

Octavia, wearing cut-off jeans and a tank top, was setting smooth, black river stones in the soft sand of the spiral pathway she had drawn. Sweat was pouring down her flushed face, and leaving dark patches on her clothing. From time to time she doused her whole head in the bucket of water she had fetched from the spring. It was the third week of such effort, and the path felt endless to her.

From a distance, Sebastián observed her toil with compassion. He remembered his own anguish when he laid the path for his mother. It had taken one whole summer holiday, just after Georgia had left, and he had welcomed the physical effort and the pain of it. He wondered what was going on in Octavia's mind. What had happened to so distance her from Lucien?

Alejandro suggested that they let her get on with it.

"She has found a way to manage something that she is not ready to talk about. I would say—have faith in her. I think she is an extraordinary person. And I do remember you, and how your mother worried. I said the same to her."

Alejandro paused.

"And my goodness! Just look at her! She is the image of Magdalena. Such a beauty already. That is also not an easy path for a woman."

Image IV

The woman is naked. She stands in front of the long mirror, and examines her image. Her body is the color of dark wheat. Next to her on the table is a carafe of oil—oil of sandalwood. She pours a little into her right hand, rubs both hands together, and starts to apply the oil to her face and neck. Taking more oil from time to time, she moves her hands over her breasts, down her arms, over waist and stomach, over the contours of her hips and buttocks; down her legs to her feet and toes. Finally she reaches behind her back, from her shoulders down to mid-back, and up from her waist, until she is satisfied that every inch of her shines.

She holds her cupped hands up to her face, and breathes in deeply the sandalwood fragrance. Strokes her black hair till it glistens.

She crosses the room to where the paints and paint-brushes are kept. Selects a tube of crimson acrylic paint, and a brush. Takes these over to the mirror. She applies the paint to the brush.

Starting at her left nipple, with her left hand she draws the outer line of a spiral—a crimson spiral—that moves across her body, below the right nipple and on and around, just touching the edge of her pubic hair; goes around—the spiral growing smaller, and ending in her navel.

She replaces the paint and brush.

From a small jar she takes a handful of coarse, crystalline salt. Sprinkles it over her hair, allowing the grains to fall and adhere to her body.

Turns off the bright overhead lamp. Lights a candle.

She crosses the room and selects a record—Puccini: Tosca. Selects the track. E Lucevan le Stelle. Repeat.

She lies down on the raised bed—the white linen sheet. Lies on her back. Her right knee is pulled up toward her, and falls out to the side. Right arm hangs loosely over the edge of the bed. Her left hand arouses her left nipple. She closes her eyes, and allows the music to fill her.

The Gallery

"Is everyone ready? We need to leave."

Georgia was taking Lucien, Octavia and Sofia in to Santa Fe.

Lucien was to be dropped at a music store, where he wanted to buy some CDs for his new CD player.

"Don't bother to hurry back. You know me. You could leave me here all day, and I wouldn't notice it." He laughed. "Enjoy the exhibition."

The O'Keeffe Gallery in Santa Fe was hosting an exhibition of Huichol Indian art; tapestries made of brightly colored yarns, the brochure stated, that were fixed to a wooden base with a mixture of beeswax and pine resin. Georgia didn't want to miss it. It was the last day.

Octavia stood in front of the first work—transfixed. Her whole body trembled. She read the title—Peyote Nealika.

It was a mandala with what looked like a dark sun, or a mysterious, dark, circular object in the middle; or perhaps it was a space, an opening, a way through to—she didn't know what, only that she wanted to find out.

She knew this place! It was instantly familiar. She could feel it resonating inside her. If only she could remember it!

From this center, like rays of the sun, serpents and lizards and small, button-shaped images—which she read from the card were symbols for peyote—streamed out.

The image was alive.

Vibrant.

The text gave a brief definition of the word "Nealika" as a power object. Nealika was a way of communicating with another world, an invisible dimension which the artist described as the Source.

Tears fell down Octavia's cheeks.

Georgia and Sofia had moved on. They were discussing a work on the other side of the room, and were so engaged that they didn't notice Octavia's response, or that she had not moved away from the first work.

It was only when they had discussed all the works in the room—and had almost come back to the beginning—that Georgia saw Octavia's tears. She left Sofia reading a long text about initiation into the shamanic profession and the uses of the peyote cactus, and moved to stand next to Octavia.

Neither of them spoke. Slowly they walked around the room together, stopping in front of every tapestry to gaze in silence.

On the way out of the gallery, Octavia asked if Georgia would buy a copy of the exhibition catalogue. All the way to fetch Lucien, and all of the way home, she bent over the color illustrations of the tapestries, and studied the text. She marveled at the photographs of the beadwork: bowls and figures, all covered with the same brilliant patterns, but made with beads—which she had not seen in the second room of the exhibition. She read the detailed account of how the beads were set in the same mix of beeswax and pine resin.

The last full page showed a carving of a deer. It was magnificently decorated with patterns of peyote, sun images, rays of light, corn plants, wolves, arrows and spirals.

With the book still open at the page, Octavia sat for the rest of the journey with her eyes closed.

When they arrived back at The Adobe, she turned to Georgia with such a look of gratitude that Georgia felt a lump in her throat.

"Thank you, mama, for taking me. This is so precious."

She turned, hugging the book close to her chest, and ran to the Black Room. Inside, she locked the door. She selected the Puccini. El Lucevan le Stele. Pressed repeat.

Still holding the book, she sat in a chair under the skylight—eyes closed.

Journal Entry 1

Dream
I am standing on a high rock.
Below me, in darkness, is a vast, empty desert.
Above me, millions of stars.
I am reaching up to touch them.
And now the sky goes dark.
Far below me I see something bright. It might be a fire.
I do not find it strange to see a fire in the desert.

I wonder what dreams mean. Sebastián told me that Magdalena, my grand-mother, never ignored a dream. She told him that dreams are like messages—only sometimes we have difficulty understanding the language, because it comes in strange pictures.

Sebastián told me she used to think in pictures. I do as well—although people don't seem to know what I mean. I used to think that something was wrong with me. Now I am so happy that I am like her.

She said if we pay attention to dreams, they will continue to talk to us. And then, one day, if we have been listening closely, something breaks through, and we can feel in our heart the power of their truth.

I wish I had met her.

Sometimes I feel as if I am a fire in the desert.

Octavia closed her journal. Tomorrow she would make a drawing of the dream.
She got back into bed. Turned off the bedside light.
Closed her eyes.
The image of a night sky, and millions of stars, was printed in her brain.

The spiral path around the Black Room was almost complete.
Octavia sat on a juniper log, contemplating her work. Something was missing.
She visualized the herb garden, with all of Magdalena's herbs growing in the areas between one stretch of the path and another. No. That was not what she wanted—although it was lovely.
She closed her eyes, and called up her dream. She could see the stars above her. So close. So unattainable. How would she ever be able to touch them? How strange, that sudden dark sky. She thought of Alejandro and his angels. What was the story he had told her? Someone who had a dream about angels? Of course. Jacob. Angels ascending and descending. She would build a ladder, going not up, but in—to the center: to the stars? Where had that thought come from? And she would paint it—what color? Gold? Crimson?

Shortly before the end of the summer vacation, the path of stones was finished.
Not far from its external opening, there was a stack of logs of varying lengths and thicknesses—all painted crimson. The laying of the ladder would have to wait a while. She would ask Alejandro to show her how to make the angels.
Octavia gave a sigh of pleasure.

The Music Men

Octavia spent very little time with Lucien and Sofia that vacation.
The musicians who worked together on the concert would include Salvador, Reuben, and a gifted young cellist from Russia, Kristiyan Bacarov, who had been engaged to play with the Santa Fe Orchestra for the opera season.
Kristiyan Bacarov was born in Russia in 1961. His parents were both musicians, and at an early age the young boy was introduced to music in general, and the cello in particular. On his twelfth birthday he was given his first cello on the suggestion of his instructors, who remarked to his parents that he had a most unusual gift.
After completing his studies at the Saint Petersburg Conservatory in 1986, Kristiyan applied for a position with the Santa Fe Orchestra, and was accepted.

"Salvador," Kristiyan said as the two entered the concert hall for a rehearsal, "may I ask you a few questions about your violin? It has the most extraordinary tone—no, not tone; maybe voice is a better word for it. Where did you get it?"

Reuben gave a shrug.

"See if he believes you, Salvador," he said.

"Actually, I made it. It is what I used to do for a while to support myself."

"You made it!"

"Yes. My father and Alejandro—you have met him, I think; the man who carves angels—they both taught me all I know. Alejandro has an ongoing love affair with wood. I made this particular violin after my wife, María, vanished. People say it is full of tears. I don't know about that, but it does seem to have a powerful effect on listeners."

"I should say."

He winked at Salvador.

"I suppose you have never considered making a cello, by any chance?"

"Not recently!" Salvador said with a straight face.

The concert was booked for early in the following spring. This gave the musicians time to learn and rehearse the score. Santiago arranged times for them to practice in the Las Madres church, where he still taught the church choir and played the organ for the services. Father Rafael Montdragón, the resident priest and Sebastián's friend from college days, had attended some of the rehearsals, and was deeply moved by the music.

"I haven't ever heard anything quite like Lucien's composition," he told Sebastián. "It is so inner—if you know what I mean." He searched for the precise words. "It touches me so deeply. Here." He put a hand on his heart.

"And Sofia's voice has something so pure about it. It is perfect for his concept of light overcoming darkness. He is calling it The Invisible World—isn't that beautiful? And such a mixture of pathos and beauty that Salvador's violin and Reuben's bandoneon bring to the music—especially to the lament for the light—so moving. Quite extraordinary."

Octavia was so engrossed in her own project that she paid no attention to—indeed, had not noticed at all—Lucien's coolness. If she did think anything, it was that he was preoccupied with his concert plans.

□□□

"Hello—I do hope I am not disturbing you. Octavia, isn't it?"

His voice was deep, and resonant; his accent slightly foreign. It made Octavia think of a dark wind moving slowly through a forest. His build matched his voice; it was sturdy, and she sensed that he was not easily intimidated. His hair was thick and reached almost to his shoulders. He was, she thought, extremely good-looking.

"Sofia told me I would probably find you here. I'm Kristiyan. I will be playing the cello in Lucien's concert."

He gave a small, formal bow.

"Do forgive me for knocking so unceremoniously."

Octavia stood half in, half out of the door to the Black Room.

"I saw you at the O'Keeffe Gallery, but I don't think you saw me. It took me a little while to learn that you were Lucien's sister."

"Half-sister. I am not a full sister."

"Oh. I didn't know—sorry—half-sister. Does it make a difference?"

"Yes."

There was an awkward pause.

"May I come in and see what you are doing?"

Octavia squeezed out of the doorway and closed the door behind her.

"Oh, it's such a mess at the moment," she said, pushing back her hair and fussing with her clothing. "Perhaps some other time. Let's go and find the others. They should be about to begin rehearsing."

She locked the door, and began to walk away along the black stone path.

Seeing that it was too narrow for two people to walk side by side, Kristiyan walked behind her.

"Do you always follow this path round and round when you leave?" he asked.

"Yes."

"Even if you are in a hurry?"

"I try never to be in a hurry when I am on this path. The stars never hurry. Or if they do, they die. That is when we see a shooting star—but of course it died long before we see it. Isn't that beautiful?"

Octavia paused, and turned to face him. She was wearing a painter's smock with little underneath it, for the heat.

"I suppose it is."

Kristiyan stared at the lovely face in front of him. What an extraordinary remark. He had heard that Lucien's sister was unusual.

"I believe you are very interested in stars—is that right?"

"Yes."

Octavia turned, and continued along the path. Kristiyan followed.

Only when they moved out into open ground did he catch up with her, and attempt to continue their conversation.

"Lucien tells me that you love opera?"

"I don't know much about opera. I only have a few arias on record, but I do listen to them a lot—particularly one from Tosca."

"Have you ever been to a live opera—at the Santa Fe Opera House?"

"No."

"It is such a beautiful experience—an opera house out in the desert, open to the stars. Do you think you might be interested in going to one? I am playing in the orchestra this season, and I have two complimentary tickets for any opera I choose. Lucien told me how you like Puccini. Tosca is on the program—I will give you the actual date. Would you like to come with someone?"

"Do you mean it? Oh, I would love to go, if you are sure you don't want the tickets for someone else—only it would be wrong to say that I like Puccini, as if I knew all his operas. How lovely it will be to hear the entire opera. I only know the aria where Cavaradossi sings of his love for Tosca, just before his execution—how he never loved life so much. To know this just before you die! This must be the height of passion and romantic love, don't you think?"

"You don't think it would be better for them to live and be together?"

"It would not. I mean—could there ever be such passion if they both lived?"

"Well, perhaps the passion would change to a deeper kind of love."

Kristiyan was intrigued by the direction the conversation had taken. Was she really only thirteen? He had been amazed when Lucien told him. He had thought she was much older.

"I think passion is everything."

They had come to the hall where Lucien and Sofia were about to rehearse with Salvador and Reuben. There were to be eight compositions in which the organ was replaced by the bandoneon, an unusual feature in music that was not tango. They were standing around and chatting as they waited for Santiago to arrive.

Sofia waved, and turned to say something to Lucien.

"Hello, Sofia. Hello, Lucien," Kristiyan called across the room.

"Hi there, Kristiyan," Lucien replied in the general direction of his voice.

"I have brought someone with me," said Kristiyan. "Perhaps she will stay and listen to the rehearsal."

He turned to Octavia.

"Would you like to stay?" he asked. "Please say yes."

Octavia blushed.

"We could all go out afterwards, and have supper somewhere in Las Madres."

Image V

The woman is naked.

She pours oil into the palm of her hand—a musky-scented oil. Rubs her palms together and works the fragrant oil into her long, black hair.

She crosses the room. Removes a small box from the shelf. From this she selects a stick of black stage make-up.

She stands in front of the mirror. Slowly she starts to apply the black cream to her face and neck. Leans forward to examine the effect.

She draws a circle around each breast, and spreads the cream to cover them. She takes care to leave both nipples bare.

With slow hands she covers her shoulders, arms and all of her torso with gentle, stroking movements. And down her thighs and calves: down to her feet. And reaching behind her back; her buttocks—until all of her body is black and gleaming.

She leans forward again to examine her handiwork. Her nipples, aroused now, and pink. With care she wipes her fingers on a soft cloth.

From its hook on the wall, she fetches the mask with the golden hair. Kisses her fingertips and touches, lightly, the half-closed eyes. She suspends it from a cord above the raised bed so that it faces downwards, the fair locks falling forward—almost touching the sheet.

She crosses over to the long mirror, and with red crayon writes four words across the top of the glass—Suffer me. Save me.

She reaches up to adjust the lamp, so that the light falls at a dramatic angle onto the narrow bed; turns to take a record from the shelf: Puccini. Selects the track. E Lucevan le Stelle. Presses repeat.

The opening clarinet solo. She climbs with great care onto the white linen sheet. She lies on her back below the mask. She draws her right knee up, and allows it to fall outward. Her left hand lightly caresses her nipple. She arches her back until her breasts are lost in the mask's long, golden hair. Right arm hangs loosely over the edge of the bed.

She turns her head.

Tears stream from her eyes.

"The stars were shining,
And the earth was scented..."

"Oh, sweet kisses and languorous caresses..."

"And I die in desperation!"

Her body trembles. Her right hand covers her face. The music builds to a crescendo.

"And I never before loved life so much...

"Loved life so much..."

"O, Lucien," she sobs—"come die in me—"

"But why won't you partner me?"

"Oh, come on, Octavia—I'm ten years older than anyone who will be there. I'm nearly thirty, for goodness' sake. And I'm your brother."

"Half-brother."

"Half-brother. It's the same thing."

"No! It isn't!"

"Surely all the boys in your class are just aching to go with you. It's your graduation—and theirs. Why not ask one of them?"

"They are such boys! That's why."

Lucien made a despairing gesture.

"Well then, why don't you ask Kristiyan? I am sure he would love to go with you."

"He's even older than you. Why is it all right to ask him and not you?"

"What's all the talk about in here?" asked Georgia, coming into the room.

"Lucien won't be my partner for the grad dance," said Octavia petulantly.

"Well, anyone you invite has the right to say no," Georgia ventured.

Octavia gave her a dismissive look.

"Please! Please, Lucien. I will only graduate once. I would love you to be the one who escorts me."

"I can't, Octavia. I would feel uncomfortable. There will be an after-party, with everyone going wild. I can't do all that stuff."

"But we can leave after the dance. We don't have to join them. Pleeeeeeeease, Lucien."

"I don't want to go, Octavia. That's all I have to say. I hope you enjoy it, and have a wonderful evening."

"It won't be wonderful without you."

"Octavia! No! Let it go now."

"But why won't you come with me, Lucien? Why?"

Lucien's fingers were making their swift, agitated movements—finger and thumb tapping each other, over and over.

He took a deep breath. His fingers became still.

"Because Sofia and I are getting engaged. That's why," he said bluntly.

Octavia stared at him in disbelief. All the color drained from her face. Her head was moving from side to side. Her whole body was shaking.

"But you can't marry Sofia! You can't!"

She ran to him and held onto his arms, her face reaching up in an attempt to kiss him. Lucien turned his face to the side, and pushed her away.

"Octavia! Stop it."

Georgia stepped forward, as if to intervene, but was warned off by Octavia's frown. She took a seat, and looked on helplessly.

"Oh, Lucien, please listen," Octavia implored. "How can you think of marrying Sofia? I am the one. It always has been—me—who you must marry. Don't you know that? You can't marry anyone else. You can't marry her."

"I most certainly can—and I will! And the name is Sofia—not 'her'. Who do you think you are, Octavia, to tell me who I may or may not marry?"

"Because I know! You are going to marry me!"

Lucien made a gesture of frustration. His fingers began their agitation once more.

"You must be out of your mind. How can you possibly think that, Octavia? You are my sister, for God's sake. And even if you weren't, you are not my type."

"But I am! I am! I can change. I can make myself be your type." Octavia was barely able to speak through her panic. "I love you, Lucien! I love you!"

Georgia sat listening, her hand over her mouth. Tears were streaming down her face.

"Octavia. Listen. You are my sister—it makes no difference that you are my half-sister. Apart from anything else, it is not permitted. But even if it were, it still makes no difference to the fact that I love Sofia."

"No! You can't love Sofia. You love me! You are going to marry me!"

Octavia was shouting.

"I am in love with Sofia." Lucien's hands clenched. "And I am going to marry her. I am not in love with you, Octavia."

Octavia flung herself into his arms, hitting his chest with her fists.

"No! No! No—you love me! You must love me!"

Lucien pushed her away.

"Octavia—listen to me. I am going to marry Sofia. And that's the end of it!"

Octavia opened her mouth to say something, and then changed her mind. She looked like a wild creature caught in a snare, her eyes large with fear and rage—or panic.

"No!"

With a sob, she turned and ran out of the room.

Georgia put a hand on Lucien's shoulder.

"Lucien—I am appalled. When did all this begin?"

"All what?"

Lucien's body was shaking with shock and rage.

"Did you know that Octavia felt this way?"

"Good heavens, no! Not at all. She has always been pushy. I thought she just liked getting her own way. I never dreamed she felt this way. My sister!"

"Perhaps you should have told her more gently; you could have prepared her in some way for the news," Georgia suggested.

"Why would I do that? I had no idea that she felt this way about me. Besides, there is no way you can say anything gently to Octavia. Everything is black or white with her. Do you realize that no one ever says no to her? They manage her. They manipulate the circumstances. They—we—all skirt around the issues to avoid her rages."

Lucien gave a helpless shrug.

"Everything is always all about her. It is time she was told no! I don't know how she could ever have thought that I would want to marry her. It's sick."

He felt around for the back of a chair, and took a seat.

"Why doesn't she have friends of her own—boyfriends? I can't always be her best buddy—and I don't want to. I have never for one minute given any sign that what I felt for her was more than a brother."

He paused.

"That is why she always insists on saying I am a half-brother. As if that makes any difference. I don't know how I am going to continue living here, as if none of this has happened. I think I will move into the guest casita—at least until she goes to art school. It will be good for her to get away from here, meet some people who have similar interests. She spends her whole life cooped up in that room of hers. God knows what she does in there all the time. Don't you ever worry about her?"

"Alejandro seems to think that she should be left to work things out for herself. He thinks that she has an unusual destiny. And not an easy one."

"Well, it's not very easy for anyone else either. Someone needs to talk to her— maybe someone who is not involved with the family, who doesn't have to live with her tantrums. I think she needs to see a therapist."

"Oh, surely not, Lucien?"

But it was a question.

Georgia sat down at the table. She put a hand on his.

"Don't let this spoil anything for you and Sofia. I will discuss this with Sebastián, and we will see what's to be done. This is nothing that you must worry about."

She sat up straight.

"And now, let's talk about you. What are you and Sofia planning?"

Lucien made a desperate gesture with his hands.

"You don't seem to realize what has just happened. This isn't just a small family disagreement, maman. Don't you see that nothing will ever be the same again?" He put his right fist up to his temple, and knuckled it. "Do you really think I can just switch channels, and talk about wedding plans?"

Lucien stood up to go.

"I feel too rattled now to even think about a wedding."

Changes

Sebastián sat on his favorite rock on the pink hill, just below Magdalena's white cross. He was thinking about all the changes that were taking place at The Adobe.

It had all begun, he thought, when Lucien moved into the guest casita—on the face of it, and bearing in mind that he was soon to be married, not such an unusual thing. Perhaps it should have happened sooner.

How had they not noticed what was happening with Octavia? It must have begun long before this painful confrontation. Surely there must have been some clues to alert them to such inappropriate expectations.

He began to gather some small pebbles while he thought.

Of course, there had been that childhood crush he had noticed. He remembered mentioning it to Sister Piadosa, but they had decided it was just that—little sister, big brother admiration. Perhaps they had been deceived.

What did she do all day in her room—her Black Room?—he wondered. Perhaps it had not been wise to allow her quite so much unsupervised privacy. Lucien was right in saying that she always managed to get her own way. She had the room she wanted, the size and shape she wanted it, and even, against his initial wishes, the color she wanted. What did she do with all the hours she spent in it? She said she was working, and he knew from all the trips she made with him into Santa Fe that she was preparing to work with beads. Why was nobody allowed in? That was not right. He wondered now how that had been established. Why had he permitted it? He would speak to her.

His left hand had laid the pebbles into the soil—the beginning of an intricate pattern, using a variety of different-colored stones.

How wonderful everything had been when Georgia arrived. Lucien and Sofia had immediately formed a close childhood friendship—and his marriage to Georgia. He still couldn't quite believe, even after all this time, that Georgia Fitzgerald had married—him!

He remembered the day that Octavia was born. What an unforgettable day. To witness the birth of this impossibly small and perfect human being—his daughter! Perhaps this was when things first began to feel different. Certainly she had been a difficult infant—an extremely willful child.

Sebastián frowned. He had no siblings, no experience of how small children behaved. And Sister Piadosa repeatedly reminded him that there was no such thing as the average child—"and a good thing, too," she would add. "How boring the world would be if such was the case."

But, nevertheless, he felt instinctively that there was something different—more than different, something singular—about Octavia that set her apart.

He recalled his own sense of alienation when he was a child—and all through his adolescence. Old Elena, who used to work at the rectory when Father Octavio was alive, had seen it immediately, and she was never wrong. "Other" she called it. Perhaps that dark wind had blown its cold breath over Octavia as well. Perhaps that was what Alejandro meant when he said she was in love with passion?

Sebastián examined his work absent-mindedly. Eight triangles; their apexes almost touching at the center of the pattern.

And other changes. Sister Piadosa had been told to take things a little slower—which meant they would need to add on an extra room for her replacement. Sister Piadosa would stay on in a more advisory capacity. She would surely not leave. He could not imagine The Adobe without her. How fast the time had gone. It seemed such a short while ago that she had arrived with Sister Ana and the nuns. But it was almost twenty-five years.

And there was something going on with Georgia. She hadn't said anything, but she just wasn't herself. He thought back to the confident, self-possessed person he had known before she went to Paris. Where had that person gone?

Sebastián suddenly felt that everything was slipping away from him. It felt to him like a handful of sand, when it is held too tightly—how, the harder you hold it, the more it slips away between your fingers.

Was he all right—happy?

It came as a shock to realize that he didn't want to answer his own question.

Lucien and Sofia? Surely they were all right? Of course, that scene with Octavia had made things difficult. It was good that they were soon to marry, and get away for a while.

Mama—you worked so hard to make your dream a reality. What is happening to all of us?

He placed a small, black stone in the center of the pattern.

Wedding Plans

The late afternoon sun was streaming in through the small chapel windows.

Sofia sat close to Lucien, holding his hand. Sister Piadosa, Georgia, Sebastián and Salvador sat facing them.

Lucien spoke first.

"A small wedding, here in the chapel. It would seem silly to have a long engagement, so perhaps we can combine the two."

"And we want to make the white doves a part of the ceremony, in memory of my mother," said Sofia. "Perhaps, when we come out of the chapel—Gregorio could release them, so we can be sure that María knows we are thinking of her."

"Do you think my grandparents—your parents, maman—will come?" Lucien asked. "I wonder what they feel, not knowing anything about us. Do you think they are sad about it? Don't you think it is time to try and heal things with them?"

Georgia's lips tightened. "We'll see," was all she said.

Sister Piadosa gave her a sympathetic smile.

"And of course we will ask Mercedes and Encarnación," said Sofia, aware of the awkwardness, "and Diego and Roberto—and all the others who were at the rancho before it was sold."

"Yes, and then everyone at The Adobe," said Lucien—"Gregorio and his wife, and Refugio, Manuel and Pedro-Manuel—and Alejandro and Santiago."

"And, of course, all the nuns. Perhaps they would sing before Salvador and I arrive at the chapel door." Sofia clasped her hands. "It is all going to be so beautiful," she said.

"And, I would like Kristiyan to be my best man now that he's decided to stay— yet another year."

"I'm surprised that he is content to stay in such a small town when all of Europe is at his feet," said Georgia.

"I'm not," said Lucien. "He's in love with Octavia—poor guy. What a fate!"

"Isn't that a bit unkind?"

"No. You must know that he hasn't got a chance," said Lucien. "He's going to break his heart over her."

"Poor Kristiyan. Perhaps you should warn him."

"It wouldn't do any good. Anyway—I don't want to interfere."

"And what else would you like, Sofia? This is your big day," Georgia said tactfully.

"Oh, so many things! Firstly, I want all of us to remember everyone who will not be here."

She made a list of the names.

"Sebastián's mother, Magdalena, and of course Father Octavio—and Catherine, my grandmother." She broke off. "I wonder if there is anyone who knows where she is. Do you think she is alive? Didn't you say Mercedes believes she is in Mexico?"

"Perhaps María's sisters will know. We could ask."

"I wonder if that would do any good? They know nothing about me, and I don't know them. I am told that they didn't even come to my mother's funeral service, and they must have heard about it. But then, maybe they didn't," she added.

"Has anyone ever tried to trace her?" Lucien asked.

"Mercedes told me that there was a rumor of a beautiful diva who used to sing occasionally at a small, intimate music venue," said Sister Piadosa, "but no one knows if it is true—or whether it was Catherine. You know how stories grow. But surely, if it is indeed Catherine, it will be a well-kept secret. She must be well into her eighties."

"I wish we could find out," said Sofia wistfully. "She and Santiago are my only grandparents—I won't ever acknowledge Lorenzo!"

Her face became flushed with anger.

"He is a cruel tyrant," she said vehemently. "I don't ever want to meet him. I can't feel any pity for him—sorry, Sister Piadosa—but he ruined so many lives. And I think that secretly you agree."

"Perhaps we can just be grateful that he won't be here."

"And what else, Sofia?" asked Salvador.

Sofia turned to her father.

"More than anything, I want to remember my mother's love and courage—and the love that you and she shared. That is the greatest gift I could ever receive: to know that I am here today because of that love—and so is she!"

Salvador managed some kind of a smile.

"Do you think that you and Reuben, and the band, could play the music you wrote for her? For our first dance together—only if you feel happy about that?"

Salvador looked down at his hands.

"How could we not?" he said quietly.

"And also—I know it is not traditional—but I would like to sing the song my mother gave me."

She looked at Sister Piadosa.

"You and Sister Ana are the only ones ever to hear it—apart from me, of course."

Sofia frowned. "And that horrible little priest who was sent away—he heard a snatch of it." Sofia paused. "It didn't do him any good in the end," she added with satisfaction.

Sister Piadosa had to smile.

"Do you think it will be all right for me to do this?"

"I think it will be unforgettable, and quite wonderful. At what point in the service would you like to sing?"

"I thought—when I am walking up the aisle, to stand next to Lucien. Everyone else will be able to see me, but I want Lucien to see me through my song."

Catherine

Sebastián sat, looking out of the plane window. He knew that Mexico City was large but flying over it now, it seemed to go on forever. How did you ever find one person among so many millions? Of course, there were places where it would be extremely unlikely for him to find her. He thought he would follow the rumor of the beautiful diva.

He fastened his seat belt, but remained looking out as the runway rushed up to meet them.

Where would he begin?

He had booked a room at one of the more up-market hotels, and hoped he would be able to glean some information there about music clubs, or places that Catherine might frequent; places that were, perhaps, small and discreet. He wondered if she had changed her name—whether she was still in Mexico; still alive.

He took a cab to the hotel, and checked in.

Diego, the cab driver, following instructions given by the doorman, took him to a different part of town. The streets were cool and shady and lined with trees, some still full of late summer blooms. The buildings were painted in bright colors. The whole area had an atmosphere of old elegance, mixed with more than a touch of bohemian eccentricity. People sat and smoked outside doorways to shops and bars, or called out to friends as they walked along the street. The place felt warm and friendly to Sebastián.

The cab stopped outside a low adobe building that seemed to grow out of the street. There were no pavements. The place looked closed. The cab driver got out, and went and banged on the door.

"Gonsalez!" he shouted. "Someone to see you!"

There was a wait of some minutes, and then Sebastián heard the sound of a key being turned. The door opened, and a man stepped out into the street.

"Si, señor? May I be of assistance?"

Sebastián explained his mission to the man, and the reason for it.

Gonsalez shook his head. He had never heard of such a lady. He said something to the cab driver, and pointed to a building further down the street. The cab moved on. But with each stop, they were met with the same shake of the head.

"Maybe further down the street, next to the big green house with the balcony, number one thirty-eight—ask for Luis."

Sebastián lost count of the times they stopped to repeat their inquiry. Nobody could offer any information about the diva, now in her eighties, who had the magnificent voice.

"Señor, perhaps we stop here—have a drink. Something to eat? Maybe this will bring us some luck."

Diego stopped outside a small pavement café.

"You order, Diego; something refreshing to drink—and to eat, whatever you recommend."

Diego ordered two Jamaicas, soft drinks that Sebastián thought tasted like cranberry juice, and two tacos al pastor.

They both ate hungrily.

"Good choice, Diego. Thank you."

They finished their meal with coffee.

He was beginning to think how stupid he had been to imagine he would ever find one person who—even if she was still alive—would most probably have taken great care not to leave any trace of where she lived or worked. In this vast city, she could be anywhere.

He got up, and went to pay the bill. As he received his change, he asked the proprietor if he knew anywhere nearby where he might hear some live music—solo artists, singers of classical music. He did not mention that he was looking for anyone.

"Si, señor. Are you familiar with this area?"

Sebastián shook his head. He called out for Diego.

Diego wrote down a name and an address. He walked to the pavement with the proprietor, who proceeded to give him complicated instructions of left turns and right turns. Sebastián waited.

Finally Diego came up to him, and said he thought he would find the place— very few people knew about it. The entrance was inside a small courtyard, almost hidden from view.

Number eight. They rang the bell outside the wrought-iron security door. Sebastián could hear it ringing inside the building. They waited.

He rang again. They heard footsteps. A woman came to the door, but did not open it.

"Can I help you?" she said through the wrought-iron security door.

The woman was tall, slim and elegant. She wore an indigo-blue dress that emphasized the color of her eyes. Her face, although lined, still showed the clean outline of her jaw and her high cheek-bones, the fine line of her brow. Her hair showed traces of red fire.

Sebastián stared at the serene face in front of him. He had only met Catherine once before, at the fated concert where María sang the love duet with Salvador. He remembered the meeting vividly; how he had never before seen such loneliness in a face. He had been mesmerized by her sadness. And he remembered so clearly the last thing she said before her husband came and literally dragged her away. They were speaking about what it was that drew a person to write poetry. He had given some answer about desert sunsets and the souls of the dead. Not really an answer to her question at all. Now he recalled her words.

"No. It is deeper than that. It is what is given if ever we would save ourselves. It is a hunger for that dark touch. It is the only way we can come through. If we lose this, we are lost."

And then her husband came, and Sebastián, astounded, watched the presence of her slide back into the shadows, right before his eyes.

And now this poised woman was asking if she could be of help.

"Yes, I think you can. My name is Sebastián Chavez. My mother's name was Magdalena. We met once, at a concert where María de la Cruz was to sing. We spoke about poetry. Father Octavio was with us. Do you remember? The composer of the music was—"

He broke off. The woman was staring at him.

"Salvador Fuentes!"

"Yes."

She threw open the iron security door.

He smiled.

"Hello, Catherine," he said.

ㅁㅁㅁ

Two weeks had passed since Sebastián had returned from his visit to Mexico City. Wedding plans and preparations were underway, the chapel was freshly painted, and the nuns had polished the pews until they shone.

Sofia was only told that her grandmother was coming to meet her, and to attend the wedding, once it was certain that this would be possible. Catherine would arrive three weeks before the ceremony, so that she and Sofia could spend time together.

ㅁㅁㅁ

Sebastián sat, drinking an espresso in the small café area of Albuquerque Airport. The Air Mexico flight was delayed by forty minutes. He had been idly watching people come and go up and down the escalator and the staircase, allowing his thoughts free rein.

He wondered what everyone would feel, meeting Catherine again after so many years—wondered what Catherine would feel. And Sofia. This was her grandmother.

How very painful their meeting in Mexico City had been.

How did you tell a woman that her child had been dead for over twenty years? How did you break such news?

All the time, while driving with Diego, he almost hoped that they would not find Catherine; that he would not have to find the words to make it sound—what—less tragic? Somehow, impossibly, less final? How would anyone be able to do this? There was no gentle way of telling it.

ㅁㅁㅁ

They ordered coffee, and sat drinking it in the courtyard of the hotel.

There was an awkward silence.

Finally Sebastián put his cup down and leaned forward across the table, reaching out a hand to Catherine. She touched it lightly, but remained sitting upright.

"Sebastián," she said, "I think you must just tell me why you are here. I can see from your face that it is going to be something painful."

There was a long silence.

"Catherine," Sebastián said finally, "María is dead."

Catherine's lips were white, but she said nothing.

"She died quite some time ago. No one knew where to find you."

"Go on."

"She died shortly after her birthday—her twenty-third birthday."

Catherine struggled to keep her composure; struggled to connect with this impossible information. But it was too much for her.

"No! No! No!" She was shaking. "No—it can't be. Not María! It is not true! Not María. Not my María. You are mistaken!"

She stared at Sebastián, searching for—what? Some way out?

"Tell me it isn't true," she pleaded.

"I can't," he said softly. "I am so sorry.

"At first we did not know why Don Lorenzo brought her to The Adobe. We could not imagine his motive. And then, when Sister Piadosa discovered that María was pregnant, María told her the whole story. She and Salvador had married secretly on the night of her sixteenth birthday."

"María and Salvador got married that night?"

"Yes. Alejandro married them."

Catherine said nothing.

"Don Lorenzo did not know this when he found them together that night, on the eve of her twenty-first birthday. They had just made love when he stormed in."

Catherine put a hand up to her mouth.

"María thought he was asleep. It was perhaps a crazy thing to do—but they hadn't seen each other for five years."

"I can't believe it! How is it possible that we didn't notice anything? For five years!"

Sebastián offered no answer.

"After he brought her back—at the time of her sixteenth birthday—he threatened to harm both of them if Salvador ever came near her again. I wonder how, in all that time, they managed to communicate. I do remember that María was unusually quiet, but I put that down to sadness."

Catherine cast her mind back.

"I know that Roberto set up a work-table in one of the empty stables. He said she was working with clay—or something like that. I didn't give it a thought. I don't suppose they could have met there."

"Unlikely. They would surely have been discovered."

"I knew nothing of the second visit. I woke that morning to find my husband in the worst rage I had ever witnessed; yelling and shouting at everyone. María didn't come out of her room. Mercedes told me a bit about what had happened. But of course no one, not even María, knew she was pregnant then.

"Lorenzo went on and on at María: that she was going to do as she was told; she was going to marry this man he had chosen. She didn't argue with him. She didn't even look at him. I remember feeling so proud when she said: 'You can shout at me all you like—but you cannot make me say yes'."

Catherine paused.

"I am trying to remember the day she left. It was such a dark time. It must have been several weeks—no, more like a month after her birthday. She came to say good-bye. She had shaved off all her beautiful hair."

Catherine burst into tears.

Sebastián waited.

"And I do remember now how Mercedes told me that María had been vomiting. We thought it was because of..."

She began to sob.

"All this was going on—and I was there! How is it I didn't know? Why wasn't I there for her? Why didn't I do anything? Why...?"

Sebastián touched her hand lightly.

"Perhaps María knew her father too well, Catherine. She knew she would never win with him; nor would she ever compromise. If she was going to lose, she would have the satisfaction of knowing that he would lose as well. I am sure she also knew that you would be the one to bear the brunt of his rage."

"I can't believe I was so ineffectual."

"Years of bullying, Catherine, will bring anyone down. Years of trying to protect María from his violence. What could you do with such a man? Perhaps María knew that this was the only possible way that she, and you, would ever be free of him."

He waited while Catherine struggled to compose herself.

"María begged us not to let a word of it be made known, or her father would come and take her and the child away; he would do to the child what he had done to her all her life. He would control her. She would have no freedom."

He looked at Catherine.

"But then, you know all about that part of the story."

Catherine nodded, but said nothing.

"So Sister Piadosa dressed her in a nun's habit, and declared that María was considering taking holy orders."

"Did anyone believe this?" Catherine asked.

"Well, yes, until she fainted one morning while Father Octavio was there to deliver Christmas presents and conduct the Christmas Mass. While he waited for help to come, he noticed her condition. When she was tucked up in the infirmary, Sister Piadosa told him the whole story."

Sebastián looked at Catherine's shocked face. "Shall I go on?"

She nodded.

"Well, Father Octavio was furious, and vowed to bring the couple together—give them a church wedding, and make their circumstances known publicly so that Don Lorenzo could not hush things up. He said he had wondered for a long time why you looked so tired and frail. Now he understood what was behind all that, and María's so-called sudden delicate health, her absence from choir practice, and her sudden absence from Salvador's concert after only one performance. He was appalled."

"So what happened next?"

"Unfortunately Father Octavio died before he could do any of these things. He suffered a heart attack."

Catherine's face was unreadable.

"I should have fought for her. I did all I could; but his sudden rages, his voice shouting in my face—his abusive language—his—his..."

Sebastián paused until she became calm.

"Sister Piadosa and Sister Ana kept her secret—even from the dreadful French priest who was sent to replace Father Octavio. He didn't last long, thank heaven. It was he who declared she was a heretic when she refused to make her confession to him. Because of this, on his orders, María was buried outside the camposanto."

He nodded at Catherine's look of inquiry.

"Yes. But Sister Piadosa granted her absolution. The Church accepted it as valid after learning some home truths about Father Jean-Luc Sel.

"María was very strong, Catherine. She was strong through all of it, right up to her death.

"It was only after it was discovered that he had betrayed the secrets of the confessional, and was deemed to have been unfit to hear her confession—and he was to be sent back to France in disgrace—that the whole truth of María and Salvador's marriage was made clear."

"I almost can't believe it. It is like something you might read in a novel; not something that actually happened. And I wasn't there for her—"

Catherine's voice broke, and she gave a sob. "My beautiful, gifted María..."

He waited while she fumbled for a handkerchief.

"There was an exhumation ceremony, attended by everyone at The Adobe. Your husband was present, and Salvador; and all the staff who worked at the rancho. They were told the whole story—not your husband, of course. Mercedes was devastated. Sofia, who was three at the time, was also present with her foster-parents. Strangely,

Don Lorenzo did not seem to notice her striking likeness to her mother."

Catherine made no comment.

"There was a ceremony, granting absolution, and then a 'marriage ceremony' before witnesses that was conducted by Father Rafael."

"How on earth did they conduct a marriage?"

"It was what many considered to be a miracle. When the coffin was lifted out of the grave, the lock on the lid burst open and bright light, so witnesses claimed, poured out of the crack. Later the lid was opened, and María's hair streamed out like a shining river, and ran all the way down the aisle. She was untouched by death. She lay just as the nuns had dressed her, in her wedding-dress, looking as if she slept."

Catherine had a hand up to her mouth.

"Did you see this too?"

"It is difficult to express exactly what did happen. I think everyone's awareness was so heightened by the experience—so beyond anyone's imagination—that what we saw could not be expressed in any rational way. There are many differing accounts of what happened. Maybe such things just will not fit into a common-sense account."

"And then..."

"Father Rafael conducted the service, with Salvador standing beside María."

"And you say my husband was there through all this!"

"Don Lorenzo looked frightened. He walked out before the end. For Jean-Luc Sel it was terrifying. But for the rest of the congregation it was nothing short of miraculous—indeed, the word 'milagro' was on everyone's lips."

□□□

"Day-dreaming, Sebastián?"

Catherine, for all her eighty-seven years, was a strikingly beautiful woman.

"Catherine!" He rose and embraced her. "You look wonderful. This is just so incredible. I wonder how we will all manage the joy, and the grief—all the emotion—and the utter miracle of this meeting."

"I must thank you for everything, Sebastián—for our time together in Mexico City; that I have had time to grieve; that I can arrive without making everyone feel bad on my account. It was a difficult message you had to bring. Thank you for your courage and your gentleness."

She smiled, and he could see a flash of the Catherine he had met all those decades ago.

"But we read each other perfectly during that meeting at the concert—didn't we?"

"Yes, Catherine," he said. "It was unforgettable."

He took her hand luggage, and together they went down the escalator to collect her bags.

Sofia watched the car turn in at the bottom of the narrow track that led up to

82

The Adobe. She couldn't tell whether she was feeling nervous, excited or terrified. This was her grandmother—her only grandmother—for Salvador's mother had died giving birth to him. There was so much she wanted to know about her mother—what she was like when she was a little girl.

Sister Piadosa had told her as much about María as she knew, but that was not about her childhood. She wanted to know all about her mother's life—her dreams at the Rancho de Las Palomas, where she grew up. She had heard all about her grandfather's tyranny, and how cruel he was to Catherine. But she wanted to know about her mother's day-to-day joys and sorrows as a young girl: the happy times.

The car stopped. Sebastián jumped out, and went round to open Catherine's door. Sofia stepped forward to greet her grandmother.

Catherine stepped out of the car and stood still, regarding the beautiful young woman who came toward her.

In front of her stood the young woman she had been so many decades ago.

In front of her stood María.

Tears began to fall down her cheeks.

Sofia went up to her grandmother, and put her arms around her.

Sebastián felt a lump form in his throat. How had de la Cruz failed to recognize the three-year-old Sofia, at the exhumation, as María's child, his and Catherine's granddaughter? The likeness, in spite of the great age difference, was startling.

"May I call you Catherine?"

"Oh, my sweetheart—of course you may."

Catherine gathered her grandchild into her arms.

Sister Piadosa was waiting at the guest suite.

"I am so very happy to meet you at last."

She reached out a hand, but Catherine stepped forward to embrace her, the tears falling freely.

"And I you. I want to hear every detail you can remember about María's stay here before she...she..."

Catherine could not bring herself to say the word.

"María told me so much about you. She said she could feel your love even though you and she were separated. She loved you so very, very much. What a dreadful time it was. I am sure you want to know everything—but you must be tired."

She took the small carry-on bag from Catherine, and placed it next to the dressing-table.

"Sister Ana will be down in a few minutes to help you unpack. If there is anything you need, please let her know. Would you like to eat supper here on your own and have an early night, or would you like Sofia to join you?"

"If Sofia is free, I would love to have supper with her. I knew coming back to New Mexico and seeing all the familiar places—the landmarks I know so well—

would be an emotional experience, but nothing really prepares you, does it?"

She paused.

"Would you show me where María is buried—now, before I do anything else?"

Sister Piadosa took her hand, and together they walked down the path to the camposanto.

Once there, the two women stood in silence.

"I know it must sound very unsympathetic—wicked—of me to say this, but I am so relieved that there is no chance that I will have to see my husband. Is that very callous, sister?" Catherine said, as they walked slowly back to the casita.

"Not at all. And if it makes you feel any better, both Sofia and I feel the same relief. I met your husband only once, and from my observation and all that I learned from María, I think it is for the best for all of us."

There was a knock at the door, and Sister Ana entered.

"I will leave you to rest, Catherine. Sister Ana will unpack your cases. Sofia will come with your supper at seven o'clock—does that suit you?"

"That will be lovely. Thank you so much, sister."

While Sister Ana unpacked, and hung up the dresses for the creases to fall out, Catherine stepped outside and looked about her.

This was the landscape her daughter had known while she carried her child. This was the last place she saw before she died. And this was the place where Sofia was born—where she grew up, knowing only love and beauty and serenity; a place fragrant with lavender and herbs; and piñon smoke in winter.

Catherine compared the simplicity of the buildings and their humble contents to the ostentatious vulgarity of the Rancho de Las Palomas, where she and her husband Lorenzo had raised their children. It was he who had commanded all the furnishings and interior décor. He knew, he said, far better than his wife what was appropriate for a family which bore the name—de la Cruz.

Catherine found a chair, and sat, drinking in the serenity of her surroundings. She looked up at the small, white cross that stood like a protective presence, overlooking the valley from the pink hill. She wondered what it signified. There was so much she wanted to know.

Matilde

Georgia and Lucien drove down to Albuquerque the week after Catherine arrived.

Lucien had not been told that Matilde was coming for the wedding, so the trip was on the pretext of collecting a shipment of goods for The Adobe.

They arrived at the airport ten minutes early. Georgia said they would have to wait a little for the goods to be off-loaded.

"Would you like a cup of coffee? We might as well sit while we wait."

They sat, sipping the strong coffee in the small alcove, discussing what still had to be organized for the wedding.

"What will we do if it rains? How will all the guests get from the chapel to the hall without getting drenched?"

"Sofia has already thought of that. She bought a dozen umbrellas, just in case. We will have to find some runners to take the umbrellas from the hall to the chapel, and back again. Maybe some children from the school."

Georgia took his hand.

"You are marrying a very remarkable woman. Not only is she beautiful, but she sings like an angel, and—she is incredibly practical."

"I know. How did I ever get to be so lucky?"

At that moment Georgia saw Matilde walking toward them. She put a finger up to her mouth, and indicated for Matilde to greet Lucien first.

"Bonjour, monsieur. Comment ça va?"

Lucien started.

"Pardon?" he said, automatically switching to French.

"J'espère que vous pouver m'aider, monsieur. Je suis inconnue à ce pays."

Lucien stood up.

"Bonjour, madame. Comment puis-je vous aider?"

"Je cherche quelqu'un."

"Oui?"

"Je cherche un petit garçon—il s'appelle—"

She paused—

"Il s'appelle Lucien. Lui connaissez-vous?"

There was a long pause.

"Matilde!" It was a shout.

Lucien held his arms out wide. Matilde ran into them, laughing. She had to stand on her toes and reach up to hug him.

"Oh, my goodness. What a wonderful surprise. I can't believe it is really you."

"And I don't remember that you were so tall. What 'as 'appened to you while I was away? Where 'as my little boy gone?"

Lucien laughed, and hugged her fiercely.

"Maman! You didn't tell me."

Georgia and Matilde hugged each other, laughing and crying at the same time.

"And when we get to The Adobe," Lucien announced, "one of the first things I want to do is to sing you your song."

Father Rafael

Father Rafael was the priest for the parish of Las Madres and the surrounding area, which included The Adobe and many other small-holdings.

His entry into the priesthood had been a complicated one owing to a strange set of circumstances, the first being the legacy of his grandfather, Felipe Montdragón.

Felipe was a Penitente who had been banished by the brotherhood after he painted a retablo of Christ on the cross, with the head and horns of a ram. At this time their morada—a small adobe church they had built—had been plagued by a series of raids by hooligan gangs, who thought it great sport to beat up the Penitentes and damage their buildings. It was thought at the time that the Cristo Carnero had attracted this evil. Felipe left the brotherhood that same night.

His son, Rafael's father, was forbidden to go near a paint-brush. So it was with dismay that it was discovered that the young Rafael, Felipe's grandson, had painted an exquisite, though unorthodox image of Christ on the cross, wearing a brightly colored Mexican serape, his head thrown back and surrounded by wild red hair—and laughing. He had never been told the family history. Now it was feared that Rafael had inherited "the taint." It was decided that he should turn his back on painting in general, and on the Cristo Risueño in particular, and enter the priesthood.

He was given the parish after Father Octavio's death, following an extremely bitter interlude involving the tormented French priest, who was later sent back to his country to face the music.

ㅁㅁㅁ

Rafael arrived at The Adobe just before lunch, and found Sebastián speaking to Gregorio outside the big barn.

"Hello there, Sebastián! Gregorio! So are you ready for the big day?"

"Good morning, father," said Gregorio.

"Good to see you, Rafael," Sebastián said. "Are you coming to put the young couple through their paces?"

"That—and I want to know what kind of a service they would like to have; what readings, and so on. Also, I want to ask them how they want to speak their vows."

"Don't you chaps have to stick to the rules?" Sebastián said wickedly.

Rafael was familiar with Sebastián's take on religion, and gave a grin.

"For an old heathen like you I would be expected to bend them a little, if only to make sure you understand what is going on."

Gregorio looked on, bemused.

"I think I'll go and see to loading the truck," he said. "I want to leave right after lunch. Excuse me, father."

He disappeared into the barn.

"I think you scared him off," Sebastián said with a laugh. "Come. Let's go and find Sofia and Lucien."

The wedding party sat in the chapel—Sofia with pen and paper, making notes.

"And here for you to read, are the words and vows we would like to exchange on the day. I hope they are appropriate. We don't want to land you in hot water."

Rafael laughed.

"Hot water doesn't scare me! Sometimes it even wakes people up a bit."

He paused.

"Your father, Lucien, will vouch for me in this. We have known each other a long, long time, and in that time we have both occasionally pushed against what is not questioned by others, with varying degrees of success—and varying degrees of hot water," he added.

Lucien chuckled.

"And you, Sofia, must have heard many times about all the goings-on and scandals of the past, from Father Octavio's funeral service—for which he wrote the words before he died, and which had all the church elders whispering about blasphemy—and on to that sanctimonious French priest, who, most thankfully, was sent back to his country in disgrace. Sister Piadosa became a literal firebrand whenever he came here. You must have a lot you would like to say to him too, Sofia."

"More than a lot!" she said.

"So, The Adobe is very familiar with hot water. I think it will be able to weather your vows."

He stood up.

"Now, let's just run through some logistics. I will stand here."

He moved into position. "Where would you like Lucien and the best man to be while they wait for you?"

"I think here is best."

Sofia took charge and moved around the chapel, indicating who would stand here and who there.

Lucien sat in one of the pews, listening to their voices and trying to get an idea of the relative positions.

"Father Rafael, where will my mother and Matilde and Sebastián be standing?"

Rafael took his arm.

"Come, Lucien, let's walk through the movements for the ceremony, so you have an idea of where everyone is standing or sitting. We will begin with you, walking in from the vestry with Kristiyan to a position on my left..."

But Lucien persisted.

"I will not be able to see my three parents. I want to be able to touch them, in the chapel, before the service begins—I want to touch them."

By midday it was all settled.

Sofia and Lucien went off to see Sister Piadosa, and Rafael went to take up Georgia's offer of lunch.

Sofia's Wedding

From early dawn the white doves had been making restless, cooing sounds in the aviary.

Sister Piadosa, on her way to the office after morning prayers, heard their agitation, and walked down to the barn to call Gregorio.

"Oh—there you are, Gregorio. There seems to be something upsetting the doves. I can't see anything the matter, but would you take a look? Something seems to have disturbed them."

Gregorio made his familiar dove sounds as he approached the large security aviary where the doves were housed at night, safe from predators. He opened the door to let them out for their morning flight.

But instead of taking to the air in ragged flight as they usually did, they flew up to settle on the ridge-pole of the roof, and jostled each other for position.

Gregorio peered inside. Perhaps a rat had got into the cage. But no. The cage was empty.

"So what is troubling you, my beauties?" he asked.

He waited.

When there was no sign that they wanted to fly, he reluctantly left them and went to complete his other morning tasks with the rest of the livestock.

The sun had just touched the top of the pink hill when Catherine stepped out of her guest casita, wearing a gown and slippers. Her long hair, with its faint traces of fire, hung down in a thick braid, almost to her waist. She was about to take a seat on the outdoor bench when she heard a rushing sound. Looking up, she saw the whole flock of doves lift up from the aviary roof with a familiar flapping of wings, and fly over her—so low she could almost reach up and touch them.

"María!" she whispered.

She arranged the cushions, and was about to lie back when Sofia came down the path toward her.

"Too excited to sleep?"

Sofia nodded.

"Come and sit with me."

She made a space for Sofia on the bench beside her.

"And you are up very early as well," Sofia remarked.

"Yes. I heard the doves cooing. They know that today is a special day."

She lay back against the cushions.

"Your mother—when she was a little girl—and I used to lie back just like this, in the big hammock up at the Rancho de Las Palomas, and watch the doves. They were a gift to me from my husband, shortly after María was born. No other gift ever gave me such pleasure."

She smiled at Sofia.

"Of course, these are not the very same doves. That was well over forty years ago. But they still carry the memory."

Sofia snuggled up close to her, and together they watched the doves. Every time they flew low over the casita, Sofia's loose hair would lift up. Catherine, looking on in wonder, would see the familiar blue sparks fly up to join them in their flight, and she would fancy that this was María, and that time had vanished.

"Sister Piadosa has told me all about your birth; how your mother gave you the only gift she had to give—your song. How she sang to you, all during her pregnancy."

"Yes. She told me as well. And now people still say that if you sit quietly in the early evening, after work is over, you can hear that song on the wind."

Sofia paused.

"She couldn't keep me—they had to keep my birth a secret. Did Sister Piadosa tell you that as well?"

"Yes—and I heard it from Sebastián as well, when he first came to Mexico. I heard all about her death, and the exhumation service two years later."

"Did they tell you how they opened the coffin and saw my mother lying there, in her wedding-dress, looking like a bride?"

"Yes."

"And how, even as they watched, her hair began to grow; how they saw it tumble over the sides of the coffin, and flow like a river of fire all down the chapel aisle?"

"Yes. All the people around here recognized the milagro—everyone except Lorenzo. Sister Piadosa told me that his face went white. She said he looked afraid."

Catherine took Sofia's hand.

"Not even death could touch the purity of her soul."

"Won't you tell me something about my mother—something that made her happy; perhaps something that she loved? I would like to be able to see her in that way—especially today."

"There is something which stands out in my mind. It is not all happy, but then nothing ever was at our home unless Lorenzo was away. But this one thing was, I think, a turning-point in your mother's life, so it is worth remembering. It will tell you so much about her spirit."

Sofia sat up to face Catherine, and listened attentively.

"It was the first day of spring, and it was the custom for Lorenzo and Diego, the farm manager, to ride out on horseback to inspect the lands. Lorenzo had María on a cushion in front of him. It was her eighth birthday, and it was the first time she would go along with the two men. I can still remember the dress she was wearing. They had just cleared a rise when Lorenzo saw a female elk that had not joined the herd for the spring migration. He reined in his horse, grabbed his gun from the saddle and shot her."

"For no reason?"

"For no reason other than sport."

"Sport?"

"Lorenzo always liked to boast that he was an excellent marksman."

"How horrible."

"Yes. When they got up to her," Catherine continued, "María jumped down and ran to hold the elk's head in her lap until she died, and when Lorenzo tried to pull her away, Diego told me that María said, without looking at him: 'Don't touch me!'

"Diego said that Lorenzo stood back. He didn't know what to do! That was a first for him!

"Diego examined the elk, and saw that she had recently foaled; that the baby must be somewhere close by.

"Against Lorenzo's wishes, they found the baby elk and brought him back to the rancho. Your mother called him Santo, and he used to follow her everywhere. It was such a love affair."

Catherine smiled at her granddaughter.

"But when Santo got a bit bigger they gave him his own paddock, and María had to stay away from him. That was hard. Diego said he had to forget his trust in people. He said they would have to take him to a safe, wild place where he could learn how to be a wild elk. He would want to be free to find a mate."

"Where did they take him?"

"There is a place called the Valle Grande. It is a vast valley high up in the mountains, and it is the wintering-place for the elk. Diego and José and your mother took him there in late autumn."

Catherine paused.

"I could have wept for her; so young, and having to learn that if you love some-

90

thing that needs to be free, you must find enough love inside you to let it go."

"You said it was a turning-point."

"She went up to the valley as a little girl. She came back, suddenly grown in some way that would be difficult to articulate. Her father would have said she grew disobedient. He would have been wrong. She was obeying a far deeper command. This was the time he lost her trust and respect—and her love. And it was from this time that she knew that nobody—and most certainly not her father—would ever tame her."

"So she lived her truth from that time?"

"Yes."

"I am so glad you told me this."

They lay in silence, and watched the doves as the sun rose over the hill and touched the tops of the cottonwoods. It was going to be a beautiful day.

The Journal

It was late afternoon on a hot August day.

Octavia sat on the pink hill, just below the small grove of yuccas. Behind her, Magdalena's white cross stood clean and stark against the sky.

She had come there to write in her journal, but it lay unopened in her lap. She had been there for over an hour, allowing her heart to catch up with the events of the past months.

Lucien and Sofia were on honeymoon. She did not want to think about that. She did not want to think about any aspect of the wedding, especially the emotional meeting between Sofia and her grandmother, Catherine. She didn't have a grandmother; not one that she was likely to see, or who would love her. To think of this made her feel abandoned in some way. No, she wouldn't think about it.

She wanted to think about her beads.

Gregorio was making her some special shelving on which she would be able to store her growing collection of bottles—bottles filled with every shape of bead imaginable.

"I am going to need space for hundreds of bottles, Gregorio—but not very deep. Only about so—"

Octavia indicated a depth of about six inches.

"And the top three shelves about eight inches apart. The lower shelves can be about half of that."

"And how long do you want the shelves?"

"I think three feet should be room enough. I can always add more shelves if I need them."

Gregorio asked questions, and made notes on a scrap of paper.

"And where would you like them to be?"

"Could you make three free-standing units? Then I can put them wherever they look best."

She didn't want to tell Gregorio that she didn't want anyone—not even him—inside her work-room.

"Good, Octavia. And I will put them on castors, so they will be easy to move. They'll be ready at the end of the week."

Octavia gave him a swift hug.

"There now," he said, taken aback. "It'll be a pleasure."

The bead collection was impressive. Octavia had found a bead shop in Santa Fe, not far from the Plaza, that sold beautiful antique beads.

"These beads came originally from Europe," the owner of the store explained, "but they found their way along the trade routes to northern Africa. They were used there as items of trade for hundreds of years."

"They look so old; sort of antique."

"That is because they have been used and handled over and over. See how the marks of their previous usage are clearly evident in the worn and pitted surfaces. Now they are highly sought after, and are being bought back—to be traded once more."

Octavia loved these beads in particular. They made her think of adobe—that mix of mud and straw, used for building—and how it gained a certain gravitas over the years through its weathering down to the soil of its origin, only to be shaped once more for building. She loved the quality—almost, she thought, the presence—that things acquired when they have been used and handled many times over the decades. It was as if memory resided within their very substance.

There were brass beads that were made in a sand-mold in Africa through the lost wax process; no two alike. They looked very ancient. What work must have gone into making one wax bead at a time, she thought. She had beads made of glass and metal and bone; some of semi-precious stones, shell and horn. In a separate glass case she found beads made of metal, dipped in gold, that made her think of icons.

It was as she was about to leave the shop that she saw the crystals—a small cabinet with crystals hanging on fine nylon thread. There were several different shapes and sizes: some tear-shaped and cut with a few large facets; others round with many small facets, like a diamond. Octavia bought four, all different. She would hang them in the south-facing window of her studio.

In a second-hand bookshop she found a book that told the history of beads. From this she read about the Anglo-Saxon origin of the word "bead"; how it came from "bede", meaning prayer. So that is where the term "prayer-beads" originated, she mused.

She learned how, long before that, in prehistoric times, Neanderthal man made beads from the teeth, claws, horn and bone of the animals whose powers he wished to carry with him; how even found stones that had a hole in them became power objects. Octavia could feel a fierce connection to their early sense of wonder: the thought that one small bead could represent the inner power or force of something else. A single bear-claw could carry the entire totem power and energy of bear protection for the wearer. She could well imagine the awe they must have felt as the enormity of this thought exploded into their consciousness.

She touched the heavy bead necklace she wore around her neck. She had made it for herself. The beads were threaded on several strands of violin-string that Salvador had discarded. They were the size of large pearls, irregular and black, and made from a kind of smoky quartz—and they carried flashes of fire when the light caught them. She was unable to discover their age; only that they came from somewhere in Africa. They held for her some dark earth power.

Together with Gregorio, she designed a work-frame for the tapestries. She had gone with him to choose the wood, and it would soon be finished.

"I think it should be fairly solid—heavy, so that it stands firmly when you are working. I know Alejandro likes cedar because of its clean smell. Would you like me to use that?"

He held up a handful of shavings.

"Smell that. Perhaps you will be able to get some of that fragrance into your work." He smiled at her.

"I will do my very best, Gregorio."

Journal Entry 2

"Erotic desire and its satisfaction is the key to the origin of the world." From The Book of Baruch. I can't find this book. I just tripped over the quote in a bookshop. I can feel its truth, but I can't really understand it. How does this translate into the world as it is now? Perhaps it is possible to experience that passion through some other medium—art, for instance. I wonder if mama ever thinks these things.

"Identification with the star is possible only to the chosen few."

I'm not sure of the significance of this, but I hope I am one of those few. Do I identify with the stars? I know I share something with them. But, why does the quote say "star"—and not "stars"? I will ask Alejandro.

"Biblically, the desert is a place of transition. It is a place of dislocation."

Perhaps this is why I feel so at home in desert places. I wonder what this transition will look like for me.

I made a note of a quotation by Esther Harding. It was written as an inscription in a book celebrating women artists—

"The woman who is virgin, one-in-herself, does what she does—not because of any desire to please, not to be liked, or to be approved, even by herself; not because of any desire to gain power over another—but because what she does is true."

I have written it out in large letters. It is on the wall in front of me where I work. How I long to grow into this!

Ever since the wedding in August, she had been waitressing in a small restaurant in Las Madres. The money she made was spent on beads and special beading-needles and thread, and black linen cloth for backing. She also had a growing collection of books, mostly second-hand. Among them was an illustrated book of Russian icons. She could feel a growing sense of excitement: that, rather like her spiral stone path, she was moving closer and closer to some kind of center—to what she wanted to do with her life.

The Icon

Octavia sat, bent over the work-frame, her eyes focused on the very precise placing of three gold beads.

Next to her, on a small table to her right, was a collection of bottle-lids, each holding a number of beads of different shapes and colors. These were the beads she was using for one small section of the total work.

In front of her, on her easel, she had clipped a tracing of the finished design, one she adapted from an early sketch of Lucien in cut-off denims, and wearing a Mexican poncho of bright colors. It showed him standing in an archway, which might have been the entrance to a church. It was reminiscent of the devotional style of painting seen in the retablos she had studied. Behind the figure, framed by the arch, was a night sky full of stars.

It was small in scale, with not too many details. Using dress-maker's chalk on the back of the tracing she had made from the sketch, she managed to transpose the design onto the black linen cloth, which was now stretched over the frame. She had been working it section by section, noticing how even the smallest beads added to the life of the work. She soon learned the value of a clear outline.

Gregorio, with great skill, had fashioned two round poles, like long rolling-pins, top and bottom of the frame, to which the fabric could be attached. These could be wound up or down and then fixed securely into place, so that the fabric remained taut, and the area to be worked would be close at hand.

On the large table to her left were several books, open at the pages she had been studying. Many of them were books that she found at Chimayo. Among them was an illustrated book on the crafting of devotions: works by local santeros, showing bultos and retablos—exquisite paintings of a religious nature, done on wood—all collector's pieces. There was something in the passion of this work that called to her; the powerful simplicity of its design. Looking at these works, she could feel how the artists had allowed the forms to come through them. Would she be able to allow this in her work? The word "sacred" came into her mind. It was not the subject-matter that drew her. Rather, it was the feeling of reverence that shone through them.

She was drawn particularly to the book of Russian icons, because of the formality and precision of their design; and a book, written in Spanish, about Huichol Indian ritual art. Indispensable was a book titled Beads Through the Ages, which contained illustrations of beadwork from all countries around the world; its different styles and purposes. Many cultures used beads as a decorative art, which simultaneously served to honor some ancient spiritual practice.

Of huge value was a work-book on how to work with beads. She spent hours making notes, especially about what to avoid.

"Work on one color bead at a time. Do not be tempted to fix a loose bead of another color section with the current thread. There may be times when you will want to unpick one area only, and it will cost you time if beads from another section suddenly become loose and fall out."

"Take note of the effects created by setting different sizes, colors and textures (shiny or matte) against each other."

"Remember to step back from time to time. It is a good idea to have a moveable light by which to see the effect of the brilliance in the overall work. Interesting effects can be obtained by slanting tube beads in different directions. This, alone, can transform the ordinary into something sacred."

"The study of the effect of light on the beads, particularly on those that have a brilliant shine, is essential. Light may also distort the desired effect."

"Always work with a bead-apron, designed to prevent beads from dropping on the floor. It will save time—and beads!"

"Make space for the creative impulse to surprise you. Follow that voice."

Journal Entry 3

I have hung my four crystals in the south-facing window! From time to time I look up to rest my eyes, and there they are, winking brightly at me. So full of light!

This work is so slow. I can feel my impatience nagging me—but there is no way I can hurry this process. I didn't realize that in every small packet of beads, seemingly all the same, no two beads are alike. I have to select each bead with care, making sure it fits the space. How strange that I, with all my impetuosity and impatience, should have chosen such a medium to work in.

I can feel a raw lament for my loss, for this betrayal I feel, rising up inside me. I want these beadworks to be icons that will, I hope, offer a response to this—will offer a lament in visual form—and maybe something else.

I am using two different shades of gold beads for the hair—one is small and shiny, and one is matte. The braids look so incredibly alive. I have added a tiny, intense purple bead to give definition and shadow.

Oh, the stars! The stars! I played the Puccini over and over while I worked the night sky contained by the arch. I think some of the music has turned into stars for me. I want to say thank you!

I want to find my own style, and yet keep the intensity—the sense of sacred presence—which the icons embrace. I want to discover for myself what I hold to be sacred.

I have fallen in love with beads.

This is the way I will speak to Lucien—and he will never be able to receive it.

The Recital

Kristiyan stood at the door of Octavia's Black Room, waiting for her to respond to his knock. The door opened.

"Oh, hello, Kristiyan—how nice to see you."

Kristiyan blushed. Why did Octavia have this effect on him? After all, he was fourteen years her senior. But there was something about her, he thought—what was it? The word that came to him was—authority.

"I'm giving a recital with Reuben, Salvador and some other musicians—together with the Santa Fe Choir—next Saturday. Would you like to come with me?

They have invited me to play for a selection of tango works, and I will also perform one solo piece by John Tavener. I would love to hear what you think of his music. It is a rather strange choice—Tavener and tango—but I think you will enjoy the music. It will end early, and then we can all go and have supper somewhere."

He smiled at her.

"Do say you will come—please."

Octavia sat in the small recital room, facing the raised stage with its grand piano, its music-stands and empty chairs. She was studying the program.

She had heard of Piazzolla, because Reuben spoke of him often, but she had never heard his music. She read the short note about him and his work, and then about the other composer, John Tavener, of whom she knew nothing. Reuben, Salvador and Kristiyan would perform Piazzolla's Milonga Del Angél, Tristeza Separación, Oblivion, and the popular Café 1930. There would be a short interval. The second part of the program would include three works by Tavener: Thrinos—a composition for solo cello; Svyati, and Song for Athene—both with the choir. The concert would end with music composed by Salvador Fuentes in memory of his wife, María. It had been the theme music for a play that he had written and Reuben had choreographed, called Tango Amor—Tango Muerte. Reuben would play the bandoneon, and Salvador and Kristiyan would accompany him on the violin and the cello respectively.

A man appeared on stage, and gave a brief introduction to the recital.

"Good evening, ladies and gentlemen. This evening we will be hearing works by three very different composers. First on the program, we have…"

Octavia tuned out. She noticed, to her surprise, Alejandro sitting next to Santiago on the far side of the room. She leaned forward, and gave a little wave. The two men waved back and indicated that she should come and sit with them, but at that moment the musicians began to file in with their instruments. She gave a smile and shook her head.

The musicians came in, made their bows and settled themselves. There were a few minutes of waiting while instruments were tuned, and notes were bowed or plucked, and then they were ready.

At the first notes of the Piazzolla, Octavia closed her eyes. In her mind's eye she saw Sofia, helping Lucien into the honeymoon car with all its ribbons and tin cans.

Saw him wave. Watched the car bump its way down the track. Saw it pause before making the sharp turn into the road, next to the large cottonwood. Then it was gone.

She felt a lump gather in her throat. All her hopeless longing for Lucien, and her pain, gathered like a tide inside her. Everything she felt—all the passion and ecstasy that she had never been free to express openly, all her loneliness, her feeling that she did not and never would belong anywhere—now sounded in the nostalgic notes of the tango. Right until the wedding ceremony, until she heard him say the words—"I do"—she had held the belief that something would happen to prevent the marriage. Now she felt as if everything she had ever believed to be true had turned out to be a false dream—a lie. Her conviction that she and Lucien were destined to be together, always, lay in ruins.

"Lucien," she whispered under her breath. "How could you do this? How could you leave me?"

At the opening notes of the second work she felt a rush of tears, and she groped blindly in her bag for a tissue.

Octavia left her seat as unobtrusively as she could, and slipped out the door at the back of the room. She found a chair, sat down, put her head in her hands and sobbed. Through the door she heard the melancholy notes of pain and separation, like the sound of a sea-tide, rising and falling—and the slow, dredging sound of its ebb as the waves were pulled back again and again.

A door opened and closed quietly. Footsteps.

Someone pulled up a chair and took a seat next to her. She felt an arm go around her shoulders.

Octavia gave herself over to her grief.

The arm held her.

At last she sat up and took the handkerchief that was offered. She wiped her eyes; dragged her fingers through her hair.

Octavia turned her head, and saw Alejandro sitting beside her.

"Oh, Alejandro! I'm so sorry."

She drew in a sobbing breath.

"You are meant to be in there, enjoying the concert."

"And I am. Listen! We can hear it quite clearly from here."

"But—"

"Shh!" he said softly. "Listen!"

The two of them sat in silence, listening. Alejandro kept his arm around her, and slowly she let her head fall against his shoulder. Her eyes closed. They stayed like that until the sound of clapping and a scraping of chairs informed them that it was time for a short interval.

The lights dimmed, and Kristiyan appeared on stage alone. To the sound of applause, he bowed and took his seat under the spotlight. He adjusted the position of his cello, shifted his chair a little and looked up. The room became quiet.

At the sound of the first somber notes, Octavia knew instantly what her next beadwork would be: an icon to the depths of grief that was all she had left of her dream.

She felt her tears start to gather, and yet they were not the sobbing tears which the bandoneon had drawn out of her during the tango. In the Tavener she heard something far beyond that lonely nostalgia. In spite of herself, and against everything she believed, she heard the note of beauty; the passion that is a part of suffering.

Octavia leaned forward, listening—listening to images that flashed before her eyes; the images that were carried in the pure notes of the cello.

Animal images! How strange, she thought. What had animals to do with where she was going with her work?

At some other level she noticed how transformed Kristiyan became in her eyes while he played. How beautiful he was. How he became the music.

And then she let herself disappear into it.

After supper, Kristiyan drove her back to The Adobe. He parked a little way from the front door, and switched off the car lights.

"How did you enjoy the concert?" he asked, turning sideways in the car seat and leaning back against the door. "I didn't want to say anything at supper, but I saw you leave in the first half, and was worried that you were disappointed."

"Oh, no—I loved all of it. I just wasn't prepared for the sadness of the tango."

"But the Tavener—the two laments—they were not sad?"

"They were, but not in the same way. In some way there was acceptance in the sadness, and that seemed to transform it in some way, and it became beautiful. I have never heard music like that before. There is something in it—" Octavia held her hands up, almost as if she was holding a bowl—"something like the passion I hear in opera, but free of—" She was searching for the words—"free of that thread or cord that binds us to the world. There was such a passionate longing—for what? Perhaps something that could rise above pain; even above longing; even death."

Octavia looked at him.

"But you know what I mean. I could see that; the way you gave yourself to the music—it was beautiful."

Kristiyan stared at her.

"Have you any idea how extraordinary you are?" he said.

It was Octavia's turn to blush. To cover her confusion, she changed the subject.

"You haven't told me anything about your country, or where you studied music; what your country looks like."

"Well, I studied music at a famous conservatory in Saint Petersburg. That is quite far north. But I grew up in a nearby apartment—they all look the same—faceless high-rise blocks, hideously ugly and badly built. I don't think there is anything comparable in your country. My parents are both musicians, so music was in my ears from the day I was born. It never entered my head to do anything else but become a musician."

"When did you decide on the cello?"

"It was just before my twelfth birthday. My parents took me to hear the famous cellist, Mstislav Rostropovich, perform in Saint Petersburg. They said this might be the only opportunity I would have of hearing the great man play. I sat transported for the entire performance."

"Is that when you began to play the cello?"

"Oh no. I had been playing the cello and the piano since I was very young; but that was when I chose the cello as my solo instrument. My parents gave me my first cello that year."

"And your country? Is it all snow? In the films I have seen there always seems to be miles and miles of thick snow. I loved the burial scene in Doctor Zhivago: you see this endless expanse of whiteness, and a small, dark patch of men standing around the open grave. It made me wonder about the weight of our personal tragedies when set against the vastness of time, history and space."

Kristiyan laughed.

"I think that is Hollywood. Russia is a vast country full of beauty, and not a little ugliness; full of extremes. Like anywhere else there is great wealth, ruthless power and crippling poverty. There are pristine areas, untouched by any kind of industry, and others that are a shameful and polluted dot on the map; a scar of abandoned and decaying buildings. In a small country such things would have to be removed. In Russia there is so much space, you can just leave a failure and move on."

"Wasn't that all very depressing?"

"You would think so, and for many I am sure life is just a struggle to survive. And yet, underneath all of this there is the powerful current of the Russian soul. It triumphs over all the political abuse that is visited upon it by many of its leaders; unscrupulous men who are power-hungry fanatics. It is revealed in its poetry and its music, and by so many writers who have suffered imprisonment, or even death, for speaking out against injustice. Again and again people, men and women, have taken a stand for freedom. I think a country's true soul is revealed when it has its back to the wall. Russia has been there so many times. Next time I come, I will bring some English translations of poems that I love."

He leaned forward, and was about to take her hand when Octavia hurriedly gathered up her bag.

"I think I must be getting in. It's late. Thank you so much, Kristiyan, for inviting me, and for telling me so much about your country. It was a lovely evening."

Before he could reply, she had opened the door and stepped out of the car.

"Thanks again, Kristiyan," she said before closing the door.

She gave a little wave, and was gone.

Image VI

It is night. The woman is naked. A row of candles throws soft light across the room.

She stands in front of the long mirror. Takes a handful of wood-ash from the black pueblo jar. Sprinkles this onto her hair. Another handful covers her face and neck.

She works with slow, ritualistic movements until her whole body is white and grey—clothed in ash.

Examines this new image in the mirror.

She takes the large, white shirt and spreads it open on the floor. Takes the mask from its hook on the wall and places it on the shirt, taking care to arrange the long, blonde hair like a halo around the face. She wraps the shirt, bit by bit, over the face—arranging it in folds to resemble a shroud.

She crosses the room. Takes a record from the shelf. Places it on the player.

Selects a track. Tavener's Thrinos. Presses repeat.

She takes a large piece of soft, black fabric, shaped like a poncho, from the table. Puts this over her head and body, so that it covers her completely. Down to her feet.

She begins to walk around the shrouded object on the floor. Slowly. Her bare feet move to the long, measured notes of the cello.

She walks a gradually opening spiral.

Finally she stands in the open doorway.

Stands, looking out into the night.

Steps outside—allows the black fabric to fall to the ground.

Stands naked under the stars.

She raises her arms. Begins to move slowly—very slowly. Allows the music to take her. She raises her arms in a gesture, somewhere between dance and worship.

The Tavener plays over and over.

The Opera

Sebastián stood on the balcony of the opera house, sipping a glass of red wine and looking out over the darkening silhouette of the desert.

Beside him stood Octavia—how like his mother, Magdalena, she looked!

He had a flashback to a time when he was not much older than his daughter was now; a time when he and his mother had been given tickets to the opera season, and he had suggested that Father Octavio, the priest in Las Madres, should accompany her. It was, if he remembered correctly, a season of Puccini. Yes. It was Puccini. And here he was, standing where his mother and Octavio must have stood together so often, looking out over this self-same landscape and talking—of what?

How shocked the people had been to see their priest accompanying a beautiful young woman.

Sebastián felt a lump in his throat at the recollection. Hardly a day goes by, he thought.

Although neither his mother nor Octavio had recognized it at the time, it had been the start of a tender love affair: tender because it was only a few moments before her death that they became fully aware of their love; tender, and for Octavio later, passionate in, and because of, her absence.

It was because of his realization of his love for Magdalena that Octavio had put off his priestly clothing, just before he died. In a letter, opened at his death, he explained how he wanted to die as a man—not a priest.

"Oh, look at that moon, Sebastián!"

A fat, red moon was beginning to slide up from behind the silhouette of the low desert horizon.

"And the evening star!"

Octavia's face was ecstatic.

Father Octavio had been a father to him: the only father he had ever known. How had they not seen the great love that held them for all those years? But it was there—was still there—like a slow, deep current, flowing perpetually.

As he looked at his daughter, he didn't wonder that Octavio had fallen in love with Magdalena. He knew that half the town, at the time, was in love with her. And here, in some strange way, was Octavio's granddaughter—named Octavia, after him—and somehow a testament to that love. And so lovely.

Sometimes life, thought Sebastián, was almost too intense; too beautiful, too full of passion and pathos to bear.

And now, by some strange quirk of fate, he stood with Octavia as those other two must have stood, sipping their wine, waiting to enter the opera house and find their seats for—Puccini's Tosca! Surely more than a coincidence? Perhaps Alejandro was right: that Octavia's fate was in some way ordained.

The audience made their way to their seats.

"Look, Sebastián. Here is Kristiyan's name in the program. Kristiyan Bacarov: visiting cellist. Isn't it wonderful? And I am going to hear my star song performed here tonight."

He looked at her radiant face. Alejandro had said that she was in love with passion. Life would not be easy for her. A part of him ached for her; for the price she would be asked to pay. It was already evident.

"The stars were shining
And the earth was scented..."
Octavia held her breath.
The scene was the roof of the Castel Sant'Angelo, where Cavaradossi was singing while he awaited his execution.
"Forever, my dream of love has vanished.
That moment has fled, and I die in desperation..."
Octavia sat—rapt: tears falling down her cheeks.
"And I never before loved life so much,
Loved life so much."

Something To Do With Stars

Octavia stood on the steps leading up to the Art School's offices for enrollment. She was standing where her mother had last stood in 1960. She wasn't sure whether she liked the idea or not. She joined the line of students who were there to collect registration papers.

"You're Georgia's daughter! Come to register for a fine arts degree? Well, you certainly have a high standard to live up to—a hard act to follow."
"You can be sure that I have no intention of following it!" Octavia replied.
The woman behind the desk stared at her disdainfully.
"What a pity," she said. "Still—I'm sure you will do your best."
Octavia collected the registration papers and left.
It was not a good beginning.

It was shortly after the summer vacation. Octavia was studying the prospectus—wrestling with how she would manage to study the courses that interested her. There didn't seem to be any category that offered what she wanted.
When Alejandro came to teach the wood-work class, she would discuss her dilemma with him. He was the one person she trusted—unreservedly. She felt seen by him—not as the impossible, always-out-of-step creature that many took her to be,

but as one who had something unusual to offer. When she spoke to him, her ideas and feelings did not elicit a response of disapproval, or condescending patience. With him her thoughts tumbled out, filled with extraordinary connections between things that at first seemed not to be connected in any way.

"So, you do have an idea of what courses you want to take, Octavia."

They were sitting in the shade of the old cottonwood that grew next to the camposanto.

"Yes. That's the easy part. It is finding where I fit this into any college curriculum that is problematic. I am interested in re-inventing iconography, and I want to work with beads. Ever since I saw the Huichol Indian tapestries and beadworks, I have known that beads would be my medium. I have also studied some of the Greek icons. There is some connection, for me, between the two. And it may sound odd, Alejandro, but I want to learn how to put, into a visual form, what I hear in music: what the music of John Tavener evokes for me emotionally—and maybe Puccini; maybe some tangos—especially that milonga they played at the concert."

"And what do you hear?"

"They are all intense and passionate—and full of longing. But they are also very different—completely different styles—and they all speak to me about a very different kind of longing."

"In what way?"

"Well, I think the tango is longing for what has been left behind. Times, places, people; things that will never be again. There is the melancholy of loss. It is sad—nostalgic. But it is also sensuous—erotic even in the way it remembers. I love it. And then again, it is different from Puccini—you know, my famous star song that everyone laughs about."

"So, what is different there?"

"Well, it is also about love and passion and death and loss. But it is telling us how life is—on a grand scale. The people are not displaced. The feelings are dramatic. We are lifted out of the petty distractions of day-to-day life, so that we cannot help but feel enriched—even by their grief. It is passionate. Larger than life. Or should I say, larger than life is allowed to be?"

"And what does that mean?"

Alejandro was endeavoring to keep track of the threads of thought.

"There seems to be some kind of cultural agreement that all those feelings should be contained; that we must be happy, but not too happy. Sad, but not too sad. We must not fall in love too passionately, or grieve with absolute abandon. It is seen to be excessive. Why is that, Alejandro?"

"Is that how it is?"

"Well, if I look at my family—yes. They are all so sensible. Their lives seem to work, day after day, without drama."

She looked at him inquiringly.

"Do you know what I am saying? Day after day—get up; do the work; go to bed."

Octavia shook her head.

"It mystifies me. They seem to be content to do what they are doing. I'm not like that—not that I want to be like them. But still..."

"Your way is too painful?"

"Yes. I suppose that's it."

"You haven't spoken about the Tavener. What do you hear in his work?"

"Stars! I hear the sound of a soul reaching for the stars—and in that, the passionate acknowledgement of our humanity. And yet..."

Octavia was groping for the words.

"And yet it is also hugely erotic. There is a strange paradox—almost as if something could be both erotic and spiritual. And yet, it doesn't pull us down the way longing for a person—longing for a person to return our love—does. It lifts us. It is almost as if we could leave our bodies. And at the same time there is tremendous compassion. There is no loneliness in his music. I think I hear stillness—silence. There is a connection I feel—I'm not explaining myself very well."

Alejandro nodded.

"Go on."

"You know that feeling of tension in the symbol of the cross—the vertical pulling against the horizontal. It is something like that. Perhaps it has to do with finding that still point in the center that holds both things. Something has to be sacrificed, given up, in the sense that it is distilled: made essential—sacred. Yet, through this, it is as if some part of us becomes honed; and we are made finer by it. Or maybe it is some kind of recognition of—perhaps some kind of connection—I think I'm babbling."

"I don't think so at all."

"There's another thing I have been meaning to ask you."

"Yes?"

"I read somewhere: 'Identification with the star is possible only to the chosen few.' Why do they say star and not stars?"

"Ah! I know a little about this—not much, because I haven't studied it; but 'The Star' is one of the cards in the Tarot pack."

"What is that?"

"It is a pack of cards with many different images. Each one has a particular significance that has something to do with learning about yourself. As I say, I have not studied it."

Octavia made a note of this.

"But, to go back to where we started: are you saying you want to give visual expression to these forces, which appear to wrestle against each other?"

"Yes."

Alejandro looked at her with wonder. In all his seventy-seven years he had not felt so close to anyone. The feeling was passionate in its own way. How he knew that longing—the same desire that drove him to stand on windy hill-tops on dark nights, counting all those bright stars trembling above him; that drove him to carve, with infinite patience, thousands and thousands of angels—one for every star he counted. And here was a young girl who knew that her destiny lay in those self-same stars, and who was following, as best she could, a disjointed line of clues that spoke to her heart.

"Do you have any idea, any visual image, of what this may look like?"

"I have a quote I stumbled over. It comes from the Book of Baruch. I don't seem to be able to find a copy—but the quote is: 'Erotic desire and its satisfaction is the key to the origin of the world.'"

"And what does this say to you?"

"I can only feel its truth. It sounds sexual, and maybe that is one of its components—but it is way beyond that. It has something to do with the work I want to make—and something to do with stars."

She looked at him quizzically.

"Do you think that sexual passion, when it is an expression of true love, elevates that passion to a kind of spiritual worship? It is something like this that Tavener's music says to me. It sounds so phony when you put it into words. I am hoping that beads can say it in a way that exalts it, the way music does."

She thought for a moment.

"I was surprised to find images flashing through my mind while listening to the Tavener; images that seemed to have nothing to do with what I think he was expressing."

"What did you see?"

"I saw images of wild things; wild animals, all in motion. Something about their fluid motion, their utter being-ness; something so immediate—almost sacred. In a completely different way, because they are static, Russian and Greek icons have a similar impact. Does that sound strange to you?"

Alejandro shook his head.

"Not at all. I look forward to watching your process unfold. But you say you can't find how you fit into any curriculum. Perhaps, if you explain to the registrar what you have just told me, she will be able to advise you. Otherwise—"

"Otherwise?"

"Otherwise you will just have to invent yourself, on your own."

Octavia's choice of emphasis for her art degree was considered unusual. She did not want to spend time on the conventional curriculum, which would introduce her to a variety of art media, and to the study of things that did not interest her. She knew what she wanted. No one at the art school had ever worked with beads?—well then, she would be the first. She wanted to study Greek and Russian iconography; symbolism in different cultures, including Huichol art. She wanted to learn how to explore certain paradoxical concepts—particularly those found in the music of Piazzolla and Tavener—in visual images.

When she informed the registrar that she couldn't find any category to fit her needs, she was informed in a brisk, sharp tone—

"Miss Chavez, this is an art school, not a restaurant! We offer a curriculum. If what you want is not on offer here, you will have to find some other avenue of study."

Octavia flounced down the college steps. Why did no one want to listen? She drove the long road home in a rage. And on the edge of tears.

"But Octavia, everyone goes through a broad study of art and art movements before they find what they want to do. It is considered really useful to have a general introduction to various disciplines before making a final decision."

Georgia was sitting at the kitchen table, listening to Octavia's account of her attempted enrollment.

"Alejandro didn't. He just began. He knew what he wanted to do, and he just did it."

"Well, you could do that too, but there is a long and ancient tradition of bead-work, for instance, and maybe it would be good to study that; to learn some of the methods that artists have discovered over the centuries."

"And then, when I end up doing what everyone else has done, they will say that my work is derivative."

"You might also consider that, without being aware of it, you might do work—a style of beadwork—that has already been done, maybe centuries ago—or more. It will not be derivative, because you hadn't seen it. But, nevertheless, it will not be seen as something new—original."

"I don't want to do oils or water-colors or life drawing. I don't want to learn other people's techniques."

"Look at Reuben—and Kristiyan. They both studied for years to reach the level of virtuosity they know today."

"And look at Lucien. He just knew what he would do."

"Yes, but he studied as well. Are you saying that no one can teach you any-thing?"

"No. Of course I intend to study, but not at art school. I have already collected several books—not only on beadwork, but on the history of early peoples and their rituals. It is fascinating. And I will find more as I go along. But no one can teach me what I know I must find inside myself."

"So what do you think you would like to do?"

"I am going to do it alone."

"Oh, my sweetheart—you are going to miss out on so much. Life on campus teaches you so much more than just your studies. And you meet so many interesting people from across the country—and from other countries."

"I don't want to meet interesting people. I don't want to meet anyone."

"Do you think that artists, musicians, poets create in a vacuum? Everything is about relationship. About how we respond to others—to the challenges that relationship presents."

"It doesn't have to be relationship to people. There are so many other things."

Octavia pushed her hair back and stood up.

"Anyway, I am not going to art school. So we needn't talk about this any further."

She took an apple from the table.

"I don't want any supper tonight."

She walked slowly up to her studio. Inside she placed the song from Tosca on the turn-table, and sat listening to it with her eyes closed.

Journal Entry 4

I can't sleep. Have come through to work. It must be after three o'clock. The night is so still. Working here, with the night and the stars above me—this is probably the closest I come to prayer. I know this is what I am supposed to be doing; I just can't tell people how I know it. Can't really tell myself.

I can see so many things I will do differently with my next work. I think the scale of this work, compared to the size of the beads, is too small. I have lost some of the detail I wanted. Also, I have hurried this work. It should have been allowed more time.

I have unpicked the Mexican poncho. It is not the image I want. All the energy is in the starry sky.

I can feel my anxiety to prove that I can do this. Am I ever going to learn if I am so impatient to get a finished result? Slow down, Octavia! What is it? A few weeks. What on earth is the hurry?

Where can I find a pack of Tarot cards?

Image VII

The figure of a man stands in the doorway of what might be an adobe church. His long, blonde hair, braided in a formal style, reminiscent of an icon, falls down on each side of his face. His eyes are closed. He has a halo of blue fire around his head. He wears a gentian poncho over denims faded almost down to white, cut short to above the knee and frayed. His feet are bare. The most notable feature is the way the hands have been portrayed. They are beautiful, large and open, out of proportion to the rest of the figure. They reach forward—the viewer is left to wonder at this. The space above the figure in the doorway opens out into a vast night sky with spirals of stars. The colors are rich and brilliant, a swirling mix of matte and shiny beads that offer a vivid contrast to the simplicity of what lies below.

We, the viewers, stand as if below the figure, looking up. At first glance the composition appears to be simple and harmonious, but there is something about the perspective which seems to contradict this. The area of stars is almost disturbing in that we cannot be sure whether the figure is entering or leaving the building, or whether it is the inside of the church that contains the infinite starry sky.

Although the beadwork is clumsy—naïve even—and as yet unfinished, it is strangely moving.

Journal Entry 5

Although I still have to finish the beadwork of Lucien, another image has come crowding into my mind. I have made a rough sketch for the design. I will call these images The Icons. I have put the colors in, very roughly, to gauge the effect.

I am surprised at the image that has appeared. This figure of a woman—I thought it would be me, but now I am not sure who she really is. Her name came to me: Our Lady of Emptiness. What a strange name. Does this mean she is the Virgin? Why emptiness? She is standing in an open space—is it a desert? Has she been abandoned? She is holding an empty vessel in her hands. What does this mean? I am intrigued to be working in this way. It feels like a journey. Who is leading?

She has so many tears. I can feel each one of them.

Image VIII

On the easel we see, in a rough water-color sketch, the figure of a young woman. She is naked. Her hair is black, and worn in two long braids. A halo of pale gold surrounds her head. Behind her is an empty landscape—it could be desert. In her hands she holds an empty clay pot. Stars are falling from the sky like rain. She is not attempting to catch them in the pot. She stands in the center of a bright, glowing light, surrounded by a jagged shape. What it is, is not clear. The stars fall down past her and vanish below—all but one; a very bright star that hangs over her. She is weeping. Her tears mingle with the stars.

The Black Mare

Octavia was sitting on a chair in the shade, outside the Black Room. She was reading a back-dated copy of National Geographic—an article about the Atacama Desert in Chile. Pictures of the night sky. Stars. Galaxies. Millions upon millions of stars.

She knew instantly that she would go there.

She was daydreaming about it when she heard footsteps, and Alejandro came walking along the spiral path.

"Hello, Alejandro. How good to see you. Can you stay and sit for a moment?"

At his nod she rose, and went to fetch another chair.

"I suppose you've heard—I'm not going to art school?"

"Yes. I did hear. What are your plans?"

"I don't have any—or rather I didn't; nothing specific, anyway, until a moment ago."

He gave her a look of inquiry.

"And—?"

"I am going to Chile. I want to go to the Atacama Desert—look! Here are some photographs. I have just been reading about it."

"Do you intend going alone?"

"Yes. I am going to ask Sebastián if he will pay for the trip. Maybe he will give me this instead of college fees."

"How long do you want to spend there?"

"A few months. Maybe five—six."

"So long!"

Alejandro was taken aback by the force of his exclamation. Dismayed? Whatever was he thinking? He had come to enjoy his frequent conversations with Octavia. They were always so filled with energy and passion. He always left her feeling alive, inspired; in love with life.

She made him think of a wild black mare that was owned by a neighbor of his. She had been purchased early in the spring—for a song, because she was unmanageable. No one could break her. Now she had the run of a wide paddock that stretched from the far, tree-clad hills to the pole-fence that ran alongside his studio. No one had ever managed to put a bridle on her. The farmer bought her because she was so beautiful.

All that summer, when he was waiting for some inspiration to seize him, Alejandro would lean on the fence and watch her swift, sleek blackness gallop up to the fence, stopping short just before she reached it; watch her toss her head and snort through crimson-flared nostrils; turn, rear up in a cloud of dust and thunder away. She made him think of a shooting star, or blue fire, or a swift, black wind. He loved her for her wildness.

And now this young woman, with the dark eyes that slanted provocatively up from her high cheek-bones, and the same sleek black hair, had turned his heart and his world upside-down.

She was an eighteen-year-old girl—for goodness' sake, man—you must be out of your mind!

And indeed I am, he thought: gloriously out of my mind. What was this sudden ecstasy?

He recognized in her a spirit that was ageless. A spirit so kindred to his own that it took his breath away. How many, in a whole lifetime, are offered such a gift?

Alejandro could sense his mind wrestling to understand something far beyond his rational grasp. And yet, a very human part of him knew—and he was unprepared for the realization—that he would miss her immensely. To discover this, so late in life! But of course, it had to be this way. This was no ordinary romantic attachment. But then what was it?

"I am going to miss you, Alejandro," Octavia said, as if giving voice to his thoughts, so that for a moment he thought that he too must have said something.

What an extraordinary person she was. She had only this moment read about the desert, and already she was on her way. That was what her family could not understand—that such clear intention moves mountains. He knew this.

"And I will miss you too," he said, as lightly as he could manage.

"Oh! Will you? Will you really, Alejandro?"

Octavia gave him her dazzling smile.

"Yes," he said simply. "When do you think you'll leave?"

"As soon as I can arrange it. Autumn is cooler for traveling. It feels strange being so free—time-wise, that is. I want to visit so many places in the desert. And I don't want to hurry. I want to lie on my back under that desert night sky, and look at the stars. And I want to go to Mexico City—and I want to find the places where the Huichol Indians do their beadwork."

Octavia stood up, her face flushed.

"I am so excited, Alejandro. I feel as if I have got hold of so many strings, and they all seem to be going the same way. The beads. The stars. The music. And the desert. They all seem to be leading me to one place. It is all one thing."

Her arms made wide, gathering-in movements, and folded over her heart.

"Sometimes I have flashes, and then I know this. You know it too, don't you, Alejandro?"

"Yes," he said. "I do."

Alejandro stood up, and carried his chair back to its place outside the door.

"I suppose I must get to my class."

"Oh! It is so wonderful to know you, Alejandro. I don't know what I would do without you."

Octavia ran to him and gave him a fierce hug.

Alejandro returned the hug, and stepped back.

"And wonderful to know you too, Octavia," he said. "Will you tell me all your plans when they come together?"

"I will."

She watched him walk away along the spiral stone path, until he was out of sight.

Alejandro was devastated.

At Octavia's sudden embrace he had felt a surge of heat ignite his whole body—he, a man in his seventy-seventh year. What was he thinking? But, of course, that was just it. He wasn't thinking. This had taken him unawares.

But looking back, he could see how he had been deluding himself. He was, he had told himself, the mentor. He was the older and wiser adult, who could lend his support and understanding. At his age he was beyond such whimsies as falling in love. What hubris!—although there had also been a certain kind of innocence in his heart's refusal to name the condition. Now that was gone.

But what exactly was the nature of this ecstatic emotion? He was at a loss to say. When did it begin? He cast his mind back. There were so many images he held of her, but one stood out for him. It was the day when, still a baby, he took her in his arms. He saw even then, with such clarity, that behind all the trouble she—as yet an infant—was causing in her family, she was a wild and passionate spirit, longing to be set free—impatient with the limitations of infancy.

He remembered what he said that day—

"She is in love with passion."

Nothing on earth could protect her from her destiny. Not even he, Alejandro, with all his angels and all his wisdom and all his very vulnerable humanity, could do that.

And still he wondered at this young woman, who as a baby and as a child had already sensed something that called to her; already knew that she was other—as old Elena would have put it.

He smiled remembering Elena, who worked at the rectory in Father Octavio's time. He thought of Father Rafael's much-loved predecessor—Alejandro refused to acknowledge the brief tenure of that thin French priest who had been sent home in disgrace. Elena could recognize other from one glance at a person's hands. When Magdalena, Sebastián's mother, first arrived in Las Madres, Elena had said to Father Octavio: "Mark my words, father. She is other."

Of course! Magdalena was Octavia's grandmother! Why had he forgotten that connection? He mused about the choice of name: Octavia. Was it chosen to acknowledge the former priest? He had been like a father to Sebastián. And such a close friend of Magdalena's.

Alejandro paused to consider.

Octavio and Magdalena? Is it possible that?—but of course. What a fool I am not to have seen it. They were in love. And I, so involved with my angels, I didn't see what was right in front of me.

This explained the priest's strange request for his funeral—that he wanted to be dressed as an ordinary man, and to be buried in the small camposanto close to the chapel at The Adobe. He remembered the outcry it had caused—all the church dignitaries huffing and puffing about how irregular it was. Father Octavio had anticipated this, and had left a clear letter of wishes. Alejandro recalled looking down at the fresh grave that lay alongside Magdalena's, and at the yuccas that—out of season—had burst into bloom.

"My mother always did have a way with flowers," was all Sebastián said when people uttered their astonishment.

And now Octavia!

How I wish Elena was here. She would set things right at a glance. She would see right through all the obfuscation. But—she would be at pains to warn him—knowing something will not change the path of our fate, which we ourselves have set in motion, though we may not recognize this; may even strongly deny it. It may not even prepare us for what is to come.

Alejandro stopped, and looked down at the black stones at the end of the path. But did he really wish to know? Perhaps, sometimes, too much light—

He did not complete the thought, but walked into the wood-work class with a new spring in his step, in spite of—or maybe because of—the wild and wonderful turmoil in his heart.

Blood on An Angel's Wings

Alejandro paced the length of his studio—back and forth—some new energy knocking urgently at the door of his heart. He both longed for, and dreaded its arrival. For it was not a star, or a cluster of stars, that was summoning him to shape its longing into form. It was Octavia's smile.

He waited for the presence to announce itself, the way he had awaited all the many thousands of angels that had come before. He felt a boyish excitement; a feeling of expectancy. To his surprise, a word suddenly filled his heart, so that he felt it would burst inside him. He walked over to his desk, and wrote it down on a sheet of work-paper. Pinned it to his design board.

Love.

Alejandro stared in wonder at this word, which had suddenly become invested with new radiance. Never before had an angel come to him in this fashion. He opened his arms, as if to make the presence welcome. He could visualize the angel perfectly: the long, dark hair—that smile, and the strangely slanting eyes. His heart was beating fast.

His first thought was of Octavia.

But it was not an angelic presence that now came to him, but another word.

Loss.

Alejandro felt a cold wind on the back of his neck. He knew what such a touch meant. He shuddered. He did not want to hear more.

To silence the voice, he reached for the small pile of post that had arrived that morning: mostly advertisements; one bill, and a letter with a New York post mark. He put the rest to one side, and opened it.

Gallery 420
1037 W 82nd
New York
Date 25 September 1993

Dear Alejandro,

You will be pleased to hear that your angel, Galaxy #08, has been purchased for $2 400.00.

We have informed the young man who had put down a couple of deposits, and was working to pay the rest, that unfortunately we could wait no longer, and that the angel is sold. We will, of course, refund the three deposits he has given us to date.

I am sure you will be happy to receive the news. We will credit your account, less our charges of $900.00, with the payment of $1 500.00.

We would like to order two more angels from the catalogue you left with us, if they are still available. We will contact you later in the week.

It is always such a pleasure doing business with you.

Warm wishes,
Frank.

Alejandro sat, looking out of his studio window. He remembered the angel vividly; remembered carving it.

It was at the time when Octavia was first wrestling with her decision to study at the university; what courses to take. He remembered so clearly the line she had quoted—"Erotic desire and its satisfaction is the key to the origin of the world"—remembered how she said she could only feel its meaning, its truth; and how he had come home later and begun work on an angel he called Galaxy #08. He had no idea why he chose that name or what it meant, if anything.

But what made his memory of the angel so vivid was that during the finishing of its very delicate wings the chisel slipped, and he had given himself a deep cut into the palm of his left hand—a first in all his years of carving. In putting the work down on the bench, blood had dripped onto the angel's wings. After he had bandaged the wound, it took him considerable time to wash off the blood and re-sand the wood to remove the stain.

But you didn't remove the stain, did you, Alejandro? The angel carried it all the way to New York. There was the stain of your blood on the angel's wings.

And what is the nature of the stain in you?

He thought of the young man, a man he had never met, who was willing to work extra hours, perhaps, to make monthly deposits in order to afford a carved angel he had fallen in love with: no mere collector; no slick interior decorator, who thought the angel would add a quaint—but not too distracting—touch to the rather minimalist white on white interior; but someone, a lover perhaps, who could hear its speech.

Loss—he heard it again.

He knew with an overwhelming clarity that he had been preparing his whole life for this moment; and just as surely he knew there would be a price.

He stood, head bowed. Waiting. His heart was filled with awe and dread.

When, finally, he heard his name spoken, he was not surprised. He could hear the voice as clearly as if someone was standing in front of him. He heard his name again. But what was it asking? He listened deeply. In his heart he heard the question—"Are you willing to renounce everything you hold dear?"

What fearful question was this? What was this everything he was being asked to renounce? He paused to consider his life. What did he love so much that he would find it painful—impossible—to renounce for this mystery? But even as he asked himself the question, he knew with certainty just what that price would be. Oh, please, God, not that!

There was only one thing, he thought. Only one! Octavia! Octavia's smile. All of her. That shining essence that was still struggling to make its way out of the rock. It was like the glory of watching a butterfly emerge from the chrysalis. So new. So virginally pure. How could he abandon that? Don't take this away from me now, he pleaded with his heart. Not now.

Never before, in all his seventy-seven years, had he ever felt torn between two things. He had always been able to say yes and no with his whole heart, without deliberation or hesitation. And now this. Surely he had a responsibility to her—to Octavia—during this very profound transition that she was, quite literally, calling up for herself. It was, he thought, like an unspoken covenant between them. How would she manage to contain that wild spirit without the steady guidance of his understanding?

Alejandro crossed his studio and threw open the window—stood looking out, breathing in deeply, filling his lungs with the clean, warm air. The quaking aspens were turning with the fall, and high up the mountain, sudden against the dark piñon, a wavy band of yellow and gold marked their autumn colors. There was not a cloud in the sky. How strange it is, he thought, to know that the countless stars are up there—as they had been for millions of years—and yet they are invisible. If he had never seen a night sky, how would he ever truly know this?

Alejandro realized—and the realization shocked him—that faith is not enough. It will be tested. And something far deeper is required of a soul invoking initiation. But why now? Why now, just when Octavia was so needing to be heard, to be seen and understood, deeply—and when he was the one person who could offer this—why now was he being asked to walk away? Why?

From far across the paddock he saw the black mare galloping toward him. As always, he felt the sudden sting of tears as he watched the beauty of her wildness.

She did not come all the way to where he stood at the window, but stopped suddenly—turned in a cloud of dust and stood, head up, ears pricked, facing the hills. Even from this distance he could see the scarlet lining of her dilated nostrils.

What, he wondered, went on in that beautiful head? Was it some sense beyond understanding that informed her? Of course. Some kind of instinctive intuition? Nothing as stupid or as slow as thinking.

He watched her stand—alert. She appeared to have heard something—something that came from the hills. She took a few steps forward, and stopped. Listening.

With a sudden toss of her head, she turned and began to trot with long, springy strides in the direction of the northern boundary. He watched her break into a gallop, and race across the open field toward the far fence that separated the farm from open land.

In his own body, Alejandro could feel a new tension in his muscles. Could feel himself being drawn out. He felt his heart open.

She showed no sign of slowing as she approached the boundary fence, but galloped on, a sleek and fluid beauty.

And now he watched with mounting horror, certain that she would crash into the stout poles. At that speed, would she ever be able to stop—or turn? He wanted to look away—to shut his eyes—not to see the bone-breaking collision. But he couldn't. She was a few bare yards away from the fence.

And then he saw her gather herself and rise into the air—a clean leap, clearing the fence with feet to spare. She landed effortlessly, and thundered away toward the hills. He watched her vanish into the trees.

He turned back from the window.

"I am."

He spoke out loud.

Alejandro studied the letter from the gallery. Found the phone number. Jotted it down on a scrap of paper, and went to the small kitchen to make the call.

Frank was not in, but he spoke to a secretary who gave him the name, address and phone number of the young man—Rav Zohar—who had wanted to buy the angel.

"I am sad that he didn't get it," she said. "He was so passionate about it. Loved it so much."

Alejandro replaced the receiver and returned to his work-room. A number of angels that had been photographed for the catalogue were floating, suspended from the taut wire that spanned the width of his room, waiting to be sent to any gallery that ordered them. Alejandro pulled up a chair, and sat considering them.

Early the next morning, in response to a knock, Octavia, her hands full of dark-brown beeswax, opened her door to find Alejandro standing on the steps.

"Oh! Hello, Alejandro—just give me half a minute while I—"

She re-appeared, wiping her hands on a towel.

"Do you have an early class today?"

"No. I have just come from the post office—I had an angel to post to a young man who lives in New York, and..."

She stepped outside and closed the door.

"Sorry I look such a mess. I have been preparing a surface for an art experiment."

"...so I came by to speak to Sebastián about my classes—and to let you know that I am going away for a while—for some time—not sure how long. I just came to say goodbye and wish you a wonderful time on your trip. You may leave before I am back."

He stopped, suddenly at a loss for words. He felt as if he was lying to her. The realization made him uncomfortable.

"Oh, where are you going? Is it a holiday? Are you going with others?"

"No. It is just a break from my routine, and I am going alone."

"Is it to do with your work, Alejandro?"

"Well, yes and no. I am going to the desert to listen."

"To listen? Listen to what?"

"To the silence."

"Oh!"

There was a long pause.

"Will you take some work with you—your tools, I mean, in case you are inspired to carve something new?"

He hadn't even thought about this. It was the thought that he should leave Octavia to find her own way through that prompted this decision. But his work! Would he take that? No! Of course he wouldn't take work with him.

The line—"blood on an angel's wings"—seemed to shout inside him.

Alejandro stood staring at her, uncomfortably aware that he couldn't explain his decision to himself, let alone to her. The clarity and certainty that had accompanied him through all difficulties and decision-making, for his whole life, seemed to have abandoned him.

And then another thought struck him. Was that what he was being asked to renounce—his work?

He remembered Father Octavio's comment when he told him what so many were saying about his seemingly impossible task—to carve as many angels as there are stars. He quoted something that was spoken by one of the famous rabbis at the time of Rabbi Hillel—"You are not required to complete the work, but neither may you abandon the work." It had reassured him at the time. Now—

Alejandro felt the ground quake beneath his feet. He could feel a deep chasm opening in front of him. He had made a promise to carve angels and, bizarre as that might sound to many people, he knew he would never renege on that promise. But then what—?

He was aware that Octavia was staring back at him. He tried to say something, but he couldn't speak.

If it wasn't his work, what was it? After all, all he had was his work! His whole life—his very identity—had become inseparable from his angel-carving. Everyone who knew him—or had heard of him—knew this. He was—the angel man. Almost every month he received some new commission. Galleries in New York had his work on display. The angel man was famous.

"Blood on an angel's wings..."

He looked down at his feet.

Yes, he thought to himself—and where has Alejandro gone?

So that was it. It had crept up on him so slowly, so insidiously that he had not noticed the subtle changes that were occurring.

Who is it then who wants to rescue Octavia? The angel man? It seems that Alejandro himself is nowhere to be found. You blind, stupid old fool—be honest with yourself. You aren't leaving for her. You are leaving—to find yourself? Forgive yourself?

Octavia repeated her question.

"Will you perhaps carve some new angels while you are away?"

"No, I don't think so," he said. "I think I will be on some kind of a quest."

"Just like me."

Yes, he thought grimly—but he smiled. "Yes. Just like you."

"I will write to you, Alejandro. I will tell you everything I see—and all those millions of stars."

"Well, I suppose...yes, of course—thank you," he stammered.

Not very gracious of you, Alejandro, he thought.

"Yes. I would love to hear from you—all about where you go and what you see. Especially the stars. I will leave instructions for your letters to be kept in order. When I get back, I will be able to read them."

Octavia looked at him closely, but she said nothing. He was uncomfortably aware that, in some respects, she knew more than he did. He wondered just when it was that he had fallen asleep.

Image IX

The woman stands naked under the light, in front of the long mirror. She weeps. Her breasts shine with tears.

She reaches to her right for the pair of scissors lying on the table. With her left hand she runs her fingers through her sleek, black hair. Selects one lock and cuts it off, close to her skull.

She replaces the scissors on the table, close to a long, narrow box. From a jar she selects a large turquoise bead. She threads the lock of hair through the bead. She raises the lid of the box and places hair and bead inside, making sure that the hair lies straight and long on the crimson fabric. The box is black. She closes the lid. Picks up a small penknife and the box, and holds them together in her right hand.

She crosses the room and selects the Tavener: Thrinos. Presses repeat.

Begins a slow dance to the long notes of the cello. Her tears begin to fall again. She moves in a slow circle around the room, the fingertips of her left hand just brushing the black-painted adobe walls. The dance becomes a spiral journey. With each turn she comes closer to the center—to the folded white shirt that lies on the floor.

She kneels, and places the black box on the white linen bundle. With the penknife she makes a swift cut in the palm of her left hand. Stretches it out, and allows the blood to fall onto the box and the white fabric. With her arm still reaching out, she bows her head and weeps. Her long, raw, keening cries mingle with the notes of the cello.

"Lucien," she sobs.

Alejandro's Dream

I am walking along a dirt road, searching for the black mare. In my hands I carry the leather bag that holds all my tools for carving angels.

As I walk, the road becomes increasingly narrow. The way is strewn with rocks and dead branches, overgrown with weeds. Now the road becomes a path. Suddenly it vanishes, and I see that I am standing at the edge of an abyss. I look down at my feet, and I see that the cliff-edge is beginning to crumble beneath me. My hand grabs hold of the branch of a bush, and I pull myself back. I feel my heart thudding in my chest. I retrace my steps till I come to a crossroad. I take the turning to the left, a road which looks as if it is used more frequently, but the same thing happens, and once more I find myself at the edge of the crumbling abyss. The same thing happens with the other two roads. And now I am afraid that the mare has fallen over the edge.

I stand still, and watch the four roads roll up like parchment and blow away in the wind. A tall being approaches me out of the mix of dust and haze. There is a bright light behind him, and at first I cannot see his features. I wonder whether he has seen the mare; or whether he, too, is looking for her. He comes closer, and I recognize him as the angel I carved for Sebastián before he left for college—the Archangel Michael, the Angel of Death.

The angel points in the direction of the abyss. I walk toward it. As I walk, the way becomes as narrow as the sharp edge of a flint-stone. I am terrified that I will slip and cut myself to pieces. The bag I am carrying becomes heavier and heavier. On either side of me, angels are falling past me. Each angel is carrying a star. As they pass, they reach out frantic hands toward me. I see dark shadows falling with each angel.

Now their stars drop and fall away from them, leaving bright tails of blue fire. With their eyes they implore me to rescue them. I want to reach out, but now both my arms are holding onto the bag. I let go of it, and watch it burst open. All my tools fall out and away. There is no sign of the black mare. I feel my heart break inside me. Now the sky is full of this blue fire. The abyss is full of shadows that seem to be alive. I continue walking along the thin, sharp edge. The angels continue falling on either side of me. I am terrified that I too will fall. I cannot see what is ahead of me. I do not know where I am going. Now all I know is this blue fire.

Alejandro woke up with a start. He was sweating. He looked at the clock. Five o'clock. He glanced around the room for reassurance. Everything was the way it always was.

He dressed quickly and went through to his small kitchen, made a cup of coffee and took it with him into his studio. There he sat at his desk, and wrote down the dream on a notepad. He made a sketch of the angel's face.

Alejandro got up and paced up and down his room. He stood for a long while, looking out of the window at the ghosting, early dawn landscape, as yet unlit by the sun. He searched the length of the paddock for a sign of the black mare. The empty field stared back at him.

He came back to his seat and examined the sketch; the face. The dark, slanting eyes were direct and fierce. He looked deeper into the face he had drawn—and drew back.

For the image had changed; had metamorphosed. And super-imposed onto the angel's face he saw Octavia's smile.

The Monastery in the Desert

He arrived toward the middle of fall.

He had with him a small bag of clothes, his warm coat, boots and his toiletries. He brought nothing else. He left instructions with a neighbor to clear his post-box each day, and store his post in the order in which it arrived. He informed him that he would not be contactable for a period of at least three months, maybe longer. He did not reveal where he was going.

He set off early the next morning—his destination a small desert monastery. It was several hours away by car, situated close to the foot of a vertical sandstone cliff at the end of a dirt road that wound its way into a wide canyon, many miles from any habitation. It was run by monks who sought to lead a life of prayer and solitude, away from the distractions of the world.

Men or women of any faith were welcome to come and spend time—a few days or a week—and let the busyness of their lives fall away from them. There were a number of guest-rooms built for this purpose.

Alejandro applied to stay there for as long as six months. Because of the unusual length of the stay he requested, special permission had to be obtained.

The request was heard, and permission was granted.

His first month was a difficult one. He discovered, with dismay, how unquiet his mind had become; that it had an intractable life of its own, something he had never been aware of before. He had always thought that he was the one doing the thinking. Now he observed how, during periods of meditation, it would wander away and begin chattering about angels and stars; his recent commissions, exhibitions and awards. It would scheme and plan, and argue that he was wasting valuable time—time which, at his age, should not be squandered on such stupidity as sitting around doing nothing.

And then, of course, there was always Octavia's smile: that smile, and the memory of her dark, slanting eyes, which became for him a haunting. And more than that, there was the awareness of a new and overwhelming desire growing inside him, which every day became stronger and stronger.

For God's sake, man—pull yourself together.

But no amount of self-chastisement made any difference. Alejandro began to panic. He had never felt out of control in his life, before this. Perhaps he was not suited to this strange observance. Perhaps the decision to come here was all a huge mistake. What did he hope to achieve by leaving all of his responsibilities—his work, his very life?

He would bring his mind back to his breath again and again, only to find it wandering off once more through images and memories, or questioning the value of this practice of silence. Or it would trick him into thinking—ah, so this is the silence—until he would be caught up again in the to and fro of some futile argument. He began to think he might be going mad.

He found sleep difficult, and spent many nights silently pacing the length of his room, counting his footsteps in an effort to still the flood of thoughts that screamed to be heard, and which seemed to be endless. He started having fantasies and strange dreams.

One recurring dream was of Octavia riding the black mare bareback, at full gallop across the desert sand. Above her the night sky was full of stars. In the dream he would, at first, be held by the beauty of the image—the fluid beauty of the mare's action and the long, sleek whip of Octavia's hair, streaming out behind her like a black wind. And then the stars would begin to fall like rain, and he would see the edge of the abyss coming toward them; and standing on the very edge of the abyss—the Archangel Michael, the Angel of Death. He would be seized by terror. He never finished the dream. He would wake just before they reached the edge—his heart beating, his shorts, t-shirt and the sheets drenched with sweat.

He found relief in the small tasks offered to visitors, and in the services in the chapel, but in the many hours of solitude each day, again and again he would find himself back in his chattering mind.

He was told that this was not unusual; that all he could do was to be with it.

"This is what minds do, Alejandro. They think. When we are caught up in the busyness of life with all its noise and frantic pace, we are not aware that it is going on. But it will be there—thinking, thinking, thinking. And it will think the same, often moronic thoughts over and over. It is almost as if our minds believe that if they stop thinking for one second, they—or we—will disappear. And the mind hates a mystery. So it will try to work things out—things it can't possibly know. It does not want to accept its limitations.

"Be still. Be patient, Alejandro. Don't try too hard. Just come back to the breath. And when you find thoughts or images coming to you, acknowledge their presence and let them go. Eventually your mind will become still."

So Alejandro sat, looking out over the magnificent spread of the land; at the striations of color in the canyon wall, and up to the three crosses that stood far above him; up at the vast, blue dome of the desert sky that reached out and out into forever. He sat for a part of each day close to the river, and watched the leaves of the cotton-woods as slowly they turned from yellow to gold: watched the leaves begin to fall.

Time came to have a different meaning for him. With nothing to do or to achieve, with no aim or ambition other than to be present—as present as he could be—in every moment, he came at last to know the faint beginnings of the sound of solitude in his heart.

Life became a kaleidoscope of sound and color, sunrise and sunset, night and day; of prayers sung or chanted in the chapel, and long hours of contemplative silence.

He had not brought his watch, nor did he keep a diary. He lost count of the days.

He woke one morning, surprised to find that it had snowed during the night.

It was the beginning of winter.

The End of Summer

"But don't you want to wait until Lucien and Sofia return? You are going to miss hearing all their news about the trip."

Octavia was sitting at the breakfast table, drinking coffee with her parents.

"No!" Octavia flicked her hair back impatiently. "I want to leave now—this week."

"But you have no idea where you are going to stay—what you will need when you are there. I'm not even sure that it is safe for a young girl to travel alone into Chile. There has been so much political upheaval; and that dreadful man—Pinochet—and all the stories that are going around about him. Octavia, I don't think you should travel alone."

"But Reuben went to Buenos Aires when he was only eighteen, and he went on his own."

"Yes, but it's different for a man."

"Why?"

"Because girls—young women—are more vulnerable. That's why!"

"Things have changed a lot since you were young, mama. Today young women are more informed, much more independent. I can get jobs, working in places if I need to. What better way to get to know a country?"

"It is not about comparing your life to mine. In fact, the world today is less safe than when I was young—like you are now!" she added sharply.

Octavia turned to her father.

"Sebastián—what do you think?"

"I would like you to speak to the agent, and have him or her give you some brochures of all the places you might visit, the categories of accommodation and the daily rates. And I would also like to know about transport and prices for trips—and what kind of supervision is offered."

"You still haven't told us why you want to go there so badly," Georgia ventured.

"I want to stand in the desert, with miles and miles of space all around me. I want to look at stars. I want to stand in a place that has not been altered in thousands of years—a place that is so vast and empty that I can hear myself breathe. I want to feel the history beneath my feet and above my head."

"But, Octavia, you can do that right here in New Mexico."

Octavia banged her empty coffee-cup down on the table. She stood up, and held the back of her chair.

"It's not the same. Everything here has been made so tidy—so tamed. Besides, I want to mix with the people and learn their customs—eat their food, speak in their language. You have told me so often, Sebastián, that your roots are in South America.

Well then, so are mine. I want to get to know them. I want to put my feet into the soil, and know that this is my place!"

"Those aren't your only roots, Octavia. You have Irish blood in you as well."

"Oh, come, mama. Do I look like a fair colleen?" Octavia made a dismissive gesture.

"I don't want this trip to be all safe and booked and predictable, with no room for the unexpected. I want it to be alive—and spacious. I don't want an itinerary telling me when and where to go. This isn't school, with rules and bells and classes."

She crossed the room, and stood looking out of the window at the chapel, the sheds and barns, and the cultivated fields.

"If all of you are happy living in a little valley, with tidy fields and tidy fences and everything under control and running smoothly, day in, day out, year after year—and mama, you painting pictures that will sell quickly, and Lucien and Sofia coming back to a cozy little casita where all will be domestic bliss and—"

She was close to tears.

"Why does this happen? Why do we make everything so small—so safe? Look what has happened to this country. Is there anything left that is fierce? We appear to see 'fierce' as a problem, and we either tame it or kill it. We have shot all the buffalo, and we are now shooting wolves and coyotes and elk and deer, and anything that threatens our tame and tidy existence—for the continuation of the biggest and the best burger on the planet. Instead of wild animals, we have cute little parks with Molly the Moose and Charlie the Chipmunk and Bugs Bunny—or some such nonsense. And look what we have done to the indigenous people. Why aren't we ashamed? Do we think we have the right to own everything? Control everything? And why doesn't anyone see that we have done this to our own lives as well? It is our own wildness that dies with all of them."

She paused to draw breath.

"And you—when did you last write anything? You told me your mother was so proud to have a poet for a son. Well! What has happened to him? And that's it, you see! You are busy all day doing good, sensible, practical things that almost any fool with two hands, two legs and half a brain could do. But where have you gone? How many people are poets? How many have that kind of soul—that kind of gift? What have you done with your passion? It seems that everything wild and beautiful—and not strictly necessary—dies or gets killed, or is tamed and made manageable and useful—while we slowly go to sleep."

With her flashing eyes and heightened color, Sebastián thought she was beautiful.

"Octavia," he said, "why do you think you are so angry?"

Octavia stared at him.

"Because—"

She held her hands up over her mouth, as if not wanting to give the answer.

Then, with a defiant shake of her head, she stared straight at him—

"Because I am frightened I will end up like all of you!"

She burst into tears and ran from the room. They heard a door slam, and through the window saw her running toward the Black Room.

PART TWO
THE WHITE ROOM

Paint

Octavia sat in her studio. The day was overcast, and for the first time the space felt gloomy. She turned to look at the sketches she had made of herself and Lucien. She sat back in her chair, and examined them critically from, she was surprised to note, a detached place. Would she keep them? And if so, why? But to destroy them also did not feel right. Then again, to keep them would only cause pain to a number of people if they were discovered; and embarrassment to her.

She crossed the room, took down the seven large sketches and laid them on the work-table with the mask, the shirt and the black box with the lock of hair. She folded each of the large sheets in half, and in half again. She turned to consider the finished beadwork and the still unworked sketch for the second one, half dreading that they too might be part of the fire to come. But no. Under her critical gaze, they did not flinch.

Octavia squashed the mask and other items into a small bundle, wrapped it in the folded paper and tied it all together with string. When Gregorio came by, she would ask him to help her make a bonfire.

Octavia, in a pair of old, faded and paint-spotted dungarees, sat next to Gregorio in the cab of the old truck. He was taking goods to Las Madres, and she had asked if she could go along. Something she needed to buy.

"Where shall I drop you?"

"Jake's Paint and Hardware would be good, if that's okay with you. I can wait there until you have finished."

"I will be half an hour at the most. Does that give you enough time?"

Octavia smiled and nodded.

"Perfect."

He watched her cross the street and enter the store before pulling away. Something was up. He knew that. It was not his place to interfere. In any case, he knew that interference would not change Octavia's mind once it was made up. He wondered what this next plan was. That air of defiance was a familiar one.

"Octavia!"

She waved in response to the young man up the ladder.

"Haven't seen you for such a long time," he said. "Wait a minute. I'll be right down."

"Good to see you, Jake. How is the new baby doing?"

"Can't you tell from this tired, care-worn face?" he laughed. "She's blooming. We can't wait for her to sleep through."

He chuckled.

"And what can I do for you?"

"I need a couple of gallons of interior white paint. Good quality. It has to cover black. A large room. Will it need two coats?"

"It would be better."

"Good. And rollers with extension handles; the walls are high. Some brushes, for around windows and the door. A rough brush and some masking tape, and coarse sandpaper. Oh—and a tray for the paint."

"What are you painting?"

"I am about to leave for a trip to Chile—to the Atacama Desert. Have you heard about it?"

"Can't say I have."

"It is the driest place in the world. So high and clean—the air, I mean. No city lights. No pollution. They have built an observatory there to study the stars. I want to spend a few months there. I want to learn everything I can about the stars. And I want to run in that endless, open desert space; feel the wind. Experience the brilliance of that light."

"And what has this to do with white paint?"

"I want to paint my studio again. I feel that I am moving into a new space in my life. I want light and clarity."

It took Octavia a whole morning to move the shelves of beads and furniture to the center of the room, to brush the walls free of cobwebs, and put masking tape around the window-frames and the door. By five o'clock she had completed the first coat of paint.

She lit a cigarette, and sat contemplating her work critically. Something was not right. Had she finally betrayed her stars? The white walls stared back at her; a blank, white stare. The room felt naked. So this was not what she wanted—but then, what did she want?

Octavia closed her eyes. What was it that drew her so to the desert? To stars? In a way the essence of each was unattainable. And so?

But it was not a night sky that she was seeking now. It was the bleached-out stare of the desert; the endless spaces; the searing heat that so often brought with it a distant haze, and the absence of horizon.

But it was not white. Of course! What she was wanting was a quality of light! She would need to visit the paint shop again.

Octavia bent over the buckets, mixing different shades of color: bleached-white sand tones in several buckets, and little more than a memory of blue tones in others. One small section of wall held some color-test daubs of paint.

Finally she began the task of painting wide horizontal bands, beginning at floor level. The bands were uneven in width, and included varied tones of off-white, bleached earth. As the bands moved higher, the tones became lighter, as if all color was leached out by the heat-haze.

Octavia stirred the paint for the upper levels. She dragged the scaffolding into place, and painted the first few horizontal lines. Stepped down to view it from across the room. The band treatment wasn't working for the sky. Why did it look so contrived?

Octavia sat with eyes closed, in an attempt to visualize a heat-haze. Of course! There were no lines! No bands of color. There was no way of telling where the color shift occurred—just a gradual change from the bleached sand into haze; into blue haze; into sky.

And yes! She wanted blue!

It was late afternoon when she finished painting. She removed the scaffolding, and considered the result. It was better, but she still had not managed to capture the quality of light that she envisaged. The walls looked too solid. She wanted to create a sense of the airiest of veils, through which only light or a dream could pass; or perhaps someone seeking a new way of seeing.

On an impulse, she picked up a piece of coarse sandpaper and sanded a small section of wall. The combination of the sandpaper on the rough adobe plaster was dramatic. Small dots of white from the undercoat shone through the top-coat, giving it a quality of transparency—of light.

Octavia executed a dance of pure ecstasy. The result was just what she wanted. She worked the high areas first, stepping down from the ladder from time to time to check the effect.

She was startled by a knock on the door, and Sebastián calling her to supper.

"Could you leave mine in the kitchen? I'll get it when I am finished painting."

"Aren't you hungry? Tired?"

"Yes, and yes. But I want to finish this first."

"Well, don't work too hard. I will be up late, working on the accounts. Come and eat your supper in my office if you like."

There was just a small section left around the door.

Tomorrow she would complete the work, when she got back from Santa Fe.

A Storm on the 285

Octavia was on her way to buy all the necessities for her trip to Chile.

The sky was growing dark, and she could hear thunder rumbling in the distance. She hoped the weather would hold until she reached Santa Fe. Perhaps she should have gone earlier in the week, she thought, but she wanted to finish painting her room while the weather was good. The forecast had predicted rain.

It was just before the turn-off to the opera house that the storm broke. She slowed down, struggling to see the road through the sheets of rain that battered against the windscreen. There was a flash of lightning, followed by a crack of thunder overhead, that all but drowned out the frantic clip-clip-clip of the wipers, as they struggled with the sheer weight of water that poured down on them.

With such poor visibility, Octavia slowed almost to a halt, and leaned forward over the wheel in an attempt to see the road.

She saw, or thought she saw a white animal—was it a dog; a white dog?

It was at this moment that a truck, speeding down the hill toward her, skidded—a long, slithering slide that ended with a crash into the side of her vehicle. In spite of the safety belt, Octavia was thrown forward onto the steering-wheel.

The impact of the collision pushed her car off the road and onto the dirt verge, where it rolled twice before coming to a halt on its side.

Cars, crawling through the sheets of rain, pulled to a halt. People rushed forward to offer help. A traffic control vehicle drew up, blue lights flashing. One officer took a look at the scene and immediately got on his phone, calling for assistance. The second began directing traffic to move on. The driver of the truck was bruised, but otherwise unhurt. Octavia's car had come to rest with the driver's side undermost. Her head was resting on the steering-wheel. The windscreen was spattered with blood. She made no movement. The officer attempted to open the front passenger door, but both front and rear doors were locked.

She could feel him close to her; very close. And the warmth of him. Could feel the deep softness of his thick, white coat. He paid no attention to what was happening outside the car. He was there with her. She could feel his breath on her.

It took fifteen minutes for the ambulance to arrive. It was followed by four police cars, and a vehicle with equipment to cut open the passenger door. The plates had been traced, and a phone call made to Sebastián Chavez, informing him of the accident. He and Georgia would leave immediately, and go directly to the trauma unit at the hospital in Santa Fe.

It took twenty-five minutes to remove Octavia from the car. The ambulance crew immobilized her head and neck, applied an emergency dressing to her head to stop the flow of blood, and placed a sterile dressing over her leg wound. With great care they managed to move her onto a stretcher. Her left leg appeared to be fractured, and was twisted at an unnatural angle. A drip was set up, and an oxygen mask. Thermal blankets were placed over her, for her body was shaking from shock. She was put into the ambulance with an attendant next to her, and the ambulance departed, siren sounding and lights flashing.

The police examined the scene, made measurements, obtained statements from witnesses and from the driver of the truck. A tow truck was contacted to collect both vehicles. The driver accompanied the police to the station for questioning.

A Long Road

Octavia opened her eyes. She tried to lift her head. She couldn't move. Out of the corner of her eye she saw something white.

The nurse pulled back the sheet, and fitted a band around Octavia's arm. She connected the blood pressure monitor and pumped in air, releasing it slowly and watching the figures on the small dial. She removed the band, and felt for a pulse on Octavia's wrist. She counted a minute on her fob-watch, tucked the sheet back and moved to make a note on the chart at the foot of the bed.

Octavia could feel panic flooding through her. Why couldn't she move?

Sebastián leaned forward.

"You are all right, my sweetheart. You had an accident. They want you not to move until they have done X-rays."

Georgia bent forward, tears of relief in her eyes. Octavia had taken so long to regain consciousness. It had been difficult not to fear the worst.

"We are here, my darling; right here. They are going to bring a big chair for me, and I will be staying here with you."

Octavia tried to speak. She looked at her mother, her eyes huge with panic. Georgia took her hand.

"Don't try to speak. Everything is going to be fine. You must rest, and keep still."

The nurse came in with a syringe, and gave Octavia an injection.

"This will help her to relax. Her body is still in shock."

Octavia closed her eyes.

*His eyes were blue, and very clear. He was standing beside her—a wolf: a white
wolf. He didn't seem to be asking for anything; nor was he doing anything. He was
just there.*

They seemed to be surrounded by snow. Where was she?

She felt the pain; oh, such pain. What was wrong? What had happened?

*She was glad that he was there, standing beside her; so alive. How strange to have
a wolf so close. His coat was thick and full. She wanted to reach out a hand to touch
him, but she couldn't move.*

They were in the snowy wastes of a vast landscape. The sky was white.

*A part of her wanted to drift away, but she could feel the gaze of his eyes holding
her. She allowed herself to be comforted.*

Sebastián and Georgia sat in the doctor's office, looking at the X-rays on a light-screen.

"There is a thin fracture of the skull here—"

Doctor Limón indicated a faint, white line running across the shadowy image.

"We will watch this very closely. At the moment there is no evidence of a build-up of fluid, but we don't want that to occur. The fracture will heal. What we don't want is any pressure on the brain."

Georgia took Sebastián's hand.

"Here we have the sacrum and the lumbar vertebrae. You can see here that these vertebrae have been pushed out of alignment, and this lower one,"—he indicated with a pencil the section in question—"has been twisted. We hope to be able to manipulate this under anesthetic."

"And if you can't?"

"Then we might have to fuse two of the vertebrae. What we don't want is any damage to the nerve."

"What does that mean in layman's language?"

Georgia was struggling not to give in to tears.

"Well—any damage could result in some kind of paralysis. At the moment we can't be sure of what she may or may not be able to feel. We don't want her to move until we have operated."

He removed the two X-rays, and slid two more up the screen and under the clip.

"Here is where most of the damage occurred—a dislocation of the femoral head in the hip joint, and a compound fracture of the left femur. You can see the bone has broken through the skin here—"

He indicated with a pencil. Georgia had a hand over her mouth. How could this ever come right again?

"Here we will have to clean the site, and she will be given antibiotics to prevent infection. That is always a danger where bone has become exposed to outside germs. And there is the further complication that the bone was crushed. You can see here that there are several pieces of bone unattached. Some of these will have to be removed. Others will have to be put back together, probably with several plates and screws. We will manipulate the hip joint. It may be necessary to do a hip replacement if it doesn't heal properly."

He removed the images, and clipped one last X-ray onto the screen.

"These are the neck vertebrae. She is a very lucky lady. Although there is evidence of severe trauma and dislocation, nothing is broken. She will however have to wear a neck brace after manipulation under anesthetic."

He turned to face them.

"It is going to be a long recovery period, and even after discharge she will have to return for regular physiotherapy treatments and evaluations."

"How long do you think this will take?"

"Hard to say. She is young, which is in her favor. Does she smoke?"

Sebastián and Georgia looked at one another.

"Not to our knowledge."

"Well, find out. If she does smoke, she must stop at once—nicotine can make the healing process take almost twice the time. But if all goes well, I would say you are looking at twelve to eighteen months."

Music

The trip to Chile was canceled.

Octavia lay on the special contour bed that Sebastián had bought for her in Albuquerque. It had a handle which made it possible to shift the angle of the bed from left to right, and to alter the elevation of her legs and her head. All of this would help to bring relief to pressure points. It could be wheeled easily. Each morning it was placed in the shade of the casita, just outside her bedroom window.

Sister Piadosa and Sister Ana came three times a day to help Georgia massage cream into all the pressure areas.

"The last thing you want is for the skin to break. She must be rolled from one side to the other frequently, and the weight-bearing points massaged. Any area that looks red must be raised slightly with a small cushion to allow blood to flow freely."

Lucien and Sofia returned from their honeymoon, and came to sit with her and chat about the holiday. Lucien was concerned about the accident, but they all felt awkward together.

"If there is anything we can do, just let us know," Sofia said.

"Thanks, Sofia."

"We have to put in some hard work for the next few weeks," said Lucien. "The concert is coming up, and we have many rehearsals to organize."

They were all grateful for this, but no one said anything.

Kristiyan was most attentive. He arrived one day with various electric plugs, and several yards of cable.

"If you give me the key to your studio, I will fetch your record player and set it up here. At night it can be passed through the window into your bedroom."

"No! You can't do that."

Octavia's voice was suddenly anxious.

"Sorry! I didn't mean to sound ungrateful. I mean—that isn't necessary. I will listen to my music when I can work again."

"Yes, but you don't need to wait. That is still weeks away. It won't take me a minute. Is there a problem?"

"Yes. I don't want my record player out here."

"Well, what if I ask Lucien if we can use his? He is so busy working on his compositions at the moment. I'm sure he won't mind."

"But I mind. It's all right, Kristiyan. I'll wait."

Was she dreaming? He was standing in the shadows next to her window. A full moon lit just the tips of his ears. She couldn't see his eyes, but she knew he was watching her. Did he want something? Was he trying to say something to her? No. He was just there. She felt strangely comforted by his presence—as if, in some new way, she was being held.

The next day Kristiyan arrived with a record player in a box, two speakers and a large packet.

"This is mine, Octavia, and I have no need of it right now. I have my CD player—perhaps we should get you one as well, come to think of it."

Octavia was about to say something, but Kristiyan put a finger to his lips.

"Shh! This will be quite painless. You will see."

He set up the record player and the two small speakers on the table next to her.

"Can you reach this if I put it here?"

He moved the player close to the bed.

"Thank you, Kristiyan. But you shouldn't—"

"Shh! And the records—here?"

Octavia smiled in spite of herself.

"Thank you very much."

Kristiyan fussed a little with the cables, taping them to the window-frame to keep them out of the dust.

"Will you stay a while and have some iced tea with me? Look! I have a little bell. Mama gave it to me, to ring if I need anything."

She laughed. "It makes me feel like such a grand lady."

"I would love to."

Georgia brought out the tea, and sat with them for a few minutes.

"I see that you have prevailed," she said to Kristiyan with a chuckle.

"Yes, at last. It wasn't easy, I can tell you! Was she always so difficult to serve?"

"Hey, you two," said Octavia, laughing. "I am the easiest person on earth. Just do it my way, and you will see that's true."

"Now you tell us!" Georgia got up to go.

"You're not cold out here? Do you need a jacket?"

"I'm fine, thanks, mama."

Kristiyan took an album out of the packet.

"I have brought a recording of Max Bruch's Kol Nidrei—a composition for cello and orchestra."

"What is Kol Nidrei?"

"It is sung by the cantor on the eve of the Day of Atonement in the Jewish faith. It is an ancient Hebraic song of penitence."

"What is it about?"

"It is about all vows and promises—that is the meaning of Kol Nidrei. All vows that were made between an individual and God are considered null and void. New vows will be made. It is like a fresh start."

"How do you know all this?"

"In the world of classical music you meet people from everywhere—all countries, religions; rich and poor. Music is a great common language. There was a Jewish girl—Hebrew: she came from Israel—who studied with me. She told me so much about her religion. It is very beautiful—and so ancient."

"Was she a girlfriend?"

Kristiyan hoped he heard a note of jealousy.

"Not really."

"Did you have lots of girlfriends when you were growing up?"

Kristiyan shrugged.

"Only the usual teenage crushes. I was very much into my music, so the whole young scene wasn't really my thing."

"Would you say it is very different in Russia to the life young people have here?"

"I don't know much about what young people do here. I would think that life here has far more freedom—but then, I'm just guessing."

"And when you were older?"

"This is like being investigated by the KGB!"

Octavia blushed.

"I'm just curious about what life is like in your country. I'm sorry. I didn't mean to be inquisitive. Well, maybe I did!"

She laughed.

"All right, I will tell you something which may give you some idea of the differences between your country and mine.

"I met someone at the conservatory, in the late seventies. She came from Poland to study at the Saint Petersburg Conservatory. Her name was Urszula Zawadzka, and she came from Kraków. She was a very gifted violinist. We sometimes gave small music recitals together with a friend of hers, who played the viola."

"Did you know her well?"

"I suppose she was my first serious girlfriend."

"Were you going out?"

"In a way, yes. We had our music in common, and were both very serious and hard-working students. You have to work hard if you want to compete with the best. But yes, we saw a lot of each other. We were close, if that is what you are asking."

"So, where is she now?"

Kristiyan looked down.

"I don't know."

Octavia stared.

"You don't know? How come?"

"She went home on a vacation to see her parents. I never saw her again."

"Did she call to say why she wasn't coming back?"

"No. I called her parents, of course. We had a very strange conversation. They said they didn't know where she was. I think they were afraid to speak over the phone."

"You mean, someone was listening?"

"It is possible. I did learn a bit from them. Apparently she had been involved in some underground activities—anti-government organizations, that sort of thing. It was just before Solidarity was formed. This was before she came to the conservatory. Many people were arrested by the communists for this. Maybe her name was on some list."

"If you would rather not speak about this..."

"No, I would like you to hear the whole story. I called her parents several times, but they could tell me nothing. Finally they told me not to phone again."

"And then?"

"That's it. I never heard another word."

"What do you think happened to her?"

"It would be guessing. Maybe she was being held somewhere. Maybe she was not still alive. People are afraid to talk at times like this. So that was it. No closure."

"Oh, Kristiyan, I am so sorry."

"It's okay," he said.

It was not long after this that Sebastián approached Kristiyan, and asked him if he would go into Santa Fe and buy a selection of music that Octavia could listen to while her leg was in the cast.

"You know what music she might enjoy, Kristiyan. I would be so grateful if you could do this."

"Would you consider buying a CD player for Octavia? They are phasing out the old LPs in favor of the new digital recordings. If you decided that, then I will only buy CDs. They have a remote, which will make it easier for her to manage."

"Good idea. Go ahead and get what you think is best."

So Kristiyan spent a few happy hours, making a selection of music—music from all over the world, ancient and contemporary.

It was late afternoon when he returned with his purchases.

The evenings were beginning to grow cool, and Octavia was in her bedroom.

"I have something for you," he announced as he entered the room.

He put the box and the carrier bag down on a table, went outside, unplugged the record player, brought it inside and put it on the floor.

"What is all this about?" Octavia asked in astonishment.

"It was your father's idea. He asked me to make a selection of music. I thought that, as you aren't able to travel right now, I would take you on a musical journey to visit many countries and their music. And while we were at it, we thought a CD player would be a good investment."

He unpacked the CD player, and connected the two speakers and the power cable.

"There! Everything is ready. I will show you how to operate the remote. Do you want to look at all the CD titles and choose, or shall I surprise you?"

Octavia clapped her hands, and Kristiyan found himself thinking that sometimes she looked just like a little girl, excited to be at a party.

"Oh! Surprise me!"

He consulted the list he had in his hand, and then reached into the parcel and drew out an album; lifted the CD out of its jewel case and placed it in the player. Octavia looked away. She didn't want to read the label. It would spoil the surprise.

At the sound of the first notes, she lay back and closed her eyes.

She heard a man's voice, singing a cappella in a language she did not know—only that it was beautiful. It rose and fell, the way an eagle floats on the wind. And now it was joined by other voices that repeated the same patterns of sound. The music reminded her of the vast, oceanic spaces of the desert; the gentle rise and fall of the landscape, with its soft gradations of color that melted into the haze.

Kristiyan saw the first tears fall down her cheeks.

And now the solo voice began to chant over the choir. Octavia could hear that it was church music, but could not place it in any particular country. It was enough that it moved her profoundly. Listening to it she could almost, but not quite visualize the icons that she wanted to make—or rather, she could sense their growing presence, which was, at the same time, an absence; an emptiness that was both endless and complete. It breathed in her like the faint memory of a day from childhood.

With her eyes still closed, she reached out a hand toward where Kristiyan was sitting. He moved his chair closer to the bed, and took it in his.

It was the first time they touched.

Everything was white. The low sky. The endless reaches of thick snow. She was running, effortlessly, in spite of it. The white wolf loped ahead of her, barely visible in all the whiteness. Only his shadow, a blue swiftness on the surface of the snow, gave him definition. He did not look round. She followed in his tracks.

But why snow? What was this country toward which he was leading her? He never faltered, but held a straight path to some place which was invisible to her. The landscape had no features. Just this vast whiteness. He seemed to know the way. What was the way? There were no landmarks; nothing to mark their progress or direction. Could he hear something?

Of all the music that Kristiyan brought back from Santa Fe, it was the Russian Orthodox chants that Octavia loved the most; the many different expressions of early Russian polyphony, and their ancient sources. It was something that Kristiyan had studied in depth while at the conservatory, and he held Octavia spellbound, telling her some of the history and background of the pieces he played for her.

It was this that she now listened to during the long hours, as she lay dreaming into the beadwork icons she would make.

She was taken for regular visits to the orthopedic surgeon, and for X-rays to see how the bones were healing.

She and her parents looked at the new X-rays, but the faint images told her nothing.

"When will I be able to book my ticket to Chile?"

"Slow down, young lady. Not this year—and not for most of next year. Not until we are perfectly certain that everything has healed, and is strong again. Toward the end of autumn we will see how you are doing."

"But that's almost a whole year!"

"I am sure Chile will wait for you."

Her physiotherapy was going well, although there was still a lot of pain. She could not put any weight on her leg, although fortunately there had been no complica-

140

tion with infection. Soon she would be able to sit in a chair. Her lower back and neck would have to remain in a brace for a while—and certainly if, as she said, she intended working in her studio, she would need a wheelchair.

In the meantime she listened, enthralled, to the music that resonated so deeply in her. She made some preliminary sketches for a series of future iconic beadworks, but almost immediately rejected the images.

Something had shifted in her, but whatever was moving through her, desiring some kind of expression, was still not clear. In the end she put away the sketch pad and listened: listened to the music, and to the longing that it evoked in her.

Kristiyan was a frequent visitor. He never came empty-handed. Sometimes he brought a book and would read to her, or he would play a rare piece of music for her and draw her attention to the particular style that made it possible to distinguish its sources. Or he would tell her what it was like growing up in the USSR when he was a boy, and how strange it was now to be living and working in the United States.

"What was it like in Russia? Everyone in this country seems to have been terrified by anything Russian. And communism, of course."

She paused.

"Are you a communist?"

Kristiyan laughed.

"You mean one of those sinister men in dark coats and fur hats, with a hammer and sickle tattooed over their hearts, who lurk behind doors and curtains, whispering into small devices, like they do in films? Or young fanatics who rush about, shooting tear gas into churches? No. I am not a communist. There were, and are, many in Russia—free spirits—who fought for freedom of speech: writers, composers—artists of all kinds. Some were put in prison. Some died. But the spirit of freedom cannot be locked up. If anything, it grows stronger under such repression."

"I cannot imagine what that must be like; to live in such a country."

"My country is also beautiful. It has a great soul. Over centuries, it has had to endure so much. You can hear it in the music—and yet there is no complaint. That is what is so wonderful. Nothing can destroy that. Next week, I will bring you an early composition by Stravinsky—The Rite of Spring. Then you will get an idea of the dramatic grandeur of that season in Russia: very different from the gentle budding that you know here. In fact, when it was first performed—as a ballet—people in the audience were so shocked that they became violent. It was never performed as a ballet again."

"I want to learn all about your country."

Octavia gave him one of her most captivating smiles. Kristiyan blushed, and muttered that he would tell her all he knew.

I cannot see him, but I know he is nearby; maybe in the shadows of the cottonwood.

I can feel some kind of response in me. Response to what? What is this presence? It feels like something sacred. Something that just is. I don't want to speak of this to anyone. It would feel like a betrayal.

Journal Entry 6

I can't wait to draw this image that came to me, like a vision. The background is desert and sky. They melt into each other. Endless space. There is no horizon. I see a jet-black horse at full gallop. I sense that this is a mare. A woman is riding her bareback. There is no bridle. On the sand is the black horse's shadow. It is blue. An upside-down horse at full gallop, and a woman. They are held, almost as if they were suspended in time. I cannot explain this—but I love it.

Is a shadow a kind of mirror?

Panic

"Mama! Mama!"

Georgia woke from a deep sleep to hear the cry of panic.

"Mama!"

She ran into Octavia's room, and switched on the light.

"What is it? What's the matter?"

Octavia was lying flat— the brace holding her back straight, a cushion under her knees.

"I can't feel—my feet! I can't feel them! What has happened?"

Her words came out in fast, panicky sobs.

"Oh, mama—what is happening to me?"

Georgia pulled the bedclothes back so that she could touch Octavia's legs and feet.

"Can you feel this?"

She ran her finger along the underside of Octavia's foot.

"I can't feel anything."

Georgia moved her hand to touch first one knee, then the other.

"And now?"

Octavia burst into tears. She turned to Georgia, her arms reaching out to her mother.

"Oh, my darling! I am here. I am right here!"

She pulled the bedside chair forward and sat close to Octavia, holding both her hands.

"There. We are going to find out what is wrong. I am going to wake Sebastián, and ask him to call the surgeon. We will see what he says."

The ambulance arrived with four paramedics. Octavia was strapped in a brace to prevent any movement of the spine, and transferred onto the portable stretcher and into the ambulance.

She turned her white face to her mother.

"Come with me, mama."

Sebastián nodded to Georgia.

"I will meet you at the hospital. He said to go straight to ward A4. He will be there. He has already called the anesthetist, in case he wants to take her into theatre."

Georgia sat, holding Octavia's hand. It was the first time her daughter had reached out to her so clearly. She felt a rush of love almost overwhelm her. Tears stung her eyes, and she struggled to stay calm. She leaned forward, so that Octavia could hear her through the brace.

"I am right here, my sweetheart. I am coming with you, and Sebastián will follow. We will both stay with you at the hospital."

She paused.

"I love you so much, my darling."

Octavia squeezed her hand.

He is sitting close to me in the ambulance. I am afraid that mama will get a fright, but she has not seen him. How is that possible? I can feel the warmth of his breath on my cheek. He is so close. If my hands were free, I could touch him. If only I could touch him.

He is close to me. They are wheeling the trolley into theatre. Nobody seems to think it strange that a wolf is in the hospital—in an operating theatre. I can feel his presence like a glow around my heart.

Sebastián and Georgia sat on the plastic chairs outside the operating theatre.

"Why is it taking so long? It's been more than an hour."

Sebastián put his arm around her.

"Oh, suppose—" Georgia broke off, not wanting to give voice to the fear that was rising in her.

"Suppose the nerve is damaged—irreparably?"

"Then we will do whatever has to be done."

Shadows

Georgia sat with Sebastián, staring at the new X-rays—seeing the surgeon's pencil point to areas in the shadowy images.

"You see here. This is where the fourth and fifth lumbar vertebrae were traumatized by the accident. We hoped, after the manipulation, that they would settle and heal. There was always the possibility that the nerve was compromised in some way by the accident; not sufficiently to cause paralysis, but..."

He removed the X-ray, and slid another under the clip.

"Here you can see that the vertebrae have not stabilized. They have moved out of alignment again, and the disc is protruding and pressing on the nerve."

He sat back in his chair.

"These are only X-rays. We are waiting for the results of the scan, which will be more detailed. Then we will decide what is to be done. In the meantime she has been put on a drip, to bring down the inflammation and the pressure on the nerve. Her back—her spinal column—has been immobilized."

"What are the options?"

Sebastián was staring at the image on the screen.

"One option is to reposition the disc, but we cannot be certain that this will settle it. The most likely solution would be to fuse the two vertebrae. That should prevent this from occurring again."

"Should?"

"Well, although the major damage was to the fourth and fifth vertebrae, her whole spine was affected by the impact of the collision. When we fuse two vertebrae it reduces the suppleness of the spine, and it puts added pressure on the vertebrae beneath them."

"What does that mean?"

"It could cause a further trauma."

The phone on the desk rang.

"Ah! Good. Bring them to my office."

He turned to Sebastián and Georgia.

"We have the results of the scan."

The scan showed that the damage was more extensive than was originally supposed. In the previous scan they had seen small, hairline fractures in the two lumbar

144

vertebrae. Now there were small chips of bone that had broken off, and were floating. These would need to be removed. The decision was to fuse the vertebrae. However, Octavia would have to wear a brace, perhaps for an extended period—perhaps, if things did not improve with physiotherapy, permanently. They could not take the risk of having the same thing happen again with a more serious outcome.

"What would that be?" Georgia's face was strained and drawn from lack of sleep.

"It could mean paralysis."

"You mean, she would not be able to walk at all?"

"Yes. And the complications that go with that."

"What complications?"

"Well, her bladder and bowel functions could be compromised, and possibly her sexual function. Then, of course, there is the need for physiotherapy on an ongoing basis; and daily massage and care of pressure areas. These, of course, are just the physical complications. She would have to see a psychotherapist. Her whole way of life would be drastically changed."

Georgia was devastated. How did you tell your child this? A thousand images of Octavia's passion and defiance flashed through her mind—her fierce willfulness; her extraordinary beauty—running like a wild creature, that mass of hair streaming out behind her.

She came back to the room, to the surgeon's voice.

"We have also noted that although the femur appears to have healed well, there is evidence of infection around the break. We will put her back onto antibiotics for this. It may be necessary to insert a drain to allow the pus to escape. Although skin has covered the wound, it has not allowed for proper healing; so we may need to reopen it and remove some of the necrotic tissue. Also, the original damage was extensive, and she has lost some bone in this area. The result is that her left leg has been shortened, and she will need to wear a corrective shoe to compensate for this."

It was too much. Georgia burst into tears.

She was floating on her back across the vast Atacama Desert, gazing up at the stars. She felt weightless. She wanted to float right up into those starry galaxies, but a thin cord attached to her hand held her back. She saw the image of a horse, a black horse, galloping swiftly through the clouds of stars. It looked like a wind. A sleek, black wind. Then it melted away into the stars. Now she saw a face, gazing down on her. Alejandro's face. He was weeping. She wanted to speak to him. Ask him why he was weeping. But now his face grew less distinct. Became fragmented. Became a fading cluster of stars. Now the great clouds of stars and galaxies began to turn and drift off the edge of the sky. The sky faded into white.

Octavia opened her eyes. Her eyelids felt heavy. She could not move.

"Hello, Octavia. Welcome back. You are in the recovery room."

The nurse bent over her, and attached a band to her arm.

Octavia felt the band tighten and slowly release. She felt the sudden throb of her pulse. Felt the band being removed.

She watched the nurse move to the foot of the bed, unclip the chart and make a note of the time and information.

"In a little while we will take you back to the ward. Your parents are waiting there. How do you feel? Are you comfortable?"

Octavia tried to speak. She felt drunk.

"Wha' dime ish't?"

"It is two o'clock. Now, you have a good sleep."

Octavia closed her eyes.

He was close beside her. Safe. She felt safe.

The door opened, and an orderly came into the room.

Octavia awoke at the sound of voices, but she did not open her eyes.

She felt the bed being turned. Felt the vibration as it was wheeled across the room. It stopped, and she heard the sound of the door being opened. The vibrations began again.

Octavia drifted back into sleep.

Georgia and Sebastián listened intently to the surgeon's account of the operation.

"It went well. We have removed those fragments of bone. We took some bone from her right leg to place between the two vertebrae. These we have pinned together. Hopefully the bone will help to fuse the vertebrae, and then we will remove the pins. She will be in a brace until we are certain that everything has settled down. It is possible—probable—that she is going to have a degree of back pain. We have her on morphine at the moment. In a few days we will begin to lessen the dose, and then discontinue it. Then we will be able to tell what she needs to manage the pain."

"And the paralysis—is there any danger that it will happen again?"

"No one can answer that with certainty. I am surprised that this has happened now. We saw the faint hairline fractures on the vertebrae when we first operated, but we expected these to heal without any problem. We don't anticipate this happening again..."

"But—?"

"Well, like I say, it is impossible to predict these things. She will have to be very patient, and not rush the healing process. Initially she must lie flat on her back. She must take care not to twist or try to reach for things. Everything depends on rest and patience."

The Waiting

Octavia was lying on her special bed in the shade of the casita. She was some-where between sleep and daydream.

It is midday. I am standing on a high place, looking out over a vast expanse of shining white desert; the glare so bright it hurts my eyes. I have been standing here for a million years; and yet it remains a vast emptiness. The light and the shadows shift, like the colors during sunrise and sunset, day and night. These are just effects. They come and they pass. They leave no mark on the land. There is no visible or tangible movement in all of this whiteness. Surely such emptiness must eventually call forth a presence; a being-ness? How else could it know itself?

I hear the first sound—is it sound or the absence of silence? Can there be such a thing? Against the brilliance of the glare I see white shadows. They are little more than a flickering in the light, as if the light itself is searching to become form. And now, is it a sound—the faintest whisper, hardly more than a breath—that comes from the flickering shadows?

Octavia half-opened her eyes, a part of her still in the daydream. Above her she saw the white doves turn against the light and disappear. She heard the whisper of air grow silent—for how long? A second? An eternity? How did you measure such things?

And then the whisper became a rush of air again as they turned out of the spiral, and flew with the light full on their wings once more.

Strange that something could appear and disappear, and yet always be there. Was there something eternal that held the transient in place? Indeed, the flight pattern was a constant, even as doves departed, died; or as others joined the flock. Was there a pattern that endured all things? What was it—emptiness or silence that was the origin of all things?

And does the emptiness long to know itself? Long to be seen? And the silence to be heard? Is this our deepest longing? To be known?

Surely, if the emptiness calls out, there must be a response. The call and the answer: the closing of the circle that never closes.

"Listen."

147

"Only listen."
I watch the white doves disappear into the empty desert whiteness.

Thoughts and words faded away.
Octavia drifted off to sleep.

Kristiyan listened carefully to Octavia's struggle to make sense of her daydream.

"How would it be if you made it immediate?"

"In what way?"

"Well," he suggested, "what happens inside you when you sit down to create a new work?"

"I feel something that has no image; no words. When I listen to music—particularly the Russian Orthodox chant, and of course the words don't interfere because I don't understand them—then I feel called to put that into an image."

"How do you do that?"

"It's not easy, because the music is not static and the image will be, so I have to find out how my discipline can take that step and yet maintain that sense of constant becoming. And then, music has a language all its own; it signifies nothing but itself. Words cannot go there. This is where the daydream tried to speak in images, but a part of my mind was still interfering. It will do that, even with an image, to a lesser extent."

"Yes," he acknowledged. "It is said that music is the language of pure connotation. Even poets envy it."

"That's just it—although in the chant I do hear a call and a response."

"So, to get back to my question, how do you make it immediate for your particular discipline?"

"I have to hear a call. It is not a voice; I mean, it is not like a person calling. It's something else. I cannot remember a time when it was not there. It comes from the stars."

"From the stars?"

"Yes."

"And what is it?"

"This will sound crazy, I'm sure, but I don't know! Or rather, I would not be able to tell you. I can't even tell myself."

Octavia looked at him, to make sure he was following what was so difficult to articulate.

"But this is my challenge: how do I introduce that moving quality?"

"Well?"

"Firstly, light is one of my tools. Ideally, the works should be illuminated by a light that moves. That way the brilliance of the beads will not be static."

"What else?"

"I think that any form must be offset by emptiness. Maybe one day I will not have any identifiable form; just light and space. At the moment I am too full of what I want to say."

Octavia laughed. "You see how perverse and contradictory I am!"

"I love it," he said with a smile.

Wolf

I asked mama to buy me this second journal. I want to keep all my notes of the white wolf apart from all the other writings. I don't know exactly why, but it feels right to do this.

What is this wild breath?

He is not asking anything of me, and yet I know that through his presence alone I am hearing something. Not words. He doesn't have words. I doubt that he has thoughts, in the way we do. And maybe he is not even trying to tell me anything. I am wounded, and he is being wolf. If there is a lesson for me, I will have to recognize it. He is not telling or teaching or giving. He is being wolf. It leaves me so free.

Is this how animals comfort one another? They are present to the one who is suffering. They ask for nothing. Not even gratitude.

He is not doing this for any reason outside himself. I don't know how I know this. He is doing this because it is in his nature to do so. Nothing is required of me! I know he has no expectation of me. I don't feel obliged to be or behave in any way. He does not require this. Whatever my fate may be, he will accept that too. What is this extraordinary acceptance? What a strange thing it is to know I am not alone.

I wonder how different my life might have been if I had been there for others as he is for me. It is not only his presence, this just there-ness of his that brings such a deep sense of communion. It has something to do with breath. It is something I have forgotten—if indeed I ever knew it. Wild breath! What have I done with mine?

I wonder where his pack is?

What is the nature of this creature; this blue-eyed wolf? I have been asking myself if he is real. I have felt his warm breath on me. That is real. I haven't touched him; nor has he touched me, physically.

The Zunis would talk of Wolf Medicine—but this is not that. That is a way of giving wolf the characteristics of humans. I think that insults the wolf. This is something so immediate, so ancient. This breath that is entering into me is something I have never known.

Sometimes I cannot see him. He is a master of stillness; so still, I lose sight of him. But when the pain is bad, there he is; close to me. I don't see him arrive. All at once he is just there beside me.

I long to touch him: and be touched by him.

PART THREE
THE YELLOWING

October 1993

"Come in!"

Sebastián was busy doing the accounts for The Adobe. He looked up when the door opened.

"Oh, hello, Kristiyan—come on in! Good to see you."

Sebastián rose, pulled up another chair and closed the office door.

"I came to visit Octavia, but she is sleeping, so I thought I would come and ask you what you would think if...if I..."

"What's on your mind?"

Kristiyan put his music-case on the chair, but he remained standing.

"Am I interrupting? I see you are busy. I can come some other time."

"It's nothing that I am not more than willing to put aside."

Kristiyan moved his case, and sat down.

"I was wondering—if you thought it was appropriate—whether I could move into one of the guest casitas. I would pay rent, of course. What I mean is..."

He blushed.

Sebastián waited.

"Well," Kristiyan continued, "the opera season is over, and I am going to be working with Salvador, Reuben and Lucien. I thought perhaps it would be easier if I was here, and we could rehearse without worrying about time and traveling and so on. But only if you have no objection."

"Of course, Kristiyan. It will be a pleasure to have you here—but you don't need to pay rent. The casita is just standing there, empty."

"I couldn't accept that. I am well able to pay the full rent and expenses. Are you sure I would not be imposing on your privacy?"

"Well, you are here such a lot, with one thing and another—I think we will be able to bear it."

Kristiyan frowned. He was not familiar with Sebastián's sense of humor.

"Perhaps it is not a good idea," he said.

"Kristiyan, we would love to have you, and I am not going to accept any rent payments. We are happy that you will be staying, and working with the music. When would you like to move in?"

Octavia's Dream

I am standing in the Atacama Desert. I am following the black mare. Now I hear a strange sound, like a wind. But there is no wind. I see an object rolling toward me. It is a white clay pot.

It comes close to me. Before I can pick it up, it is back where I first saw it. It rolls toward me again.

Finally it stops in front of me. I reach out to lift it up, but it changes into the sound of emptiness.

Octavia awoke—her heart beating fast. She looked at her surroundings for reassurance. Everything looked as it always looked. Or did it? She could not see the wolf.

She reached out to look at her watch. Four o'clock. Kristiyan would be here soon. He was bringing some new music for her to listen to.

She did not want to go back to sleep. She would just close her eyes and rest.

But the dream was waiting.

Moonlight. Again the clay pot is standing on the desert sand in front of me. How beautiful it looks. So clean and shining.

And now I see the black mare once more. She is moving at full gallop. I see that all the desert sand is slipping away behind her as she runs. And now she leaps into the sky. All the stars are falling. Falling out of the sky—falling down into emptiness. Thousands of stars.

I want to take the pot, to catch the stars; to save them—but once again it has vanished. Again I hear the sound of emptiness.

Octavia opened her eyes. Kristiyan was sitting in the chair beside her. He was reading. At first she thought he was part of the dream. But then he turned, and seeing her awake he closed his book.

"Hello there. That must be some dream you were having. You have been calling out in your sleep."

He put the book into his briefcase.

"Shall I go? I can come another time. Perhaps you want to stay with it—your dream, I mean."

Octavia smiled sleepily.

"No. I'm awake now. It's good to see you. Have you been here long?"

"About ten minutes. Do you want to speak about it?"

"Not right now. But tell me what you have been doing."

"Two things. Do you remember, before you had the accident we were speaking about Russia, and I said I would bring you some Russian poetry, translated into English?"

"Yes, of course."

"Well, I have a small book with me now. I will leave it with you. There is a marker at one of my favorite poems by Marina Tsvetaeva.

"Then I went to select some music for you; something different. But I kept coming back to Russian music. And it's not just because it is my country. There is something in that deep Orthodox chanting that is so strong—as if it would be with you through all circumstances. It sounds as if it comes out of the bowels of the earth—like an ancient root. And it can withstand all things."

Octavia stared at him.

"Did I ever play you any basso profondo singers?"

She shook her head.

"They sing below the general bass range—something which seems to be peculiar to Russian choirs. People have been fascinated by them for hundreds of years—the power and beauty of those incredible, deep vibrations of sound."

"Can we listen to something now? I would like to hear it with you."

Octavia closed her eyes. She was back in her dream.

Moonlight. I am naked. I am gazing down at a vast circle of desert. At the center of the circle I see the white, clay pot. I hear the rise and fall of an ancient chant. It is coming out of the clay pot. Above me is one bright star.

Fado

Octavia lay staring up at the autumn leaves of the cottonwood, willing the pain to let go its hold on her body; willing the small voice of fear to cease its whispering at the back of her mind.

Georgia had sat up all night with her, hoping that the painkillers would bring some relief and enable her to sleep. She had made cocoa, brought a hot pad and given Octavia's feet a massage; all to no avail. If the pain persisted, they would have to go back to Doctor Limón and see what he could do.

Just before dawn Octavia fell asleep, and Georgia lay down to catch an hour's rest before the day started.

Octavia lay outside in the shade, trying to get her mind to lift her out of the awareness of pain. She could feel tears of anger and helplessness, and a growing sense of defeat, building up inside her like something solid and immovable; something that felt like an adversary with a will of its own, challenging her to defy it. Would this pain be with her always? She stared directly into her fear, knowing that this was a possibility—a probability? How would her life look? What would she be able to do—and not do? It took so much of her energy just to manage the demands of her pain, before the day had even begun.

Where was that wild breath now? Why was the white wolf not present, all through that pain-filled night? And where had he gone—now?

The tears broke through her hold on them, and ran silently down her cheeks. She closed her eyes, and lay in the deep loneliness of unremitting pain.

Footsteps. The sound of someone sitting down in the chair next to her bed. She did not open her eyes.

She felt a hand take hold of hers.

And now the tears burst out of her, and with them, the raw sounds of pain and grief.

"I am right here," Kristiyan said.

Octavia wept helplessly, till there were no more tears.

"I am here."

He held her hand until she fell asleep.

It was some time after lunch when he came back.

"I am so sorry, Kristiyan, about my melt-down this morning. Things just got the better of me for a while. I'm fine now."

She pointed to the small packet he was carrying.

"What have you there?"

He took out the CD and gave it to her.

"Fado?" she read. "What is fado?"

"Let's listen to it first, and see what you hear. Then I will tell you what I know about it."

He put the disc in the player, and pulled his chair closer to Octavia's bed. She closed her eyes, and allowed the voice to take her.

He sat, watching the small shifts of expression play over her face: the smallest flicker of a smile; a look of sadness; a flash of surprise—tears. He watched her face change as she listened through all the songs; listened to all the varied renderings by a range of different artists. As he watched, he saw her whole body relax into the music.

When finally it came to an end, Octavia opened her eyes and smiled at him.

"Whatever it is—I love it."

"Say more."

Octavia gazed up at the leaves of the cottonwood.

"It speaks to me with such compassion," she said slowly. "With all the yearning, the joy and the utter grief that life can bring."

Kristiyan nodded.

"Where do you feel it the most—in your body, I mean?"

Octavia thought a bit.

"I feel it here—in my chest, and up into my throat; mostly in my throat. It feels as if someone is saying everything I need to say, right now; as if they truly know this place that I am in—or that is in me!"

She placed her hands on her throat as she spoke.

"But some of those deep notes sink into me; right into the depths of me," she added.

Kristiyan nodded. He was about to say something when she continued.

"But it goes far, far deeper even than that. I feel something move in me like a strong, deep ocean current that is unperturbed by transitory things."

Octavia was thoughtful.

"It is as if these songs hold all that is best and worst in us. But they make no judgment. Something like that."

She was quiet again.

"They know all the terrible things that happen to us, and still there is no complaint."

"Yes?" Kristiyan waited.

"That is what I hear."

He nodded.

"I was about to ask how you saw it compared to tango, for instance."

She gave him a quizzical glance. "Why are you asking me all this? You are the musician—not me. You tell me what you think."

"I will, but I would like to hear from you first. Your impressions are heartfelt. You have not been taught the traditional wisdom, so it is refreshing to hear an original response."

"All right then. There are some similarities, but I hear more differences. I think that tango is nostalgic. It yearns for a time that cannot be recovered. It looks back—but shame on you, Kristiyan. You are making me sound like a pompous idiot."

"Go on."

"Okay. I get drawn in by tango. I start remembering better times. I feel sad, thinking that the best is over."

Octavia gave a laugh. "This is just what I feel, you know."

"Yes. And *fado*?"

"I hear how the past is somehow always with us in the present. It is part of us. It makes us who we are. Perhaps it is only we who make that separation. In those voices I hear what perhaps only those who have suffered much and survived can know: that the acceptance of fate is always now! Does that make sense?"

157

"Go on."

"I hear the pain we feel when bad things happen; the questions that cannot be answered. And yet it is both wild and mysterious, and it brings with it such a strong sense of celebration; in spite of everything."

She repeated the phrase.

"In spite of everything. Isn't that remarkable? I hope one day I will be able to say that with all my heart."

She thought for a moment.

"I feel naked—and I feel held by it."

There was a long silence, broken only by the rustle of the leaves above them.

He is close. I can feel him, moving silently through the shadows. He has his own kind of silence; wolf silence. Did he learn this from forest places?

Finally Kristiyan spoke.

"So you have said it all. That is *fado*. It means fate or destiny."

Another silence.

"So now, you tell me—the educated version."

"Okay. So here comes the formal history lesson.

"Lisbon gave birth to *Fado* in the middle of the nineteenth century: a time of hunger and disease and horrible suffering in Portugal. And yet they created a response which could accept and embrace all of it. It differs from many other genres in that it is not just listened to; it must be felt deeply. It is truly an art form. It is not enough to have a perfectly trained voice. In fact, that might, almost certainly would be an impediment. "You really want to hear all this?"

"Yes."

"It requires that the artist should have an exquisite sensitivity, and a specific vibration of the voice to lift us into an unknown place. It is almost impossible to learn to sing fado unless life has marked you deeply. It is the duende's touch; it is that blessing, or curse, that is heard in the voice. They call it blood in the throat. It is said that if you have to choose between a conventionally beautiful voice, however remarkable, and one with this raw touch, it will always be the voice of deep knowing that will touch the heart. A perfectly trained voice may impress you; fado will move you deeply, into yourself."

Octavia gave him one of her smiles, and Kristiyan blushed and dropped the history lesson.

"But forget all that. Those are just some facts. You have told me so exactly what fado is."

He replaced the CD in its sleeve and handed it to her.

"I thought it might be of help, when you are having a lot of pain, to listen to it."

He paused, and added: "And I think that you—your art, your passion, the way you live your life—that too is *fado*!"

The Rectory

Sebastián sat on the familiar chair on the back porch of the rectory, in the shade of the old cottonwood whose leaves were turning all the yellows of autumn. He was eating a burrito from a packet, waiting for Rafael to return.

Nothing much had changed here since the days of his boyhood, when he had spent many an hour in conversation with Father Octavio. He had felt very lost then, and now it seemed that he was back at the beginning again, not knowing what to do next. He felt that he had come to the end of something, but what would follow was completely unknown to him. He thought he might leave The Adobe, but now—with Octavia's accident—that would not be possible till she was on her feet again and healed. And, anyway, leave and go—where?

"Hello there—hot, isn't it?"

Rafael sat down next to Sebastián. "How is Octavia doing?"

"Oh! I didn't hear you coming. Yes, it is—hot." He offered the priest a burrito.

"She's coming along. It will take time, but the surgeon is happy with her progress."

"That's good. So what brings you here?"

"Why can't this just be a friendly visit?"

"Oh, come, Sebastián. You know you never put a foot near a church unless you are in extremis." Rafael gave a chuckle. "Besides, I saw you yesterday. What's up?"

"I'm not sure. Everything is going perfectly. Sofia has taken charge of just about everything. She's amazing. The Adobe is running like clockwork."

"So?"

"Well—I don't quite know. I feel, sort of, redundant. What am I supposed to be doing? I am sitting in an office, doing accounts and paying bills. I don't want to spend my life in a little room with bits of paper and lists and—I need a change."

"So?"

"I am tired of myself—that's what's so."

"So?"

"Is that all you can say? So?"

"You know exactly what is up with you, but you want me to do the work and draw it out of you."

Sebastián stared at him—then gave a nod.

"Do you remember that strange meeting I had with the condor up in the Sangre de Cristo Mountains, just after my mother died?"

"Yes. Very vividly."

"Well. I keep having this dream. I am back on that mountain ledge. Only now there is a thick, yellow mist that rises up and stains the sky. Out of this, the condor rises up and flies straight at me, until all I can see is its open beak and its eye staring into me—and I hear that harsh cry over and over. It's like it is inside my head, my brain. And it is calling—or maybe warning me. And I feel ashamed."

"Ashamed? Why ashamed?"

"It is so fierce and alive and vibrant. And I feel as if I have abdicated in some way. I am not living fully. I was, but something has ended—ended some time ago, actually."

"What does this yellow mist say to you?"

"I'm not sure, but I think it has something to do with things that have been packed away for a long time. You know—shirts, old linen, that kind of thing. They get that old, yellow stain that only bleach and strong sunlight can remove."

"And how does this relate to the condor?"

"Well, I suppose he is still in the same place, doing the same thing. It is almost as if he can't move on."

"Can everything run at The Adobe without you?"

"Certainly."

"Then, you have honored Magdalena. You have brought her dream to a new level. Maybe it is time to let go."

"And do what?"

"Well, if you don't know what to do—do nothing. Do nothing until you are so bored with yourself that something gives way—breaks, explodes; till some new possibility reveals itself to you."

"I'll go mad."

"Good. Go mad. It's what you need."

"A strange way you priests have of spreading the good news."

"Indeed."

Georgia

Georgia sat in her studio, staring at three canvases—her most recent works. Her paintings were famous for the quality of light—an almost transparent quality—that she brought to them; whether to landscape, or more recently to her unusual portraits. It was this that made her work distinctive. One art critic had gone so far as to liken her treatment of light to that of Vermeer—high praise indeed. And now, these lifeless paintings. Where had all the light gone?

What was happening to her?

She got up and poured herself a glass of water. Sat down again. She felt the edge of panic push its way up toward her throat. She took a deep breath. She examined the works again, critically. They were dull. Sluggish. They looked, she thought, the way you feel when you have a migraine—or the way an animal looks when it has just died; as if a light has gone out, not only in the eyes but in the form, which now becomes dense—heavy.

Georgia put the glass down. She was on the edge of tears.

Had she come to the end? Lost her gift; her talent? What if she could not paint—would never be able to paint again? What would she do?

She struggled to hold down the panic that was rising in her—a cold sweat that seemed to confirm that something had ended. But just what was that? Surely not her creativity. Then what?

Maybe she could re-work them. Yes. That's what she would do. She just hadn't given them enough time. With all the crises around Octavia's accident, she had lost her focus. That was all. Now that everything had settled down, she would get back to where she was before it happened.

An hour later she was in tears again. She took off her smock, threw it over a chair, and left her studio.

On her way back to the house she met Sister Piadosa.

"Georgia! Oh, my dear, whatever is the matter?"

Georgia drew in a sobbing breath.

"I have just finished three paintings, and they are awful. I think I have lost—" She searched for the words. "I seem to have lost my—my vision. I don't think I can paint any more. I can't feel the forms. I can't feel anything. What will I be if I can't paint? Nothing. Octavia was right."

"Right about what?"

"She said we had all gone to sleep. That I was just painting pictures that would sell."

"Isn't that a bit harsh?"

"I think not. Why am I painting? Once I had something to say. Now I am just saying it over and over again—as if I had found the winning formula. This is what people want. They are comfortable with these calm landscapes. They do not feel confronted in any way. They don't have to think about them. I feel as if I am one step away from painting images that will match the curtains or the furnishings. Like an interior decorator."

"Most people would not agree with you."

"That's the problem. I don't want to paint for most people."

Letting Go

Octavia received the news of Sofia's pregnancy in silence.

Of course she knew that Lucien and Sofia would have children. But still, the news came as a shock to her. It should be happening to her. She should be carrying Lucien's child. She would have been the better choice. Lucien was tall and big-boned, and Sofia was such a tiny slip of a thing. How would she carry—and deliver—a big infant?

She felt a cold wind blow through her—saw again the white pot; heard the sound of emptiness; saw the black mare leap into the night sky, with the stars falling down like rain.

I can feel his gaze resting on me. His blue gaze. I feel the clarity of that blue light—that haunting, blue gaze—enter me; fill me—with such peace.

Let it go, Octavia, she told herself. Just let it go.

"Good! Now try again. Come to where I am standing."

Octavia was learning to walk again. She was wearing a pair of shoes especially designed for her comfort. The left shoe had a raised sole to compensate for the shortening of her leg. It had added support for the arch of her foot. She was still wearing the neck brace.

"A year ago I wouldn't have been seen dead in these things."

It was late autumn. Although the mornings and evenings were cold, the sun was still hot during the day. The leaves on the cottonwoods were falling, blown into untidy tides of color by the autumn wind. The land had lost its summer green, and was turning all its shades of brown and pink and pale grey.

Octavia was walking between two rails that Gregorio had built in the long, covered cloister that led from the main building to the nuns' rooms. This was the second week of daily exercises, followed by these first steps—putting some weight on the left leg.

She held the rails, her face tight with pain. She took uneven steps along the passage to where Severo, the physiotherapist, was standing next to Sister Piadosa, who was watching closely. He had shown her all the exercises that Octavia was required to do several times daily, and everything that she had to avoid during the walking exercises.

"How does that feel?"

"Awful."

"Let's do it one more time, and that will be enough for today."

Octavia turned, switching arms and grabbing at the poles.

"I don't seem to have any sense of balance."

"You must give your body time. Remember, it has been through an ordeal. Your muscles must strengthen again, and then you will feel your balance come back."

Octavia made the return journey, over to the wheelchair.

"I never thought I would be so relieved to sit in this damn thing."

Georgia stepped forward with a towel, and Octavia wiped the sweat from her face.

"Thanks, mama." She flashed her mother a smile, and Georgia's heart gave a lurch.

"And thanks, Severo. I'll try and show you some new tricks when you come next week."

Sister Piadosa had a quick word with Severo, and then helped Octavia wheel herself across the uneven stretch of yard and back to her room for a rest.

"You did well. I could see he was very pleased with your progress. We will try and give him a surprise next week."

She helped Octavia onto the bed.

"Aargh! I feel about a hundred years old. Look at me. Fifteen—twenty steps, and I'm finished."

"But remember, a week ago you could hardly stand."

"Do you think this is what babies feel when they are learning to walk?"

"I don't know about that, but I have seen babies learning to stand before they learn how to sit down again. They stand and cry and cry from tiredness, until someone plops them down. But then they stand up again, and repeat the whole thing. However, I never saw one fail to learn in the end."

Sister Piadosa took off Octavia's shoes. She massaged both feet with oil, paying special attention to the heels; adjusted the pillow for her left leg.

"Is that comfortable?"

"It's perfect, thanks."

"Would you like the cover, or are you warm enough?"

"The cover would be wonderful, thank you, sister."

"I'll bring you some tea, and then perhaps you will have a sleep before lunch."

Fall

It was Kristiyan's idea to bring the music over to the cloister when Octavia was doing her walking exercises.

"Maybe it will help with the pain. I have read that the mind cannot hold too many stimuli simultaneously. Some dentists use sound in place of an anesthetic."

"Well, I'm happy to try it as long as you don't try the dentist bit on me!"

So for the first weeks, when the going was slow and painful, he brought the same music he had played once before—the Russian Orthodox chants, featuring the slow, deep voice of the basso profondo chanting over the rise and fall of the choir's voices.

"Can you hear in the music—there is beauty in suffering? My country is so vast. So much of it is silent. Frozen. You can hear the heaviness of the cold. It has suffered so much, and yet this beauty comes through all of it. You can hear it in the voices. They are not called 'profondo' for nothing. There is something invincible in the human spirit—at its best—that resonates deeply in each of us. It is like bowing a cello next to another cello, and hearing the vibrations well up in response."

"I love it, Kristiyan. It is beautiful."

Octavia listened to the timbre of the voices, and managed to put her pain into those deep vibrations, and into the background rise and fall of the choir's melody. Like an ocean, she thought. Like some kind of eternal presence.

If only this pain would go. And the weakness. Would she ever run again? Or sleep? That long sleep that leaves you fresh and rested. Ready for anything.

Days passed.

Octavia could still not trust her sense of balance. She still had to grip the poles to make her way down to the end of the passage. And there was still the scary moment when she had to let go of the poles, and turn.

It was a cold, windy day, with the promise of a storm blowing in from the south. Octavia, bundled up in a sheepskin, made her way to the end of the poles with Sister Piadosa walking beside her.

He is standing at the end of the rails. He is facing me. He is standing, alert but relaxed; his blue gaze on me. Sister Piadosa has said nothing about his presence. Hasn't she seen him? Is he waiting for something? No, he is just there.

The nun watched Octavia swing her arm across the space between the bars. She saw the left leg crumple under her weight; saw her make a frantic grab for the rail—miss it—and fall.

Gregorio, who happened to be walking by at the time, ran up to help the nun lift Octavia onto her feet.

"Can you hold her while I get the chair?"

He fetched the wheelchair, and together they lowered Octavia into it. Her face was white, and she was shaking.

"Oh, my dear! We'll get you back inside and into a warm room."

She pushed the chair across the yard as fast as she dared for the unevenness. Even so, Octavia gave cries of pain. Georgia came running out.

"What happened? Oh, my sweet! Look at you. Here, sister, let me help to lift her onto the bed. I'll get her some sugar water."

When Octavia was made comfortable, she phoned the hospital. The surgeon was in theatre, but the sister on duty advised them to bring Octavia in, and that he would see her at around noon.

While Sister Piadosa sat with Octavia, Georgia went in search of Sebastián. She found him in the concert hall, chatting to Salvador and Reuben.

"It's Octavia," was all she could say.

Together they ran back to the house.

"I'll get the station wagon ready with a mattress in the back, and bring it to the door. Better get an overnight bag ready, in case they want to keep her there."

Sebastián ran off.

Georgia tried to look calm as she entered Octavia's room.

"We are going to take you through to the hospital. Doctor Limón will see you as soon as he finishes in theatre. I am going to pack some toiletries in case he wants you to stay. Is there anything else you would like me to do?"

Octavia shook her head.

"Sister, they are delivering the feed for the winter today. Could you see that they store it in the big shed, please?—I think that is all—we will call you once we have spoken to the surgeon."

Octavia was lifted onto the mattress in the back of the station wagon, with pillows wedged on either side to prevent her from rolling from side to side, and then they were off. She closed her eyes, and gave herself up to the pain.

I can feel him. He is lying next to me. My hand can feel his wolf coat. I am touching him. His breath is close to my face. I am breathing in his warm breath; all the way down my body. I can feel his wet nose on my cheek. Is he breathing me—or am I breathing him?

The Return

Alejandro unlocked the door to his adobe house and studio. He entered. Walked through to the small bedroom, and put his suitcase on the bed.

He entered his studio, and stood staring at the piles of wood. The tools. Sketches pinned to his work-board—a black horse at full gallop; the drawing of Octavia's smile.

He walked over to the window and stood for a long time, staring out at the fenced pasture—and beyond it, to the wooded hills. The pasture was empty. The dream that had been haunting him had faded away. It left him feeling strangely uneasy.

He went to the kitchen, made himself a cup of black coffee and took it outside to the back porch. Drank the coffee. Sat for over an hour.

Toward evening he saw his neighbor return from work.

He was in two minds about fetching Octavia's letters. One part of him wanted to rush over like an eager, young boy—read everything. Another part cautioned him to wait.

The boy won.

"Evening, Juan. As you see, I'm back."

"Alejandro! How good to see you. It has been so quiet with no sound coming from your studio. Welcome! Welcome! Come in and have something to drink. Coffee? Some wine? Come and tell me where you have been all this time."

He bustled about, getting glasses; wine from the cupboard.

"Perdita will be back soon. Stay and have supper with us. I'll light a fire."

Alejandro took the glass of wine—nodded his appreciation.

"Thanks, Juan, but I'm a bit tired. I think I'll just collect my post, and have an early night."

Juan handed him the box. A few bills, pamphlets; a letter from a gallery in Albuquerque—that was all.

Alejandro stared. "Is this all?"

"Yes. I didn't bother to keep them in order. There was so little."

"I was expecting several letters—from Chile. Do you think they might have gone astray?"

"Nothing has come this way. Maybe check at the post office."

Alejandro finished his drink, thanked Juan for the post and left. What could have happened to Octavia's letters? He would pay a visit to The Adobe tomorrow. Maybe she had sent them there. No. Why would she do that?

He did not sleep well.

Alejandro made the familiar turn into The Adobe. It felt strange to know that Octavia was not there. He pulled up next to Sebastián's truck.

"Alejandro! So glad you are back. Where have you been all this time? Come in. Have some coffee."

Sebastián led the way into the kitchen. He poured two coffees from the machine, and put milk and sugar on the table.

"Good to see you. So much catching up to do. Want to hear all about your time away."

"In time. It's good to be back. How are things here?"

Sebastián put his coffee down on the table.

"No one knew how to contact you."

He paused.

"We wanted to let you know, but..."

"Know what?"

"We wanted to let you know about Octavia's accident. It has been a difficult and painful time."

"What has happened to Octavia? What accident? Where? In Chile?"

"No. She never went to Chile. She had an accident on the 285, shortly after you left. A truck ran into her car during a rain-storm. She has been in and out of hospital—theatre—since then. And now there has been a serious setback. We can't know for sure what it will mean in the long term, but at the moment she cannot walk..."

"Can't walk!"

"No. And she has a lot of pain that is being managed with medication."

Alejandro had not touched his coffee.

"Where is she?"

"Georgia has taken her in to the hospital in Santa Fe. The surgeon wants to run a new scan. She will be back shortly."

There was a knock at the door, and Kristiyan came in, holding some musical equipment.

"Oh, hello, Alejandro. We have missed you. The place hasn't been the same without you." He nodded to Sebastián. "Sorry to interrupt. Where would you like me to put this? It's all fixed. No charge."

"In her room—I think that's best for now. It's too cold for her outside."

"Right. I'll speak to you later. See you around, Alejandro."

As he was about to leave, he remembered Gregorio's message.

"Oh, yes. About those footprints. Gregorio has seen them too; most frequently very close to your house—and once near the cottonwood, where Octavia often rests in the shade."

"Okay—thanks, Kristiyan. Don't mention this to her. I don't want her to get frightened. There is probably a very simple explanation. But we can speak later."

The door closed.

"Tell me what has happened."

"You mean—the footprints?"

"No! The accident!"

Briefly, Sebastián gave him the details: the accident; the two operations; the fall, and the subsequent paralysis of Octavia's left leg.

"She has been very strong through all this, and Kristiyan has been a life-saver. He set up a new CD music system. Says he is going to take her traveling through the music of various countries. He says that, until she can travel physically, he will make sure she gets to know something about the world through its music. So far, it is the Russian choral chants that she likes the best."

"Yes. Yes. But what is the prognosis? Has the surgeon said anything about what to expect?"

"That is the reason for the new scan. He has a team of doctors who will all look at it. They are familiar with the whole history. We will have to wait and see. So at the moment she is in a wheelchair."

"Octavia! In a wheelchair!"

"Yes."

An image of the black mare flashed through Alejandro's brain. And Octavia, running; running like the wind. And his dream. The black mare galloping toward the abyss.

"What can I do to help?"

"At the moment, all anyone can do is to be around. Help to keep her spirits up. Most of the time has been taken up by physiotherapy, and—until the fall— by her learning how to walk again. Now I suppose we must wait. I know she wants to get back into her studio. I think it will be very good for her to work again—that is if we can manage the pain adequately. It has been a tough time, but it appears to have brought out the best in her. And the new bond with Georgia—that feels like some kind of miracle."

"Oh, my God," Alejandro groaned. "And all this time I have been away."

"And now you are back. And that is good. She will be thrilled to see you."

Sebastián took away the cold coffee, and poured a fresh cup.

"And, what are your plans—angels?"

"Not sure. I have been doing quite a bit of thinking—re-assessing. Too many shadows right now." He took a sip of the fresh coffee.

"And you? I haven't heard about all the rest of you. Lucien and Sofia—did they have a good honeymoon? And how is Georgia bearing up?"

Sebastián thought for a minute. So much seemed to be happening; one thing on top of another. He wasn't sure what he thought about anything, least of all himself.

"So much has changed—in all of us. All I can say is that it feels as if it is time to wake up. Octavia has been a kind of catalyst. I think you are not alone in the self-examination. And it is interesting to hear you talk about shadows. I think we have all been in a kind of sleep—all except Octavia. Nothing will ever be the same again. Uncomfortable, but necessary."

"And Lucien and Sofia—do they feel the same?"

"I don't think so. Perhaps because they are at a beginning. They are so full of energy. Sofia is a dynamo, and Lucien is writing the most beautiful songs. There are all kinds of projects in the wings."

He paused. "But Georgia is having a rough time."

"In what way?"

"She feels as if she is just repeating herself—as if she has come to some kind of end. Perhaps we are all questioning the meaning of what we are—were—doing so comfortably."

He pulled his chair closer to the table. Leaned forward.

"Do you see the changes, Alejandro?"

"What kinds of changes?"

"Small things; maybe not so small. Signs of some kind of disintegration."

"Disintegration? I hadn't thought to put it quite that way—but yes! Where do you see this?"

"Well, for instance: for many years I have been delivering goods to Santa Fe and Albuquerque. People have greeted me by my name, and I them by theirs. We know a bit about each other's lives. There has been a feeling of fellowship, of con-nectedness—just like we experience here in our community."

"And now—things have changed?"

"Not radically—but yes. When I look at what is happening just in my small world, I am dismayed. I have become just another delivery, or just another customer. People no longer make eye contact. They are too busy—often at the cost of friendli-ness, and sometimes even respect."

"Yes. What else do you see?"

"I see a loss of trust in the other—and because of this, a disconnection; a loss of dialogue. Have you ever noticed—in a crowded mall, for instance—how many people are not aware that they occupy space? It is almost as if they are sleep-walking. They seem to be cut off from what is around them."

"In what way?"

"Well, for instance, if we drove cars the way people walk in malls, we would be arrested. Everyone is locked into their little bubble—no hand signals; just sudden stops and turns, cutting in front of someone else. On the road we would at least hoot or shake a fist! Increasingly there is no sense of us; no consideration for the other; no true awareness even. Just an onslaught of 'me, me, me'—all in our separate little bubbles. We think we have a global consciousness, and yet we remain compartmentalized into our countries, and cities, and towns, and suburbs and our little houses; living in ever smaller and smaller worlds. Our fear is making life smaller, until we end up living in our heads."

"But aren't we getting more connected? More aware of what is happening in other countries?"

"It is not a question of knowing. It is a question of response—that we actually care about what is happening. And that we do something about it. But instead of responding, we react. We take our fear out into the world."

"So, what are you leading up to?"

"We have forgotten that everything we do has an impact. It may be so small that we dismiss it as a mere detail. That is where the trouble begins. Is it ever a mere detail? I don't think so. We think these small things don't make any difference.

"But when we make decisions as a country, there is an impact felt throughout the world, whether we like to admit this or not. And how we yell when a reaction comes back at us!

"We talk about progress, but do we count the cost of this? Have we ever? Look what we have done to the indigenous peoples of our own country; and to the land. For a long time it was others who felt the cost. Now it is all of us."

Sebastián paused to draw breath.

"Do you remember when they cut down that vast tract of the redwoods in California, to create jobs? Such a short-term view. And what do we have now? A change in the climate there. We never even considered the impact that those trees had on the weather. And now they are just gone, after being there for centuries before us. And the rain-clouds that used to be pushed up by those tall trees—thousands and thousands of feet high—and dropped their rain, now blow somewhere else, and carry their moisture with them. And the jobs have run out.

"Almost every day you read about another species that has dropped off the endangered list to become extinct; another thousand square miles of forest that has been cut down. Do we care? Maybe we say: 'What a shame'. But does it touch us?"

Sebastián banged the table.

"What I am saying is—it is touching all of us now! All around us. In the world. A loss of meaning and values. And many people pretending that it is not so—or that it will go away. This feels like a world that has no center. And I feel as if I have lost mine."

Sebastián took a deep breath.

"Sorry about the rant," he said apologetically.

Alejandro leaned back in his chair.

"How strange to be having this conversation—now," he said. "I have been at a place in the desert—a small monastery—to contemplate. To listen. I have been feeling so much of what you describe. I feel as if I have gone to sleep, carving angels—beautiful little angels. Everyone wants to own one. People hang one in the doorway, and they feel reassured. Yes. Life is good. Nothing bad will happen while this little angel blesses us. How sweet! How immensely dangerous!

"I think I have been guilty of turning my back on shadows, particularly my own—until now. And now they are pressing in on me, demanding to be seen. And why? Why do you think this has happened?"

He pushed his coffee-cup away.

"I can speak for myself. Because of pride and ambition. Because I had begun to work for fame and acknowledgement—to have a place in galleries; my name in art magazines. To have people say: that is a Jaramillo angel—how beautiful."

"Is there something wrong in that?"

"Yes. Because I have never stopped to examine what I am about. Or rather, I have looked only at myself—my own self-interest. My responsibility—or let me rather say my response—has been only to my own needs. Purely selfish. I have not examined all the changes that are occurring in the world around us. I have been living in my own little world of stars and angels. I have taken no interest in what is happening to our own planet. Much easier to leave that to others to worry about. It has not affected me—or so I thought. Now I see that no one will escape the consequences of what we all—every last one of us—have done, and continue to do to the natural world." Alejandro shook his head. "And to ourselves," he added quietly.

"And just look at that thought: 'the changes that are occurring'—as if we have no part in all of it. I have kept myself so busy that I have failed to hear the knocking at the door. Well, while I was away, and when my head at last became quiet, I heard the knocking. And I opened the door. I have to tell you, my heart was pounding."

"And...?"

"You are the poet around here, so I am sure you know the D. H. Lawrence poem—The Song of a Man Who Has Come Through."

"Yes. Very well. But I didn't know that you went in for poetry."

"Oh, I don't really, but someone gave me a copy of it because of the angels. So there they were: the three strange angels."

"Yes?"

"I wondered why he called them strange. You want to know what I think?"

Sebastián nodded. He was fascinated. This was a side of Alejandro he had never met before.

"We think they are strange because we haven't seen them before. How could we possibly recognize them? They are within us. They always have been—although we may deny this, because it is not rational. I think we fear them because they do not fit into the world as we know it. We see them as foreigners. Are they going to want something—take something from us? In our chaotic world, we have been taught not to trust the stranger who approaches us."

"So why should we open the door?"

"Perhaps because we have been waiting for such a long time."

"Go on."

"And maybe they bring a gift? A strange gift that will also demand something of us—something almost inconceivable; will demand everything that we are. I think so."

"What might that be?"

"I don't think we can know this. And yet, when it comes we will recognize it."

"That sounds like a contradiction."

"We both know that something has to happen; that all the 'isms' and other great ideas have failed. So it is something else; a call that still only sounds faintly, because we are too afraid to listen. And the message is being brought, very traditionally, by three angels. What Lawrence is saying is—'Admit them. Admit them.' We have to go against our sense of survival, which reaches back to the early reptiles—against so much that is in our nature; our strong sense of self-preservation—and allow ourselves to be open—vulnerable. We sense, probably correctly, that we will also lose something; something we think is a part of us."

"And why should we do that?"

"Because it is time? Because there is not a choice?"

"And if we don't?"

"Well, if we don't open the door and don't open the door and don't open the door—eventually they will come with bombs and the like, and blow us to pieces."

"Angels will do that?"

"If it is necessary."

"And why are we so afraid?"

"Because we know that if we want this unknown thing, we will have to surrender everything."

"Good lord, Alejandro! Whatever has happened to you? I think you have spent too long at that monastery; too long in your head. You can't possibly mean that."

"It has nothing to do with my head. In fact, my head is part of my problem. I can see that my head has been deciding what I may think for far too long. No. It is something else that is calling.

"Look, Sebastián. We both know something is amiss, but we don't want to admit it. There's that word 'admit' again. It would really interfere with the good opinion we have of ourselves. This mess that is all around us; it starts with us—each one of us. Things don't just happen out of nowhere."

"What do you think this means?"

"I think it is the end of the world as we have known it. And if we don't wake up soon, we will all pay the price."

"That sounds rather radical—almost apocalyptic."

"Yes. But not almost. Why are we afraid to even speak that word: 'apocalyptic'? We are told to stop being so negative; that the scientists exaggerate. Well, it is traditional not to listen to prophets. We think—if we think at all—that prophets are dreaming into some unlikely time yet to come. We don't realize that prophets do not see the future—they see the present. Yes! It is already happening."

172

Alejandro shook his head again.

"But that is not all. What we see happening out in the world is happening inside us. You are quite correct. We have lost our center. We are like a wounded hawk in free fall. Chaotic. No direction. Blaming someone else; waiting for some new messiah to come and save us from ourselves. Well, I don't think he's coming this time."

Sebastián was quiet. But he could feel Alejandro's words resonate inside—his mind? No. Inside his heart.

"If you recall the second line—'A fine wind is blowing the new direction of Time'. And Lawrence goes on to say: 'If only I let it bear me'. What a beautiful word—'let'. But we are much too clever to let anything persuade us to change direction—or are we? It is as if there was a conversation going on between some part of us that we do not acknowledge, and what we like to call our rational mind. And we listen to our mind. And all the other minds."

Alejandro paused.

"But what of the other voice? Is it dead?"

"Surely not."

"But maybe, yes. Or is it that we have not been listening? I think we—let me rather say I—have allowed the lesser man in me to take over. I have slowly and unconsciously sold out to him. Maybe this is what is happening in the world. I have become so proud of my achievements, and of a certain power that follows them, that I have become intoxicated—or addicted to them. Is it possible that this is our highest value? Power? Oh, Sebastián, I think the world has gone mad—and I with it."

Sebastián was about to say something when they heard the sound of Georgia's car pulling up outside.

"They're back. Come and help me unload the wheelchair, and help Octavia into it."

Alejandro felt unexpectedly awkward, but he followed Sebastián out into the yard.

The passenger window opened.

"Alejandro! You're back!"

He felt his heart quicken.

The Cornerstone

It was some weeks later. Octavia's face was drawn and white with pain as Sister Piadosa wheeled her across the courtyard for her morning walking exercise between the parallel bars.

"Please, can't we skip the session today?" Octavia pleaded. "I feel exhausted. I didn't sleep last night. I am so sick and tired of pain. I feel this pain like an entity inside me. I can't even tell where it begins or ends; only that it seems to be growing. What is the point of making it worse? All this effort, and then what? Another fall? Another operation? Surely just one day of rest won't do any harm. Maybe it would be better for me than forcing myself to go all the way up that agony path and back again."

Sister Piadosa eased the wheelchair over the uneven ground, taking care not to jolt her passenger.

"Octavia, you know what Doctor Limón said; that daily exercise, always pushing it a little further than the day before, is essential for muscle tone. You can rest afterwards."

"You are not the person living in this body. Neither is Doctor Limón," Octavia said with feeling.

They arrived at the covered walkway where Gregorio had set up the bars. Sister Piadosa positioned the chair at the one end, and set the brake.

"That is indeed true," she said as she moved the foot-rests to each side, "but we all have something that obliges us to face up to our individual challenge. This is yours, and you are doing so well. Look at the progress you have made. Today is a bad day, but there are other days when you feel so good."

Octavia said nothing, but prepared herself to move from the chair to the bars.

"Good. Now remember to keep your posture straight, even if it is painful. It is natural to try and compensate by putting more weight on the other leg to avoid the pain, but by doing that you set up yet another problem. You have to push through the pain."

"Easy to say that."

"I know."

Octavia stood up straight, waited to find her balance, and began the walk between the bars.

Where is the wolf? Surely he is here? Is he watching? I cannot see him but...

"Good. Head up. Take even steps. Good. And now—turn."

Octavia executed the tricky part of turning, which involved letting go briefly and changing her hands from one side of the rails to the other. She bit back a cry of pain, and began the return journey. Back at the chair, she sat down.

"I can't do any more. Let's leave it for today."

Sister Piadosa said nothing, but she fetched a chair and sat facing Octavia. She leaned forward, and took Octavia's hands in hers.

"Octavia," she said, looking directly into her eyes, "I would like to tell you something about my life; my story. May I?"

Octavia nodded. She was close to tears.

Sister Piadosa's voice suddenly carried a different tone from the pragmatic, seemingly carefree one she used as a rule. This was a new and unfamiliar side of her; a seriousness that Octavia had not seen before.

"I was the youngest in my family. My brother and my two sisters all went to university. But just as I finished school my father suffered a stroke, and he had to leave a well-paying job and find work that he could manage. Financially, things became difficult. So it was decided that I would not go to university; that I should enter a convent and become a nun."

Octavia did not take her eyes off the nun's face.

"I wanted to study psychology, and work with children. That had always been my dream. And now, almost overnight, it came to an end. Shortly after that I entered the convent, and began the difficult task of letting go of the future I had planned, and doing everything I was told to do."

She gave a smile, and shrugged.

"Like you, I felt rebellious. I felt that life had cheated me. I could not find meaning in this new life. I felt very sorry for myself—and for quite some time, I must add.

"After my first year in the convent, when things with me were no better, I asked for permission to speak to the mother superior. I will never forget the day. Nor will I ever forget her."

"What did she say?" Octavia was intrigued.

"She spoke about discipline."

"Discipline?"

"Yes."

"How on earth was that going to be helpful? Didn't that make you furious? It is the sort of thing teachers say at school. It never seemed to bring good results there."

"At first, yes, I was angry. But she had a completely different take on discipline. It was this that brought meaning into my life."

"And what was that?"

"She invited me to take a closer look at the word 'discipline', and where it comes from. I had never considered words in this way. The word 'disciple' carries the meaning: to learn; to learn by following another person's example, or by following a calling that may present itself to us in a way we don't immediately recognize. In other words, she was suggesting that we make ourselves disciples of life, and whatever life brings to us."

"How did that bring any meaning to you?"

"Well, she asked me what it would be like if I made myself a disciple of what was right in front of me. In a way it made sense for me to do this. After all, it was all I had."

"Couldn't you have left, and found a way to do what you wanted?"

"She spoke about that as well. Yes. It was an option, she said, but there was something else I needed to consider. Our first idea is not necessarily the best one for us, and it is certainly not the only one. Too often we don't look any further."

Sister Piadosa paused, and then added:

"This is my one argument with the straight and narrow way—don't repeat this to Father Rafael! Don't look to left or to right. Why not? What is the great fear? Of course I know all the traditional arguments for this. Let us just say that there is still a rebellious spirit in me, and I guard it with my life."

Octavia leaned forward, utterly fascinated.

"Father Octavio always encouraged such questions. He used to say that if we become fixated on one idea—or on a goal—we see only that. Our goal fills the whole screen."

"I wish I had met him."

"You would have loved him. Everyone thought he was such a dear priest—and, of course, he was. But he was also fierce about responding to the inner call—no matter what people thought. This is why he wanted to die a man, not a priest."

"Why was that?"

"He was no longer the same young man who took vows to be a priest. Life shapes us, and what was absolutely true for him when he was a young man was no longer true. He heard a different call. That was his response.

"Too often we think we can—or should—control everything; be able to dictate how things ought to be; make it happen! There is so much in our culture that encourages this. But there may come a time when we are compelled to listen to this inner voice. It is like a command. Often our actions will upset those around us. Friends will be upset to see us suddenly making a radical new choice. That is too bad. If we don't respond to it, we do ourselves such harm. We need to listen, deeply."

"Listen to what?"

"Perhaps our heart. Perhaps I had to ask what being of service meant to me, right here and now; not according to some abstract idea I may have had. Perhaps I had to ask the uncomfortable question: who was I truly serving? The children—or my idea of myself?"

She smiled at Octavia.

"I will never forget her. Nothing changed, and everything changed. It became the cornerstone of my vows."

"And then—"

"Well, I knew I wanted to be of service, but I was only looking at one way I could do this. I needed to enlarge my idea of what carried heart and meaning for me. I had to see beyond the limitations I had placed on that commitment."

Sister Piadosa stood up and replaced her chair.

"And, most importantly, I had to get myself out of the way! We don't know yet what this accident, and this pain, and this struggle will bring you; or what they will mean in your life. This work is testing your mettle; testing whether you are fit for what is to come. This is the hard part. You need to proceed in the faith that this is necessary for some future you still cannot see."

She helped Octavia to stand and take hold of the rails.

"But—rest assured: life will surely tell you."

Icons

Octavia sat in her wheelchair, feeling herself into the space of her studio. She wheeled herself slowly around the room, touching the walls she had painted just before the accident. How beautiful they are, she thought. I must have been inspired. She smiled at the small unpainted area around the door, remembering how she had planned to finish it the next day; but that was the day of the accident. She took in the beads in their glass bottles, the two tapestries, one unfinished, and the crystals hanging in the high window.

"I am sorry that I kept you waiting for such a long time," she said aloud.

Gregorio had taken her there, maneuvering the wheelchair over the stones of the spiral path with difficulty.

"I think we may have to come up with some new idea for this if you are going to come here alone," he said. "I'll think of something soon. I have a lot of time for thinking."

He pushed the wheelchair over the lintel, and left her there.

"Ring the bell when you want me to fetch you—a good, long, loud ring."

"Sure. Thanks, Gregorio."

Now she sat, listening to the stillness. This was her space. She experienced a sense of home-coming—almost, she thought, a sense of recognition. So much had happened since she last sat here, planning her trip to Chile. It felt to her as if everything before today had occurred in another lifetime.

She circled the room again, again touching the walls—these walls that carried in them such a sense of place. Crossed the room to the old record player. The album with the song from Tosca was still on the turn-table. She lifted it off, and removed the dust with a cloth. Replaced it and selected the track. Sat with eyes closed, listening to the faint, gritty sound behind the song she loved. But it did not hold the power it once had. She turned the player off.

She recalled a day she had spent sitting in on one of Alejandro's classes at The

Adobe. He was addressing one of the students. The youngster had finished a section of his work—an arm and a hand, the fingers very sensitively carved, and resting on a knee. However, he was struggling with the proportions of the figure. Alejandro stood behind him for a while, observing his difficulty—watching him make adjustments to his drawing, all to no avail.

"Sometimes we fall in love with a part of a work, but a part that will not serve the whole. We need to have the courage to let it go in order that the whole may come through."

She remembered the young man's horror at these words. She watched him struggle through the three-hour class, attempting to make any possible compromise to the original drawing in order to keep the hand. At the end of the class he was almost in tears.

"The creative muse will not allow you to get away with anything. If you have learned that today, you have not wasted your time."

Octavia cast her mind back. The Black Room. The erotic drawings. Her obsession with the song from Tosca. It all belonged to another time. Another person.

And no, she realized now; she had not wasted her time either.

The wolf is sitting next to my chair. I didn't see him come in. He is just here. Does he know that his are the first eyes, apart from my own, to enter this room? I am happy that he is back. Where does he go when I can't see him? How stupid my questions are. He is here because there is a space for him. I wonder what I mean.

Journal Entry 7

I wonder who she is, this Virgin of Emptiness? Why is she naked? All I know is that she is bringing about the fall of the old.

I can see a series of images: forests burning—whole mountain ranges; city people wearing masks, running beneath a smoke-filled sky; piles of skeletal animal corpses in dry river beds—they all speak of destruction. Alejandro has always said to trust the voice—the images—that want to come through. Stay with the image. Don't try and work it out. These are apocalyptic images—some beautiful; mostly terrifying. Will I be able to convey this quality in the beads? I also have a sense of wild animals somewhere else, but they are not here yet. I think that they are the innocents who will witness this destruction. Is it too much to hope that they will escape most of it? I intend to work these images into a series of icons.

178

Vision

I am looking out over a vast, empty desert. Maybe it is the Atacama Desert. I hear a wolf howling. I see a black cross, like the ones you find at Chimayo with all the little milagros tacked onto them. It stands on a rocky outcrop. I see that there is a figure nailed to the cross. It is the figure of a man with a wolf head. Behind his head I see a circle of light—a bit like the aura around the Virgin of Guadaloupe—burst into flame. I know I must make a work of this vision: the crucified wolf-man.

Journal Entry 8

I have just read an account of new incidents of wolves being shot by ranchers. I am so angry. How is it possible that we do not see what we are doing? What should— what could I be doing to have any impact? What can one person do? I feel so helpless now. Am I fooling myself? Does this work I have chosen have any merit? Sometimes it feels as if everything has been said, been done before—and the world is in a bigger mess than ever. I almost envy Sofia and Lucien the simplicity of their lives.

A phrase has come into my head, and it won't leave me—the mercy of wild things. I don't know what this means. I know, when I feel such a passion about some- thing—like these five words—that it is the tip of an iceberg. I will wait. Impatiently. Oh, God! I am in such a rage, and I am in love. I feel so helpless, and I feel so alive. Sometimes it feels as if this passion will deliver me. Or kill me.

Vision

I see the image of the crucified wolf once more. The man-body has gone. This is wolf. And now I see the faint shadow of an image in the sky.

What does it mean—the mercy of wild things?

A Day in Albuquerque

"But I would love to take you."

Kristiyan was trying to persuade Octavia to come with him to Albuquerque. He knew that she wanted to go to a bead shop she had read about, but everyone at The Adobe was too busy to take her to it.

"There are one or two things I need to do there," he said, "so why don't we make a day of it?"

"It will be too complicated; and then there is the chair—oh, and everything. I'm just not ready to go out in public, and have everyone feel sorry for me. Or, worse still, feel sorry for you."

"Nobody is going to feel sorry for me when they look at you. They will probably feel very jealous."

"And I get tired so quickly. What if I fall asleep in my chair with my jaw hanging open?"

"Well, I admit that would be the end of it. I would have to park you in some cul de sac, and leave you there."

"Oh, be serious, Kristiyan."

"I am asking you to come to Albuquerque with me. That is serious. I have heard you say that you need some smaller beads."

"I will need them some time, but they can wait a while—but thank you, Kristiyan."

"But it needn't wait. And it will be fun. I am going there anyway. It will be good to have company for the drive. I'll pick you up at eight o'clock tomorrow morning—no! No excuses," he said as she was about to protest. "I'll see you tomorrow. Dress warmly."

The bead shop was Octavia's idea of heaven. Kristiyan left her there in the good hands of Louise, the owner, who was delighted to have an artist in the shop—someone who would be making artworks with beads. It made a change from the many who came to buy beads for necklaces or clothing.

"Let me show you some of my more unusual beads."

She pulled out a drawer filled with small packets, opened one and shook a teaspoonful of tiny beads into a little saucer.

"These are the smallest beads I have ever received."

Octavia leaned forward.

"How do you pick them up? They are too small for fingers. They look like jelly powder—or very fine sand."

"You need to catch them on a needle."

"Do you have needles that will go through these? And what about thread to go through the needles?"

"Yes. I have everything, but you may need to buy a pair of magnifying glasses when you work with them, or you will strain your eyes."

"Will they even be visible on a bead tapestry?"

"You will be surprised at the difference they make. You don't notice the bead as much as the effect—an added definition: a touch of brilliance."

Louise opened another drawer.

"These beads are dipped in gold. They will not tarnish. There are several sizes, and different shades of gold. Expensive—but so magnificent.

"And here," she said, opening yet another drawer. "I think that these are my favorite bead. They are very old. They were made by hand by the Bushmen in South Africa."

Louise put some into Octavia's hand.

"What is the red stain on them?"

"It is juice from some kind of henna plant, I believe. The beads are made from broken chips of ostrich egg. A hole is drilled by hand. Then the pieces are threaded onto a piece of twine, also hand-made. Then all the chips are pasted together with this red, sticky juice. When this dries, the whole string of chips is made smooth on a rubbing-stone."

"It must take ages to make just one string."

"Ah! But I don't think the artists who made these beads were in any hurry. They did not live in the insane world we inhabit. They had time; they did not measure it. And these were not made for sale. They would have been for personal decoration, or a spiritual symbol, or to aid them in the hunt. Perhaps to give thanks.

"You know, many books have been published about their rock paintings, and theories have been put forward about what they might mean. Still, no one actually knows for sure. And I remember reading about a woman who wrote down stories told to her by some Bushmen. They were being held for sheep stealing. These give us some idea of their lives. They were extraordinary people—ancient people with very few artifacts; only what they could carry, because they followed the animals that migrated to follow the weather patterns. There is an account of the misery one of them felt over a tobacco pouch that went missing. It was a prized possession; possibly the only possession he had. They felt the wonder of life so deeply—one of their surviving story-tellers said: 'We are the Star People. We are Heaven's Things.' Can you believe that? Isn't it an incredible insight?"

Octavia clasped her hands.

"I know just what they meant!"

She lifted a handful of beads and examined them closely.

"They are beautiful—particularly their unevenness. It makes them come alive."

Oh, to be one of the Star People; to be one of Heaven's Things.

When Kristiyan returned, Octavia had a heavy bag full of beads, and threads and packets of needles. Louise also gave her sample sheets of beads.

"If you need anything, just phone me, and I will put the order together and send it up to Santa Fe. It will save you the trip. I have your card details. Will it be all right to charge any order to it?"

"Of course."

"And don't forget. I want an invitation to the exhibition."

Octavia laughed.

"With these beads, you may have to wait quite a long time."

"I'll wait."

They had lunch in a small restaurant recommended by Louise, not far from the bead shop. When they were seated, Kristiyan put a packet on the table and took out a small book.

"I love bookshops, and while browsing I found this."

Octavia picked it up. Read the title: "Psyche Speaks—A Jungian Approach to Self and the World: Russell Arthur Lockhart."

She gave Kristiyan a searching look.

"I read the contents page and a few random passages. I think you will love it, particularly because you are an artist—or so I believe. I'm still waiting to see some of your work."

"Not yet. I'm not ready yet. But one day—"

He reached into the packet, and pulled out a second book: Jung and Tarot.

"Is this the book you were wanting? I bought it anyway."

At that moment, the waitress came up to take their order.

"It's a special occasion. What about a glass of wine?"

Kristiyan paid the bill.

"I'll take you to the rest-room before we leave."

So in the end it was easy. Before she could object or make any excuses, Kristiyan pushed the wheelchair into the room marked "Ladies."

"Excuse me, ladies! Is there someone who would like to assist Octavia?"

"Of course there is," they laughed as they pushed him out the door. "And don't come back. We will bring Octavia out when she is ready."

Kristiyan brought the car to the door. He helped Octavia out of the wheelchair, made her comfortable on the front seat; did up the seat belt.

"You okay? Comfortable? You look a little pale."

"Just a bit tired. I haven't had so much excitement for a long time." She fished around in her bag for her pills and bottled water. "I'll be fine soon."

But they weren't five minutes out of Albuquerque when her head fell sideways against his arm. He shifted his position to make it more comfortable for her.

They arrived back at The Adobe at six o'clock. As they made the sharp turn and bumped their way up the narrow track, Octavia woke up.

"Oh! Are we home already? Oh, how rude of me. Have I been asleep all this way? Kristiyan, I am so sorry. How awful of me. And after such a lovely day; and being spoilt with these two books, which I can't wait to read."

"I have enjoyed every minute of the day—even seeing you with your jaw hanging open for the last twenty miles, while you slept."

"You are impossible. My jaw did not hang open, and you know it!"

Georgia came out to welcome them back.

"What is the laughter about? Did you have a good time? Here, let me help you, Kristiyan."

Together they unfolded the chair, and helped Octavia into it.

"Stay and have supper. Sebastián will be back just now."

"I would love to."

After supper, while Georgia helped Octavia prepare for bed, Kristiyan and Sebastián sat talking over a cup of coffee.

"Gregorio says he saw the prints again when he was up at Octavia's studio. They are large—too large for a coyote; could be a very large dog, although he says they don't look like dog prints. He said that if he didn't know better, he would think they were the prints of a wolf. But we haven't seen a wolf around here for many decades."

"What does he suggest?"

"Nothing, as yet. He did try following them, but they just vanished. Very strange."

"I think we should contact one of the wolf sanctuaries, and ask if they know of any animal that has escaped. I'll get onto it tomorrow."

The two men stood up.

"Don't say anything to Georgia till we sort this out."

"Of course not. Say goodnight to both of them for me," Kristiyan said, "and thanks for the supper."

There were no reports of escaped wolves or wolf dogs, Sebastián was told.

"Perhaps it was a coyote, and the soft sand made the prints look larger," one keeper at the wolf sanctuary suggested.

He scratched his head.

"Certainly there are no wolves around these parts."

Journal Entry 9

Sofia has gone into labor! She is in the birthing-room where she and I were born. Isn't that strange? And Sister Piadosa and Sister Ana will deliver the baby. They must have delivered so many. Lucien is going to be present for the birth. I am happy for both of them. I wonder if it is a boy or a girl. They have said nothing about names. Salvador says he will come and tell me as soon as the baby is born. He is going to be a grandfather! He doesn't look like my idea of a grandfather. He looks happy and worried. It is a big baby. Sebastián says they may have to take her into the hospital for a caesarian if things don't look good. What a thing women go through. Poor mama. And then, when I was born, I put her through an even worse hell. And still she loves me. I am not going to have children.

I am spending the day in bed. Too much pain. Even Sister Piadosa has relented. But for a day like yesterday it is worth it.

The tiny beads I bought are so small; they look like grains of sand in the packets. And so many colors!

This changes my idea of how I will work these images. I was wondering how I would be able to include small details that you will only really see if you are close to the work. I want them to offer an experience of discovery—of shock, perhaps—to the viewer.

I want to make a series of mandalas—reminiscent of icons, but a little different.

I would like the viewer, at first, to be taken by the beauty and brilliance of the beads, so that at first glance the works will appear to be about something sacred. Will they all be circumscribed by golden haloes? Not sure.

On closer examination, the smaller details will inform the viewer of the horror that is taking place. It makes me think of the beauty of the atomic mushroom cloud— and how only later we saw the hideous devastation it caused.

These works will be my vision of the ecocide that we are bringing about. They will speak of the apocalyptic times to come; no—that are already here, and have been for a long time.

Kristiyan bought me two books yesterday. I have just begun reading the one by Russell Lockhart. I am going to love it. I feel that I am on the right track. So affirming to read this. So much is new to me. I have never read anything about or by Carl Jung. A whole new world ahead.

And I want to have animals—everywhere. I love how this writer delves into words to reveal their original connections. "Animal" from "anima": vital life— breath—soul! They are what animates us. Is this alive and well in our world today? I think not.

How is it that I feel such excitement about this project, which is about so much suffering? Perhaps it is because this work is taking me on a journey of revelation. Perhaps this is what my spiral path was showing me; that the journey outward and the journey into ourselves is one and the same. We make that separation—if indeed we make the connection at all. But they are not separate journeys. And there is that word: "revelation." I long for, and fear the voices coming through.

Kristiyan and I were discussing what happened when the Greco-Roman world collapsed. He told me that this was when the Book of Revelations was written. It felt like the end of the world then—and in a sense it was the end of the world as people had known it. Why can't we see that this is what is happening now?

At last I am going to read about the star card in Jung's tarot.

What is the mercy of wild things?

I feel so awake. So alive.

Are we really going to lose all this beauty?

What do the white doves mean to me?

Sebastián has just come to tell me that they have taken Sofia to the hospital. She will have a caesarian section. He says Lucien is going with her. Poor Lucien. Sometimes it is hard not to be able to do anything—but wait.

Journal Entry 10

It's a boy! The caesar was not complicated. Just as well they decided on it—he weighs eight and a half pounds! His name is Caradoc—it is Celtic, and it means "beloved." He is going to have red hair, like Sofia. Yes, I am happy for them.

It is hot today. I have left the door open to allow some of the north wind to blow through the studio. And what magic! The sun is reflected off the facets of the crystals, and they are turning slowly in the draught. My studio is full of rainbow fireflies! Bright rainbows are dancing on the desert walls! Small rivers of light. My studio is full of energy.

Why have I not seen this before? I love the moment when they all change direction; that momentary stillness when the twist in the nylon reaches a certain degree of tautness. And then the slow reversal of direction: slow, but growing faster as the force of the crystal's weight and the sun playing on its facets create new streams of light.

It reminds me of the flight patterns of the white doves.

I wonder what the stars think of this! Is this what they do in stellar slow motion? I wonder if, every hundred million years, they stand still for several centuries, and then reverse their paths.

"The world hangs by a thread and this thread is the psyche." I am quoting Carl Jung.

"The mercy of wild things." I am quoting Octavia's muse.

The Presence of Absence

Alejandro sat at his desk, his head in his hands. In his mind he was going through his conversation with Octavia.

"I am not going to have angels in my designs, Alejandro. I want to have animals as a different kind of messenger. I want to be able to feel every animal somewhere inside me—to experience that connection to earth and river and sky."

Alejandro regarded the smooth, round stone on the desk in front of him. It was a gift from Octavia.

"Can you feel it, Alejandro? That this stone is not dead matter? I wonder if anything is ever dead. And can't you just feel its history? How did it get to be such a perfect sphere? How many centuries did that take? But the animals—surely they are our angels. They are our connection to what is sacred."

Have I been staring at the stars all this time, he thought, and not seeing what lies right beneath my feet? Why have I neglected the whole warm earth-blood of life?

He was amazed at the change in Octavia. No. Not change: something far more radical. He didn't want to call it transformation—it sounded so abstract— but he could not think of a better word. Perhaps this is what, even as an infant, she knew was her destiny. And now, through all the pain of this traumatic event, it has found her. And she has recognized it! There lies the true artist. I wonder what it is going to look like in the end, he mused. He would love to see her work—her designs—but no one was allowed to enter her room. She had painted it white, Sebastián said. No one would ever see the Black Room now. How strange. But perhaps she was right to keep everything away from curious eyes. A butterfly in a cocoon lies hidden while the transformation occurs.

He got up and went to stand at the window. He missed the black mare.

Alejandro, my friend, maybe it is too late for romantic love, but love is what you need. To give it freely, and to receive it. He donned his jacket, and went out into the street. He was, he thought to himself, a man on a mission; a man in search of his soul.

Alejandro walked the length of the street that led to the small village plaza. Several people waved to him, and called out.

"Alejandro! Where have you been all this time? We've missed you."

"Good to see you back, Alejandro. But why aren't you working? It's not like you to be walking around at this time of day."

"Hello, Teresita. Good to see you too. But I am working. I'm on a quest. Do you happen to know any family with new puppies?"

"Puppies! Why, yes—unless they've all been homed. Gervacio and María's bitch had eleven pups. Maybe go and ask there."

One small, black puppy sat in the middle of the large box on the back porch—his head on one side, ears cocked.

"I'm afraid he is the only one left. He is the runt of the litter, and no one wanted him. All the others were so big and beautiful. He seems to have missed out somewhere."

María lifted the strangely misshapen pup out of the box, and handed him to Alejandro.

"If you want him, you can have him for nothing. I will be so pleased to know he has a good home."

The small dog wriggled, and strained up to lick Alejandro's face. He had the sweet, warm smell of puppy.

"I have never owned a dog before. I don't know what you feed them or anything. If I take him, can you give me a list of do's and don'ts?"

He looked again into the eager little face. What am I thinking? I must be mad even to consider this.

The puppy barked. Alejandro jumped in surprise, and then laughed.

"He's small, but he has courage," said María. "He has stood his ground against the rest of the litter—and that took some doing, I must say."

"I'll take him."

If Alejandro thought that he had chosen El Elegido, he was soon to learn that the small creature was under the impression that it was he who had made the decision to live with and guard this tall man, and that he took his new responsibilities extremely seriously. His protective sensibilities were highly developed, and no one was permitted entry into the house until Alejandro acknowledged the visitor and signaled that he was a friend.

Alejandro was delighted to experience the joy of having another living being in the house. He purchased a dog basket, and placed it close to his bed so that El Elegido would not feel lonely. It proved to be unnecessary, however, for El Elegido had other ideas, and as soon as Alejandro was asleep he clawed his way up onto the bed, and moved surreptitiously forward to sleep in the crook of his arm. When he grew too big for this he slept, stretched out in bliss, back to back with Alejandro.

And then there was the joy of finding chewed slippers, shredded socks, overturned bins—indeed, anything that was seen by the instigator of these actions as needing to be re-cycled. Alejandro consulted María, and learned about teething and the wisdom of keeping shoes and the like in a puppy-proof cupboard, as well as the value of having bones and hooves and chews on hand.

If Alejandro wanted to enter the blood and bone of the world, he could have found no better way. He had not once thought of an angel since El Elegido entered the house.

So it took him entirely by surprise to receive a call from a gallery in New York, making inquiries about the possibility of an exhibition of his carvings there in June. After he put the phone down, he crossed the room and sat down in his big chair, and tried to get in touch with what he was feeling.

He had some work already completed. Not enough for an exhibition. And he didn't feel sure about how his work might change in the future, if indeed there was a future for his work. He wasn't prepared. That was certain.

All right, Alejandro, what is it you think you don't know? You can be ready in time—you know that much. It is a simple yes or no.

But still he didn't move from the chair—until El Elegido, tired of the lack of action, took hold of his jeans and began to tug at them.

"Oh, all right. Come on, Granuja—you scamp!" Alejandro used his nickname. "We are going to pay Octavia a visit."

Granuja

"What kind of a dog is he?"

Sebastián crouched down and held out a hand to the small dog, who ran up, sniffed it, and then jumped up to lick him.

"Yes," said Alejandro, and both men laughed.

"And his name?"

"Officially, El Elegido—the chosen one—because he was the last in the litter to go, and I don't want him to think that I didn't choose him on his merits. But I think his everyday name will be Granuja."

"Suits him." Sebastián stood up, and Granuja ran back to sit at Alejandro's feet.

"Do you remember my mother's dog—the stray with the blue eyes, Perro Mestizo?"

"Who could forget him?"

"Well, this little dog of yours reminds me of him. Not in looks, but there is something about him that is similarly unique. I think it is his air of authority. Look at him now. So young, but already he is taking care of you." He called the pup again, but this time he just ran once around Alejandro's legs and sat down again.

"You see that? He knows whom he serves. I remember Father Octavio saying that he wished his congregation was as faithful to God as Perro Mestizo was to Magdalena. He said that her dog had found a great love—I think that was how he put it—and something about finding meaning in life through being committed to this."

188

"Then he will be my teacher, I am sure."

"What do you think he has, that you still need to learn?"

"He knows he is here to serve. He doesn't have to be reminded. I realize now, that it must be examined regularly—just in case your success has put you to sleep."

Sebastián raised an eyebrow.

"Oh, just doing a little more soul-searching," Alejandro said. "And now we are off to introduce Granuja to Octavia. Do you know where I'll find her?"

"She's up at her studio. She and Gregorio are discussing ways to make it possible for the wheelchair to manage the spiral path."

"I've brought someone to meet you."

Alejandro walked the spiral path, and Granuja followed at his heels.

"Hello, Gregorio. Good to see you."

"And you too, Alejandro."

"Oh, Alejandro!" cried Octavia. "He's adorable."

She bent forward and called to the pup, who ran to her and jumped up into her lap, put his paws on her chest and licked her face.

"Oh, look at you," she laughed as he rolled over, and had his tummy tickled. "When did you get him? What's his name?"

"Granuja—and I've had him for ten days."

"Granuja!"

"Yes. His real name is El Elegido."

"The chosen one." Octavia held him up, and nuzzled his neck; then she put him down on the ground, and he ran back to Alejandro.

"Lucky man. He knows where he belongs. But any time you need a dog-sitter, I offer my services."

She turned back to Gregorio.

"Just to finish this—I think we should pick up all of the painted ladder section, and make that a smooth gravel path. That way we needn't move any of the stones."

"I'll get onto it right away."

Gregorio left, and Alejandro pulled up the old chair that stood outside the doorway.

"So, you are about to get back to work. The beads?"

"Yes. I can't wait to start."

"And your back? The pain? Won't you get very tired—all that bending forward?"

"Probably. But Kristiyan had a marvelous idea. He bought me a weight-lifter's belt. It helps to support the back. I suppose I'll look a little strange—but so what?"

"Have you had the results of the scan?"

"Yes. The various specialists are debating whether it is worth my while going to see an orthopedic surgeon in Washington. He specializes in back injuries."

"And what do they think he might be able to do?"

"That's what they are discussing. They are sending all the reports through to him. There is the slight possibility that he might be able to do a very delicate operation that would make it possible for me to use my leg properly again. It is a new technique for rescuing a nerve, provided it has not been damaged. They seem to think that this might be the case."

"But that is good news."

"Yes."

"You sound—reluctant?"

"Oh, not really. It's just that this has been going on for such a long time, and I am so ready to get back to work. I am boiling inside with ideas and images. I am terrified that I will lose this momentum if I have to stop again for something that will take months before I am back here again."

"But if it means you will be able to walk—"

"Yes, of course. And I will keep up the conversation I have begun in my journal. I just can't promise I won't explode! But what about you, Alejandro? What work are you doing?"

"I suppose right at the moment I am doing puppy-work. I have never known a dog before. Well, other people's dogs, yes, but I have never shared my life with one."

"And?"

"It's a full-time job! But I am grateful for it. I am not sure just how I want to proceed with my work. Something has changed. I thought I was clear about what I wanted to do, and now I have been invited to exhibit in a gallery in New York—and I find I am not clear in my mind. Not yet."

"What were you thinking?"

"I have been examining my commitment to carve angels—made when I was ten. I am asking some questions about that. So far, I have no answers. But I made a promise—"

"And?"

"Well, I have been carving angels for over sixty years, but I find that I am not sure now who or what I am any more. You are right at the beginning; it is all new and exciting. But I feel like an old carpet that has been walked over—too often."

He paused.

"I remember something Father Octavio once said. He said that in any relationship—be it with a lover or your work or God or yourself—there are always three stages, and you will know them as they repeat and repeat, many times over, during a lifetime: the period of romance—that is at the beginning, when everything is so new and clear and wonderful. Then comes the period of disillusionment, when we feel disenchanted; that we have made the wrong choice. And finally, if—if we can see what we have with new eyes—the period of joy. Most often, when we are disillusioned, we think something is wrong outside us, and we discard the idea or the person—or whatever—and we find a new one. Well, that is where I am—looking for the gold."

"You aren't going to abandon your angels!"

"No, never. Indeed, I have one in the car that I made for Caradoc. It just presented itself—out of a dream, I think—so it was simple. But for others—just how I am to serve them is the question."

"Well, how will you not serve them?"

Alejandro looked at her, and smiled.

"Not bad!" he said. "A good question—right on the jugular."

Well here I am, he thought, the famous mentor; and the pupil has put an elegant finger on it—just like that. He didn't know whether to be proud or humbled. Or both.

"I think that I will not serve them by accepting this invitation to exhibit. Yes! That's it! I have turned the angels into a commodity. That's where I'll begin."

At this point Granuja, tired of this inactivity, sat in front of Alejandro and gave a bark.

"You see," said Octavia. "He agrees. Time for play."

"Please let me know as soon as you hear from the doctors—promise."

"I will. And don't forget the offer to dog-sit—any time."

She watched the tall man, followed by Granuja, begin to walk the spiral of stones. She had never thought of Alejandro as getting old, but today there was a spring in his step that was quite new.

In any relationship—always three stages. She wished she had known Father Octavio.

Washington DC

She was aware of him the instant he appeared; aware of how his presence changed the energy of the room. She felt her body let go of a certain tension, one that she had not been aware of holding. It was only as she did this that she noticed how she had prepared herself to resist whatever was to follow. The wolf stood close to the bed. He was not looking at her. He was relaxed and alert. She could feel him as if he was in her body; could feel a new sense of expansive awareness that did not waste energy by wrestling with a future that had not arrived.

Octavia lay on the white bed. She was wearing the hospital gown, cotton boots and cap, looking up at the ceiling. The sister had prepped her earlier—it was barely light when she came into the room—and she had just returned to give her a pre-med injection. A hospital orderly and a nurse wheeled her into a room close to the theatre. Now she was waiting for the familiar drowsiness to claim her. She closed her eyes to visualize the beadwork of the crucified wolf and the strange shadow in the sky. The image began to spin. The sound of voices. Bright light. She was sinking, slowly...

In a small room nearby Sebastián and Georgia sat, holding hands. There was nothing to say. Now, only the long wait.

She could feel the agony of the crucified wolf—the pain of it—in her body. And the men who have done this—where are they? Oh, the pain! How long would he take to die? How many times must the other—the outcast— be crucified? Forgive them, for they know not...Too late for that. They should know by now. Too late for forgiveness. It's all too late. She could feel the world shaking beneath her. Just the pain of the world...

Only a momentary glance from those astonishing eyes, and then he was ahead of her once more, running at an easy pace through the snow. She followed. Everything is white, she thought; even the sky. I am in the middle of nowhere. How does he know where to go?
Now they were in forest. How did that happen? Why did she not see it?
The wolf slowed to a walk, and when they were deep into the trees he stopped and lay down.

She opened her eyes, and saw the swimming image of her parents standing at the bedside.

"It went well, my sweetheart," said Georgia.

"We are both here in the next room," Sebastián said. "Now you must sleep."

Octavia sank back once more into the ocean of sleep.

He was looking at her. In the half-light and shadows it was his eyes that held hers. She moved over to him, lay down and curled herself into his warmth. She could hear the steady heartbeat; feel his wild breath enter into her. She was home.

"She's out of theatre. It all went well, he said. It is a little early to be certain, but he feels extremely hopeful about the outcome. Apparently the nerve was not harmed. He widened some place between the vertebrae, I think. I couldn't follow all the technical details. So now we must wait. He wants to keep her here under observation for at least two weeks, maybe longer."

Sebastián listened while Sister Piadosa gave him all the good wishes from everyone at The Adobe, and a message from Kristiyan.

"You say he is coming to Washington?"

Sebastián was quiet again.

192

"Well, I must say she is fortunate to have such a dedicated friend. And he seems to have contacts everywhere. What about the music? Aren't they booked for a concert?"

He was making notes in a small pocket notebook.

"Yes, I'll tell her. And how is everything else? No problems?"

There were a few more exchanges, and they said goodbye.

Sebastián went back to Georgia.

"All is well at home. The concert date has been moved to early August, and would you believe it? Kristiyan is coming to Washington. Apparently he has a friend with an apartment, where he will stay for the two weeks that Octavia is here. If all goes well, he will fly back with her."

"I wonder what she feels for him. He has been such a loyal friend. Lucien says he is mad about her. Perhaps she hasn't let herself feel too much because of her condition. But if this operation is successful, I think she might have to come to some kind of a decision."

□□□

The flight back to Albuquerque was uneventful.

Severo had flown down to be with her, and to make sure that nothing went amiss on the return flight. He and Kristiyan sat close to where she lay on a stretcher, her body immobilized against any sudden bumps or air-pockets.

The pilot, who had been informed of the stretcher passenger, touched down at Albuquerque Airport as light as a feather, and was rewarded with a round of applause by the passengers.

While Kristiyan saw to the luggage, Severo supervised the stretcher-bearers. Sebastián and Georgia stood waiting at the station wagon in the special area.

"Kristiyan says we will follow in his car with the luggage," Severo said when Octavia was made comfortable. Georgia sat in the back with her to make sure that she was secure.

"We'll meet you back at home."

He was standing under the cottonwood that marked the turn-off to The Adobe. Octavia stared out of the window. He looked different. What was it? The way he held himself? Something different in that unforgettable blue stare? They were turning the corner. Soon she would not be able to see him. She made one last effort to see out of the window.

The space under the cottonwood was empty.

New Steps

A small group stood waiting at the top end of the covered cloisters—Sebastián and Georgia, Sister Piadosa and Sister Ana, Gregorio, Kristiyan, Alejandro with Granuja on a lead, Lucien and Sofia, who was holding the infant Caradoc wrapped in a warm shawl.

At the far end, Octavia sat in her wheelchair with Severo standing beside her. He was holding a light-weight aluminum stick. He bent down to tell her something. She smiled and nodded a reply; then, taking hold of his arm, she allowed herself to be pulled up and out of the chair.

She took the stick from Severo, and stood for a little while, finding her balance. Then, leaning heavily on the stick, she took a step—and another—and another. She walked, her face grimacing for the pain of the effort, the length of the cloister. Severo followed with the chair.

At the end there was a burst of applause. With relief, Octavia sat down in the chair again.

Everyone came up to congratulate her, and to say how proud they were to see her walking on her own. Georgia whispered something in her ear, and Octavia reached up to give her mother a kiss.

Lucien, holding Sofia's arm, came and put out a hand to touch her face.

"I am so happy for you, 'Tavia," he said.

She took hold of the hand, and held it.

"Thank you, Lucien," she said. "That means the world to me."

The last one to come up was Kristiyan. He had in his hand a leather cuff with beaded tassels onto which many small animals from the Southwest, made of silver, were fastened.

"It is for your stick," he said as he fastened it tightly just below the hand-grasp. "The silver charms were made by a local man—all your fierce, wild animals."

He leaned forward and whispered something in her ear—

Octavia looked down. Her face was scarlet. She took his hand, and held it for a moment.

"And thank you for such a lovely gift. I was wondering how I could transform this stick into something I will come to love."

With cheeks still flaming, she nodded to Severo, who took hold of the chair and helped her to cross the bumpy yard to her house.

□□□

Kristiyan passed the envelope to Octavia.

"I didn't want to say anything about it until it was a reality. It has taken a long time. So many forms. So much waiting for things to be approved. But here it is! This opens so many doors for me."

Octavia took out the card, and gave a cry.

"Kristiyan! Your green card! When did you apply for it?"

They were sitting in the shade outside her studio, drinking iced tea. Granuja was sitting next to her feet. Alejandro had left to go to Albuquerque, and she was looking after him for the day.

"As soon as the Santa Fe Opera Company made my position with the orchestra a permanent one."

"But, that was years ago."

"Yes."

"More than six years! And it has only come through now?"

"Do you know how many people are in the queue?—and they all have to be checked. It must be a nightmare for the authorities."

"I'm so happy for you, Kristiyan."

"Thank you."

There was a long and slightly awkward silence. Octavia reached for the jug of tea, and refilled their glasses. The silence lengthened.

"Octavia," Kristiyan said at last. "I want to ask you something."

"Sure."

"I want to ask you how—" He took a deep breath—"how you feel about me."

She stared at him, a flush of pink coloring her cheeks.

"I suppose I am asking you if you could think of me as more than a friend. I didn't want to say anything until this card came through—I didn't feel I had the right—but now..."

Octavia put out a hand. "Before you say any more—"

She paused.

"If you are asking me what I think you are, I need to tell you some things about myself. I don't have any boyfriends—never have had. Don't really have any friends at all. I guess I'm a loner. And I don't seem to want the things that all the girls of my age want—parties, boyfriends, lovers, marriage, children, the house, the car, two cars—it goes on and on."

"What do you want?"

"I want my life to be about my work."

"And does this exclude any kind of relationship?"

"No. But it would be an unusual one."

"Is it possible that I might fit into that unusual space?" He took her hand. "I am telling you that I love you. I love the artist in you—the passion. I want to be with you—I would like to share my life with you. Do you think—?"

Words and courage failed him, but he kept hold of her hand.

"Do you know what I am afraid of?" Octavia said. "I look at my mother and Sebastián—both artists; both were passionate about their work. And look what has become of it. Housework and office work and running this whole place—and children.

Look at the enormous drain that I have put on them with this accident. Look at all the bills. But no poetry. No great art. What happened to their dreams? And then I look at the world, and I see this mirrored everywhere—a terrible loss of soul until, it seems, we stop feeling the soul in anything. Have you ever noticed how so many people look as if someone turned off the light inside them?"

Kristiyan smiled at her.

"Octavia," he said, "have you any idea how much I love you? Just the way you are, and because of the way you are. I love the things you say—the way you think. I love the way you challenge yourself—and the world. It is not written that you have to lead a life of domestic bliss—or domestic lethargy—just because you love someone. There is no script you have to follow. You—we—can write it the way we want it."

He paused.

"I am saying I want to be committed to you. And that could be marriage—or if you don't like that, I want to live with you. I am not hung up on the form it takes, and I don't yearn for children. I too have my work, my music."

"And what if suddenly I can't walk again? It's not impossible. As it is, I will never be able to walk without the stick, and even then not far. I have nightmares that I am not able to walk at all, that I become dependent on everyone—a burden. I still have a long way to go with the physiotherapist. I still have pain. Maybe it will be with me for my whole life. I have had this pain now since the accident, and I know how it drains my energy. What right have I to involve anyone else—you—in that drama?"

"Well, what if anything happens to my hands—an accident, arthritis—and I can never play the cello again? There are never guarantees. That's what the 'for better or worse' is about. I want to share it all with you. With you!"

Kristiyan stood up, took both of Octavia's hands, helped her to her feet, put his arms around her—and kissed her.

"I have wanted to do this since the first time I saw you." He kissed her again.

"I love you, Octavia."

Journal Entry 11

Kristiyan kissed me today! I have never been kissed by a man before—not like that.

He says he wants me. Loves me. Wants to marry me. Me!

Oh, my God! What do I feel? Am I betraying Lucien? Am I that shallow? That fickle? I don't know what I feel.

Is that true? No. Not really.

If Kristiyan left, I would be—so empty? I don't want him to leave. I suppose I don't want him to leave me. I feel so comfortable with him—or I did. And now? I know I want him to kiss me again. Yes, Octavia—be honest with yourself. You are falling in love. The one thing you said you would never do.

Alejandro's Shadow

It became patently clear to everyone at The Adobe that something had happened between Octavia and Kristiyan. This was not revealed by their behavior. Outwardly they appeared to be the same. But everyone could feel the heat of the flame that burned between them.

And so did Alejandro, when he came to give his weekly wood-carving class.

He found Octavia with the musicians, down at the hall. They were about to begin their practice session, and were enjoying a mug of coffee and some cookies.

Octavia sat next to Kristiyan on the edge of the platform, her stick with its fringe of silver animals across her knees. Lucien, Salvador and Reuben had arranged the chairs and music-stands. Now they were waiting for Sofia, who was giving Caradoc his morning feed.

"Hi, Alejandro—want some coffee? There's some here in the pot, and cream and sugar on the tray."

Reuben poured the coffee, and gave it to Alejandro.

"Thanks, Reuben. So what are you rehearsing now that the opera season is over?"

"We are doing a benefit concert in Santa Fe, to raise money for the wild horses of New Mexico," said Salvador.

"Why? What is happening with them?"

"Some ranchers want to have them all shot. They say that they are taking all the grazing away from their cattle."

"So, what is the money for?"

"There are several organizations, each raising funds to solve one aspect of the problem. There is one that works with the Navajo people, working to set up a wild horse preservation area—horses are sacred to the Navajo. Another—the one that we are supporting—is campaigning to get effective legislature passed, so that the treatment of these horses can be closely monitored. Shooting the horses would be humane compared to what is happening now."

"And that is—?"

"Trucking them down to Mexico—with no food or water for days—to be slaughtered."

"Why were the horses brought here in the first place?"

"They weren't brought in at all," said Octavia. "Some are wild horses—mustangs; others are horses that have been released onto the range, and have become feral."

"And ranchers want them shot?"

"Yes. There are very heated meetings carrying on right now. Already, many of the horses have been rounded up and slaughtered for pet food."

An image of the black mare flashed through Alejandro's brain. He wondered where she was. Was she safe?

"And this music," he asked Salvador, "is it instrumental, or do you have voices as well?"

"Both. It is based on something that Octavia wrote—it's called Requiem for a Broken World."

"Something Octavia wrote!" He turned to her. "When did you decide to start writing?"

"I didn't. I was dreaming into a design for a beadwork, and I heard the word 'Requiem'. I had been reading about the fate of the wolves and the wild horses of New Mexico, and before I knew it the words just came to me. I am busy with sketches for beadworks I want to make about this. It is still too early to know where they will take me."

"How interesting—and the music?"

"Kristiyan has written the music for the requiem. He studied the patterns of medieval Russian choral works when he was in college, and he has written parts for the solo voice and for all the background voices. They evoke the sound of something forever changing, forever changeless; like some eternal, oceanic rise and fall."

"And Sofia, I take it, will be the soloist."

"If Caradoc will spare her."

"I like it that the solo voice is a woman's—especially when it is Sofia's."

He turned to address Kristiyan. "I didn't know that you composed music. Is this something new?"

"Not really. It has never really called to me before now. But these words—Octavia's words—who could resist them?"

"Who indeed?" said Alejandro. "Well, I suppose I must get to my class, and leave you young people to get on with it. Ah! Here comes Sofia now."

Alejandro did not go to his class immediately. There was too much churning around inside him, and he needed some time alone to assimilate what he had heard—and more importantly, what he was feeling in response to it.

There was Octavia, his protégée, the odd one out whom only he could truly understand—suddenly, it would seem, comfortable to be included in a group project—in fact, a project she had initiated.

And now—Kristiyan? Suddenly he was close to her. Well, of course he had been very good to her after the accident, and through all the operations; but this, now, was different. Very different.

Alejandro found a log, and sat down.

Is he in love with her? What had he said about the requiem—about Octavia's words? "Who could resist them?" Of course, you silly old fool—he is in love with her, and has been for a long time. Why didn't I see it?

Alejandro felt something ugly turn over in his heart. He felt cold and sick. He didn't want to listen—or look at it. But he saw the angels from his dream—falling, falling—and the deep abyss with all its shadows, and he on the knife-edge path.

He heard a voice say: "You are jealous,"—and he turned around to see who spoke, but no one was there.

It must have been me.

Yes, I am jealous. It was, in a way, a relief to own it.

But there was more. Something much worse. He could feel it coming up into his throat like food that had gone bad, being rejected by the body.

And then he knew what it was.

Alejandro put his head in his hands.

"No. Oh, God—please, not that!"

But it *was* that.

It had been so comfortable for him to be the one who understood her; the one who had her trust. It was comfortable for him that she was lonely—he would save her; that she felt an outcast—he would be there for her. Her aloneness made him feel strong. He had been living through her; off her energy, like a parasite. It was he who was lost—not her.

And now a young and gifted man had taken his place.

It never was your place!

And was she in love with him?

Yes. He had seen that, the instant he saw the two of them sitting together.

Alejandro felt as if all the layers of self-deception were being flayed off him like skins, so that now his flesh was raw; raw right down to the bone.

And there it lay, at the bottom of it all—his grief; his huge and overwhelming grief for the life he had not led.

How is it possible to delude yourself for sixty years?

He thought of all the friends he never had time for. All the women who loved him—who would have married him; women on whom he had turned his back. And why? So that he could stand out in the dark, counting stars. So that he could count stars and carve angels that would make him famous.

Was it too late?

Oh, God—if only it was not too late.

A Christmas Benefit Concert in Santa Fe

Octavia entered the empty concert hall. In spite of her cane, her limp was more noticeable than usual. It always happens, she thought, just when I am nervous, and the last thing I want is for people to pity me.

She had come early to oversee the setting up of the large screen for the visuals she had prepared on her laptop. It was her idea to have ceiling to floor images projected onto a screen behind the performers. These were images of the wild horses—images that slowly faded from one into another, so as not to be a distraction.

She chose a seat in the empty auditorium, and watched the technicians run cables from the projector to where the computer would be; watched how they taped the cables to the floor so that no one would trip over them.

Now that the day had arrived, she felt apprehensive. How would people receive the requiem? The concert was advertised by the title: Requiem for a Broken World. She read the program again. How strange to see her name in print. This stepping out into the public world was a scary experience—more so because this was not, and never had been her field of expertise. What on earth was I thinking when I agreed to this? She felt like running away to her studio, and locking the door.

The Adobe Chapel Choir, under the guidance of Santiago and Salvador, had been rehearsing for weeks. The Requiem for a Broken World, with words by Octavia and music by Kristiyan, was to be the main feature of the evening.

The words of the requiem had a direct bearing on the work of the organization, Save the Wild Mustangs. As things stood, farmers could round up thirty or forty mustangs and sell them to "killer buyers" who trucked them down to Mexico. There had been no serious discussion about how to contain the breeding of the growing herds, and there was little effective legislation to protect the horses, or monitor their transport and subsequent slaughter for pets' meat. It had become a lucrative business.

In its brochure, the organization gave a detailed account of what the horses had to endure before being killed. A series of very graphic photographs illustrated this. Beneath the images and the text was a question:

"If you were here, could you stand by and watch this happen?"

A technician came up and asked her to bring her computer to the desk at the back of the hall. She waited while he made the necessary connections, and then he asked her to start the program so that they could check the placing of the screen and the levels of the projector. The concert hall became quiet, and stage lights were dimmed.

All her nervousness vanished when she saw the life-size images of the wild horses filling the screen.

Who could not see their beauty—could not feel the terrible loss New Mexico would suffer if they were no more? Their disappearance would leave such an absence in the soul of the land. And in mine, she thought.

Only the cello, violin and bandoneon would be on stage when people came in to take their seats. They would be playing a piece by Lucien. This would introduce the emotional tone for the evening.

Octavia, looking at the images that faded in and out, could feel in her mind what an impact those elegiac sounds would have on the audience.

□□□

The hall was packed.

The concert had been widely advertised, and the people of Santa Fe and the surrounding area had donated generously to the project. The audience was abuzz— some reading the program, others pointing out the names they knew.

Salvador Fuentes and Reuben Mendoza were names that most people recognized from their evenings of tango, and a few opera-goers had read something about the Russian cellist, Kristiyan Bacarov. Lucien, and Sofia—who was the soloist for the requiem—were known only to the locals of Las Madres. No one had ever heard of Octavia Chavez.

The introductory and closing music was composed by Lucien. For the first piece he had crafted his own vision of a broken world—a sightless vision—through sound: the sound of music losing its center; the harmonies slowly disappearing into the sound of empty wind.

His closing composition evoked the sound of breath moving over empty spaces. The program notes referred to the passage from Genesis in which a breath moved over the face of the waters.

The program notes stated that the images and the slow cello music were the work of Bacarov and Octavia Chavez.

Who was this Octavia Chavez?

The introductory music came to an end. A hush fell as the choir filed onto the stage. Santiago stepped into the spotlight, and took a bow. He welcomed everyone; thanked them for their support.

By way of an introduction, he read aloud some words by Chief Seattle, whose message to the world was that we are only one thread in the web of life, and that what we do to the planet and all living things—animals and all of wilderness—we ultimately do to ourselves; that we are all inter-linked in this web of life.

201

There was a burst of applause. Octavia felt close to tears.

Once the room was quiet again, Santiago turned to face the choir. He raised his hands, waited until he had the attention of everyone, and then made a gesture to bring in the voices that would provide the sustained background to the work.

These low voices—tenor and bass—began as little more than a vibration, which swelled into a drone. It was elegiac in tone, and introduced the mood of the work perfectly. Into this background the female voices were introduced, bringing an added pathos; voices that rose and fell in a series of complex harmonies. The effect was electrifying.

"This is a song of loss and betrayal,
Of broken things and endings..."

An image of the wild mustangs fades slowly onto the screen.

"This is a song of ancestral memories,
Of ancient covenants and forgetting..."

The introductory words are chanted by the women—a slow, solemn chant— while the men's voices hold the drone.

And now Sofia's voice rises out of the chant; shocking in its clarity.

"There is a rage in me...
And a sorrow...
And a song of grief so deep and full...
My soul suffers the singing..."

With subtle variations, the drone rises and falls seamlessly, like a great ocean swell.

Some of the older members of the audience felt sure they'd heard this voice before—it was not a voice that could be easily, if ever, forgotten. And something about her looks. That amazing red hair!

They wondered at the name—Chavez—and looked in the program to see if there was any information. And who was Lucien Chavez? All they could find about the artists was where they studied, and what and where they had performed. There were references to various awards. Nothing to shed any light on their names.

"There is a wound in me that shall not heal...
The deep wound of your kingdom...
The wound of your kind..."

From her place in the wings, Octavia listened to her own words coming alive through the vibrant voices. This was her vision, in sound, she thought. This is the intensity I have to capture in my bead tapestries.

And all the while, the almost ghostly images of the wild mustangs—flying manes and tails, and wild eyes—filled the screen behind the performers.

All of a sudden, Octavia saw the crucified wolf—could feel in her body the pain; taste the blood. Why was there so much suffering in the world? And so much beauty? And this wolf, crucified in the empty desert—is this me? Is this my wound too?

"In my heart a sorrow for all wild things and their passing..."

She gripped the stick with its fringe of silver animals. Am I the one who is broken and wounded? Is this why I can feel their pain?

"Breathe one last time your wild breath into me...
That I may not forget you...
That I may remember who I am..."

Please God, I never lose my wildness, however broken my body may be.
It was a prayer.

"Breathe one last time your sweet breath—into me..."

Alejandro, sitting next to Sebastián, searched through the many images for a glimpse of the black mare. Was she one of these wild horses? There were many that might have been her. How could he be sure?

And then he saw her: a series of images that the photographer had captured perfectly!

She had broken away from the herd, and as one frame faded into another he saw her running straight at the riders who were driving them. She was still well within the wide arms of the corral, and it looked as if they had her.

Alejandro prayed to all the angels he ever knew that she would make it.

"You can do it," he whispered, so loudly that Sebastián inclined his head toward him and raised an eyebrow.

And then the mare did what he had seen her do before. As image followed image like a slow motion dream, he saw her race toward the pole-railings; clear them effortlessly. She was gone.

"Thank God," whispered Alejandro, so loudly that Sebastián nudged him.

"Is something the matter?" he whispered.

"Nothing."

The final composition was a sensitive evocation of a world in waiting. The music did not reach any conclusion. It ended, poignantly, on one long, drawn-out note—scarcely more than a breath.

They received a standing ovation.

Christmas came and went in the usual excitement of small children, decorated trees, gifts and delicious food.

And snow!

Rafael conducted a special early Mass at The Adobe early on Christmas Day while the silent snowflakes covered the hills and valley, muting all sounds.

After all the greetings were done and the blessings for Christmas exchanged, the members of the congregation left to finish their preparations for the day. The nuns hurried off to finish their work, and Rafael prepared to leave. Sebastián and Gregorio helped him to put the snow-chains on his car, and after a hot coffee, with a tot of something that Sebastián said would do him the world of good, he left for Las Madres to conduct the nine o'clock Mass.

A Trading Store on Old Arroyo

Santiago was sitting at the organ in the Las Madres Church, playing through some music that had been chosen for a funeral that was to take place on the following day, when Alejandro walked in. Hearing the footsteps, he turned round. Seeing Alejandro, he waved a hand, but he did not stop playing.

Alejandro took a seat at the back of the church, and sat with closed eyes, listening.

He knew that the funeral was for the wife of old Mr. Isaacs, who owned the ancient Isaacs Trading Store in Las Madres. Benjamin Isaacs had married outside of the Jewish faith—a matter that had caused a rift in the family at the time. But that was long ago, and now all of his family, his parents and siblings, were dead. Now there was no one to object to his giving his wife a Christian burial service. As a kind of compromise, he had chosen the Kol Nidrei to be played at the funeral—which, although composed for a very different Jewish ceremony, was written by a man of the Christian faith. He had discussed this with Santiago, who had suggested that Kristiyan should play the cello voice which was so important to the whole composition. This was duly arranged.

Alejandro was not familiar with the music or its history, but as he listened he felt his tears begin to fall.

As if the music had called her up from the past, he suddenly saw a tall woman walking toward him. He recognized her at once: Francesca Ortega.

Alejandro sat, shocked into memory. Francesca! Where had she gone? No, Alejandro—where did you go?

Now she stood in front of him, lovely and luscious as a ripe pomegranate, in a white cotton dress that revealed the swell of her breasts—a soft gold against the crisp, white linen. He remembered the summer they fell in love. It was a short but passionate love affair, one in which he felt that he was being drawn up into a realm so far from his angels that he could only wonder about the nature of heaven, and how the angels fit into it.

He did no work that summer, but was happy to bathe in the glory of that flame. Days came and went. Barefoot days of sun, and nights under stars—watching a plump New Mexico moon, the color of a ripe plum, slide up over the hills to bathe their naked bodies in soft light.

He was aware now of how he must have broken her heart when he told her—abruptly—after looking into his studio and seeing the tools lying untouched, that he must get back to work.

What had become of her? He had just walked away, and buried himself in his angels and his stars. He had never stopped to inquire about her, or what she made of her life.

Alejandro felt a chill run down his neck. How could he have been so unaware? So callous—so unbelievably cruel?

Now, in front of his closed eyes, she turned away from him, and he watched her run away down a long, narrow road—run swiftly on those long legs he loved to caress; run away like the wind.

That was fifty years ago.

He was surprised to find Santiago looking down at him.

"You look as if you've seen a ghost. What's up?"

"Do you remember Francesca? Francesca Ortega? I think I met her the summer before Salvador was born."

"Yes. A very lovely young woman. What became of her? One minute you were all over each other, and the next she was gone."

"That's what I am wondering. While you were playing that music I suddenly saw her in my mind, as clearly as if it was yesterday."

"What happened between the two of you?"

"I walked into my studio one day, and saw all my tools lying idle—and that was it."

"What did you tell her?"

"That's just it. I can't remember that I said anything much. One day I was just back at work. Carving angels! This is the first time I have thought of her in—what is it?—fifty years? How old is Salvador?"

"He will be fifty this year."

There was a long silence. Santiago put his hands in his pockets, and waited.

"I wonder how I find out what happened to her; where she went."

"There must be people here who knew her. Why not ask around if anyone knows?"

"Yes."

Alejandro looked up at his friend.

"I don't know what I was thinking."

He stopped. "Obviously I was not thinking. How could I have done this terrible thing?"

Santiago said nothing.

"What if I cannot find her?"

"And if you do find her—what then?"

Alejandro looked up helplessly.

"I suppose it depends on her circumstances. If she is married and happy, with a whole bunch of children and grandchildren, who am I to barge in with my guilty conscience and ask for forgiveness? Just so that I feel better! I think I must first try and find her. Maybe the circumstances will show me how to proceed."

He shook his head.

"Fool!" he said. "You stupid, arrogant fool."

He could only imagine what she must have felt, being dropped so ungraciously.

And unkind, Alejandro! Don't forget that, you famous Angel Man! Worse than unkind; that would have required at least some measure of awareness. No. Just completely self-obsessed. That's what your life has been for fifty years, and you think you have kept a promise!

□□□

Ortega's Trading Store was located in the middle of a narrow street, named simply Old Arroyo. It was built in the old style: adobe with a low, flat roof of vigas, covered with latillas and the traditional mix of straw and mud. Over the front façade a long, low overhang of weathered latte created a shady porch. On its dusty wood floor a motley selection of comfortable and well-worn easy-chairs spoke of a bygone era. The obligatory bleached steer skull hung on the wall at the far end, and a Navajo weaving was nailed to the rough adobe wall between the entrance and a small window. An old bridle, its cracked leather faded almost down to white, hung on the wall next to a pair of spurs.

Alejandro stood in the dusty street, and looked up and down. The street was empty. Even so, he felt that he was being watched. He felt as if he was, in some way, trespassing on a life he had abandoned.

This is not the time to lose your nerve, Alejandro, he said to himself. He hitched up his jeans, crossed the street and entered the store.

He walked across the room, past a shelf carrying blankets, tin mugs and an assortment of pots and pans, to the counter where a white-haired man, in a check shirt and denims, was busy sorting out a number of small boxes. He pushed them aside when Alejandro walked in.

"Yes, sir," he said. "How may I help you?"

"The name is Alejandro," said Alejandro, extending his hand. "Alejandro Jaramillo."

The man raised his eyebrows, and smiled.

"Ah! The Angel Man!" He reached out a hand. "Joe López," he said. "See!" He pointed to the space over the entrance. "Your fame precedes you."

Alejandro turned, and saw one of his angels hanging above the doorway.

"I forget how we came by it—maybe it was always there—and I didn't know what it really was until a customer told me. He showed me a catalogue from some exhibition—in Santa Fe, I think it was. It had your photograph and name in it. Good to meet you!"

He followed this with an inquiring glance.

"I am looking for someone who used to live in Las Madres—about fifty years ago. I am here because of the name on your store. The person I am trying to trace is, or was an Ortega—she may have married since. Francesca Ortega she was then."

The old man shook his head.

"Can't help you there. I bought the store in 1945, after the family moved away. Don't know where they went. Don't even know if it is the same family you are looking for."

He thought for a moment.

"Tell you what, though," he said. "Old Rachel Esperanza—she lives two doors down, same side—she will know. She has been here forever."

Alejandro thanked him, and left to go in search of old Rachel.

He found the house easily, and knocked on the bright, blue-painted door. He heard the shuffling of feet, and then the door opened to reveal a tiny, shrunken woman with long white hair in a braid, and skin the color and texture of a dried peach. Alejandro introduced himself, and gave the reason for his visit.

"You would be looking for Arturo and his family. They moved to Albuquerque in the early forties. Not quite sure of the year. There was some trouble in the family. No one ever learned what it was. Just suddenly they upped and were gone. Odd, we all thought it. Did you know the family well?"

"If it is the same family, I only knew the daughter, Francesca, for a short while."

"That's the family, all right. A lovely girl. Well, good luck to you. I hope I have helped."

Alejandro thanked her, and left.

He drove to the post office, and asked if they had a directory for Albuquerque. He leaned on the counter and searched for F. Ortega. It was a long shot, but he could think of no other way. There were two names. He made a note of the phone numbers and addresses, thanked the postmaster, went back to his car and drove home to think things over.

Francesca

Alejandro stood, facing the entrance. His heart was racing. Now that the moment had arrived, he felt reluctant to knock on that door; to resurrect something that had been laid to rest for so long.

He knocked twice.

Footsteps, coming down a passage. The sound of the lock being released.

Alejandro stood in front of a tall woman with white hair, cut stylishly short. She was dressed very simply in a well-tailored linen dress of some neutral shade.

"Come in, Alejandro. Here—let me take your jacket."

She led the way into a small, elegant sitting-room, furnished in a minimalist style. The absence of clutter gave presence to each piece of furniture, each artwork. The effect was one of stillness.

Alejandro sat, awkwardly aware of his faded jeans and his boots.

"Will you take tea or coffee? Or perhaps something cold?"

She put his jacket over the back of a chair.

"Coffee would be good, thank you."

While she was gone, Alejandro looked around the room. A bookcase with, he noticed, several books about interior design; one photograph of a young man with two young boys. A low table, covered by a Navajo weaving. A vase with one stem of yucca blooms. His heart missed a beat when he saw one of his angels, high on the wall above the doorway. He remembered the day he gave it to her.

□□□

"It's a gift for you."

They had just made love, and were sitting naked on the crumpled, white sheets. The late afternoon sun streamed in through the small window, making a pool of light on the bare wooden floor.

She untied the string, and removed the brown paper; folded back the tissue.

"Oh, Alejandro!" she cried. "For me?"

"To watch over you, always."

□□□

She came back with the coffee.

"Francesca," he said. He was suddenly tongue-tied.

"Do you still take it without cream and sugar?"

"Yes, thank you."

She put the coffee down in front of him. Poured herself a cup. Added a little cream, and took a seat opposite him.

"I think the last time we took coffee together was up in Taos, at that little corner coffee-shop. That must have been toward the end of summer in 1943. Do you remember what a cold day it was? They had those very early snows that year."

"I remember."

They drank their coffee.

"Francesca," he began again. "I came to apologize—" He searched for the words. "—for the callous way I turned my back on everything we had—that summer. It was unforgivable."

She said nothing.

"Are you married? Do you have children?" he blurted out before he could take the words back.

"No. Not married. I do have a son, Mariano. He's all grown up now."

She did not offer any more information. There was a long silence.

Come on, Alejandro, he thought.

"I am so, so sorry, Francesca."

It was hopelessly inadequate.

"You don't have to be, Alejandro. And I stopped being hurt and angry years—decades ago. Life goes on, and I have been blessed in many ways."

He was about to say something when there was a tap at the front door, and a man's voice called out: "Are you busy, mama? Can you spare a moment?"

A tall man of about fifty entered the room.

"Oh, I beg your pardon! Sorry, mama, I didn't know you had company. I'll come back later."

"No, it's all right, Mariano. There's someone I want you to meet—an old friend from way back. Alejandro Jaramillo. Alejandro—my son, Mariano."

Alejandro stood up and shook hands with the tall, good-looking man. Stared at the face. The incredibly blue eyes.

"Good to meet you," he managed to say.

"Mama," Mariano said, turning to Francesca, "I brought you the letter. Won't you cast an eye over it? I would just like to hear your opinion before it goes off. I'm sorry, Alejandro. This must seem very rude. I have to post this early tomorrow."

209

Alejandro made a gesture with his hand. "Not at all," he managed to say. He was struggling to sound normal. He was far from feeling it.

While the two of them were discussing the letter, Alejandro took in the tall frame, the so familiar profile. Surely not! Not that!

Mariano was standing in front of him, saying something. Alejandro stood up, and mumbled an apology—something about wool-gathering.

"I said it's very good to meet you, Alejandro."

He turned to his mother.

"Sorry I interrupted. I'll let you know the result."

The front door closed.

"I didn't know he was coming, or I would have warned you. I would have asked him to wait until this evening."

"Are you telling me what I think you are?"

"Yes."

"Mariano is my son?"

"Yes."

He looked at her. He was almost in tears.

"Why didn't you tell me?"

"I have never been one to shirk responsibility for my actions, Alejandro. You chose your work. I wasn't about to come and whine to you."

She said it matter-of-factly.

"I have had a good life. I have a wonderful son, and two very bright grandsons—oh, yes, of course! You are a grandfather! Mariano is married. A lovely woman. She has been like a daughter to me."

She gave a laugh.

"That angel you gave me," she said, pointing toward the doorway, "has been extremely dedicated. I have never wanted for anything. I must thank you."

Must thank him, he thought—for what? All the years that he was being a second parent to Salvador, his own son was fatherless. The image from his dream came back to him. The angels falling into the abyss. The shadows. The black mare. He had thought it was about Octavia. But she was only a trigger—there were so many similarities. No. Not only a trigger. But in truth, this had nothing to do with her. In what part of his heart or mind was he aware of what he had done? And why had it become conscious—now? Why now? Why not forty—no, fifty years ago? Then he would have been able to do something. To make it right. This was a cruel punishment indeed, and justly so—to see his folly when it was far too late to undo it. A punishment you deserve, Alejandro, he thought.

"Did you ever marry?" he asked. "You said that you are not married now, but—"

"No. I never married. I never wanted to marry anyone—anyone else, that is. And then, one day, suddenly you are old, and there are different priorities. My two grandsons. They are such gifted boys. The older one is studying design. He wants to design jewelry. The younger one is still at school, but carving must be in the blood somewhere. He wants to be a santero."

"And financially—how have you managed?"

He did not want to think of her facing being a mother—an unwed mother—at the age of twenty, twenty-one; going through pregnancy, which should have been a joyous time, alone. And the birth.

"My parents were very understanding. They gave me this house, and paid for all of Mariano's education. They just adored him. I worked for an interior decorator. Very interesting work. I learned so much from him."

Alejandro looked around the room again, and compared it to his own functional but rather loveless living arrangement. His studio was full of the energy of his angels. But where were his demons? Hidden, you idiot.

The rest of the house had received no attention. Not even curtains! The occasional sweep and dust. That was all. He saw his commitment in a new and frightening light—saw that he had been hiding behind it. He had served the angels, but he had not served his life. That would have taken far greater courage.

He felt like an impostor. The wise Alejandro. So many people loved him, looked up to him. The Angel Man.

If only they knew.

The Confessional

Alejandro sat in the small confessional cubicle of the Las Madres Church. He had last sat there as a boy, shortly after his confirmation. He could not remember what he had confessed that day; nothing memorable, he was sure. All he wanted then was to get back to his angels.

So you thought you could make it alone, did you, with no guiding discipline; that you, of all people, were beyond such things? And where, pray, oh arrogant one, are all your angels now?

Alejandro sat, elbows on knees, his head in his hands, while a litany of questions and harsh thoughts assailed him. Finally he sat up.

"Bless me, father, for I have sinned."

He fell silent once more. The priest said nothing.

"I am an arrogant fool. And I have fooled so many people. The worst of it is that I have fooled myself."

He paused.

"I don't know just when this began; just when it was that my youthful innocence and enthusiasm became calcified—hardened into self-satisfaction." He bent his head and stared at his shoes, deep in thought. "Maybe it was always there?"

It was a question.

The priest said nothing.

"I was always so certain of my path. My destiny." Alejandro made a gesture of desperation. "It must be fifty years—well, forty at the very least—that my life has been a lie."

Alejandro looked toward the curtain behind which the priest sat, as if begging for comfort of some kind, but the priest maintained his silence.

"I thought I was living a committed life—committed to my angels; to my promise that I made when I was ten years old. And on the face of it, I have been just that. But I have denied the world in doing so. I have turned my angels into idols. I have seen my own image reflected in them, and I have not truly seen all the people who love me. I have not been true to what I thought I held sacred. I have been so blinded by what I saw as my calling that I have not seen what was right in front of my face."

Again Alejandro looked toward the curtain.

"Are you there, father?"

"I am listening, Alejandro."

Alejandro sat, agitatedly rubbing his clenched fists back and forth across his faded denim jeans. At last he summoned up his courage.

"I have a son, father; and two grandsons, one of whom wants to be a santero. And there is a woman whom I loved one summer, fifty years ago. And then, without any consideration for her feelings, I left her—dropped her, to tell the truth, for my angels. I don't even remember what I said—or indeed whether I said anything at all. It never even entered my head to ask her how she felt. I was so self-obsessed. I have no memory of our parting."

The words came out in a rush. Alejandro pushed against the sides of the small cubicle, as if to prevent them from closing in on him.

"I did not know she was pregnant. With our child; our son."

There was a long silence.

"Would your choices have been different, had you known?"

Rafael's voice was soft but clear.

Alejandro paused to consider this. What would he have done? Married her? Had a family life? And what of his promise to carve all the angels in The Heavenly Host? Could he have done both, and honored each commitment truly?

"I would have married her, of course," he said, "but I have no idea how I would have managed."

"I seem to remember you telling me that a commitment to an impossible task did not mean that you would have to complete it—only that you would not abandon it. I don't remember hearing anything being said about the need for exclusivity with the angel-carving."

The priest paused to consider.

"I think there are two issues here that need to be teased apart. One is your pledge to carve the angels as an act of service—a promise. The other is the need to examine your motives in doing this. Have they changed over time?"

Of course they had. Alejandro sat back on the bench, and considered. Just when did everything change? He couldn't mark a specific time; an event. It had happened slowly, so slowly that he had not noticed the changes. But now, he realized, he didn't know who he was any more.

"I think it was when the galleries began to collect the angels. I was flattered. My angels were now fetching extraordinary prices. They were in demand. And I sold out. I became a factory—the angels, a commodity."

The priest was quiet.

"I am going to marry Francesca—if she will have me."

Alejandro faced the curtain, and knelt on the small cushion.

"Will you bless me, father?"

The familiar words from his boyhood felt like a soothing balm. Alejandro wept.

Dream

I am back in the dream—searching for the black mare. In my hand I carry the leather bag which holds all my wood-carving tools.

The dirt road stretches out in front of me. There is no sign of the black mare. The road crumbles beneath my feet. Again I retrace my footsteps. Once again I find myself at the crossroad. I try the other roads, but again the four roads roll up like parchment and blow away in the wind. Once again the tall being approaches, and I recognize the dark Archangel Michael, the Angel of Death. The angel points to the abyss. I am standing on the narrow strip of rock, sharp as a flint-stone. I am terrified that I will slip and fall into the abyss. Now angels begin to fall past me. Each angel holds a star. My bag of tools becomes heavier and heavier. The angels drop their stars, and reach out their arms to me. I want to reach out to them, but now both my hands are holding the bag. And now the bag of tools falls from my grasp, and bursts open. All the tools fall out and away. There is no sign of the black mare. I feel my heart breaking inside me. The sky is full of blue fire. The abyss is full of shadows. I see the Archangel Michael beckon to me.

In his sleep, Alejandro cried out. The bedclothes were a tangle of sheet and blanket, slipping off the bed, but the dream would not let him go.

I hear someone calling my name. Over and over. I want to answer, but my mouth will not shape the words. And now I see the black mare, galloping toward the abyss. I try again to call out. I try to run and stop her, but my legs are rooted to the ground. I hear the Archangel Michael laughing.

Alejandro woke from sleep with a sense of dread. His cheeks were wet with tears. Dawn light was coming through the open window. He smelt the earthy scent of the dew-wet desert, and the familiar, tangy aroma of the juniper bushes. But his world was not the same.

Octavia

She lay still—looking up at the ceiling, feeling sleep fall back into night. Something was different—something very wrong. Pain! The pain was back. Not the familiar, dull ache that she had disciplined herself to push to the back of her consciousness. Now a sharp, cutting stab in her lower back. What was happening?

Octavia moved her head and neck from side to side. Nothing there. She attempted to sit up. Gave an involuntary cry. Fell back onto the pillows.

From the kitchen, where she was making coffee, Georgia heard the cry and came running.

"What has happened, Octavia?"

"I don't know. I can't sit up. The pain is back."

Tears of shock or panic on her cheeks.

"Oh, mama! Not again! Not all over again! I can't bear it!"

"Don't move. Just lie still. I will phone the hospital, and leave a message for Doctor Limón to call us when he gets in. Sebastián left early to go to Albuquerque. If we need to go to the hospital, we will have to request an ambulance."

Georgia pushed her hair back off her face.

"What am I thinking? I will order it now. The sooner we get you there, the better."

She tried to gather her thoughts.

"Let's see. I will call Sofia and ask her to take my place, checking the goods for Las Madres. Oh, and yes! Sister Piadosa is interviewing the new nun. I will speak to her as well."

Octavia turned her head to her mother.

"Would you also let Kristiyan know what has happened?"

"Of course, my sweetheart." She turned to go. "I'll only be a minute."

□□□

Octavia sat very straight at her work-table. The new surgical corset, which had been fitted after her manipulation under anesthetic, was designed to protect her unstable lumbar vertebrae from slipping and pressing on the nerve. The surgeon was very reluctant to operate again, hoping that in time the body would correct itself.

"No lifting or sudden turning. If you need to reach down for something, let your legs do the work, not your back. And don't let up on all the exercises that you have been shown. There is no short cut to recovery. You will have to work hard at it. And keep walking."

"Do I have to sleep in this thing? I can't believe anyone could manage a wink with all these straps and hooks."

"We have a slightly less invasive one for sleeping. Remember, Octavia," he said, seeing her grimace, "this is a crucial time. If we can just give your body time to heal itself without any more interference on our part, it will be a blessing."

Journal Entry 12

My mind will not focus on this work. Too much going on inside me, and all around. Things are moving too fast. I have scrapped all my beadwork designs. I wonder what the connection is between stars and wild things—for me. I feel as if something is falling to earth; like the stars. I don't even know what I mean by that. I only know—can feel so deeply—my connection to wild things, and to everything that is happening on the planet. Wilderness is shrinking. Where will all the wild creatures go? Look at what is happening to these wild horses. Sometimes I think that we humans are spreading like a cancer over the planet, destroying more and more wilderness and driving more and more species over the brink.

Journal Entry 13

I feel remarkably unsexy in this corset. Never thought I would say such a thing. Kristiyan is, as ever, so cheerful about it.

"Think how far you would have to look to find another beautiful woman so well-protected. It is almost medieval!"

In spite of all of the frantic activity, the excitement and success of the concert for the horses—and not least my feelings for Kristiyan—I am looking for stillness; a return to my inner solitude.

I still have the image in my head, from my dream of the naked woman in the desert, and the bright star overhead. Is it calling to me? Guiding me? Is this what the white wolf follows?

Maybe that is what I love about stars: that unchanging stillness. And yet, I have changed. The stars are not enough. What a line. It sounds like the title of some trashy love story! But it is, nevertheless, true. I feel as if the earth has claimed me. Maybe I have finally fallen to earth from my star. What does it ask of me—or is it the dark earth that calls? Don't ever speak of this to anyone, Octavia. They will think you are quite mad.

Journal Entry 14

I am over the moon! Sebastián has just given me the most precious gift. It has come in its original box. I can't believe it! It is a rosary, carved by one of the great Zuni grandmother carvers on request from my grandfather—Sebastián's father, Antonio, whom he never met—and given to Magdalena, my grandmother, on the evening he asked her to marry him. And—every bead is a carved animal. The card inside—I can hardly bear to hold it—says: "So that your beloved animals will be close to you always—and in your prayers. Tonio."

Such a treasure. Sebastián says I look just like her. Oh, I do hope so!

Ah! I know where I am going with the beadworks. I am going to place wild animals, standing at the edge of desert landscapes; edge of the world places; apocalyptic landscapes that are both dead and beautiful—the way bones are beautiful. I want to make art that disturbs people; that is a statement of protest against the way the world is so blindly heading—do we not see what we are doing? But, at the same time, I want to make images of beauty. I feel as if I have come home.

The New Frame

Octavia sat in front of the beadwork-frame that Gregorio had adjusted for her. It was now higher, with the fabric stretched vertically.

"Will you be comfortable when you reach behind for the needle?" he asked. He had just delivered the altered frame up to the house for Octavia to inspect. "See, here—I have put the frame on a swivel, so that you can turn it without having to bend forward or turn yourself."

"Gregorio, you are such a genius. However did you work that out?"

Octavia gave him one of her smiles.

"When you get to my age, Octavia, you have time to sit and think about such things. It is one of the great gifts of growing older: you have time."

Octavia was testing all the screws that tightened and loosened the two big rollers which held the fabric.

"Oh, wait! Wait! I have a needle somewhere here—where did I put it?—oh, here it is. Let me try."

Gregorio watched closely as she put an imaginary bead onto the fabric, pushed the needle through to the back, swiveled the frame and retrieved it, placed it once more into the cloth, swiveled it back—and she had the needle once more.

"It is perfect, Gregorio! Oh, I want to begin work today!"

She moved the frame from front to back, back to front—and again.

"Now here is something," she said thoughtfully. "I have often thought about the effect of light on beads, and I've wondered how I would begin to explore this; but now you have supplied an answer. I know that beads appear to change their color, texture and brilliance when they are set at different angles to the light. It is almost as if the image moves. This is going to give me an opportunity to work with light as a vital component in my work with beads."

She smiled up into his face, and he beamed with pleasure.

"Shall I take it up to your studio for you, or...?"

He hesitated, knowing that no one ever went into her room.

"I think leave it here, thanks. I want to show Sebastián and mama when they come in—and Kristiyan when he gets back from rehearsal."

She stroked the smoothly sanded sides of the frame. "How beautifully you have made it. It feels like silk. Thank you a thousand times, Gregorio."

She took his work-roughened hand in her slim, brown one, and held it to her cheek.

"You have always been so good and patient with me, Gregorio—even when I least deserved it. This means the world to me. I can't begin to thank you enough."

"There now," he said. "Your happiness is all the thanks I need, Octavia. It is so good to see you..."

He hesitated, not sure if he should go on.

"I think you have come home to yourself," he said, holding her hand in both of his. "That is good to see."

"I have something I want to show you! Close your eyes, and follow me."

Octavia wheeled her chair into the kitchen, Kristiyan following—his hand on the back-rest. She came to a stop.

"There! Now you can open your eyes."

Kristiyan stood in front of the new frame.

"Just touch it. Feel the wood. Isn't it lovely?"

She watched as his hands and fingers explored the intricate wooden cogs that held the rollers in position.

"Gregorio altered it for me so that I won't need to bend forward."

"It is beautiful, Octavia; so beautifully made. Gregorio is to be congratulated."

He turned to her to say something, but she was already speaking.

"Oh, Kristiyan! I want to begin working right away. And look. I have a surprise."

Octavia pulled the small box out of a pocket, and put it down on the table. "Sebastián gave it to me." She opened the box and pulled back the tissue-paper; removed the card.

"My grandfather gave this to my grandmother on the night he proposed to her."

Octavia lifted out the rosary—the pale, iridescent beads gleaming in the late afternoon light—and passed it to Kristiyan.

"Every bead is an animal of the Southwest—my animals again! Something is speaking to me so clearly. And see all the doves that mark the Mysteries."

"It is very lovely, Octavia," he said, examining each bead closely. "Why do you say something is speaking to you?"

"Well, first you gave me all the silver animals for my stick, and now more animals have come with this; and I am reading such a fascinating book, and I have been dreaming into the work I want to do. So much is coming together. I am so excited."

She paused, and looked up at him.

"Can I ask you a favor?"

"Of course. But first there is something—"

"Will you help me take this up to my studio?"

"Sure. Right away, but—"

"Please say yes!"

"You have stolen my line."

"Yes, I have—but I mean it." She made a gesture of supplication with her hand. "And will you carry it in for me? Please."

"Carry it in—you mean take it into your studio?"

"Yes."

"But no one goes into your room. Are you sure?"

"Yes." She took his hand. "I would like you to be the first person to come with me into my studio."

Kristiyan flushed.

"There is really very little to see; a few sketches, and one beadwork. I haven't finished the other one yet—and anyway, I have changed direction. I suppose I must complete it, but—oh! I'll tell you all that later. Can we take the frame up now, or are you busy?"

"Not busy, no," he said, bemused. "I do have something I want to share with you. Can you manage the wheelchair on the path?"

"Gregorio, bless him, has laid a smooth path between the stones. I'll follow you."

Kristiyan lifted the frame. "It's surprisingly heavy!"

"Yes. Gregorio chose heavy wood so that it would stand firm."

"Right. Here we go."

At the door, Octavia took out the key and unlocked it. She flashed a smile at Kristiyan, and took his free hand.

He left the frame outside, and accompanied her into the room.

He stood still for a moment.

"I thought the room was black," he said. "Am I confused?"

"It was black. I painted it just before I had the accident. It was like a new beginning." She gave a shrug. "Some beginning."

Kristiyan stood surveying the room, marveling at the effect of the painted walls.

"Am I really the only person who has ever been into this room?"

"Yes."

The late afternoon sun was slanting through the high windows. Overhead, through the skylight, they could see the evening sky just beginning to turn pink. The room itself had taken on the quality of a desert sunset. There was a sense of space and stillness. The walls seemed to recede, allowing anything placed against them to stand out.

He took in the three sets of shelves full of small bead-bottles, arranged according to color and size. Beyond this he saw a collection of Zuni carvings—many of the animals of the Southwest; found objects: bones, stones, shells; small, gnarled pieces of weathered desert wood.

There were two easels. One had a large sheet of paper clipped to it, with many sketches of a howling wolf: the position of the body; the angle of the head; details of the eyes and mouth. The other, like a flip chart, had dozens of sheets hanging down its back, with the front sheet showing the image of an exquisitely drawn dead tree in a barren landscape. On the far side of the room, a beadwork was tacked to the wall. He would look at it later. Another work lay unfinished on the bench. A line of rough sketches which, to Kristiyan, looked rather abstract, occupied a space on the wall beyond the bead collection.

He was particularly drawn to a small painting of a white wolf that was hanging on the wall, close to her work-chair. He stood for a long time, examining the expression of the face. He remembered seeing a Russian icon at an exhibition in Saint Petersburg, showing a saint—was it Saint Peter the Lame?—with the head of a wolf. He remembered it having the same expression in the eyes.

He stood, allowing the energy of the room to come to him. No one but Octavia had ever been in this room for—how long was it? Over ten years. And now she had invited him into her very private space. He felt as if he had entered a sacred place—like a church. Or a hidden chapel. The room had the same feeling of presence.

He was surprised that there was not more finished artwork on display. He would ask her later.

He noticed, with interest, the red angel high up on the wall, facing east.

"Is that one of Alejandro's angels? It looks so different from the many I have seen. Red!"

"Yes, he brought it as a gift when I was a baby. Everyone thinks it is rather strange, but I love it. I have put it there so that it will see the sunrise every morning."

"And what do you make of the color?"

"I don't know yet. But Alejandro said the angel demanded it; so I trust that. I think for me the red brings a touch of something—almost pagan."

"A very earthy angel!"

"Yes. Sort of—elemental."

"I suppose you know that to many people this conversation would seem beyond strange."

Octavia laughed.

"I think it is my ancient, pagan ancestors that speak through me. I have always thought things that others considered to be very odd."

"How does that make you feel?"

"It used to make me feel lonely. Now I value it above all things."

He pulled up a chair so that he could face her. They sat in silence.

"I have something for you," he said at last. "I think perhaps this is just the right time and place to listen to it."

She looked at him questioningly.

"A friend who has recently returned from Argentina told me about it." He took the CD out of his pocket and handed it to her.

Octavia looked at it.

"Misa Criolla," she read. "A Mass for Latin America."

"Can I play it for you? It is part of your history. I hope you will like it. It is like no Mass I have ever heard."

"In what way?"

"It is a Mass set to the rhythms of Hispano-America. You have this in your blood, from both your grandfathers—just what you were talking about. Such a rich mix."

He crossed the room, and inserted the disc into the player. Adjusted the volume. Stood there. Listening.

Octavia, with the rosary still in her hands, sat—her eyes closed, listening to the woman's powerful, guttural voice. She could feel its power and beauty resonating inside her. This, she thought, is what I want my work to be like. And that voice. She could hear something ancient in its timbre that was arousing; sensual.

She read from the booklet that the singer was part American Indian, part Hispanic. Was it the ancient Indian sound that stirred her blood so—or the mix of the two very different cultures? It was something she had recognized in the Huichol beadwork as well: a place where wildness, contained by art, becomes both erotic and spiritual.

She closed her eyes once more. She saw high mountains, disappearing into mist; wide plains. And wild horses. And now she stood in a high place, looking out over the Atacama Desert—endless space, with all the variations of dry and bleach; and sudden, deep shadow. She felt herself floating on the rich sounds of music. Her body ached with the need to express this earthy, spiritual beauty in her own medium. How she had longed for this. Would she ever be able to bring it forth? It felt so large—something inside her, which had been there since ever she could remember, demanding a presence in the world. She felt tears from such a mix of feelings and—what? A prayer, perhaps, that something would take her into that magnificent country?

Kristiyan came back to her. Took her hands and, pulling her up gently, gathered her into his embrace. As the last notes died away, he brushed away her tears, and kissed her.

"I love you so much, Octavia. You are beautiful."

He kissed her again.

Octavia could feel the passionate response rising up within her.

"Oh, Kristiyan," was all she could say.

And then she let his kiss take her.

Journal Entry 15

Kristiyan came into my studio today! It was good. So good. I could feel the change in the room the instant he stepped over the threshold. It became more spacious.

I am thrilled with the desert walls. Now they—and I—have work to do. Some time last week Sebastián read me one of Rilke's poems—Oh You Darkness. I love the last lines, and I can feel them when I enter my room: "And it is possible that a great power is moving near me. I have faith in night." I do feel as if I am about to step into my true life. I find it strange to receive this poem now that the black has gone. Maybe I couldn't really see the night with the black all around me.

And the frame is ready. Kristiyan carried it in for me. I need to begin a bead-work right away. I can see the image hanging in front of my eyes. It will be for Alejandro and Francesca—for their new house. Santiago told me all about Alejandro's black mare. How strange that we share this image. I can feel her presence as if she lived inside me. The black mare, and wide-open space. I know just how she feels. How I love this sensual image: the sculpted curves of the desert. Bright moonlight, and shadows. And the sleek swiftness of her form—her wild mane and tail streaming out and away from her like a night wind. And reaching out ahead of her, the aura of her wildness, drawing her—and me—onward. I can see every detail of it.

Kristiyan's comments about the red angel have set me thinking. I wonder—why a red angel?

A New Design

"I want you to design it just the way you want it."

They were surveying the large plot of ground next to Alejandro's studio. The farmer had been more than willing to sell a corner of land for which he had no use. Now they were feeling into the fall of it, and the magnificent, uninterrupted view across grazing-land, to the trees which marked the start of the foothills. From there the inter-weaving hills grew more and more ethereal with elevation and distance, so that they appeared to be floating on the soft mist.

To his dismay, Alejandro found himself visualizing the black mare. This was the corner of the field where he used to stand, drinking in her wildness. Stop it, Alejandro, he told himself. What is the matter with you?

"Of course it must face this way—all this quiet space." Francesca took his arm. "I can't believe this is happening! Oh, Alejandro. How is anyone ever allowed to feel so happy?"

Alejandro looked into her bright face. God, man!—you are such a mess, he thought. But he was thinking the same thing. So late. It had come to both of them so late in life. I have been unforgivably slow in waking up. Am I awake now? Will there ever be time to make amends for this?

"I want to give you so much, Francesca. Everything I have. Think of anything that will make you happy; anything that will make this a home—a place where Mariano and María will be happy to come and visit. And the boys. I want to hear all about what Roán is going to do; what his dreams are.

"And I want to teach Nicol everything I know about what it means to be a santero. It is not just a matter of painting or carving—no matter how skilled he may be. It has to be personal—a way of life. A deep communion."

You are such a phony, he thought, but he carried on doggedly.

"Does he believe utterly in the work, do you think? Does he have a passion for—a personal connection with the stories? And even then, he must go to university and study anthropology, like the great Charlie Carrillo. He must learn everything about the history of this rich culture: the symbolism of numbers and colors."

"There is a man who supplies the interior decorator I used to work for with folk art. He uses an art piece around which to build a color scheme."

Alejandro put an arm around her.

"I think there is a difference. You would not buy a santo to match your drapes or cushion-covers. Santos are not the same as folk art!"

"Is there such a difference? There are museums for folk art. It is held in high esteem. It also tells us about our culture; our customs."

"True. Folk art is seen as fine art, and it is valuable as an account of culture and customs, as you say. But the work of a santero is considered to be sacred work. Santos are sacred, not just art—even fine art. It may be a fine line at times, but it is an important one. Any santero worth his salt would agree. You would buy a santo because of its deep significance for you."

"So what does this make you?"

Alejandro laughed grimly. "My dear, that is a question I have been asking myself for some time now. When I began, I would say I was some kind of santero. And then, somewhere along the line, I lost the plot."

"What happened?"

He laughed again. "Fame."

"Fame? What's wrong with that?"

Alejandro gave a rueful grimace.

"Nothing intrinsically. But it's what it can do to you. Fame and money, if you are not wide-awake, may seduce you. I became a salesman; a very successful one. This is where the preparation for the work, the study—I would say the reverence for it—is essential. And this is where it is good to have a mentor to challenge you. I thought I didn't need one. But it is very clear to me now how arrogant that was."

He looked out to the far boundary fence; to the hills, almost expecting the black mare to come galloping over toward them. Wanting her to come. What was it with him? He looked back at Francesca, remembering how the long, sleek mass of her black hair would fall over her face when she bent to kiss him—when they made love. And now, here they were—both white-haired; both in their very late years, and all that life they could have shared—gone.

"I began my work when I was only a boy. I never went to college. I was seen as this strange man who carved angels."

"Why strange?"

"I suppose because no one else did that. And I did it obsessively. I had made a promise—a commitment to the work. But I see now that my life was out of balance."

"Would it have made such a difference if you had a mentor?"

"It would have been good for me to have someone, bringing me down to earth. I was so sure of myself. I thought I didn't need anyone."

He turned to her. Sudden tears in his eyes.

"Oh, my dear—how is it that you can forgive me for such blindness? I am such an old fool. How could I not even have seen what was right before my eyes? In my hands—"

He stopped. Looked away, out at the hills. This is what hell must be like, he thought. Finally aware of all your folly, and unable to escape it.

"How is it that I never valued any of the gifts that were given to me? Especially your love. And even my angels."

He paused again.

"Arrogance! Pure, unexamined arrogance!" He kicked the dirt. "Will you ever forgive me?" He looked into her eyes. "Will my angels forgive me?"

For an answer, Francesca took his arm. "Do not be so hard on yourself, Alejandro. We all have such things in our lives. Why should you be different? Come, let us take a walk around our new estate."

ooo

He was dreaming again. Empty desert.
Now the black mare is galloping across the desert sand.
In his sleep, Alejandro groaned.
Something is wrong. Something is missing.

He turned over in his sleep, and in so doing shed the blankets. This woke him. He lay still, the dream in front of his eyes. He felt sick.

He got out of bed. Threw on a dressing-gown, and went into the small kitchen. Switched on the light. Put the kettle on for tea. When it was made, he crossed the room. Sat, looking out of the window, holding the warm cup close as if for comfort.

What was missing? What was the black mare showing him in the dream?

He rinsed the cup, turned out the light and went back to bed.

But the dream was there, waiting for him.

My legs will not move. I watch the black mare gallop away from me. Now I can no longer see her.

In front of me stands the Angel of Death.

Raho's Visit

The tall man stood in the doorway of Sebastián's office.

He was well over six foot, even with the slight stoop. His long, white hair was braided down his back. His face was clean-shaven. He wore a loose white shirt, blue jeans and sandals. Around his neck, a strand of dark wooden beads, shiny from much handling. He stood firm for all that he carried a cane in his left hand.

His gaze took in the greying head, the papers that lay scattered about the desk in untidy piles; took in the thick ledger, the small calculator and the cup of coffee, untouched.

"Is this the way you greet an old friend?"

Sebastián turned around—then leapt up, uttering a shout.

"Raho!"

He threw his arms around the man, and gave him a fierce hug. "Is this real? Oh, how wonderful it is to see you! Unannounced! What brings you here? Oh! This is such a great surprise! Wait! Let me call Georgia!"

He shouted out of the window to where Georgia was standing, talking to Gregorio.

"Come and see what has blown in with the south wind!"

He turned to Raho, his face beaming.

"Come! Let's leave this dismal room, find some shade and have something to drink. You can tell me the whole story. You can't just pop up out of nowhere, and not explain yourself. How long is it?" He counted on his fingers. "Good heavens! It must be all of ten—fifteen years. Whatever the number, it's too long. Much too long."

He turned to Georgia as she entered the room.

"Georgia! Look who is here. I don't think you have met." He laid a hand on the tall man's arm.

"Raho—my wife, Georgia."

He turned to face her.

"Proceed with caution, my dear. You can drown in those eyes—or lose yourself in them! This man is not to be trusted for one second. He will turn your mind and your life upside-down with a gesture. You have been warned!" He laughed.

"Will you have some iced tea? A glass of wine? Of course, I was forgetting. Do you have some of that strange herbal concoction with you?"

Raho smiled. "Iced tea will do very well, thank you."

Georgia brought the tea and sat for a while, listening to them talk about times past; about Father Octavio, the much-loved priest who now lay buried in the camposanto, and about the eccentricities of Raho, his closest friend.

He and Octavio had both entered the priesthood at the same time, but before long Raho left to become a Buddhist with strong Zen tendencies, while Octavio, just before his death, put off his priest's robes and died a barefoot man.

"Do you remember all the fuss it caused among the local priests?"

"Indeed, I remember that circus well. And what about the following one—involving that rather deranged French priest who came to replace Octavio? I heard all about that. I would have given anything to witness it! Poor man. He had no idea of what he was up against."

"Nevertheless, he made things extremely painful during his brief stay." Sebastián gave a chuckle. "I think it was María's hair, flowing down the chapel aisle, that finally finished him."

"And don't forget the weeping, wooden eyes of the figure of Christ—I heard all about that too!"

She listened, fascinated, as they spoke of the history of The Adobe.

Finally she rose and left the two men talking, saying she had promised Gregorio that she would not be long.

"So what does bring you here? Where are you staying?"

"I am staying with an old friend of Father Octavio's—Father Ramón. We used to spend such pleasant times together when we were young. He has come home from South America, where he established a small mission station. He is not well. I don't know how long I will be staying."

He paused.

"And I came in response to your call."

"But, I—"

"Yes, you did. I have been very patient with you, waiting for the time to come."

"The time? What time?"

Raho raised both his arms, upward and outward, as if inviting heaven to speak.

"You must only pick a fruit when it is ripe—that is the secret. Not over-ripe, not green—or it will never have its full flavor. There is an exquisite timing needed for such things—don't you agree?"

He fixed Sebastián with the direct fullness of his extraordinary blue gaze.

"Pick it too early, and the green fruit will not ripen. It will shrivel." He smiled. "Pick it too late, and the energy is already turning into something else. A certain moment—perhaps I should say a critical moment of soul—has passed. The fruit is already dying into new life."

"I suppose you are aware that I have not the slightest idea what you are talking about!"

"I am talking about picking fruit."

"Yes—right," Sebastián said. "But why?"

"Ah!" Raho leaned back in his chair, and took a long draught of his iced tea.

Sebastián waited.

There was a long silence.

"Well?" Sebastián asked at last.

"Do you want the long version or the short version?"

"Let's start with the short version."

Raho leaned forward, and stared deep into Sebastián's eyes.

"Wake up, Sebastián!"

It was not a shout. Indeed, the voice was almost quiet, but Sebastián felt as if he had been struck across the face. He sat up straight.

"Get yourself out of that dreary little room, with all those stupid bits of paper. Leave this place to all the many capable hands that are here. Step off the cliff! Go and do what you have been avoiding—your whole life! You can find excuses forever, if that is what your game is. Then you can feel sorry for yourself. You can pretend not to know what is going on. But you do know! You know bloody well. And take that lovely woman with you, before you both die from the weight of your unlived lives!"

"Raho! How can you come here after all this time, and pretend to know what is happening in our lives? You know nothing about what we have come through; what has been achieved! And all this talk about fruit. You remind me of Father Octavio. He used to speak about apple trees in much the same way. What's with you guys that you are so hooked on fruit-trees?"

"It is called a metaphor," said Raho, smiling.

"Well, I am speaking about important things that have really happened, right here—things that have changed our lives; that have made demands. Not fruit-trees!"

For answer, Raho lifted his cane, and with one gesture swept all the glasses and dishes, and the tall glass jug, off the table and to the ground where they smashed, leaving dark patches of moisture between the fragments of glass and china.

Sebastián leapt to his feet.

"Raho!" he shouted. "What on earth has got into you? Look what you have done. All these things broken! Why?"

"Sit down, Sebastián. Sit down and listen to me."

He leaned forward, and fixed his stare on the younger man.

"These are things, Sebastián! Only things. Just as all those pieces of paper, crowding out your life, are things. You can sort them all out, and tomorrow there will be more. And the next day. Do you think you will finally get to the end of them? Do you think that is when your life will begin?"

His voice was quiet, but Sebastián felt as if he too had been struck with the cane.

"Don't you see?" He paused. "Of course you don't. It is not important how I came to be here. There is just this one thing—you cannot see yourself any more. Not in this web of earnest doing. Get out. Not next week! Not tomorrow! Today! Pack a small bag: jeans, jackets, your writing materials, Georgia's easel, paints, whatever—just the essentials. You can buy what you need along the way. But get in the car and leave. Follow the road. Don't worry about time or maps or bookings. Drive on until all your meaningless chatter leaves you. Until you finally find the silence inside your-selves again. And then drive on further—and on. Get lost on some byroad. The world will support you. Just go."

Seeing that Sebastián was about to protest, he added:

"Do you think you are indispensable? That the world will grind to a halt without you? No one is indispensable. If you die tomorrow, who will miss you? Of course those close to you will grieve—a year, maybe two; three. And then other lives will move into the space that you leave. People die. Sometimes they are missed; are mourned. And then history sweeps them up. The world shakes her feathers, and settles back into being. Some may be given a line; a page. Maybe even a chapter. But it is a very big book. What is significant about our lives, and to those around us, is how we lived. This is the most powerfully creative or destructive legacy we can leave. What impacts on those close to us—or on the world, if we are a high-profile figure—is the truth and impeccability of our lives."

He smiled.

"Above all things, it matters that we live in integrity with ourselves and those around us—and," he stressed the word, "and that we bring forth all the fruits—the fruits!—of our love, our passion and our imagination. Then we have truly lived."

He paused. "I am off to find Alejandro."

He put a hand on Sebastián's shoulder. "I look forward to our next meeting."

He got up to go.

"If you are still here, of course."

Summer Plans

Sofia pushed her hair off her face, and retied the black ribbon that held back the mass of red curls. She was sitting in the office, waiting for Sister Piadosa and Sister Clemencia, who would be relieving the older woman of many of her duties, to arrive. They were going to discuss all the new developments at The Adobe, and prioritize the most urgent ones. Lucien had gone with Salvador and Reuben to Albuquerque to buy supplies for the music-room, and would be back in the late afternoon.

***

Sister Clemencia was the oldest of four siblings—older than her brother, the next in line, by ten years. She had grown up helping her mother, who was a women's rights activist, with the three younger children. Her father was a distant figure, who was away a lot of the time doing only he knew what, and bringing home very little money at the end of the day.

She was ten when her baby brother was born; twelve when her sister appeared, and fourteen when the youngest child was given into her care.

"I am trusting you with the care of your new brother. Make sure that he is safe always. Don't leave him unattended. That's a good girl."

With both parents away so much of the time, it fell upon the young Clemencia's shoulders to raise the three younger children, learning how to do things as she went along. This she did with great joy—and approval from all three of them—because of her inspired way of turning even the most boring tasks, like dishwashing and bed-making, into a game. The first to finish could choose how he or she wanted to spend the afternoon.

Clemencia remained at home until the youngest had finished his schooling, and gone to college. Then in her early thirties, vowing never to marry, she entered a convent and became a nun. The Adobe was her first position.

***

Sofia straightened herself to ease the ache in her back. She did not remember feeling this tired during her first pregnancy. Maybe she had more time to rest then. Caradoc was now an energetic handful, and although she had help during the day when she was working, there was still his evening bath, supper and quiet play-time. Lucien kept him amused and told him stories while she cooked the evening meal, but the task of putting him to bed and getting him to settle took up to an hour. He was teething now and was, for him, being unusually demanding. Often it was close to midnight when she finally got into bed.

She heard the familiar swish of Sister Piadosa's veil, and stood up to greet the two nuns.

"Hello, sister," she said as she stepped forward to hug the woman who had delivered her as a baby, here at The Adobe.

"And hello, Sister Clemencia—how are you settling into this madhouse? You have arrived just in time for all the changes that seem to be happening—some quite radical."

"My dear, there is nowhere I would rather be. And I love change. It's like spring-cleaning. Things are discovered that have been forgotten, and sometimes never seen."

Sofia took in the new sister's radiant energy; the clear, young face. How old would she be? Not much older than I am. And yet today it was she who felt older; much older.

I wonder if raising children is what makes us feel so old?

"Let's go and sit outside," Sister Piadosa said. "It is such a lovely day. We can take a few chairs, and sit in the shade. I have asked Sister Ana to bring us some iced tea and cookies."

She led the way to the covered cloister, and pulled up three chairs. The three women put their papers down on the table, and sat back.

"Before we begin," said Sister Piadosa, "how are you feeling? Lucien says you have been very tired."

"Oh, not too bad; just back-ache. Caradoc is getting so heavy. Soon I won't be able to lift him."

"Shouldn't be lifting him at all, my dear. Leave that for Lucien, and the rest of us. Sister Ana can't wait to get her hands on him. She loves babies. I will ask her to come and help out in the evenings—no! No objections. It's an order." She smiled.

"And I too would love to have some toddler duty. I come with good credentials," Sister Clemencia said with a laugh. "I raised my three younger siblings, so I know a trick or two."

"You raised three children? From what age?"

"From when they were babies. I was just ten when the first one arrived. My parents were out most of the time—my father working, my mother busy with her activist duties."

"You were ten years old?" Sofia looked at her with growing respect. "How long did you take care of them?"

"I left home when the youngest went to college. Then I entered the convent—and now, here I am. This is my first position."

"And after all that you are still soliciting baby duty! I thought martyrdom had gone out of fashion!"

Sister Clemencia chuckled.

Tea came with cookies, and then they set to work.

First on the list was the blessing of Alejandro and Francesca's new house, and the house-warming party. This would happen in early autumn. Sofia made notes as they discussed it.

Then came all the early preparations for Christmas. That, Sister Piadosa thought to herself, was when The Adobe was always at its busiest, with extra goods and products to be packaged and delivered.

In addition, there were two christenings and a marriage to prepare for, and there were the presents to be distributed to all the local children who attended the school and the clinic. God willing, old Tila, who used to work in the kitchen, would last to see in the New Year.

Then there was the Christmas concert on the day before Christmas Eve. This had been widely advertised, and they anticipated a full house.

Father Rafael would come to conduct an early Christmas Eve Mass in the small adobe chapel, which had been named by the community, when they restored it to its present, humble beauty, La Capilla de Nuestra Señora de Sofia.

Sister Piadosa brought her mind back to the present.

"Do we know how many people are expected to come to the house blessing? We must get an estimate for catering. Alejandro has carved thousands of angels—what if all their owners turn up to see what the Angel Man has been up to?"

She turned to Sister Clemencia, and explained the reference to angels.

"And we must freshen up the chapel. The people who named it must have known that you were coming, Sofia!" Sister Piadosa laughed. "But that was long before my time. I only arrived here in September of 1966, shortly after Sebastián's mother died, and that was two years before you were born. They restored and named the chapel twelve years before that. I have no idea why they chose the name Sofia—maybe Sebastián remembers—but where were we?"

The three women worked until lunchtime. The last event on the agenda, the marriage of Alejandro Jaramillo to Francesca Ortega, would take place in late spring, when the quaking aspens were drawing their horizontal lines of brilliant green through the piñon and ponderosa on the mountains.

"Such a dear man—he says they met at that time of year. I wonder why they never married—then."

***

"I hope I'm going to have enough room left in me for air to sing!"

They were discussing the program for the concert.

"Would you rather choose something less demanding?"

Lucien had written a song that celebrated the inner quiet of the season—the winter snow-storms, the silence of snow; a time for introspection. The song demanded a sustained mood; quiet joy, and the expression of an inner inquiry—not the usual merriment that many associated with Christmas.

"Oh, absolutely not! This baby will just have to take a back seat for one evening. Do you think I am going to pass up such an opportunity? Never!"

But as the weeks went by, and Sofia grew bigger and bigger, it became clear that taking a back seat was the last thing the baby was planning.

"I'm having a scan next week—I was never this size with Caradoc. And look

231

at the rest of me." She flexed an arm muscle. "Not an ounce of fat! This baby is eating me out of house and home."

Salvador and Reuben laughed.

"You know, no one but you will sing this song. It will keep. Perhaps we can re-think the program."

Lucien put an arm around his wife.

"Not on your life!" Sofia said with spirit.

The Blessing

Beneath the simple, carved angel that graced the entrance of their new house, Alejandro and Francesca stood, greeting the steady stream of guests that gathered at the front door for the blessing. The ancient cottonwood, which stood between the house and Alejandro's studio, was shedding the last of its autumn leaves, carpeting the ground with gold and adding a rustling sound to the proceedings.

Everyone from The Adobe had come early to prepare the refreshments, and to set out chairs borrowed for the occasion. The doors of the spacious main room were thrown wide open, showing a porch shaded by latte, and a view of the foothills.

From the size of the gathering it appeared that all the people of Las Madres had come to participate in the house blessing of one of their most loved and legendary sons, who was, at the age of eighty, preparing to marry Francesca Ortega, the love of his youth, in the spring.

Father Rafael stood waiting at the entrance, with the choir of the Las Madres Church and the nuns' choir from La Capilla de Nuestra Señora de Sofia, just as the last out-of-town cars pulled up into the shade.

When everyone was quiet, he began the blessing.

"Estamos reunidos aquií, en esta occasion con el propósito de consagrar esta casa a Dios. Nos regocijamos con esta familia..."

Father Rafael spoke the familiar blessing to the quiet gathering.

"Que así sea, O Dios."

Sister Piadosa thought she had never heard a response more beautiful than the hush of several hundred voices. She turned her head to smile at Alejandro, and was surprised to see tears in his eyes. Such a gentle man.

"Que estas puertas estén siempre abiertas para todas las personas..."

"May the doors of this house be always open to those who need friendship, love, bread, and solace."

What a long time it had taken him to realize how lonely his life had been. Sister Piadosa looked at the beautiful, white-haired woman who was soon to be his bride, and felt a surge of happiness for both of them. But what is time, anyway?

She stood, drinking in the beauty of the evening, and listening to the ethereal voice of Sofia as it soared above the two choirs in a hymn of praise.

To the unsophisticated eyes of the people of Las Madres, let alone to those from the homely dwellings in the valley, the minimalist style of the adobe house was a wonder: the space, the clean lines, the higher than customary walls.

"I remember the old Ortega place. I used to sit on the front porch with her father, Arturo, where that bright serape was tacked onto the wall. Do you remember it? It wasn't Mexican, though people thought it was. He wove it, you know, on that old foot-loom he had. Old! It must have been well over a hundred years old—then! And inside—such a comforting jumble of things." He glanced about him at the absence of clutter.

The two old men followed the large group that was being shown all the rooms of the house, looking about them with a mixture of pride and awe.

"She worked for an interior designer, you know. In Albuquerque."

He was well-informed.

Finally everyone collected on the porch to take some refreshments, and to chat to people they hadn't seen for a while. Francesca's grandchildren poured drinks, and passed snacks to the seated guests. All the younger children spilled out into the farmer's paddock and ran off to talk to a pair of mules, who were viewing the unusual activity with interest.

Octavia sat on a chair, with Kristiyan beside her. On her lap she had a gift for the house, wrapped in brown paper. She stood up when Alejandro and Francesca, with Granuja at his master's heels, came up to speak to them.

"No, my dear. Don't get up. We'll pull up some chairs. Kristiyan, will you have a seat?"

Octavia handed Alejandro and Francesca the gift.

"I hope you like it. It is for the house."

Francesca took a seat, and unwrapped the gift. She stared at the artwork in her lap; then looked up at Alejandro, astonished.

Together they examined the beadwork, marveling at its meticulous detail. At first glance it appeared to be abstract—a subtle interplay of shades of light on a moon-bleached desert, with deep shadows and open space. Looking more closely, Alejandro saw, to his amazement, the black mare—small but perfect in every detail, crafted with the tiniest of shiny, blue-black beads—galloping off into the distance. Around the racing form, Octavia had made an aura of pale gold beads like a halo, but one that reached out ahead of her. It looked to Alejandro as if the mare's wild soul was stretched out in front of her, and as if her form was being drawn forward by it. The image of the horse, although small when compared with the surrounding space, was haunting, and dominated the work. It was, Alejandro thought, strangely erotic. The thought surprised him. He found his eye constantly returning to this form, this passionate flash of life and movement in an empty and static landscape. It was utterly beautiful.

He stared at Octavia.

"My dear, how can we accept this—this—" He searched for the word. "This sacred work of yours?"

He and Francesca both looked at Octavia in wonder.

"It is yours. For the new house. I know it belongs here."

Francesca went over to Octavia, and kissed her.

"I have no words. This is such exquisite work." She examined it closely. "I love the presence of the black horse in all this silence! This is so unique—so powerful. We feel a little overwhelmed by such a gift."

She turned to face Octavia.

"Whatever can I possibly say that will express all that I feel? You are so gifted. I have never seen work like this before. So original. I don't know what else to say except thank you."

She embraced Octavia warmly.

Alejandro had been studying the work, listening with half an ear to the conversation.

"I know the wild horses have become something of a mission for you, but why did you choose this one for me—us?"

He marveled again at the exquisite perfection of it.

"I was speaking to Santiago about the benefit concert, and he told me how you seemed to be praying for one horse in particular—who looked like a black mare—to escape. So I thought I would show you that she was free."

It was night-time. There was no wind. He was alone.

Alejandro sat in his studio amid pieces of wood and wood-chips, half-finished angels and piles of paper covered with sketches and rough notes, two empty coffee-cups, empty biscuit-boxes, a bare light bulb and an ancient and very dusty chili ristra, hanging in one corner. The room was functional. That was all. It needed a good clean; the walls needed painting. The cupboards were stuffed full of a mix of things—mostly rubbish.

Everything was coming together in his life. Soon he would marry the woman he loved, and they would move into the beautiful house they had designed together, and which she had decorated. Why then was he close to tears?

Alejandro looked at his work-worn hands, his chipped nails, with something close to loathing. He was not ready for this—this sudden change. He felt as if he was putting on someone else's clothes. Or like an actor in a play, donning an identity that was not his. How could he go through with this marriage?

He put out the light, and went to bed.

It was waiting for him.

I am standing at the edge of the abyss. Shadows all around me. Flying around me, like black angels.

Now I am walking down some black stone steps. I am at the very bottom of the abyss. In front of me is a pool of black water. I know the water's depth is beyond any measure: it is infinite. I look at the still surface, and see images moving over it; images that float up toward me. The black mare. I see her take that free leap over the paddock fence, and race away. And now, the image of Octavia's face. Her smile. I see black angels, flying like shadows across all the images. And now I see Francesca as a young woman, running with the wind. A small boy sitting in a playground, praying. So many images. The moon. The black night wind in the cottonwoods. And all the time, the angels flying across the images like shadows. I see two small boys, running down an arroyo; a room full of little wooden angels; a night sky full of stars. And I see another image, below all of these, floating up toward me. I lean closer. All the shadows fall away. I am staring at my own face.

Alejandro cried out in his sleep, but he did not wake up.

Everything has vanished. I am standing alone in a vast desert. The sun has set. I begin to walk toward the east. I walk and walk. It is dark, but there is a strange light from the stars. The sky is alight with cold fire.

He woke, feeling cold and stiff. It was late, past midnight, but he was afraid to go back to sleep.

He wandered into his work-room; tidied his work-bench, his chisels; swept the floor. He noticed that some of the chisels were rusty; some needed to be sharpened. He fetched the electric grinding-stone, and some water in the old, cracked cup. He took up the first chisel, removed the chipped edge and made a new, clean bevel, dipping the hot metal into the water frequently to prevent it from losing its temper. He worked on eight chisels in this way. When he was done, he took them over to his chair and began the finer sharpening on the oil-stone. He felt the old familiarity as his fingers held the blade true to the bevel, refining the sharp edge. When he had worked the first chisel for about five minutes, he removed the last scrap of feathered metal with a small, white stone, wiped the chisel with oil, and put it back onto the oily cloth. Picked up the next one.

He worked for an hour, two hours—afraid to go to sleep, where he felt sure the dream was waiting; but eventually his eyes began to close, and he went to bed.

He did not dream—or if he did, he had no recollection of it in the morning.

235

Alejandro woke to the sound of chopping. He knew that his neighbor, Juan, regularly cut away the dead wood at the end of autumn, chopped it into pieces and stored it, ready for winter. He lay, savoring the sounds of activity while enjoying the last five minutes before rising.

In the shower he sang snatches of the solo Sofia had sung at the house blessing. Everything was all right after all.

When he was dressed, he went to the kitchen. Fed Granuja. Made coffee. Gave himself a moment to muse about the dream.

He took his coffee, and went to sit outside in the cool morning air. The sun was not up yet. He could smell the damp desert earth and the fresh tang of piñon, juniper and sage. He felt happy. Almost happy.

But as the morning wore on, he began to feel strangely tearful; sad.

I am about to marry my true love. Everything is working out. Why then am I sad—fearful?

Raho Visits Alejandro

It was midday when he heard a knock at the door.

He opened it to see Raho standing there. For a moment there was silence. Alejandro stared, thinking that perhaps his dream was playing tricks on him. Then, with a bellow of laughter, he stepped forward and embraced the tall man.

"Raho!"

He stepped back again to inspect the slim figure standing in front of him.

"Greetings, Alejandro!"

"This is truly the most wonderful surprise! What brings you here? Have you been to The Adobe—catching up with all that has been happening?"

"Let us just say that I have been channeling Father Octavio. It is so in fashion these days, isn't it, to channel entities from some other dimension? However, his voice is as clear as ever it was."

"But seriously, what does bring you here?"

"Well, I could say the wind was blowing in this general direction."

Alejandro nodded and waited.

"Or perhaps I just wanted to greet old friends."

Silence.

"But in truth it has something to do with a black mare."

Alejandro was suddenly alert. He stared into Raho's blue eyes.

"A black mare?" he said. "What do you know about a black mare?"

"I am hoping that you will tell me."

They went to sit in the studio. Alejandro moved the grinding-stone and the cracked cup, and pulled two chairs to the small table. It showed a random pattern of stains from over fifty years of varnish, paint, coffee-mugs and wine. All the tools and sketches he pushed to the far side of the work-bench, and closed the cupboard doors against his collection of paints and glues and old rags. In an attempt to make the space look less bleak, he placed a faded cloth over the table.

"What would you like to drink? Coffee? Wine, perhaps?"

"I never drink coffee if I can help it. I think wine will do justice to the day, thank you."

They clinked glasses, and saluted each other. "So tell me about the black mare."

"Are you some kind of a magician—a psychic? Did you bring a crystal ball as well?"

"Tell me about the black mare."

"It is a long story. It begins with my meeting with Francesca, when I was a young man."

Briefly, he sketched the series of events that led up to the present.

"And now, here I am. I should be the happiest man on earth, about to marry the woman I love, and yet..."

"And yet—what?"

"These repetitive dreams—nightmares. As if the dream was telling it this way and that, so that I would finally understand."

"Tell me about the black mare."

Alejandro glanced out of the window at the large, empty paddock.

"Some time ago the farmer next door bought a beautiful, black mare. A mustang. She had been brought in off the range. Wild. Untamable. But such a beauty. Breath-taking to watch her move. The farmer did not want to have her turned into dog-food."

He grimaced. "You know, they are trying to round up all the indigenous wild horses and have them destroyed. A petition is being signed to protest against this. But farmers want more grazing for more beef—more profit. It is a shocking reflection of the values of those who permit this. And this is not just a few people here and there. Our country is changing, Raho, and not for the better."

"Yes—but to get back to the black mare."

"I loved to watch her. She had an electric aliveness. Watching her, I could almost remember something—something very important. I would often find myself in tears, just looking at her—her wildness; her beauty. No one had ever put a bridle on her. Not even a halter. Not a hand. She was herded into a horse-box and brought here. But after a while I could feel that now she was once again trapped in this small, grassy prison."

He refilled their glasses.

"Then, one day, she seemed to hear something—a sound coming from those hills. I watched her closely."

Wine-bottle still in hand, he moved to the window and indicated the direction.

"She started off at a trot, which broke into a gallop. She was heading toward that far boundary. I wanted to yell; to warn her not to run into the high pole-fence. But she galloped on. I almost couldn't look. How, at such speed, would she ever be able to stop? She would break herself on that fence."

He looked toward Raho.

"But she didn't. She cleared it with a foot to spare—galloped away, and disappeared into the trees."

He came back to the table and sat down; sat in silence, thinking.

"And then, later, I remembered the day when I last saw Francesca. We had spent the whole summer together—delighting in each other, talking, going out at night, dancing. Making love. And then, one day, I think I told her that I was going back to work."

"You think!"

"Yes. I don't really remember."

"Did you know it is said that only those who have memories can live in the infinitely fragile present?"

"I haven't heard that—no. What about the people who don't have memories?"

"They don't live anywhere."

Alejandro stared at him. "So—?"

"So what happened next?"

"I just went back to work!"

He cast his mind back, and tried to remember.

Raho waited.

"What I do remember is watching her run off, beautiful and tanned from our summer days together. It was like looking at a beautiful creature, running away as fast as the wind."

"Just like the black mare."

"Yes. But I didn't think of that then."

"So what came next?"

Alejandro gave a sigh. "About half a century of carving angels, and making some serious money."

Raho did not speak.

"Then, the most extraordinary thing happened inside me when I first met Octavia. She was a baby, only a few months old. Sister Piadosa called me in after it was discovered that this baby—can you believe it?—grew quiet at night if she could see the stars through her nursery window."

He looked at Raho, as if asking for a comment, but Raho said nothing.

"Well, I went round for tea one morning, and picked Octavia up out of her pram. Usually she screamed if any stranger came near her. But she didn't scream. I walked a little way with her; asked her what all the trouble was about—of course she couldn't answer. But in some strange way, I did connect with her; deeply. What I heard in the silence was—" He hesitated, and thought for a moment. "What I heard was that she felt alone; and that she was in love with passion."

Raho raised an eyebrow. "That is all?"

"Yes."

"What did that tell you?"

"I could feel the truth of it more than understand what it meant. Later, as she grew older and continued being a troubled hell-raiser, it told me that perhaps she was born into some particular—should I call it a fate, or a calling?—and that, even at that young age, she was aware of its demands; was perhaps impatient for it—impatient with her youth, when she knew how exacting it would be. I think some part of her knew it even as a baby, when she was unable to speak or walk. I think she felt her baby body to be such a frustration—knowing, even then, that what she wanted to be doing hadn't arrived, and that she wouldn't be able to truly meet it, even if it had. It was there, you see—fully realized. But it was still too big for her. That is a hard fate."

Raho listened intently.

"She loved her brother, Lucien, with a passion; had eyes only for him. But later I was the one she felt she could talk to. And then, of course, we had this love of stars in common. She used to sit and listen to stars. Later still, when she built her studio, she requested a large skylight and high windows. And no one was allowed into that room. She said she had to keep the stars safe. She used to play a song from Puccini's opera, Tosca—E Lucevan le Stele—over and over. It drove everyone mad, until she moved the record player out of the house and into her studio."

"And what were you feeling during all of this?"

"I wanted her to feel that she wasn't alone; that in some way we shared a kind of passion."

"Yes. But what were you feeling in your own self?"

"At first I felt blessed that I could be a mentor to this passionate soul; that I would be able, in some way, to contain some of her frustration while she grew into her calling."

"And then?"

"She was so extraordinary! She was never a young person in her conversation. She could go directly to the essence of things. Only people didn't recognize that. She was too young for them to take her seriously. They thought her strange—not normal in some way. It is difficult to be so ahead of yourself, especially when you are not yet in your teens."

"Are you deliberately evading the question, Alejandro?"

"Yes!" Alejandro laughed. "Then, in 1987—she was just thirteen, but looked twice that age, so beautiful—many things happened. It seems that Lucien fell in love with Sofia, and that this felt to Octavia like an utter betrayal. They did not speak. At the same time, a young Russian cellist called Kristiyan Bacarov joined the other musicians at The Adobe, and began to perform with them. He was very smitten with Octavia."

"And you—?"

"Yes, Raho! I was jealous. There I was, well over seventy years old, and acting like a teenager. Well, not acting it outwardly, but certainly feeling like one."

Alejandro gave a rueful smile.

"Well, then. Lucien married Sofia. Octavia was eighteen; I was seventy-seven. She decided that she would not go to university. She wanted to spend some time in Chile, and in particular in the Atacama Desert. They have a wonderful observatory there."

"And so?"

"I was devastated." He looked at his hands. "I went home, and did some soul-searching."

"And—?"

"I began to have these repetitive dreams. Sometimes they varied; grew more intense. In them, I am always searching for the black mare. I come to a crossroad; the Angel of Death points toward an abyss—that sort of thing. Dreams full of fear and confusion. I decided that I needed a break. Long story short, I went and spent some time at a small monastery in the desert. I came back in February. It was only then that I heard about Octavia's accident. By then Kristiyan had moved into one of the spare casitas, and had become part of the community. He was very attentive to Octavia."

He looked down into his glass of wine. Raho shifted his position, and leaned forward.

"How would you understand the command to carve angels—as many as stars—if you heard it today?"

Alejandro looked surprised.

"Have you ever asked yourself that question?"

"I am beginning to ask it."

"So let's ask it again, now."

"It never entered my head, until recently, to question it."

Raho was silent. Alejandro got up, and paced up and down the room.

"I can't imagine that I could ever have thought or done anything differently."

"I am not suggesting that you should do anything else. I am asking you where you are now with the command."

Alejandro said nothing.

"You were a ten-year-old boy. In all this time, have you never wondered what the angel from the Heavenly Host might have meant by his command?"

"No."

"Would you say that this was a sign of devotion and commitment? Or maybe a sign of laziness?"

"Laziness! How can you say laziness? I have worked long hours, every day of my life."

"This suggests to me a certain lack of curiosity. What in a ten-year-old boy is admirable might need to be re-examined five, ten, twenty years later at the most."

He rose.

"Good to see you again, Alejandro. I will be staying at The Adobe for a few days. We can chat some more if you would like that. Or we could just sit and drink some more of this excellent wine, and gaze into the sunset."

Alejandro walked with him to his car.

"I think I would like to talk further."

"You think!"

"No. I would most definitely like to talk further, Raho. Good to see you too."

Alejandro did not go inside immediately. Instead, he walked round the studio and went to lean on the paddock fence—the place where he used to watch the black mare in the past. What was it about her that always brought tears to his eyes? Indeed, just thinking of her now, he could feel his eyes begin to fill. Not just her beauty, although that too. But her wildness. That was it. No compromise. She would accept no rope; no hand on her. And no fences. Only the free wind, and wild places.

And what about you, my friend of so many years? Can you say the same about yourself?

A Conversation Continued

Raho and Alejandro returned from their walk up the pink hill, where they had sat just below Magdalena's white cross and the yuccas—looking out over the desert, watching it turn crimson beneath a sunset sky. It was, Alejandro thought, like a pilgrimage. He'd brought a stone with him to place on the growing pile around the white cross, in memory of Sebastián's remarkable mother.

It was several days since their previous conversation. Now they stood in the warmth of Georgia's kitchen yard, two glasses and a bottle of wine on the table between them.

"What are you thinking?" Alejandro asked, pulling out a chair.

"I was thinking that so much of what constitutes our modern life—unless we

241

stay awake—leaves no space for silence. It is as if we have to prevent, at all costs, an inner voice from drawing our attention to something that might shatter our complacency, and change our lives."

He glanced at Alejandro.

"But perhaps it might return us to our true inheritance."

Raho poured the wine. Lifted his glass to Alejandro.

"When I listen to very fine music, especially music that has endured for centuries, there is one thing that always strikes me: how eloquent the silence is between the notes. Have you heard that too? Like the negative spaces between one form and another in a sculpture; between trees in a forest, or shapes in a landscape. It speaks beyond words. Beyond thought. A silent emptiness that fills the heart."

He paused.

"Some people are afraid of the desert because of its vast space—and its silence. They need people, walls, noise, distractions—to drown out that little voice, and its forbidden question."

"And what is this question?"

"Ah! I am waiting for you to tell me that. I have done enough talking, I think."

"Are you saying that I have spent my life carving angels so that I can keep that voice at bay?"

"Perhaps you are saying that. Are you?"

Alejandro shifted on his chair, and uncrossed his legs.

"I am not aware of having done so—well, maybe just recently, with all those dreams—and the feeling that I have lost... Well, I don't mean I have exactly lost—"

"Lost what?"

"I mean, I have felt lost. But that does not mean I have been deliberately drowning out this voice you speak of—surely!"

"Do you want me to do the work for you? Lost what? What were you going to say?"

"Octavia. I have lost Octavia."

"Did you ever have Octavia?"

"You know what I mean."

"I am not clairvoyant, Alejandro. I can only hear what you say. If it is not clear to me, I must ask what it is that you mean."

Raho considered for a time before he spoke again.

"Let me ask you this: who would you be if you stopped carving angels?"

"Are you saying...?"

"I am not saying. I am asking a question."

"I am not sure that I understand what you are asking."

"It's very simple." He repeated the question.

"Who would I be? I would be who I am," said Alejandro.

"Ah! And who are you?"

242

There was a long silence.

"When we spoke a few days ago, I asked you what you heard when you listened to the infant Octavia. You appeared to hesitate. Was there anything else that you heard?"

Alejandro looked at his hands. "Yes, there was," he admitted. "I thought it wasn't important—or that I had perhaps imagined it."

"So you just edited that bit out?"

Alejandro said nothing.

"Talking to you is like drawing blood out of a stone! What did you hear?"

"I heard: 'Don't abandon me'."

"And that came from the infant?"

"I'm not sure."

"Well—where else would it come from?"

"From me," Alejandro whispered. His eyes were fixed on Raho.

"And who was speaking those words?"

There was another long silence. The light was changing into that shade of blue which seems to be the bridge between sunset and evening. As the silence lengthened, the blue grew in intensity until the pink hill became a dark silhouette against the sky. It would soon be night.

"I cannot say."

Raho sat, as if contemplating whether to speak or not.

"Alejandro," he said finally, "has it ever struck you that you have spent your entire life looking up—up at the stars; up at the light?"

Alejandro shook his head. "I have not thought about it that way."

"And what might you discover if you allowed yourself to grow down—down into the earth?"

"I cannot say," Alejandro muttered.

Raho finished his wine, and put the glass on the table.

"May I make a suggestion?"

Alejandro nodded.

"Sebastián is sure to have a copy of one of Goethe's poems. See if he has, and if he won't mind lending it to you for a day or two. The poem is called The Holy Longing."

He stood up.

"Thanks for the wine, Alejandro."

***

It was early morning when Alejandro arrived at The Adobe. He found Sebastián down at the barn, loading one of their cows onto a small trailer.

"Hi there, Alejandro—what brings you here so early?"

He gave a nod to Gregorio, who was holding the cow's halter.

"One moment, and I will be with you."

The tall man and Granuja watched with interest.

Sebastián gave the cow a slap on her rump, and she jumped forward. Simultaneously, Gregorio gave a tug on the halter—and before she could back away she was up the ramp, and Sebastián had lifted the back of the trailer and slipped the bolt.

"She's having a day off." He laughed. "She has a date with old Joe's bull."

He went to have a word with Gregorio, who was getting into the pick-up; then returned to stand next to Alejandro. Together they watched truck and trailer rumble away.

"Yessir! What can I do for you? Why don't you come and have some coffee? Have you eaten? I'm starving."

The two men walked up the path, and across the yard to Sebastián's house—the dog everywhere at once, excited by the farm smells.

They were in Sebastián's office, both replete with Georgia's breakfast of eggs on chili beans with nachos, and strong coffee. Sebastián was hunting through the books in his poetry section.

"I keep promising myself that I will put everything in alphabetical order, but..." His voice trailed off. "Ah! Here it is."

He paged through the contents.

"Yes! The Holy Longing. A challenging poem. Beautiful! And a good translation, I think."

He sat down next to Alejandro.

"I didn't know you were interested in poetry."

Alejandro gave a bashful laugh.

"Rather a lot going on in me at the moment. Raho suggested I should read this."

"Well, keep it as long as you like."

"Thanks." He patted the book. "I will take good care of it."

They parted—Sebastián to do the bills; Alejandro to go home, and read the poem.

Christmas 1995

The snow-storm began the night before Christmas Eve.

By morning the valley lay beneath two feet of snow—and the strange silence that accompanies it. It covered the rooftops of the buildings, and obscured all the details of the fields, paths and courtyards, the camposanto, the orchard and the herb

244

garden, creating a vast, white emptiness. It was only the presence of the snow-clad cottonwood standing at the turn-off that indicated the whereabouts of the road into town.

Father Rafael was due to come to The Adobe to conduct an early Christmas Eve service, before returning for the evening service in Las Madres. At mid-morning he called to say that the roads were impassable, and that all traffic had been advised not to attempt driving anywhere until the snow-ploughs had cleared away the deep drifts. Small roads would only be attended to once the storm had passed. The priority was to clear the Interstate and other major roadways.

Half an hour later Alejandro called to give the same information, and to wish everyone a blessed Christmas.

Snow continued to fall all morning, and by midday the fences around the paddocks and fields were only just visible above the thick blanket of whiteness. Everyone took turns shoveling snow away from doorways, and clearing the paths that connected the various buildings to each other and to the chapel.

In the afternoon there was a fresh snow-storm, making it impossible for anyone to move out of doors.

By evening the storm had passed.

Sister Piadosa stood at the window of what used to be María's room. She was watching Gregorio plough his way through the thick drifts of snow toward the doves' aviary. She watched him bend to release the catch and open the door.

In that instant she felt the presence of María, standing next to her as together they watched the familiar, ragged cloud of flapping wings rise up into the white sky.

They watched the individual doves become one unit, informed by a single will; watched them circle the valley, swooping low over the white landscape. They watched how they appeared to vanish in their wide turns into the light, only to reappear seconds later, dark against the white sky.

"Aren't they beautiful, sister? When I look at them flying, I know exactly what silence sounds like."

"They are indeed, María. There is something timeless about those patterns in the sky—the endless repetition; always different, always the same."

She smiled at the young woman, dressed in nun's clothing.

"But they followed you here, and they are watching over you. Now that is really something different. I have never heard of anything like it before."

"They are like music, sister. I think they are my song. I sing it every day."

Sister Piadosa conducted the evening service in the chapel.

She offered a special prayer for María Fuentes, Salvador's wife, who had given birth to their child, Sofia, here at The Adobe, and whose death and unusual exhumation ceremony had made history in the small community. In the hearts and minds of many, she reminded the congregation, María and the Virgin were still fused into one holy image. The word "milagro" was still whispered when María's name was mentioned.

She gave thanks for the lives of Magdalena and Father Octavio, both of whom had worked so hard to establish the bonds of goodwill that were shared to this day by the inhabitants of The Adobe, and by all the members of the surrounding community.

After the service blessings for a happy Christmas were exchanged, and then everyone returned to their warm houses.

Christmas Day began with carols sung in the chapel, after which the women went home to prepare the Christmas meal, and the men went to help Gregorio with the livestock—making sure they were all fed and watered, and that the doves were let out for their morning flight.

Evening brought a crimson sunset that stained the snow and the flying white doves pink, and filled the whole valley with its soft light.

The Birth

The pains began just after midnight. Sofia woke Lucien, who sat with her and rubbed her back while she timed the intervals between each pain.

"Twenty minutes! We must phone through to Georgia and Sebastián right now. Will you do that, while I pack an overnight bag? I would so much rather give birth naturally. You don't think—"

"No, I don't think so for one minute," Lucien said nervously as he dialed the number.

He spoke briefly, and put the phone down.

"They will be over in a minute. Sister Piadosa and Sister Ana are coming as well, to stay with Caradoc. Can I fetch anything?" he said, hearing Sofia breathe her way through another pain.

"Could you put my toiletries into the sponge-bag? It is hanging behind the bathroom door. Oh, and a hairbrush. The baby's suitcase and special car seat are in Caradoc's old cot."

Lucien returned with everything just as Georgia and Sebastián arrived, with the two nuns on their heels.

"Fifteen minutes apart," was all Sofia could say, just as another pain gripped her.

"Into the car, then. No time to waste."

Sebastián showed Lucien to the place where he could sit with Sofia. Georgia climbed into the passenger seat—and they were off.

"Caradoc's food for play-school is in the fridge!" Sofia called out of the window to Sister Piadosa, and then they were gone.

"Nearly nine pounds! No wonder you had back-ache!"

"Yes! And thank heaven and all Alejandro's angels that you didn't go for a natural birth," said Lucien. "There would have been nothing natural about it."

Georgia looked at their new granddaughter, lying so peacefully in the crook of Sofia's arm. Caesar babies always looked so peaceful, she thought, with none of the pressure marks that so many infants had from being squeezed during birth. She turned to Lucien to describe his daughter to him.

"You and Sofia have a very definite pattern. She looks so much like Caradoc did when he was born. The same shape of the face. Same little mouth. And she is going to have the famous red hair." She took his hand. "Here, let me show you where her hand is; such perfect, tiny fingers."

Lucien felt for the infant's hand, and thrilled to the grip of a tiny fist on his thumb.

"She is strong!" he said in wonder. "Can you believe it is really true, Sofia? This new little person."

"I have believed it all too well for the past six months!" Sofia said with feeling. "And I don't wonder she is strong! So she should be—just lying there at her ease, and eating away. Do you know how much weight I gained? And look! I am practically down to a bone. It was all her ladyship, who lies here so unconcerned."

They laughed.

"Have you settled on a name?"

"Yes!" they both said simultaneously.

"You tell them, Lucien. You thought of it."

"Her name is Erin," he said.

One Question

It was mid-morning when Raho arrived unexpectedly at The Adobe. He wandered casually into Sebastián's office.

The winter snow-melt had completely disappeared, and everywhere small, indomitable shoots were breaking through the earth's crust, announcing the onset of spring.

"Would the new grandfather have time in his busy day to drink a little wine with an old friend?"

"Raho! Of course. It will be a pleasure. Let us go and find a place that is sunny."

They seated themselves at the small table in the kitchen garden. Sebastián poured the wine.

"Your health, Raho."

They clinked glasses.

"Alejandro was down here some time before Christmas to borrow a copy of Goethe's poems. He said you recommended he should read The Holy Longing."

"Yes."

For some reason he could not explain, even to himself, Sebastián felt uncomfortable. For a while they sat in silence. Finally Raho spoke.

"This is a beautiful valley. What a lovely place to live! Did Magdalena plant this lavender?" He pointed to the bushes that grew against the low wall. "You must be so happy living here," he said serenely. With his arm he indicated the fields, the row of cottonwoods at the far end, and the pink hill.

Sebastián was not fooled.

"You didn't come here to look at the view, Raho. Don't play innocent with me. It doesn't suit you."

"I am not playing. I am appreciating the beauty of this valley."

"What did you really come about?"

"Oh! You don't know?"

The two men drank their wine. The silence lengthened. Raho appeared to be enjoying the peace of the valley.

"All right!" It was Sebastián who spoke. "You have come to berate me for working hard."

Raho shook his head.

"I came to ask you about a condor."

Sebastián's hand, holding the wine-glass, froze in mid-air. Raho said nothing. He sat, watching.

"Why do you ask me this? What do you know about a condor?"

"Ah!"

Raho took a sip of wine, and put his glass down on the table. He leaned forward, his face close to Sebastián's.

"I know it is a kind of vulture. And, like all vultures, it is a prophet of death—as some would have it known. I think it could also be described more literally: it circles around a dying animal, waiting for it to fall and die. Of course, that is not nearly as poetic."

Sebastián stared at him. Raho raised his glass, and took another sip of wine.

"Excellent wine, Sebastián."

248

"I don't know why you are talking about vultures."

"Is that true?"

Sebastián frowned.

"Don't lie to yourself. You are fighting your own truth—not me. And you know exactly what I am talking about. Do you want to know what is going on? Or are you going to waste more years, with your brilliant intellect protecting you from knowing it?"

"You don't understand. You see a peaceful valley, Raho. You do not see how much work it takes to keep it so."

"Of course, Sebastián. I must apologize. You are quite correct. Without you, this place would undoubtedly fall apart."

"That is not what I said."

"What did you say?"

"I am saying that I have to complete what I started here."

"And how long will that take?"

Sebastián looked away.

"And I am talking about poetry."

Sebastián said nothing.

"I am talking about the only true responsibility you have—have ever had, in your whole life."

"And what is that?"

"I am asking you to name it."

Sebastián banged the table with his fist. "Why don't you just come out and say it? Why must you always play this game?"

"I don't play games. I am speaking about the duende that is shadowing you, every step of the way."

Sebastián stared at him. Had Magdalena told Raho about his birth; about the shadow that had blown down his throat? The women who delivered him had crossed themselves when they saw it. "The duende!" they cried. Did Raho know about this?

"Don't you think you have fooled yourself long enough?"

Sebastián was about to speak.

"No. Don't give me reasons—excuses." He stared into Sebastián's eyes.

"To deny a calling is dangerous. I am speaking about the condor."

Sebastián stood up. He leaned forward—both hands on the table. His chair fell back into the dust.

"Well, I don't know what you want from me! I am not complaining. I have a lot of work, but I don't call that a problem. Why do you keep—?"

"Don't you see, Sebastián? You don't have a problem—"

"I have just said—"

Raho held up a hand.

"You don't have a problem," he repeated. "You are the problem!"

"How dare—"

Raho bent down, and picked up a small stone.

"Do you see this pebble?" He held the stone up between his thumb and forefinger for Sebastián to see.

"Here! Take this! Take it! This is your gift. I want to watch you throw it away. Take it!"

When Sebastián hesitated, he leaned forward and put the stone into his hand.

"There! You have your gift in your hands. Now! Let me see you throw it away!"

"Stop it, Raho," Sebastián muttered, but he held onto the stone. "You have said enough!" He was close to tears.

"But is it enough? How much will it take to be enough?"

Raho leaned forward again. Put a hand on Sebastián's shoulder.

"Don't waste any more time. You have a gift, Sebastián. Unless you embrace it with all your heart, it will destroy you. The duende is a formidable adversary if you turn your back on it."

"What do you know about duende? Why do you keep saying this?"

"Oh, Sebastián." He held his hands out, palms up, as if making an offering of their emptiness.

"I—"

"You are living your mother's life," Raho said, so gently that Sebastián was taken aback. "Very noble. I am sure many think you are a wonderful son because you carry on your mother's dream. But hear this: this is not your life—or your dream. You have nothing invested in this place. You are comfortable here because you cannot fail."

"That is not fair, Raho!"

Raho leaned forward, and looked Sebastián straight in the eye.

"Who are you?" he asked softly.

"That is the only question."

A Vulture in the Mind

It was past midnight. Sebastián lay awake, watching the moon cast its light over the shawl that hung on a rod opposite the window. He remembered how it had been wrapped around the painting Georgia gave him when she graduated from art school.

250

He recalled so vividly the day he asked if he might see her work.

***

"But only if you feel comfortable with that. I know that these things must not come out into the light before they are ready. I shan't be offended if you say no."

But she had given him her heart-stopping smile, and taken his arm.

"I am so happy that you will be the first person to see the finished paintings. They will soon go on exhibition, and then all eyes will look at them—and I will have to surrender them to their future, like a mother letting her grown children step out into the world."

He remembered the moment as if it was just yesterday. He had been told that Georgia's work was in a league of its own, but not even that had prepared him for the dynamic power of her huge paintings. He was at a loss even to describe them. They were landscapes, and yet not like any landscapes he had ever seen. They were more like the energy of landscapes. One had the brooding weight of an electric storm, about to break; the last rays of brilliant sun lighting the trees so that they vibrated, green against the purple sky. Others were hardly more substantial than the light in which the land appeared to be floating. He remembered walking around the large room as one would walk in an empty church—feeling the power that was contained in the architecture, the walls, the high, north-facing windows and the magnificent images. He could still summon the memory of that almost palpable silence.

He pulled up a chair, and sat gazing at one particular painting—a painting that called to him. It was like a not-quite image of something he almost remembered. It was at once unknown and familiar.

He remembered the thrill he felt when she stood behind him, her hands on his shoulders. He still couldn't believe that she had chosen him out of all the hundreds of students at the university.

"I would love to buy this one, Georgia," he said. "I almost know this place. Would that be all right?"

"It is yours, Sebastián. I would love you to have it."

He had protested, but she was adamant. It was only at the exhibition, when he saw the red sticker and read: "By courtesy of the owner: Sebastián Chavez", and saw the prices on the other works, that he felt ashamed and stupid. He would never have been able to afford to buy one of these. How could he have been so naïve?

She called it Where the Pink Hill Waits.

And he remembered, when college closed for the summer break, the excitement of setting off with her and two friends for a holiday of painting and poetry, and the open road.

And love-making. The thrill and the terror of that new experience, coming to meet him, kept him distracted for the whole of their first day's drive to the small hotel, and their first stop.

He would never forget that first night.

And then the telephone call, early on the first morning.

And suddenly, so unexpectedly that at first he could not believe it, she was gone: gone to Paris to take up a scholarship, leaving him feeling rejected and abandoned.

He returned home to The Adobe like an injured creature—to lick his wounds, and to shout his rage at God in a summer storm. That night, while he stood in the drenching rain, a bolt of lightning struck the white cross he had set on the pink hill in Georgia's name; a cross that was usually a sign that someone had died.

And indeed, it felt as if she—or perhaps he—had died.

Poetry had been his only solace then.

* * *

And now this strange conversation with Raho. And the condor. And the reference to the duende.

In his mind's eye, somewhere between waking and sleeping, he saw Raho lift up the top of his skull, the way one lifts the lid off a cooking-pot. Simultaneously, a large vulture alighted on its rim, perched there, and inclined its neck and head to examine the contents.

To Sebastián's horror, he saw the bald head disappear into the cooking-pot of his skull, tear out pieces of thought, and begin to devour them.

What had Raho said? Yes. He said that a vulture appears in anticipation of death. What was this vulture looking for as it tore these pieces of—of what—out of his brain?

Sebastián knew the answer, and he tried to push it away, but it would not leave. And then the vulture lifted its head. Something dangled from its beak. Something barely alive. Such a small, mewling cry it uttered—like a creature not quite stillborn. Sebastián strained to see what it was. Something like a piece of parchment. Yes. A fragment of a page, torn from a book. He strained to read what was written on it, but the letters were too small. And then the page came closer to him. On it he read the one word—"Poetry."

He shuddered. He felt a cold hand touch the back of his neck. Felt all the hairs on his body rise, the way hackles rise on a wolf when it senses danger.

He put his hand up to his head, and gingerly felt to make sure it was all there.

"You know what you have to do." It was Raho's voice, echoing in his brain. "Do you not realize that you are the vulture—the condor?"

Sebastián sat up abruptly—so abruptly that he woke Georgia.

"What is it?" she asked sleepily. Then, looking at his face, she gave an exclamation.

"You look as if you have seen a ghost!"

"It's nothing," he muttered as he lay down once more. "Just a dream."

252

Sebastián stepped out into the early morning sunshine. This was his day to take some goods into Las Madres.

As he made his way over to the loaded pick-up, he tried to resist the temptation to look up—and couldn't. To his relief, there was nothing above him but the vast, blue dome of the New Mexico sky.

But all morning he could not rid himself of the dream. He could feel the vulture, perched on his shoulder as he drove the pick-up along the dusty road, its head thrust forward so that he could not ignore its presence.

"I must be going mad," he muttered to himself. "Damn you, Raho!"

But a small voice at the back of his mind said: "It isn't Raho. You know this very well. You must own this voice. What is it you cannot—will not—surrender?"

And now the cruel, hooked beak came directly toward his face. He heard its terrible cry, and the fierce eye bore into his—and he was back again on that cliff-edge where he had gone on the day after his mother's funeral, where the condor had risen out of the gloom and terrified him with that same fierce cry.

Sebastián shut off the engine. The pick-up rolled to a halt. He put his head down on the steering-wheel, and gave way to huge sobs that rose up from the very depths of his being—sobs that felt as if his very flesh was being torn out of him.

"Oh God—no! Not that!"

But it was that. He did not want to feel this pain. Not ever. And now he heard Raho's voice again. Clearly.

"The duende is a formidable adversary, Sebastián. If you turn your back on it, it will destroy you."

He looked about him, helplessly. For what? For anything. Anything that might take this sudden clarity from him. But nothing would ever be able to change this now. He got out of the cab, and lay down on the dusty grass. Huge sobs racked his whole body. He rocked himself from side to side. Where were his mother's arms now? He could only feel the absence of them.

Where were they now?

They were in the valley she loved; in the pink hills and the cottonwoods. They were in the scented labyrinth of the herb garden. They held the entire, shining valley in their embrace. And him with it.

He sat up. The vulture had vanished.

"Oh, mama," he said, his voice raw with pain. "I cannot bear it. How can I lose you a second time?"

One Path

Sebastián reached the center of the labyrinth just as the sky was turning from pink into all the many tones of flaming scarlet and gold. He stood there, his arms raised as if to touch that fire. Tears streamed down his face.

In his mind, he was back in the summer of 1960, just after Georgia had left for Paris. He had come back to The Adobe, lost in grief and rage. Magdalena, seeing him unable to come to grips with anything, had the idea of establishing a labyrinth, which would also serve as a space for a herb garden. Sebastián was to lay the path; a path of black river stones.

Standing here now, he could see her strong feet, bare in the dirt and dust, and the stick she held as she drew the complex pattern of lines which led to the center. From time to time she scuffed out a line with her feet, and redrew it. He sat watching her then, without any enthusiasm.

It took the entire summer to complete the work. Magdalena, watching him stripped to the waist and toiling in the hot sun, thought that perhaps the work was too much for him. Perhaps it was not a good idea after all.

It was only many months later that he learned about her conversation with Father Octavio.

"Leave him be, Magdalena," Father Octavio said on one of his visits to The Adobe. "He needs to suffer his loss, and what better way than through such a task? And the significance of it—of laying a sacred path—has not escaped me."

So he bent over the task; wheeled load after heavy load from the pile in the driveway, and set the thousands of stones into the single path that doubled back on itself, this way and that, until it arrived at the center.

He could still hear her voice now.

"There is only one path, Sebastián, although it looks as if there are many. This is not a maze, where there are many paths that lead nowhere, and you can get lost. Here there is just one path, and provided you stay on it for its entire length, and don't lose faith, you will arrive at the center."

As he stood now, with the glory of the sunset above him coloring the valley, the scent of all the herbs and the lilacs that hung over the wall filling his nostrils, and the sultry notes of the music he had just listened to—de Falla's Nights in the Gardens of Spain—echoing in his heart, he felt once again how joy and grief, loss and beauty were one thing. And through all of it, in the combination of somber, fiery Andalusian notes and the dramatic sky above, he felt the dark and powerful presence of the duende rise up in him as never before.

Word was put out through the grapevine that a memorial service would be held for Magdalena Chavez at The Adobe. All who wished to come were welcome.

There would be no official service, but those who wished to could walk the labyrinth and hold Magdalena in their thoughts, or sit in the Adobe chapel, offering whatever prayers came to them. It was to be looked upon as a celebration of her life. There would be iced tea and snacks; lemonade for the children. Wine would be on offer to sanctify the occasion. People were invited to stay as long as they liked, and to leave when they needed to. Magdalena would have wanted it that way.

People began arriving just after nine in the morning. Soon many people, young and old, were walking the elaborate pathway, each remembering Magdalena in their own way. Sofia invited the small children to come with her to visit the ponies, while the older boys climbed up the steep path that led to Magdalena's white cross. Each of them was given a stone, to place on the pile of stones that had been growing over the years; each stone carrying a prayer of thanks for the generosity of her life.

By mid-morning there was a palpable sense of tranquility hovering over the valley, as people made their silent pilgrimages.

Sebastián took himself off to sit next to his mother's grave. He spoke aloud to her, telling her how many people had come to honor her memory—some walking her beloved labyrinth, some sitting in the chapel.

"I also came to let you know that I have finally understood your words to me, that summer when we created the labyrinth. I remember, as if it was yesterday, how you said to me: 'There is only one path...'

"I did not truly hear what you were saying then. I heard only superficially. So now I am here to tell you that my feet are going to set out on that one path—at last. I hope I will make you very proud and happy, mama."

He bent his head, and offered a prayer. Then he went back to join the others.

The End of One Road

There were lines that jumped out at him, even though he would not have been able to say why.

"Tell a wise person or else keep silent..."

How could you tell if a person was wise? How often our less than wise humanity intrudes, full of so-called wise counsel.

And what was meant by this praise of *"what is truly alive, what longs to be burned to death?"*

He could feel, deeply, the truth of that paradox, even as his rational mind argued with it. When was he truly alive? Carving angels? Talking to Francesca—Octavia? Standing outside in the night, looking up at the stars?

It couldn't be determined by the outer event. It was his quality of being, his real presence in the moment, that made him truly alive. It was, he thought, the difference between being and doing. And yet, even that was debatable.

Alejandro left the book on the table, and went to make coffee.

It was, he thought, impossible to do nothing. Even doing nothing was doing something. Why was that?

He made some strong coffee; black.

And yet there were many times, when he was working on an angel, when he disappeared; when time disappeared. He would only realize this when he noticed how the light had changed. There were other times, he had to concede, when he wondered which gallery might want this angel. At times like these, he knew that he was measuring the work against its possible commercial value. So—there was a distinction to be made between doing when time vanished, and doing when it didn't.

Something changed, he thought, when he disappeared—he being the observer who measured, planned and evaluated the worth of what he was doing.

Alejandro walked up and down in his studio—touching things, throwing bits of paper into the waste-bin, pausing to look out of the window; to look out at the absence of the black mare.

What did it mean? *"To die and so to grow?"* He wiped the table-top and straightened the chairs. And what was needed to experience this? What died?

Intuitively he knew that he needed this, but he had no idea what was meant by—*"to die."*

You are finally losing it, Alejandro.

Was he *"a troubled guest?"* Certainly he was troubled, but why *"guest?"* And why did the poet call the earth—*"dark?"*

He decided it was time to take Granuja for a walk.

□□□

He remembered vividly the day when he first met Octavia. She was a small, fretful baby—only a few months old, and driving everyone mad with her tantrums. He had been asked to see if he could understand what was behind all the noise and tears. He remembered lifting her out of her pram, and walking some distance with her—to everyone's amazement, because she screamed if a strange face so much as came near her—and listening to her heart. It was through some kind of wordless speech that he heard the cry: "Do not abandon me!" And then, his spontaneous reply to those present—"she is in love with passion." Why did this come to mind again—now? And what did it mean?

Was it not precisely this—this uncompromising passion for life, for its own sake—that he loved in her? And was it not precisely this that he had lost; had thrown away?

256

If there was one thing he wanted above all others, it was this: to die and so to grow. And he knew that the dying would not come easy.

□□□

Evening came early now. Still autumn, but he could feel a new chill in the air. He spent an hour in his studio—sweeping it clean, dusting away the cobwebs. He cleaned the window; looked ruefully at the absence of drapes or shutters. This room, he now knew, would have to change before it could welcome any guest.

He fed Granuja, made his own supper and ate it; washed the few dishes. He knew that he was deliberately postponing going to bed. He wrote out a copy of the poem and pinned it to the kitchen wall, where he would see it every day. Finally he went to bed, and instantly fell into a deep sleep.

I am naked. I see that I have the body of a young child. I am about to enter a very dark place. Rising up behind me is a flight of steep steps that has brought me to this place; steps carved out of rock. I stand in bright light. In front of me is an opening in the rock; a cave-like entrance. On the lintel I see some writing. I step closer to read what it says.

Do not abandon me.

I take one more step, and the light vanishes. I am in a dark tunnel. I walk, reaching out with my hands to feel my way. Now I am in some kind of a tomb that is lit by a strange glow. All around me I see shapes. They appear to be stone coffins. Some of them look very old—the stone grown darker with age. I am drawn to one that looks new and clean. I see that there is something carved into the stone. I move closer to read the inscription:

Dying into Life: Alejandro Jaramillo 1996

The Opus

A bright light shone down on the tapestry, stretched between the two rollers on the wooden frame. The rest of the room was in darkness.

Octavia found that she could work best at night, when everything was quiet; when everyone was sleeping. She liked the knowledge that, in a sense, she had the world, the night—and the stars above—to herself. She had found herself repeating, like a mantra—"I have faith in night." And she knew that this meant far more than she could literally understand about it. There was something about the deep silence of starlight that called to her—had always called. Something so ancient, it had no name;

something it was impossible to speak about—that reached back to a time, perhaps, before humans could make fire, but stared in awe and wonder at the stars. It was this that she wanted to serve, and make visible in some way, through her work with beads.

Journal Entry 16—April 1996

I feel such a need in me to create a ritual for this work. Of course there will be music, but what music? In spite of loving all the music that Kristiyan has brought me, none of it fits what I hear inside me. And something else. I don't pray, and yet I feel as if I want to offer a prayer—to whom, to what?—in thanks for the gift of these images. I think I will begin each day by making some offering to the work I am doing. I must think what this might be.

I have decided not to make any sketches. I want to trust the images to find their own way through me. I know only two things: that the work will speak to landscape— the most ancient of the earth; and that it will speak to wild creatures—in particular the animals I know.

I have been having such strange flashes of images: apocalyptic images. Landscapes with dying trees. Rivers growing small. And always the animals, running away—whereto? The edge of the world? They are leaving us, and taking parts of our souls with them. I want to make them small in relation to the whole work, but nevertheless have them dominating it. I don't want to tell anyone about this. I can feel myself handing over—what? Control? The illusion of control?—to this energy of the night, and the images that want to come through me.

I am so in love with all of this!

Why did animals disappear from Christian teaching? Their images run powerfully through the ancient stories. When did we begin to separate ourselves from nature? Was it a fear of our own nature? Of its appetites? Fear of the body? Whatever it was, it patently hasn't worked. Only consider how those same repressed and forbidden instincts have gained power in society.

Stone-age people knew the animal powers intimately. Cave-paintings show how deeply they observed each animal. They did not see themselves as separate from them.

What is the mercy of wild things? Why can't I answer this question? I can feel it tugging at me.

I can see a form being born under my fingers, bead by bead. My progress is so slow, my fingers somehow leading the way. This is like a slow birth.

I am beginning to see him! A crucified wolf! I am using my smallest beads to capture the look of agony. I want this to be both beautiful and terrifying.

How I love this wolf. The drawn-back lips. The snarl of pain. The sudden whiteness of the teeth. And yet I have the sense that here, nailed to the cross, a god is being born in the underground cave of my imagination.

What do I mean by that? I can't say, but I seem to know it.

The wolf has taken me by surprise. I see this image as, perhaps, the first of a series of animal icons. They must each stand alone, the way an animal painted on the wall of a cave stands alone, not as a part of a picture. It is the whole story.

This wolf is my soul-brother. His body is being crucified, but you cannot crucify his presence in our consciousness. There is blood on the land, and we will pay for this. Tomorrow I will give him a blood-moon for a halo and a cross of ponderosa pine, the wood often chosen by santeros for their devotional paintings. I must still work out how to make his coat look alive; electric.

I know I must also show an image of a free wolf— perhaps almost invisible. In a forest?

Octavia sat back to examine her work, and to give her back a rest. What she saw brought tears to her eyes. She could feel the pain in her own body; could know, in the animal of her imagination, the scent and silence of wolf.

It was with surprise that she noticed that dawn was breaking.

She closed the lids of the bead-bottles, and tidied her work-table. She took off the special apron she wore to catch any falling beads, and hung it on the edge of the frame. She was still held captive by the mood of the work. She read the notes she had made, and added a further thought.

I remember now! A photograph I saw of dead wolves, hanging on sticks; wolves that had been shot for the one-dollar bounty that would be paid for every wolf-hide.

Is this how it all ends? All these ages it has taken to create this splendid diversity—centuries of history, from the earliest beginnings; everything that has ever been. Is all this splendid life and passion going to pass away?

I know what my ritual will be! I will make a series of miniature iconic sketches—all the animals that present themselves to me. Maybe I will paint them. And the music for these?

Of course! Tavener's Svyati!

She moved outside, and locked the door. The sky was just beginning to turn pink. Suddenly she heard a rush of air and a flapping of wings as the white doves, released from their aviary, lifted into the sky.

As she watched them fly their timeless patterns, swooping low over the fields and rising to clear the cottonwoods, they brought to mind Sebastián's voice, and two lines he was reading aloud from Blake's Auguries of Innocence—

"Hold infinity in the palm of your hand
And eternity in an hour."

This is it! This timeless moment! This instant lives! *This* is Blake's eternity. She sat in her wheelchair, and surrendered herself to the day.

Journal Entry 17—April 1996

Last night's dream:
I see the image of a wolf in the night sky. He is a grey wolf with a white mask. And tufts of white fur on his throat and neck. His eyes are closed. I see only his head and neck. The head is thrown back in a howl. I see fire leaping out of his mouth. Instead of a body I see a series of geometric shapes, like a collection of overlapping triangles of different sizes. They are made up of warm colors—pink, orange, red and lilac—and are strangely erotic.
What is this? I see threads hanging down from these shapes; threads of the same colors. Maybe they are ribbons—or streams of blood? I think the wolf is alive. I can see what looks like his fiery breath, reaching up into the night sky. I think he is a pagan god. Maybe, with this fiery breath, he has created the stars.
But he has no wolf-body.
Is this the idea of wolf that cannot be crucified or killed? My overall sense of this work will have to change—has changed already. It has taken on its own life. All I can do is follow. Is this like the resurrection of the wolf? I don't want to interfere with what is coming out of me—from where? I must have this image in the sky. The two wolves are intimately connected; inseparable. What do they say to me?

Journal Entry 18

How I love this wolf-creature! My progress is so slow. I am sure it is a blessing, because it allows time for the complete image to emerge. I am so impatient! I love the process; but now I cannot wait to see the end result. This must be what pregnant women feel. I hope this doesn't take nine months!

Journal Entry 19

This beadwork is taking me on a journey. I said I wasn't going to make any drawings, but I have changed my mind. I need to catch the visions that are coming to me so fast—or like a dream not written down, I will lose them. I have drawn how I see the finished work. It may—and probably will—change.

What I saw today, when I came into the studio, was the connection between the two wolf images. I still have only a sense of what this means. I want the long threads of beads hanging down from the sky-wolf to reach over the lower wolf like a veil. Brides wear veils because there is a sacred change happening in the woman— not for the world to see. Only on completion is the veil thrown back. It is like a caterpillar transforming into a butterfly, hidden in the chrysalis.

I now see the crucified wolf in a new way. Here too there is something sacred taking place. I have drawn the beads hanging down below the actual frame of the work.

These images come to me like visitors; strangers with gifts. I do hope I will serve them well. I must hold them in my mind's eye; listen with my heart. Where these images come from is not the question. The question is: what do they want? All I can offer is this response—this wolf image; this blood sacrifice, as my gift to the stranger.

What is the mercy of wild things? I have been excavating the meaning of "mercy" the way Russell Lockhart does. Such a discovery. It moves from "merci"—thank you, a gift—to a pledge, a solemn promise, a contract—a covenant!

That is it! The animals have not broken the covenant—but we have. We have broken the ancient covenant we made: that we would be stewards of the earth; would serve it and all its creatures. And now, how can we not see that we are dying with them? Soul-death; little by little.

I weep for this.

But what is their mercy?

The first miniature is almost finished. Of course it is the wolf!

And why is Alejandro's angel the color of red earth?

Bach

The Adobe Concert Hall was abuzz with people—sweeping, placing chairs, setting stage-lights, checking the stage curtain and making sure that everything was in working order. The auditorium lights were programmed to be very low during the performance—to show a little light on the audience. This was at Kristiyan's request.

"It is rather disconcerting to play to an utterly invisible audience, which may have walked out for all you know," he said with a chuckle.

On the stage, in the center, one chair was placed directly under the spotlight.

Octavia had printed the invitations to the solo cello recital. They had been sent to all the residents of The Adobe, and their neighbors in the surrounding area.

"Do you think we will have enough chairs?"

Octavia was counting on her fingers the people who were certain to come; but you never knew with country people. They all had friends and cousins in Las Madres, and who knows, she thought, how many of them might also come?

"Well, I don't think you can fit another chair in here," Sister Piadosa said, watching Gregorio place the last row of chairs up against the back wall.

"What about seating all the Adobe residents on stage, behind Kristiyan? With the spotlight on him, they will not be visible."

So dining-room and kitchen chairs were hunted down, and set in place.

"Anyone else will have to sit on cushions in the aisle."

"You look amazing," Octavia said as she straightened his black tie. "Are you nervous? I am, and I am not doing anything."

"No. Not nervous, but I am hoping that you will like the music. I played it for my final practical music exam, and I chose it then because of what it says to me. I have been learning it for years—ever since my twelfth birthday, when my parents gave me my first cello. It is a work that never ceases to challenge the artist. As I grow older, I hear new ways of expressing its many moods. I look forward to hearing your impressions and feelings. But I must warn you that it is very different from anything you—we have been listening to."

Octavia sat at the back of the auditorium, and opened the program booklet.

J. S. BACH
Cello Suites Nos. 1—6
For unaccompanied cello
Cellist: Kristiyan Bacarov

She read the short note about Bach's life and works with interest, but it was the notes about the work itself that fascinated her. The six suites were, she read, written somewhere around 1720. She read that they were considered by many to be the most challenging pieces for a solo cellist. She was intrigued to learn that Albert Schweitzer had described Bach as a "painterly" or "pictorial" composer; that there was a visual quality to his work.

Music that had a visual quality? She liked the idea. Could the reverse also be true?

Just then the lights dimmed, and the curtain was raised on an empty stage— apart from one chair.

Octavia's heart skipped a beat as she watched Kristiyan enter with cello in hand, and take a bow under the spotlight to the sound of enthusiastic applause from a house that was packed to overflowing.

He seated himself, taking care to place the cello at the correct distance; shifted his chair slightly, looked out over the silent audience; paused to come back into himself. Then he began to play.

At the first rich notes, Octavia was transported to some other place. She felt the hair stand up on the back of her neck. She leaned forward on her chair, as if wanting to touch—or to be touched by those gentle notes. The music was beyond any words she could put to it. But she saw images of landscapes—of evening skies, vast plains and forests. She saw rivers, and wind blowing through wild grasses. In her mind she saw Alejandro's black mare, running like the wind; an image of beauty. She heard in the music such a reverence for the natural world. How she wanted to be able to move people in this way; to let them know that life—all free life—was beautiful.

Octavia was unaware of anything but the music, and the movement of Kristiyan's hands; those incredibly strong and sensitive fingers. How did a person teach his hands to remember all those notes, every nuance? Surely you had to make yourself and the music one and the same. She marveled at how some notes were so gentle that it was as if they grew under his touch, while others felt almost like a blow, such was the force with which he bowed them.

She had a flash of what it might feel like to have those hands touch her.

She was brought back to the room by the applause that signaled the interval— so soon? How could time collapse in this way?

The audience made its way to the courtyard—some to get a glass of wine and finger-snacks; some to talk; others, who wanted to be alone and quiet, to find a place to sit and hold the music inside them.

The second part of the evening was like one eternal now for Octavia. When the last notes died away into the silence before the applause, she knew that she had been touched; a touch that was the confirmation of everything she so passionately believed to be essential.

Journal Entry 20

Things are moving so fast. I can hardly keep up with myself. I went to Santa Fe with Kristiyan to buy a CD of Bach's six suites for solo cello. There was a recording by Yo-Yo Ma, and another made by Rostropovich when he was in his sixties. I took both. This is the music for my studio; just this. I will not play anything else while I am working. I want to feel these notes etch themselves into the deepest part of me. And into my work.

Yesterday Sebastián and I had tea together. He and Georgia are leaving The Adobe! I can't believe it! For a year! Maybe longer. They are going to follow the road wherever it takes them. And he says he is going to find his voice again. And mama will take all her art things.

I feel so thrilled for them.

And scared.

Sebastián says he wants to reconnect with an experience he had after his mother died. He was hiking along a cliff-edge in the Sangre de Cristo mountain range when a huge bird, a condor, rose out of the gloom and came straight at him. He said he would never forget the rage in that fierce eye, so close to his face. He said the condor gave him a taste of his own death.

"And yet," he said to me, "when I returned to The Adobe, I decided to carry on my mother's work. Her dream. That is where I took a byway."

"Didn't it feel sad—turning your back on your poetry?"

"I didn't see it then. And of course life took over, and I became immersed in all the small day-to-day crises of The Adobe."

"But no poetry?"

"No—no poetry. And yet—look what it brought me: Georgia, Lucien and you! The richness of all that has happened here. How could I not be grateful for that? So sometimes, it seems, we do have to step off the straight path."

"Isn't it just a waste of time? Think of all the poems you could have written— could have published—in all that time."

"Well, yes—and I may be making excuses. But I think not. Maybe there was something I still had to learn before I could truly embark on the great work." He gave a laugh. "Some kind of testing." He paused. "Maybe that was also a part of the path."

"And did you feel tested?"

"Oh, yes. But you were quite right that day, when you said to us that we had all *fallen asleep. There has been no great art, and no poetry. It seemed as if I had turned my back on the most mystical experience of my life."*

He took my hand, and held it. "I am telling you this to acknowledge you and your clarity that day, and to thank you for it. It started me thinking—not very clearly, but thinking nevertheless.

"I have been living my mother's life—as Raho has recently made me recognize with his infuriating riddles. And yet, I have no regrets—whatsoever."

"And so, now—"

"Now—it is time for me to seize the condor's terrifying gift. I am ready, at last."

Sebastián has never spoken to me like this—not as a father to his child, but as one equal to another; with respect. I saw my father as I have never experienced him before—his passion! The depth of it! I can still feel the intensity of his commitment to life, where everything is accepted and everything has its time and its place.

I felt such a rush of love fill me—something I could not name. Not awe. Something else. Something that is beyond joy. Something that has no name.

Then we were crying and laughing together.

Oh, I am so happy to be alive.

I have begun work on the second icon miniature: an elk.

An Evening at the Adobe

The station wagon was parked outside the casita, packed to the roof with everything they would need for their respective work. A small battery refrigerator, which would be charged by the car's motor, was secured close to the back door for easy access. On the roof-carrier a tarpaulin covered their two suitcases, Georgia's easel, two light-weight, collapsible canvas chairs and a camping-table. Georgia added two sleeping-bags at the last minute. "Just in case," she said. "You never know where we may choose to stop and work. Better to be prepared."

Sebastián paused in the middle of what he was doing to watch her walk toward him, carrying a box of books. He thought he had never seen her look more beautiful. Gone were the signs of weariness. With her hair tied back in a pony-tail, and her cheeks flushed from all the activity, she looked like a young girl. All over again, his heart filled with wonder that she had chosen him.

The white doves had just been released from the aviary for their evening flight. Sebastián watched them fly their familiar patterns over the fields and the cottonwoods, and back to the room where María had lived, awaiting the birth of her child.

All of this had been so much a part of him. He knew, without regretting his decision to leave, that he would miss this life terribly. So many partings in a life, he thought. Why did they always feel so painful? Why did the memory of each one seem to endure so vividly?

He looked up toward the pink hill. It was there that he had first read the poems of Rilke from the library-book Georgia had given him while they were both in college. How it had changed his life—poetry. He had instantly recognized his destiny—only to cast it aside in favor of what felt like a greater need. And now he would have to face himself, fully, at last. Would he ever write anything that even approached Rilke's Duino Elegies, the poems he valued above all others?

As he stood, watching the doves, some lines came back to him from the First Elegy:

> *"Listen, my heart, as only*
> *saints have listened..."*

Whether he succeeded or not, Sebastián knew that he would never rest until he had at least touched that deep listening; could hear the voice that longed to come through him. He knew it was there. If only he let it speak.

ㅁㅁㅁ

Sofia arrived at Sebastián and Georgia's casita at six o'clock with the food and wine for the informal supper. Because everyone who lived and worked at The Adobe would be present, she had arranged with Gregorio to have trestle-tables and chairs set up outside to accommodate them. All the family members, from Catherine down to the youngest—Caradoc and Erin—would be there, together with Kristiyan and Reuben, Sister Piadosa, Sister Ana, Sister Clemencia, Alejandro and Francesca, Raho and all the nuns. Gregorio would be helping Sofia to pass the food, and to see that everyone had something to drink.

Ever since it had been announced that Sebastián and Georgia were going to take a year's sabbatical, The Adobe had been in a frenzy of activity, organizing who would undertake to pick up the duties which the two of them had carried for so many years. Sister Piadosa said that she was more than happy to take over admin duties, if Sebastián would just show her the ropes and bring her up to date with daily matters.

Sister Ana was thrilled to be taking over Georgia's children's art classes. "Georgia," she said with a beaming smile, "it will be such a joy for me!"

The supper was over. Gregorio and the nuns cleared the tables, and Sofia took the little ones off to put them to bed.

The rest sat, drinking their wine, and listening to de Falla's Nights in the Gardens of Spain. They breathed in the fragrance of the roses that hung over the courtyard wall, and enjoyed the warmth of the evening. The music, with its sultry passion,

266

recalled the ancient links that connected the early Hispanic and Spanish cultures. The listeners thrilled to the fire and darkness in the slow, haunting opening with its taste of blood.

The music ended, leaving everyone with the huge silence of the night. Still no one moved. They wanted one thing more from the evening.

As if in response, Sebastián suddenly sprang onto a table and—to everyone's amazement—struck the pose of a flamenco dancer. Gone was the keeper of records and accounts, the earnest overseer of the day-to-day running of the busy community. In his place they saw a man, stepping into his mixed Indian and Andalusian heritage.

He began to dance.

Everyone started clapping, calling out in Spanish, urging him on—everyone except Georgia. She sat in shock, watching a man she did not know. This was a man she had never met before.

The dance came to an end. Still the people cheered, and banged the table for more.

But Sebastián stood still. When everyone was quiet, he addressed them.

"I would like to take you back to a time when I was still in college. Georgia had left for Paris, and I had thrown myself into my poetry lectures. One evening—an evening just like this one with its absence of moon, its stillness—I found myself writing my first ever poem.

"Tomorrow I intend to pick up where I left off, almost thirty years ago."

Sebastián stood, his head inclined as if he was listening to a voice within him. He waited, his eyes half-closed, drawing up into his body all the grief and pain, all the dark feelings of that night; his memory of the extraordinary voice that broke through the barrier of his intellect, like a flash of lightning.

His voice, when he began to speak, seemed to leap out into the night. The listeners sat, astonished, hearing a voice that held blood in its throat, and the shudder of death.

> "*A dark wind is eating me*
> *I feel it in my bones;*
> *this fierce communion*
> *this shuddering black song.*
>
> "*Oh, what rapture! What rapture!*
> *This night without a moon;*
> *this fierce communion—*
> *this shuddering black song.*"

The Young Lover

There is no future. This now—this is the future!

Who said that? Or had he read it? It sounded like one of Raho's infuriating quips, but he couldn't remember just when—or if—Raho had actually said it.

He glanced at the woman beside him. Her eyes were closed, and her head was resting against the window-frame, allowing the warm wind to blow her white hair this way and that as the car sped south, down the Interstate.

They were married! She was his wife! He was her husband!—how extraordinary, those three statements.

We measure time, he thought, but what we get is an illusion. In a way, an hour is not an hour; a year is not a year. And fifty years? Only look at how those fifty years had vanished in one breath. They, and everything that ever was and ever will be—all one: this instant; this eternal now.

Out of the corner of his eye he saw a young woman, barely twenty, relaxed in the passenger seat next to him. He noticed with pleasure how lovely she was; her black hair that streamed out of the open window, with a few stray tendrils caressing her face. Her cheeks were flushed from the heat of the day. Her lips were parted, as if to taste the wind.

And then, super-imposed on that image, he saw the black mare, racing across open land—wild; free. He tried to keep her in sight, but soon she was just a dark speck, dissolving into the heat-haze.

He felt a mixture of relief and sadness. Relief that she was free. He knew, although he had not been aware of holding onto her, that he had let her go.

And the sadness?

It was a feeling, he thought, of being very solid—trapped in a body; trapped in some other reality, which prevented him from running with her.

And yet, he asked himself, isn't there also something else—something that draws us ever onward? What is that?

Again he visualized the black mare. Such beauty! That perfect wildness—so unattainable. In some way that he would have been unable to articulate, she was for him the young lover—always out of reach. He was not exactly sure just what he meant. Always out of reach. Yes. But that did not mean that there was not something in his soul that still yearned to touch her.

And who then was this beautiful woman, sitting beside him? And what had all of this to do with his angels? There was a connection. He knew it!

Alejandro negotiated a small detour where there were some road-works, and then bumped back onto the tarmac.

He recalled Raho once telling him about the Japanese tea ceremony; that it was a spiritual art form. He remembered listening intently, intrigued by its delicate complexity.

"The tea-bowls used in the ceremony are made by master-potters. No two bowls are ever the same. With each one, the potter aims at the ultimate perfection of size, shape and proportion; and yet he never quite achieves this. That does not prevent him from dedicating his entire life to the discipline.

"You see, Alejandro—all down the years, while he is reaching for the perfection of a tea-bowl, although he is not aware of it, he is learning a parallel discipline: he is honing his own soul. That is what he works at. And this is not an acquisitive act. He is not doing this in order to gain anything, the way we in the West would. He is innocent of any intention, other than to make this bowl—now.

"Compare this to us, in the West. We learn to meditate so that we can gain enlightenment—which of course provides the perfect obstacle to ever achieving it, whatever it is! It condemns us to a life of struggle.

"We do things in order that—you can fill in the space with money, recognition, fame, whatever.

"And that is not the end of it. This whatever-it-is—it is supposed to bring us happiness. And when it doesn't, we do more and more of the same. But then, of course, we must ask ourselves: what is happiness?"

Alejandro brought his thoughts back to his recent conversations with Raho. He realized that he had never managed to answer the one question Raho had asked him.

"You received a command from the Heavenly Host, when you were ten years old, to carve angels—as many as stars. How else might you have interpreted it when you were twenty, or twenty-five?"

The image of a tea-bowl hovered in front of his eyes. For a timeless instant, he stared at it.

He drove automatically, his mind focused on his inner dialogue.

Unseen, the landscape with its dry plains, and the mesas that looked like huge vessels steaming across a vast ocean. Unseen, the gathering thunderheads and the small ripple of the distant horizon, the mountains dwarfed by the immensity of the sky. Unseen, the long stretch of road ahead of him.

Just one small tea-bowl.

A humble object that is to be used, he thought. The potter makes a small bowl—how many thousands in a lifetime? Where they go, who uses them, is not his concern. It is the impeccable attention to the making of each bowl, one at a time—as if his life depends on it, as it most surely does—that is required. He is the craftsman, and he is the tool that shapes the emptiness within. Anything imaginable might come out of it.

Alejandro pulled off the road, onto the soft shoulder. Francesca was still asleep.

On a whim, he decided to look inside the bowl hovering in front of him. In his mind's eye he tipped it forward. There was something in it after all!

He stared at the tiny wooden angel that fell out; stared at the seemingly endless stream of angels that followed it, rising up like a mist, a cloud—flying out into the ether above him to become a galaxy of tiny wooden angels.

Next to him, Francesca gave a yawn and opened her eyes. Then, with a cry, she sat up.

"Alejandro!" she exclaimed. "Look! All your angels! They are flying away! What happened?"

Alejandro took her hand, and smiled.

He looked out at the vast plain that reached out into the haze, and the still mesas with all their silent history hidden within them.

"We set each other free," he said.

Journal Entry 21

So much has been happening; so many changes.

This is the first time my parents have gone away—for a whole year. I feel so vulnerable. What if anything awful happens? I never realized how much their presence made everything feel safe. I am ashamed now, looking back, at what a brat I was—that I took them so for granted. And here I am still, thinking only of myself! Oh, mama, I will tell you this when you come back. But for now I send you both so much love and gratitude for all that you are, and all that you have been and done for me—for all of us.

Coming back to an empty house each night is strange.

I feel disconnected from the work I was doing. This scares me. What if I cannot find my way back to that voice which speaks to me?

I am glad I have the miniatures, which I promised myself I would work on every day. I am busy with a mountain lion.

Alejandro has left with Francesca. I never realized fully, until now, what an important part he has played in my life. I have felt so utterly seen by him. Will I ever see myself as clearly?

I remember his remark to me, after the house-warming. It was about the bead-

work gift. He said: "I love your work! It has a quality that instantly arrests the eye; an emptiness that comes as a relief—like clean, cool water in the desert; like something we take for granted in our lives. And this sense of an eternal present. When I contemplate this work, I disappear. And there is nothing to say."

Yes, Octavia! You have taken a lot for granted!

Journal Entry 22

Where has that feeling of being in love with these images gone? I feel so dead inside. Have I been living off other people's energy?

And why must Kristiyan have his tour right now?

Stop complaining, Octavia. It isn't your style. Still, this is how I am feeling. I can't even connect with the Bach! And only a week ago I thought I could listen to it forever. This must be what Sebastián felt about his writing, and mama about her painting. Maybe, as a punishment, I will inherit the admin duties. That would be very poetic.

Yes, Octavia. You learned a lot from the accident; from all the pain—did you think that was all there was to learn?

Octavia wheeled herself over to her work-frame. She removed the dust-cover, and sat looking at the unfinished work. She felt like putting the sheet back, and leaving the room. Instead she collected some jars of beads, needles and the fine thread, and brought them to the work-table.

Go on! Put in one bead—just one bead; then you can leave.

Three hours later she packed the things away again. She sat, contemplating the area she had just worked: the closed eye of the wolf in the sky.

It was beautiful.

Three hours to work an area she could cover with the tip of her thumb!

She covered the frame, and left the studio.

Sofia

"I don't know what's the matter with me."

Sofia and Sister Piadosa were taking tea together in the nun's office.

"Nothing is wrong. Caradoc loves his morning play-school, and Erin is the easiest baby ever. She just eats and sleeps. Lucien is writing a new piece for piano and cello. He can't wait for Kristiyan to get back, so that they can work on it together. So he is happy. Everything in my life is working perfectly. So why—?"

Sofia burst into tears.

"So why am I always crying? Sometimes I wake up in the night, sobbing, and I have to run into the bathroom so I won't wake Lucien."

She blew her nose, and looked at Sister Piadosa.

"I don't want to cry in front of the children—or Lucien. This has nothing to do with them. I make excuses and say that I have to do this or that, and then I go down to the cottonwoods, and sit there and cry. Then I go back, splash some cold water on my face, and carry on. Why am I doing this? It doesn't make sense to me."

She blew her nose again, and wiped her eyes.

"I don't want to trouble my father. He is so protective of me, and he would drop everything to help me. But this is not a broken leg. That would be easy. What could he do that he doesn't already do for me? He has been like two parents, and given me so much love. And he has told me so much about my mother—how beautiful she looked on the night they got married. Did you know that he came to fetch her in a neon-green lowrider, all painted with red roses? Isn't that romantic?"

"I didn't know that. How lovely," Sister Piadosa said, smiling. "But tell me what you have been thinking about recently."

The nun pushed the tea-tray to one side, and leaned forward to listen.

"Oh, nothing new, really. I have been speaking to Catherine about her life. For some reason that makes me sad—which is silly, because she is so serene. And yet here she is, toward the end of her life, and what does she have to show for it? Six daughters—well, only five now; a horrible husband she doesn't ever want to see again, and a gift that got lost somewhere along the way.

"And look at my mother. She tried so hard to break out, but—"

Sofia burst into a fresh bout of weeping.

"Are women born just to have babies? And to run around, seeing that everyone is fed and dressed and happy? That all the laundry is done? And then, next day, to do it all over again?"

Sister Piadosa waited.

"It is very wrong of me, I know, but my life feels meaningless. How dare I even say that when I have so much—so much love from so many people?"

"Tell me, Sofia, what brings you joy—or what gave you a different feeling about yourself in the past." Sister Piadosa passed her a tissue.

"Oh, my singing! But that seems to be falling away now. The musicians are busy composing instrumental music; and even if they wrote songs, I don't have the time—or the energy—or even the inclination to sing them now. I look at the years ahead, and I see more and more of the same. And I know I chose this! That is what makes me feel so—so wicked! I think, if this goes on, I will poison everyone close to me with this—"

Sofia got up, threw herself into Sister Piadosa's arms, and sobbed. The nun held her and rocked her, back and forth, back and forth, until the sobs were done; held her still while Sofia took great, heaving breaths. Only when she was quiet did Sister Piadosa relax her hold.

Sofia sat up, and dried her eyes.

"What am I going to do? I can't go on being this miserable creature. Sooner or later the children will sense the tension—and Lucien—and then they too will become less and less happy. Do you think my mother, and her mother before her went through all of this?"

Sofia went back to her seat, sat up straight, pushed her hair back and retied the ribbon which kept it off her face.

"Sofia. This is what I think. I don't think that there is anything the matter with you. Far from it. What I do think is that you are ready to take a very big, very important step in your life. I am talking about your voice; your singing career. Why do you feel sad when you speak to your grandmother, even though you can see how serene she is? I think it is because you are looking at her, but you are seeing yourself in her—seeing all the wasted years of her life. Perhaps you see a place where you fear you will be in fifty or sixty years."

The nun sat forward again, and took Sofia's hands in hers.

"But she had one thing that you do not have. She had rage!"

Sofia's eyes widened in surprise.

"She had to fight the bullying of her husband. It is a wonder she came through. It was this rage that saved her in the end. All the fire and energy she would have brought to a singing career, she harnessed to withstand his irrational and violent tempers. She only stayed with him for your mother's sake. And when María was sent away, and Catherine could not discover where she had been taken, she packed a bag and left. She just disappeared—and no one, not even de la Cruz with all his power, could find her. It was her rage that saved her in the end."

Sofia had not taken her eyes off the nun's face.

"You have a very special gift, my dear. You know this. It is a gift that has been carried, virtually in silence, through two generations. And now it is yours. I think it is time for you to step into your destiny; a step that neither your mother nor Catherine—although they fought so hard—could take. In this way you will bring meaning not only to your life, but to theirs."

Sofia clasped her hands.

"If only I could." Her eyes brimmed again with tears. "But I have made choices. I cannot suddenly say: 'Sorry, but I have changed my mind.' I have Lucien to care for, and two very young children. I cannot—no—I would not ever abandon them. So what's to do? Maybe this gift is, in fact, a curse. It doesn't seem to have brought any joy with it—to anyone. Only terrible pain."

"A rare talent, my dear, is not the same as a Christmas present, where all you have to do is untie the ribbon. It has to be birthed. It has to be earned. It is like the steel out of which a very rare sword is made. It has to endure the furnace and be beaten into shape, over and over, until its strength is without a single flaw.

"If we are given such a talent, and we do not step into the life it requires, we do ourselves terrible damage. No amount of sensible talk, no amount of rationalization will make that fire go away. Instead of serving us, it will begin to destroy us, little by little—until we feel dead inside; until we no longer really feel at all."

Sofia rocked back and forth on her chair, her hands pressed against her throat.

"People say they envy great writers, musicians, famous painters—singers, like you. They only see the moment of glory. They do not see the grueling years of training, of dedication to a discipline; the sacrifices that have to be made in its name. They do not see the weeks, the months of desperation; the failures. They have not had to endure those critics who, although they do not have the gift to create such a work, think they know enough to tear it to pieces."

She smiled at Sofia.

"But enough of that. Now we must work together to see how this is to be achieved. You and I and Lucien will discuss this first. Then we can look at how we will make it possible in such a way that no one gets left out, and you do not have to abandon your family. All this is possible. You will see."

She paused.

"And something else. This will be the greatest gift you bring to your family: the example of stepping, heart and soul, into what you are called to do. If you want to know how to make your children happy, be happy within yourself. Not to do this—well, you can already see what that looks like. And how happy will Lucien be to develop his gifts, his compositions and future performances, if he looks at you and sees a very worthy, careworn and bitter drudge?"

Sofia had to laugh at this.

"You see, my dear, in the end no one feels grateful for the huge sacrifices that are made, ostensibly for them. They become, increasingly, a tremendous burden on the one who is supposed to feel grateful. We very soon begin to resent them. Martyrs are always rather dreary people, I think. They are so awfully worthy. They have denied themselves so much. And yet they bring up such a rage in us—we want to kill them, the way they are slowly killing us.

"No, my dear. There is nothing wrong with you. This sadness—this depression you have been feeling—is a sign of spiritual fitness. It is the health of a soul that refuses to go to sleep.

"Sofia, my dear, I was there at your physical birth. I heard the song your mother gave you, even as you were coming into the world. She knew that you would be taken from her. Such pain at a moment that should have been filled with wonder and joy. But she knew what she was giving you: the one thing that no one had been able to take from her—her song. I look forward now to watching you give birth to yourself, and claiming your inheritance—your particular and utterly unique song.

"I am sure that María is watching over us with such joy, even as we speak."

Journal Entry 23

I have spent an hour sitting in front of this beadwork of the two wolves. I felt so happy about it before. Now there is something that disturbs me about the wolf in the sky. It is a beautiful image, for sure; but why is he disembodied? Where is the warm blood and breath of his body, the fire within that makes him—Wolf? I think I mistook the message of my dream. This is a flat image. Why did I see a wolf without a body? What does that tell me?

This image robs him of his vital aliveness; his physical presence in the world. It has no soul. It is the kind of image you see printed on T-shirts and fridge magnets; on a logo for a brand of merchandise.

And what does it tell me about myself? Am I living a one-dimensional life?

I have been asking this wolf in the sky what he wants. I can feel in my own body his struggle to find his voice. He is so far removed from it, hanging there in the sky. Can people see the extreme cruelty beneath the beautiful image?

Is this what we are doing to animals?

Have we ever stopped to ask why—why we are robbing them of their souls; their wild breath—and finally, in increasing numbers, of their physical presence?

And where does that leave us?

Perhaps there is more soul in this disembodied wolf than there is in all of us, in this increasingly sanitized world.

I want to spend time in forests; to be in the places where wolves once ran wild. I want to sit there, and just listen; feel into their landscape. I want to let those grey shadows that melt into the forest enter me through the misty labyrinth of my ancient history. I want all that is wolf to breathe into me—body and soul; all that fierce wildness. I want to feel the electric energy of their immediacy travel down my spine. Feel the hair prickle on the back of my neck.

275

I know that I will make a beadwork—an icon—of the white wolf!

Postscript: I have just flashed on what this image means to me. We have killed—crucified—the body of the wolf. What we have now is the disembodied spirit, floating in the sky—a beautiful image with no soul; the idea of wolf. How safe! How satisfactory! Now we can pretend to love him. Is this what we are doing to our soul-life? In our culture, is it only the image we project that is important? Is this a result of religion's denial of the body and its hungers? Or do we begrudge him his fierce independence?

A Day with Gregorio

Octavia sat, watching Gregorio groom the ponies. The bay pony skittered this way and that during the whole process, jerking the halter-rope that was fastened to the railing, and giving kick-ups whenever the brush came near a ticklish spot. But the grey stood—relaxed, head lowered and eyes closed, enjoying the rhythmic movements of the brush.

"Another minute, Gregorio, and you will put him to sleep." She laughed. "Does he always respond like this?"

"We got him when Sofia was a little girl; nine or ten I think she was. He was still a foal. She felt sad for him because he had to leave his mother—she knew what that felt like—so she used to bring him apples and oats, and stay with him while he ate them—playing with his mane and scratching him between the ears when he lowered his head. She could lean against him, and daydream; and he never moved. They became very close friends."

He gave the pony a shove, asking him to move over so that he could groom his other side, but the grey just leaned into him without budging.

"You see that?" Gregorio moved to the other side.

"Young children see animals as equals, as friends—and the animals recognize this. The bonds that are forged then are very strong. Animals never forget. You want to see him when Sofia comes to visit. He behaves like a foal all over again."

Octavia compared this information with what she knew about her wolf in the sky. What did wild animals feel about humans? They probably didn't think about them at all—until they were caught and abused. Then they learned to fear humans. They moved away into the mountains, coming down only to hunt or to take a sheep or a young calf. Then they were labeled as bestial brutes, and shot.

But was it possible for her to have a relationship with a wolf? And if so, on

276

what terms? Certainly it would require that he was not removed from his world of un-
tamed spaces: forests and mountains. Not tamed in any way. Free to come and go. And
why not, she thought. Animals were here long before we were a speck on the horizon
of history. Long before we lived in caves. Then she thought of the rescue wolves she
had read about—the price they paid for their safety.

She watched Gregorio lead the ponies to their paddock, and remove their hal-
ters.

"And why are you not in your studio today, working?" he said on his return.

"I needed to get some distance from the tapestry I am doing. I wanted to get a
feel of animals. Apart from Alejandro's dog—and he's not very big—I have had very
little to do with large animals. I have a lot to learn. And especially about wild animals.
Doing the work I am busy with has made me realize that true wildness is only an idea
for me. I have no experience of it. Of course there are videos and so on, but that is not
a true experience. There you are shown what has been selected and edited; what will
be of commercial benefit to the program."

Gregorio cleaned the brush with the curry-comb and turned to replace both in
the saddle-room.

"I don't have a busy day today. How would you like to visit one of the wolf
rescue places I know, not far from here? It will not be wolves in their natural state, but
maybe it will give you a sense of them. Some of them are wolf-dogs that people have
bred, thinking they will have an exotic pet. But when the wolf character comes out,
they abandon them. Turn them loose to fend for themselves. But of course they are
now ruined for that as well."

"I will be ready in five minutes."

Journal Entry 24

I am in such a towering rage.

*I bought a book at the wolf sanctuary, and I have been reading up on the his-
tory of our country's wolves.*

*What our people have done—not only sanctioned, but often instigated by our
government—over the past hundred years is a stain on humanity.*

"The wolf is the only species to be deliberately
driven to the brink of extinction by humans."
That is a quote.

And in the archives, reprinted in the book, there are old photographs of wolf-

skulls and skins, piled high; wolves shot by bounty-hunters. I am ashamed to be human!

I read how we have now learned that wolves are a keystone species. This means that they are essential to wilderness if it is to remain in balance. Yet the battle still rages on. Ranchers think that they are entitled to spread further and further into the remnants of our pristine wilderness, while environmentalists seek to redress the imbalance and to bring the wolf back to this country.

I feel so depressed, reading all of this: the extent of human ignorance and greed.

Such brutality. Such deliberate blindness.

It might interest the ranchers to learn that we humans are not a keystone species! Neither are their cows!

Journal Entry 25

The image in my mind's eye has shifted. It is now about blood. Blood on our hands. Blood on the land. I want to put all of my revulsion into a beautifully crafted image, and to set that against the horror of what is being done. I wonder if anyone will get the message—or will they think the artist is mad?

What I thought might be ribbons hanging down from the disembodied wolf are actually threads dripping blood.

In the sky I see brilliant stars, but the light they shine turns into tears of blood. Very radical stuff, Octavia! Let's see if you can make it work!

A New Chapter

Octavia sat, holding her cane with its fringe of animals. She was in a place where she could see Kristiyan's car the moment it turned into the narrow track that led to The Adobe. He was due to arrive any time now. She was surprised to admit to herself that she felt excited.

Perhaps she should walk down to meet him at the corner. No, that would look silly. Perhaps sitting here looked silly; like a child, waiting for a special gift to be delivered. She was shocked to hear an interior voice say: well, he is just that!

"Stop this now, Octavia," she said out loud.

At that moment she saw the car turn into the drive, and bump its way slowly toward her.

She stood up, and waved a greeting. Then, as casually as she could, she walked over to open the door for him.

But there was nothing casual about Kristiyan. He sprang out of the car, took her into his arms and kissed her hard.

"I have missed you so much. I thought the tour would never come to an end." He held her close. "You smell so nice; of lavender and country air."

He pressed his face into her throat, breathing in the fragrance of juniper and herbs.

"Are you staying here on your own? It must seem strange with your parents away—and Alejandro too."

Octavia nodded.

He drew her close. Kissed her again; a long, slow kiss.

Octavia laughed. "I am so glad you are back," she said.

"And I am so glad to be home; to find you here—looking great, by the way. I had forgotten how difficult it is to breathe in the city. In the streets, so many fumes from the traffic; and then the sterile air of air-con hotels. And worst of all—you were not there."

"I don't seem to remember being invited!"

"So tell me how you have been. I see you haven't lost your nerve! What have you been busy with? What new developments here? Have you heard from the honey-mooners, or from your parents?"

Octavia laughed again. "So many questions, and you haven't even had lunch. I want to hear all about the tour."

She stepped back, and smoothed her hair; retied her pony-tail. She had spent all morning anticipating their meeting; trying to imagine what she would feel. What she would say. And now it was so easy, so natural after all.

"Why don't you take your things to your place—especially the cello in this heat," she said practically, "and then come back here, and we can eat and share all our news? I also have so many questions to ask you."

Octavia cleared away the dishes, and poured two tall glasses of iced tea.

"So tell me about the tour. Did you enjoy working with the new people? Do you have any plans to repeat it in other places? Might you even take it to Europe?"

"I enjoyed it, yes, but I am not looking to go to Europe with it. I might think of a tour in South America, because I would love to visit many of the places I have read about. But not right now. I want to stay, and work right here for a while. I will tell you about the tour later, but first I want to hear all your news."

He took her hand.

"Did you miss me? Just a little?"

Octavia laughed, and blushed.

"I did. And I put all of that feeling into my work. I have come quite a long way toward recognizing what it is I want to say."

"In what way did you miss me?"

"You don't give up, do you?"

"You should know that about me by now."

"Yes, I did miss you. I thought about you a lot."

"Did you think about us?"

"Yes."

"Often?"

"Oh, you are impossible! Yes. Every day. Most of the time. I missed you a lot."

There was a long silence. Kristiyan looked into her eyes so intensely that she had to look down.

"Would you think of moving in with me—of us living together?"

Octavia said nothing. When she looked up, there were tears in her eyes.

"I didn't mean to make you cry. You don't have to do anything unless you really choose to."

"There is a part of me that longs to say yes."

"Then why—?"

"Because I am so afraid it would ruin everything. I think passion lives and grows in the absence of something—not when it is satisfied."

"What makes you think that?"

"I suppose I am reaching for something—I can't even say just what it is. And yet, it calls to me—all the time. If I could name it, and if I could reach it, it would be just another thing. There are so many things we have. Have you noticed how they do not satisfy us for long?"

"So are you saying that if we lived together, we would each become just another thing to the other? You don't think, perhaps, that you already have this unattainable something which you reach for, in your work—and I in mine? A relationship between two people does not have to come between those two disciplines. But it could give us a supportive base; a place to return to when we are not stretched out in the work."

"But what if one of us is deeply involved in work, and the other isn't?"

"Then the other must make a plan. This would not be a gruesome twosome, where there are no spaces between us. You would have your work; exhibitions. I would have tours, rehearsals and other musical commitments. I would never ask you to drop your work and play with me; nor, I am sure, would you ask it of me."

He smiled at her.

"Let's leave it there for now. See how we feel about it. We can talk about this again. "And now, I want to hear all the news."

"Well, my work has been going well. I am seeing more clearly where I am going. I can see a context for this exhibition."

"You are planning an exhibition? How soon?"

"Not for ages. Beadwork is a very slow art. A few years, I would imagine."

"You must have a lot of patience."

"But I haven't! That's just it! I want it finished—now! But I can see that it is the slowness that allows some subterranean part of my mind to surface with insights and images that would be lost if I could finish in a day; a week. Anyway I can show you this later."

"And what else has been happening?"

"The biggest bit of news is that Raho would like to stay here for a while. He does not know for how long that will be. He says that he has found the visit very revealing—whatever that means."

"That would seem to be an odd choice for such a Zen kind of a man."

"Yes. But I hope he does stay. Talking to him is such an extraordinary experience. He does not appear to say anything, but when I leave my mind is full of questions."

"What sort of questions?"

"Questions that don't have answers."

"Tell me about one of them."

"Well, what would it be like, when I have this exhibition—which I think I will call Endangered—if you and Lucien were to compose a requiem for it, and perform it at a concert before the opening? You would play the cello, Salvador the violin, Reuben the bandoneon, and Sofia would sing a song without words. That is one question that I am incubating."

"But surely that can be answered very easily."

"Perhaps. Perhaps not as easily as you may think."

"Let us say that it is at least answerable; an exciting challenge. There is no danger of falling asleep while you are asking such questions."

Kristiyan gave her a nudge. "I am going to enjoy living with you—if, of course, that is what we choose."

"Mmmm." It was non-committal, but she said it with a grin.

"Now, let's go and see the others." He took her hand. "Are you happy to walk?"

"Very happy."

The Proposal

"Do you have any idea what Octavia has in mind?"

Santiago and Salvador were walking together to attend the lunch-hour meeting for the musicians in the concert hall.

"Not a clue. I know she is very focused on her artwork now. Amazing, after all that she has been through, that she has so much determination—not to let it get in her way," Santiago said. "The testing time has brought out the best in her."

"Kristiyan said it has to do with her work," Salvador said, "but he didn't elaborate on that. Obviously it must have something to do with music. I must say, I am intrigued. Whenever Octavia gets one of her ideas, it is time to pay close attention—or you will be in it, up to your neck, before you know it. Ah! There is Reuben." He waved a hand. "Reuben! Hi there. I thought you said you were doing a tango evening tonight. Was it canceled?"

"No. I will go there straight after the meeting. There is enough time. I've got the car and the bandoneon, and a change of clothes waiting. An hour and a half on the road, and I will be there. "By the way," he added. "Do you know what this is about?"

"No, but we're all sure as hell going to find out. You can be certain of that!"

They entered the hall, where Sofia and Lucien were sitting next to Raho. He had asked if he could attend the meeting. "Just to listen," he said.

Octavia and Kristiyan greeted them as they entered. Octavia moved to a chair, facing the small group. She hooked her cane over the back of it, and sat down again.

Everyone grew quiet, and looked toward her.

"Firstly—thank you all for making the time to be here," she said, "especially as you don't know what it is all about."

She paused to give them a smile.

"The short version is that this is about a beadwork exhibition—and a concert in the early evening, before the exhibition is opened. I want to ask you to compose, arrange and perform a piece of music that will introduce the theme of the exhibition."

Salvador was the first to speak.

"Oh, is that all?" he said lightly. "We thought it might be something really big!"

"You will have years to think about this! I promise you. I foresee my work taking at least two years to complete, and that is not allowing for unexpected interruptions. That would bring us more or less to the end of '98, or possibly '99. Between now and then, we will be able to come together at regular intervals; to put forward ideas, and see how they fit in with the whole concept."

She paused while Sofia gave everyone coffee, and passed around a plate of sandwiches.

"The exhibition will, I think—I hope—spark much controversy. I sincerely hope it will. I am so appalled at what this country is doing to almost everything that is natural and indigenous."

She stood up, reached for her cane, and began to pace up and down.

"Our wilderness—its biodiversity, and so many species—all vanishing before our eyes. Why? Because people don't want to look! Don't want to think."

Kristiyan thought he had never seen her so beautiful; all lit up, eyes flashing. This, then, was the passion that had made for such an uncomfortable youth. He had heard about some of that from Lucien. No wonder, when this fierce energy was all bottled up in one small child. And here she was, finally stepping into it with her whole heart.

"Our way of life is not sustainable." Octavia stood, looking at the attentive faces. "And there is the other loss—something so insidious that we are hardly aware of it."

"What would that be?" Reuben asked.

"It is the loss of our own wildness—our inner wilderness. Every species that becomes extinct takes a piece of soul with it, leaving us and the world that much poorer. Look at us! How tame we have become. We live in little boxes, with so much brain-washing that we have stopped thinking. Actually, for an individual to remain aware means fighting against a culture that appears to be soul-dead—deaf and blind to what is occurring. Look at our world today. I could scream!"

Octavia was aware of Raho saying nothing.

"The concert would introduce the exhibition, and would also raise money to aid animal activists, and those fighting to preserve indigenous areas from mining ventures and the insatiable ambitions of cattle-ranching. We all know what happens to any species that gets in the way of these things. It is shot, trapped or poisoned; hunted for a trophy-wall—or just for the thrill of shooting a wild creature. We have managed to completely vanquish the bison—hundreds of thousands of them. Now you have to go to a farm if you want to see one! Grazing with cows! And the wolves and condors and mountain lions—the list goes on and on. The Big Horns for their fur, exotic birds to donate their feathers to fashion or to furnish a corner of a grand house, elk for their magnificent antlers..."

Kristiyan thought she looked like a spring—wound so tight that something could break at any moment. His heart went out to her, fighting for what she felt so passionately.

"The indigenous peoples have always respected the animals; all of nature. They take only what they need. But look at us today. "Unless we take a stand—every one of us—and support all the efforts to fight against this continuing rape of the natural world, and do all that we can do individually, we too will be complicit in its loss. "That it is happening at all is an appalling indictment of the human race."

"So what do you hear, Octavia, for this music?" Santiago asked gently.

"I hear a lament for creation. A lament for what has already left for all time—

for creatures that we will never see again. Think of that. It is like falling off the edge of the world, into an endless night. I want to hear in the music the voice of that one animal—the last of its kind—the moment before it takes that final step into oblivion. Does it know what has happened? What does it sense when it cannot find a mate? I want the music to make everyone who listens feel the immensity of what we have done; to offer a prayer of thanks for every single extinct species, be it fauna or flora, for the unique part it has played in the web of nature.

"And I would like to hear your voice, Sofia, in a lament without words. The animals have no words, so you will be their voice.

"And I hear, as well, the beauty of a world before humans arrived. I heard this in the opening of Stravinsky's Rite of Spring, which Kristiyan once played for me. It sounds like the dawn of the world."

"You don't think you are setting your sights rather high? Stravinsky!" said Reuben with raised eyebrows.

"I am only trying to give you an idea of elements that I hope to express in my work, and would love to hear in the music. But that is not all. I hear the brutality we bring to the natural world. I hear the cries of animals caught in traps, held in cages at zoos, slaughtered for sport. And in the music, I want to hear the rage that every one of us should feel at this betrayal."

Octavia was deeply aware of Raho's presence.

"Who are these people? Are they all brutes and criminals? No! Many of them are people of faith; people who think that they are good, principled men and women. That is how dead we have become—living in our heads, not our hearts; living with eyes closed, and mouthing words that have lost all integrity. Empty words."

"And what do you think is the bottom line in all of this?"

It was Santiago who asked the question.

"The bottom line! I think the bottom line could be that we—humans—are the most endangered species of all. Can't you hear the uproar if someone suggested that? We can't see it, because we don't want to see it. We don't seem to understand that there is an interwoven web of animals and habitat, which we share; and that every time you destroy one species, the consequences are far-reaching."

"You seem to know so much about it. On what do you base all of this?" Reuben was concerned. "You may wish to be provocative," he added, "but you had better be prepared to face a firing-squad of questions."

"I have been reading everything I can find about what is happening to the natural world, including the climate change issue. Since I began these new beadworks, I have become so aware of the deliberate ecocide for which we are all responsible. Every time we kill a species, or destroy a forest, we kill something in ourselves. This is what so many environmentalists and animal activists are writing—that unless we stop this destruction, even if we don't care about the animals or the forests, we will be looking at the possibility of our own extinction."

"Isn't that putting it a bit too strongly?"

"That's just it! That is what we say, because we hope it isn't true; that it will go away. Look at those perfect mountains! The wide plains. Our rivers. How could anything be wrong?"

Octavia was almost in tears.

"Don't you see? It is happening so slowly now, we can still dismiss the small signals. But there comes a critical time when it all begins to unravel. The activists are our modern-day prophets, and like all prophets before them they are called madmen, who think they can see into the future. But it is not into the future that they are seeing. They are seeing the present! They are talking about what is happening right now.

"For months I have had a phrase, a question in my head that will not go away: the mercy of wild things. And I have been asking myself, over and over, this one question: what is the mercy of wild things?"

When the meeting was over, everyone dispersed to go back to their various duties. Kristiyan said that he would see her back at the house in about half an hour.

Octavia was left standing with Raho.

"I was very aware of you, Raho—the way you listened. What did you make of the meeting? What are your comments?"

Raho looked at her.

"Tell a wise person or else keep silent," he said.

He gave a small bow and walked off.

Journal Entry 26

I find Raho's economy with words both exasperating and intriguing. And what appear to be riddles. The way he seems to casually drop a line, smile, and walk off! So, what did he mean? I know it is not some clever, throw-away remark. He wants me to think about it. I saw him listening so intently to every word I spoke. It made me very conscious of what I was saying.

So what does he mean—"Tell a wise person or else keep silent?"

He didn't exactly stay silent!

How else do you wake up people's awareness? Is he saying that it is not possible, unless they are wise? Then, of course, it would not be necessary.

I wish Sebastián was here. He would recognize the line instantly.

Damn you, Raho!

"Tell a wise person or else keep silent?"

Silent! But he spoke.

I have spent an hour just looking at this unfinished beadwork. It is saying so much to me, but I can't explain, even to myself, what it is about.

Ah! But it is not telling you, Octavia! So what is it doing?

Oh! I am like a dog who can smell a bone close by, and is running around—looking here, looking there, no bone—until he discovers it is in his mouth all the time. Except, I haven't got the bloody bone!

I have just finished tidying all the bead-bottles, and sweeping the floor. It is amazing how quickly things get dusty. Also, all the revolting, dirty cups and glasses are now clean.

Little Miss Virtue!

So now, Raho—what would it be like to have the concert and the exhibition, with no introductory speech; no titles for the beadworks; no explanations of any-thing?

You arrive. You hear a piece of music. You see a room with beadworks. The rest is up to you.

Does that satisfy you?

Journal Entry 27

It is said that extinction has always been natural and ongoing. Why then all this fuss? The fuss is because in nature a species eventually becomes extinct because another species gradually evolves to replace it.

This is not the same as the extinction that we are bringing, in this case to the wolves. And they do not die alone. A long, interwoven chain of birds, insects and other animals, fish in rivers—the rivers themselves, and their vegetation—all begins to vanish with them.

I find it painful to look this in the face. Painful to learn how few people are fighting for the rights of the natural world. And such small gains. How is it possible that wolves, who survived for three million years before the cows arrived, are on the brink of extinction? Less than a dozen true wolves in this state. How is this possible?

Today I feel hopeless in the face of this huge tide that is moving over the land like a dark shadow, leaving in its wake a depleted earth. We put nothing back. The domestic herds are moved relentlessly on to new, pristine grazing—and on and on and on, leaving an exhausted land in their wake.

Why am I doing this work? Why the intended concert? Do I think it will change anything? Possibly not.

But it has changed me.

This is not a fight against the tide; that would only strengthen it. (I can see you nodding, Raho!) But I will not passively accept it! This is a fight for integrity. I will do everything I can to honor the life of every creature that lives and breathes me.

Perhaps there is only one breath in the world, and we all share it—everything that has life, from microscopic plant forms to the largest mammals. This is surely the soul of the world.

I am excited to have learned the Hebrew word for the spirit that moved on the face of the waters in Genesis. It is "Ruach"—which means spirit wind or breath. It is this vital breath that animates us. It is there from the instant we are born, and leaves us only at our death. How terrible it is to consider the possibility that one day the world might lose this breath, and become a dead planet.

What would it be like to stand with the last mountain lion—or wolf, or condor—and watch it take that last step over the edge; to watch it falling into that deep and forever darkness?

How would it change a person's attitude if he was the one who finally had to push it over the edge?

We have made ourselves so separate from the natural world. I feel a profound grief—as if my heart were breaking. How will I live with this?

I am hearing what Raho was saying—far, far more deeply than I first did. And with such sadness.

This is personal.

Tell a wise person or else keep silent.

The Promise

Octavia read the short note pinned to her door—

Come to my place at seven this evening. I am going to make supper for us. K.

She sat down on one of the chairs outside her studio, holding the note. Absent-mindedly, she noticed a hawk circling in the clear, blue sky, high above the pink hill. Perhaps it had a cottontail in its sights.

She read the note again. On the face of it, this was a simple invitation to come for supper. Octavia knew that it was far more than that. Why was she so frightened of this commitment? She knew that she would be devastated if Kristiyan left— if he found some other woman! She knew that she would feel betrayed, just as surely as she knew this was irrational. Did she want Kristiyan? Love him? Of course she did. Then what was it?

Into her head floated the song from Tosca—the famous star song from her early youth. Lucien? Surely that was laid to rest long ago. What, then, was the hook that had snagged that song up out of the depths?

The hawk was still circling—lower than before, riding easily on the thermals.

No, it wasn't about Lucien. She felt sure of that. Then what?

She sat up—amazed by a sudden memory, and the image of her nine-year-old self gathering four small stones that had starlight in them; keeping them in a small tin, in a secret place in her bedroom. Instantly she knew what all this resistance was about. *It was about the stars!*

She suddenly remembered, so vividly, a childhood promise she had made. No one knew of it. It had been the secret that sustained her, all through her turbulent childhood and early youth. It was the deeply earnest promise that only a child can make: never to abandon the stars. It had felt at the time like a mating for life.

Octavia smiled at the memory of the ritual that followed the promise: the secret escape through her bedroom window—candle-holder, candle, matches from the kitchen cupboard and the small tin of stones in her hand—and then the silent walk to a clear space where she could see the whole of the night sky. There she lit the candle, and placed it on a stone. Around this she laid the small stones—north, south, east and west—at the cardinal points. Then she lay down on her back, the candle-light shining on her face so that the stars would be able to see her, and gazed up at the heavens. She lay there for the two hours it took for the candle to burn down and gutter out.

What was it that occupied her childhood mind; that she had now forgotten? Whatever it was, it must have been appropriate at that age. It was now time, she thought, to renegotiate her commitment in a way that would not betray the integrity of that child's promise, but would now serve her as well as the stars.

A clear image of that night floated into her mind—and she saw, instantly, what she would do. She would make a beadwork of that small ritual: the child, lying alone in open desert, her night-dress white and sudden against the red desert earth. And she would place the tiny, lit candle on a rock altar—with its ring of glittering stones—at her head. Above this small halo of light she would work the immensity of the night sky, with its millions of stars. This she would do in remembrance of that passionate child, and her extraordinary hunger for stars.

And she would go and have supper with Kristiyan.

As she got up to leave Octavia saw the hawk drop out of the sky like a stone, and disappear behind some rocks and juniper bushes, only to rise up again with a cottontail held in its talons.

The First Supper

It was only when she reached the door of Kristiyan's casita that she became aware of her dress—her white dress. She hoped he wouldn't see it as some kind of bridal hint. Oh, come on, Octavia! What on earth are you thinking? Such nonsense! That is in your head! Perhaps she still had time to go and change. But suddenly, there he was to greet her.

"Good evening, Octavia," he said formally, and gave a small bow. "I am so glad you were able to make it. Come in."

He led the way into the sitting-room, with its kiva fireplace and its row of windows on either side, which offered a clear view of the pink hill and Magdalena's white cross.

"I brought some wine," she said, handing it to him.

Kristiyan read the label. "Such a fine wine calls for a celebration. Have a seat, and I will get the glasses."

He came back with the glasses and a plate of nachos. Octavia fussed with her dress and then sat back, not knowing what to do with her hands.

"Are you comfortable there? Do you need an extra cushion?"

"No. I'm fine, thanks."

She took the offered glass of wine, and waited for him to take a seat close to her.

"Well, Octavia! This is a very special evening—I hope the first of many. Shall we drink to that?"

In answer, Octavia raised her glass. Kristiyan reached out to touch glasses with her.

"Za zdorov'e!"

He smiled at her look of inquiry. "It means: 'Your health'."

"Your health too, Kristiyan," she said. "I like the way you have re-arranged things," she added, indicating the new placement of the chairs and coffee-table.

"Thanks. I like to look out at the hill when I am listening to music."

"Oh, yes." Octavia tried to think of something to say.

"So when is your next musical engagement?"

"I've only just got back!" he said, laughing. "Can't a fellow have a little time off? Besides, someone I know has given all the Adobe musicians a huge project to work on. And she will be a fierce task-master!"

A long silence followed this.

"Would you like to talk or eat first? The supper is ready, but it can wait."

"Let's eat."

"Octavia," Kristiyan said when they had finished their coffee, "can we talk about us? Have you thought some more about the idea of—of sharing your life with me? Of us living together? Perhaps—perhaps getting married?"

"I've thought about it—yes." Octavia blushed. This wretched dress!

Kristiyan knelt in front of her.

"I am asking you to marry me. I want to—"

His nerve failed him, and he waited for her to speak.

Here is the moment, she thought. This was the one thing she had vowed never to consider. This was what turned a free spirit into a half-person. This was where a sense of ownership reduced you to someone's wife or someone's husband. All the old tapes crowded into her mind. Don't do it, they cried. You will live to regret it! Look around you! Look what happens in a marriage!

"Oh, Kristiyan!" she said, "I would love to marry you!"

Raho Visits Octavia

"Raho! This is a surprise. Good to see you again. Come in!"

Octavia stood aside to let the tall man enter her studio.

"Would you like to sit? There is a rather old, but fairly comfortable chair in the corner. I will fetch it for you."

"I will stand for a little while, thank you, Octavia," he said, "and then I will fetch the chair."

He stood just inside the door—not moving, apparently not looking at anything. Octavia had the sense that he was feeling into the depths of the room—listening, beneath the surface, to its language; waiting for it to speak to him in its own tongue.

She found herself listening to his silence.

Raho crossed the room to fetch the chair. Finally he spoke.

"So much has happened in this room. So many voices. I am glad they have all come home."

Octavia listened.

"Tell me when you first heard the stars."

She considered this.

"I don't think there ever was a first time. I always knew they were there. I could hear their silence, but I couldn't see them. That was difficult."

"That was when you were still an infant?"

"Yes."

"And what do you hear when you listen?"

"The stars don't speak words, so it is hard to answer you. But somewhere I know that there is a space of incredible innocence and timelessness; a place which is not an actual place—which just is."

She thought for a moment.

"Well, not exactly innocence as we understand the word. Not the unknowing innocence of a child. More like the sharp intuitiveness of a wild creature. A kind of knowing intuition that fulfills itself."

He nodded.

"The last time we spoke, you told me about your rage at what is happening to the natural world."

"Yes. I was on the war path. In a sense I still am, but not in quite the same way."

"Tell me what has changed."

"I remembered something from my childhood. No one knows about it. I kept it as my childhood secret." She laughed. "I must have known that line of yours: 'Tell a wise person'—"

"Actually it is Goethe's, not mine."

Octavia said nothing, but she made a mental note to research this later. Then she recounted her childhood ritual with the candle and the stones.

"I have only now remembered what the child knew then: that the stars do not explain themselves."

"And what do you gather from that?"

"I can be what I am, and do what I do; but there is no need to explain any of it. People will see what they see, do what they do and say what they say." She indicated the tapestry on the frame. "And these beadworks have their own life. They constantly surprise me with their demands. I must let the images speak for themselves. I am doing the physical work, but something else is guiding me. How can I explain them to others when I too can only feel into their truth? And it is a truth as profound and mysterious as the desert. When I interfere with this, and try to influence the process, I find that I have a lot of unpicking to do. I end up with what I call bead muesli."

"And this is one of the images you are working on at the moment? May I look at it?"

"Of course."

Raho moved his chair so that he could sit in front of the beadwork of the two wolves. He looked at the drawing she had made, which was clipped to the easel; at its suggestions for color, and the roughly sketched parts that offered a hint of what might follow.

"You could not explain this to anyone who cannot feel it; who does not know it in himself. To others, it is not necessary."

Raho got up and moved around the room, glancing at sketches—some black and white, some partially painted, and already suggesting possible color options.

He stopped in front of the small, round painting of the ominous, black wave and the yellow-eyed serpent; stood for a long time, examining it closely.

"And this?" he said, without turning to look at her.

"I did that a long time ago. I may or may not work it into a bead tapestry."

"It is very different from the other one. Does it have a story behind it?"

Octavia told him about seeing the black wave and the serpent in the jug of water.

"And what do you make of it now?"

"I think it carries a prophetic message. I think this is what might be unleashed in the world if we continue to ignore the warning signals. Something cataclysmic. The end days—that sort of thing."

"And does it have any significance for you, personally? Were you very angry when you saw this vision?"

Octavia blushed.

"Yes, I think I was."

"You think you were?"

She could not meet his eyes.

"No. I was very hurt and frightened and angry."

He moved his chair back, sat down and made himself comfortable. He sat for a minute, regarding her.

Octavia met his incredible blue gaze, and waited.

Finally he spoke.

"So tell me this: where did you put that rage?"

Octavia thought about everything that had happened since that day.

"I think, perhaps, it has left me," she said.

"Ah—you think, perhaps..."

"All right, then! I don't know!"

"What don't you know?"

Octavia stared into his blue eyes.

Raho said nothing.

Shedding

"I am taking you for a walk. Bring your stick."

Octavia looked at him. What a strange request. But was it? No, it was not a request at all, she thought. It was a very clear statement.

She reached for her stick with its collar of little silver animals.

"Where are we going?"

"We are going up the path to Magdalena's cross."

Octavia stared at him.

"But I will never make it up that steep path."

"Why not?"

The answer was so obvious that she discarded it. Raho was well aware of what had happened to her in the accident. She repeated her reply to herself. It sounded clear; and yet he had challenged it. But had he? No, she had to admit, he had not challenged her. She had added that. He had just asked her why she believed she couldn't go up the path.

Octavia stood still, stick in hand.

Raho appeared to be looking at the sky.

"I should have said that I don't think I will be able to walk up that path."

"Have you tried to?"

She had to concede to herself that she hadn't. In fact, she had not even considered attempting it.

"No," she replied.

"But you sound very certain about this. You must have some basis for thinking so."

It was not a question. She had no reply.

"It is a lovely day. See! The doves have been released for their morning flight. Let us too enjoy the clear sky above us. We can continue this conversation as we walk."

Raho did not appear to notice her silence.
"How lovely the cottonwoods look today."

Octavia's mind was not on the cottonwoods. It was darting this way and that. She could feel her face getting hot.

They walked on, Raho apparently enjoying the serenity of the day. The path up the pink hill was narrow and steep. Here and there, weathered basalt offered comfortable seats. It was to one of these that Raho led her after they had walked for a few minutes.

"Come! Let's sit here for a bit, so that we can talk some more."

Octavia sat down. She could feel her anger rising in her throat. She did not look at Raho.

"Now, where were we? Ah! We were looking at how we determine certainty."

Octavia was in a rage. How could he be so insensitive? She spoke now with some vehemence.

"In this case—firstly, I consider my physical condition, and the limitations it places on me. Secondly, I know this path well. I have been up to Magdalena's cross and the yuccas, many times in the past. I know, therefore, that I will not be able to climb it now. That is the basis for my decision."

"I see."

He rose, and set off again up the path. Octavia followed.

He was being ridiculous. Why couldn't he appreciate what she had been through? It was all very well, his clever questions, his silences. He didn't have the painful hip; the tired back in a corset. And why was he so insistent on climbing this wretched hill, anyway?

Octavia used her stick to help her over some loose stones. Ahead of her, Raho had found another build-up of basalt scree.

"This is a very good place to sit. If we are very quiet and still, we may get a glimpse of some lizards. Sebastián tells me that the hawks hunt them, but they rarely make a kill. The lizards have chosen an excellent habitat."

Why was he rambling on about lizards and cottonwoods?

"Raho," she asked. "Why are we doing this?"

"Doing what, Octavia?"

"This ridiculous walk. This talk of sky and lizards. If there is something you want to tell me, why can't you do it in a comfortable place—in a chair, in the shade? With something to drink!"

"Shh! Look! There is a lizard. He is starting to shed his old skin. How well he blends into the rocks."

In spite of herself, Octavia noticed how he held himself—so still that she almost lost sight of him. His head-turns were lightning-swift; so swift that it was as if he had not moved at all. A hawk would need very sharp eyesight to see a lizard sunning himself on a rock. But then, a hawk could see the slightest movement, even from a great height.

The lizard vanished. Octavia noted the raven high above them.

They walked on, Octavia struggling over the loose gravel. She was determined not to say a word about it. She would not give Raho the satisfaction of hearing her complain; not one word.

After several pauses—to sit on convenient stones, and for Raho to extol the serenity of the day—they arrived at the cross; the white cross that held the entire valley in its protection.

Just below the cross a small grove of yuccas, Magdalena's favorite plants, seemed to be thriving on the barren slopes.

Raho turned to face Octavia.

"So, here we are. We have arrived."

Octavia was so angry that she could hardly speak.

"Would you like to tell me now what all this is about?"

"Octavia," he said quietly. "You can see for yourself. I said I was going to take you for a walk."

"So?"

"As you so correctly said previously: I do what I do, and you do what you do." He smiled gently. "You agreed to accompany me. I don't feel any need to explain anything."

Octavia just stared at him.

Madame Jolie

Madame Jolie came to Santa Fe, New Mexico from Paris in 1989. In France she had studied singing and voice production under the legendary Pierre Bouget. After her husband's death she decided to travel, but after seeing Santa Fe for the first time she knew that she would live and die there.

She was a voice trainer for professional singers, and lived in a small adobe house, not far from Canyon Road. Adjacent to this, on a small, empty plot she had purchased, she built a music studio which she used for teaching. It was to Madame Jolie that Sofia was to go for instruction three mornings a week. She had been highly recommended as a teacher by the Music Society, and by several singers who were studying opera.

Sofia was to be at Madame Jolie's door at ten in the morning, and was expected to be on time.

"If my pupils cannot manage that simple commitment, they will never be able to handle the rigorous training that is demanded of them."

Madame Jolie was a tiny woman with extraordinarily large, bright eyes. What she lacked in stature she made up for by her authoritative presence. She wore black—only black—and she always looked the same as the day before. Her students wondered if she ever changed her clothes, or whether she had a wardrobe of identical black dresses. She was somewhere between sixty and seventy—she had never admitted her precise age to anyone—and wore her black hair pinned back in a tight chignon. Not one grey hair was visible, and although her younger pupils were eager to find out whether she actually dyed her hair, this was never discovered. If Madame Jolie dyed her hair, she did it impeccably, and no evidence of it ever came to light.

Meeting this ten o'clock time requirement would mean an early start for Sofia.

The drive to Santa Fe took approximately an hour and a half—and that was provided there was no accident or other delay on the road. To be safe, Sofia decided that she would leave The Adobe at eight in the morning. She would take a packet of sandwiches to eat on the way.

On the days when she was to go for lessons, it was arranged that Sister Ana would come to Sofia and Lucien's casita at seven-thirty. While Sofia fed the baby, she would dress Caradoc and make breakfast for him and Lucien. Gregorio would take Caradoc to his play-school, and Sister Ana would take care of Erin until Sofia arrived back at about two. Lucien would spend the morning working on his music, and would have lunch with Caradoc at half past twelve, after which both children would hopefully have a rest.

Sofia would undoubtedly have shone as a pupil with Madame Jolie because of her extraordinary voice; that, and because she was a punctual, hard-working student. That would have sealed it. But when Madame Jolie, on asking Sofia from whom she inherited her flaming red hair and fair complexion, learned that Sofia's great-great-grandfather, Henri Jacques Latour, had come from France in 1869—and that her mother, her grandmother and great-grandmother all had the Latour hair, she immediately became Madame Jolie's most favored pupil.

Their work together began with an assessment.

"Sofia, I would like you to sing your favorite song—a cappella."

Sofia sang the song her mother gave her at her birth. Madame Jolie listened attentively, watching for posture, breath and any signs of tension.

Sofia then had to sing songs in a variety of styles, to test her technique and her vocal range—reading, sight unseen, from sheet music. Madame Jolie's accompanist, Theresa, played softly on the piano so as not to overwhelm Sofia's voice. Madame Jolie made notes about pitch control, diction and the flexibility of the voice. Most importantly, she watched how Sofia used her breath—if or when she strained her voice, and how easily she reached high notes and low notes. Her face did not reveal anything to Sofia.

Finally Madame Jolie asked Sofia to take a seat.

"You have a rare gift, Sofia." She smiled. "I am sure you know that. You are what is called a natural."

She shuffled through her notes.

"Nevertheless, there is still a lot of work we can do together. You have an extraordinary range, and I think we may even be able to extend it in the lower register by working on posture and breathing. I will show you how to think down to a note; how to pick it up effortlessly."

She turned to the first page of her notes.

"I would like you to tell me about the first song you sang—your favorite. I have never heard anything quite like it. Where does it come from?"

Sofia hesitated. How would she explain such a song?

"When my mother was carrying me, she knew that I would have to be taken away from her immediately after my birth. It is a long story. All through her pregnancy, I'm told by the nun who delivered me, she sang me that song. She sang it even as I was being born. She knew it was the only gift she would be able to give me. She died a few months later. I never met my mother."

Madame Jolie sat in silence for a little while. Finally she spoke.

"Are you telling me that you learned that song as a newborn baby?"

"Yes."

"And you never heard it sung anywhere else later?"

"No one else knows the song. I am told that I sang the first few bars at my christening. It caused quite a stir."

"I am sure it did!" She shook her head in amazement. "So your mother had a beautiful voice as well?"

"Yes. And my grandmother before her. She was not permitted to sing. My grandmother's husband would not allow it. And when he heard that his daughter had the same gift, he stopped her too. So I am the third generation to receive this voice. My grandmother managed to leave her husband after he sent my mother away. She went to live in Mexico, and there she became known as a diva. She is just over ninety years old now. She lives with us."

"But what an extraordinary story! Extraordinary—and very sad. Is your grandfather still alive?"

"He is—just. We don't see him."

"And no wonder." Madame Jolie stood up. "We are going to make sure that you will sing for both of them, and for yourself—and let anyone try to stop us! They will regret it."

"I promise to work very hard not to let you down."

"We will both work hard."

She smiled. "I will see you tomorrow at ten."

Journal Entry 28

We haven't decided when the wedding will be—but soon. We will have a second blessing service when my parents return. Kristiyan has written to his parents. I wonder how they feel about this. He hopes that they will come for the wedding. I do hope they like me. Will they be disappointed to find that he is not only marrying an American, but a disabled one at that?

How strange that, in spite of my doubts, this feels like the most natural thing in the world.

I am enjoying these visits from Raho, even though he is rattling my cage. Perhaps, Octavia, you have had things your own way for far too long.

I have done a lot of thinking about this exhibition, and the music for it. I had thought to speak about it—explain it; justify it, really. Then, after my conversation with Raho and our walk up the pink hill, I saw that the exhibition could speak for itself. The speaking I was considering was about my rage, and whatever is beneath it. Not about the work at all. I must look at this.

His question—where have you put your rage?—disturbs me. What was that strange vision all about? I have decided to bead the black wave and serpent image. Perhaps, during the working of it, it will speak to me.

I have thought of so many titles for the exhibition and the concert—and cast them all aside again. How do you name something, and yet not name it? Naming anything makes it smaller. Ursula Le Guin wrote about this in a short story she called She Un-names Them. In it she allows the animals to give back the names that were given to them, and set themselves free.

How strange to think of our own names; how they too make us smaller. I am one of billions who have a name in record books; have a number that proves I exist. But when I truly commune with myself there is something else, and it does not have a name. And yet it is to this other—I don't know what—that I go, and come back with what I call sacred gifts. For me, this—and the slow process of giving it an image in my work— is like prayer.

I know I am rambling, but I am also aware of something that wants to be known. Something—where? I cannot answer that.

We had a meeting in the concert hall this evening. I gave an overview of my ideas, and then we all discussed possibilities for how Lucien could compose the music.

For the first movement I hear the early beginnings of life, and the spirit breathing on the face of the waters. Land appearing. The slow development of small organisms, the growth of grasses, plant life and trees. And rivers and rain, and a great wind—and out of all of this the animals are born.

This is where Sofia's voice comes in. She is the voice of all creatures. The instruments will introduce the sounds of wild spaces, with Sofia's voice moving through them.

From there the music will develop into the fierce life of the wild—the matings and the kills—from small, creeping things to the thundering of hooves; the great herds.

All of this lives and breathes, free of any naming.

The second movement will bring the advent of humans—their early, supersti-

tious fear; and their wonder. Tools are made, and weapons for hunting. But even so, the hunting is no different from that of the animals.

And then the great separation.

I wonder when it was that we first stepped out of that harmony. Maybe, like a young child, when we first said "I." What a huge and lonely step that is. I think I was born knowing it.

Was it to compensate for this new vulnerability that all the rest followed? Language; the naming—and then the power of writing; guns, and eventually weapons that have the power to destroy all life forms?

Was it only with mechanization and industry that the greater plunder began? Or was it earlier? What drove wild animals into the mountains—into distant, inaccessible places? When did their voices change? I hear the cry of wilderness, over and over—a howl; an echo. For how long will they have voices?

Who listens? A few?

The animals fall out of history. An empty wind.

I weep for them. How I weep for this loss.

And where will we be?

It has been staring me in the face.

Lament.

Lucien

Lucien sat at the kitchen table, drinking his morning coffee. The coffee was cold. He couldn't be bothered to warm it again. The rush of getting the children off to their respective places for the morning had just concluded. Sofia had been gone for half an hour, and the house was quiet.

He sat, listening for any outside sounds that might tell him people were around, doing—anything.

He heard nothing.

The rush of wings from the white doves would have been consoling.

"Must the whole bloody world go dark a second time?"

The sound of his own voice startled him.

Grow up, Lucien. Go and work. Must you have your hand held for everything?

He reached for his cane, and made his way to the concert hall.

Lucien sat at the piano, his hands in his lap.

He sat for a long time. Thinking.

Go on! Find a chord—a beginning for Octavia's concert. But his hands would not move.

Where is everyone? How can I find them when I can't see?

He banged a clenched fist down on the keys. The sound was strident, and he welcomed it. He could feel his rage in it.

He repeated the action, and felt empowered by the discordant sound.

Perhaps he would go and visit Octavia. But why would she want to see him—of all people? Still, surely the past was the past—or was it?

With difficulty, Lucien found his way to the path and, by letting his cane guide him, managed to negotiate the narrow spiral path that led to the studio.

Would she be there?

He gave a soft knock at the door.

"I'm coming! One minute."

And then the door opened.

"Lucien! How amazing! Would you like to come in?"

"I don't want to intrude if anyone—if Kristiyan—is with you—if you are working."

"I'm alone. I was just sitting. Thinking. Come in."

He took her arm, and stepped over the threshold. Octavia pulled another chair close to hers, and they both sat down. There was an awkward silence. How would he begin this?

"I wondered if we could go back to before your accident, to the time—"

He began again.

"Octavia. I want to say I am sorry for being so unkind to you over the graduation dance."

Octavia stared at him. This was the very first time he had been in her studio. She thought back to the mask with the long blonde hair; the aria from Tosca—the famous star song. How strange to be sitting together, alone, after all this time.

"Oh, Lucien. I am so sorry for my part. I was totally unreasonable. I really must apologize. I didn't question my childish fixation on you. You had just always been there for me. With you I felt so secure. I just couldn't imagine a time without you close. I never even thought about it from your side. I am so sorry."

She brushed away a tear.

"When you came up to me, the day I did that first walk with the poles, after the accident—when you came up and touched my face, I hoped we would find a way to a new kind of intimacy—something beyond my childhood obsession and dependence."

She took his hand.

"Do you think perhaps we could?"

It was his turn to be tearful.

"'Tavia—if you knew how many times I wished for this, and didn't know how

300

to do it. And I was afraid you would say no, and then it would be worse. And then you and Kristiyan got close, and I didn't feel I could interfere."

He squeezed her hand.

"I will always be there for you, 'Tavia," he said.

The Composer

Lucien sat at the piano in the concert hall—his hands in his lap, his head full of words.

He had been sitting there for more than an hour, going through everything that Octavia had said about her vision for the music.

With Sofia away three mornings a week, and the two children being taken care of, much of his time was free and uninterrupted: a perfect opportunity to work on his music. But no music was forthcoming.

This was the first time that he had been asked to compose music for someone else's vision—a vision he could not see or feel. To him the natural world was more a concept than a physical reality.

"Damn!" he said, and closed the piano.

He reached for his cane, and once again made his way to the path that led to Octavia's studio.

"You see, I don't seem to be able to feel the world you describe. I can't hear it. I go down to the hall every day, but nothing comes. The silence is rather terrifying. Almost like not being able to see all over again."

Octavia passed him the cup of coffee she had made, and sat down next to him.

"Something to eat?"

"No, thanks. This is fine."

They sat for a while in silence, sipping the hot coffee.

"I don't think I will be able to do this, 'Tavia," he said at last. "My head works in a different way. I never thought about it before. And now, here it is—staring me in the face. We live in two completely different worlds. I don't know your world."

Octavia considered his words; heard the devastation in his voice. She too had never fully appreciated the vast difference between their ways of perceiving things— particularly the world outside human interaction; human speech. Suddenly she caught a glimpse of his world. It had all the inner richness of listening—perhaps of hearing the subtle nuances of feeling in people's voices—and certainly the richness of his own inner landscape. With all its terrors. That was the world in which he moved—that, and the few known routes between places that were necessary to him.

"But you will," she said. "I have a plan. I am going to introduce you to all the sounds and smells of my world. To the wind—its many voices; how it speaks in grasses, in forests, in empty spaces. I want you to walk barefoot and feel the earth, the sand with all its textures; to touch rocks, walk in rivers. And to feel what it's like to hide in tall grass and keep very still. That is what the jack-rabbits do when they see a hawk overhead. That is something every wild animal is attuned to: a constant and vigilant attention to the slightest sound or scent that might warn it of the presence of a predator."

She paused.

"Can you imagine what it must feel like to be so aware, at all times, that the smallest sound—a twig snapping—will alert you to possible danger? This is what it means to be wild."

"I wouldn't survive such a life. It's another world altogether."

"Yes. It has only one law. To be effective. It is a world so different from ours. And it is a fierce and unforgiving law. In spite of this, the animals have thrived. But nothing in their sense of survival has prepared them for long-distance, telescopic rifles; for the mass slaughters that humans perpetrate. We are their most treacherous enemy."

"And that is freedom?"

"Yes. That is what so many people think they want."

Lucien shook his head.

"And we will listen to as many animal calls and howls as we can find. And I want you to get up close to animals; to touch them, and feel their energy. We can begin right here, with our animals; notice how they respond to you, and you to them—until you can feel some kind of a bond. Animals that have been treated well are so trusting. You will see. Our horses will pick up that they must be more considerate with you. Of course, not wild animals. But we may even get a sense of some of them if we are lucky."

She touched his arm.

"We have a project! And we need a driver. I wonder if Kristiyan would like to join us. Or I could ask Gregorio."

Lucien stood in wonder, listening to the wind tearing through the forest. The wildness of it. Octavia took his hand, and led him over to a tree.

"Put your arms around that. Feel it."

Lucien felt the huge life of the tree, bending to the wind. He could sense the deep roots holding it fast to the earth, and the strong inner core of the trunk—not unlike his own—allowing itself to be tossed and bent. He heard the conversation between wind and forest; how it was the presence of the trees that gave the wind its voice.

He placed his cheek against the rough bark—feeling; listening.

Octavia saw the tears on his cheeks. She waited. Finally she came to stand next to him—holding the tree with him, her cheek close to his.

"What would it be like if all the trees in the world were no more?" she whispered.

Mr Bojangles

"Make a left here, Kristiyan."

Octavia was comparing her map to the written directions.

"And then take the third right."

They were moving into a rural area, about a mile outside Santa Fe.

"There it is—see! Guide Dog Association. On the left."

Kristiyan turned into the driveway, drove up to the house and parked the station wagon.

A woman came out, with a dog close to her heel. She waved to them.

"So you found it all right!"

Octavia and Kristiyan introduced themselves, and shook hands.

"My name is Cindy—Cindy McLean. I believe you are interested in a guide dog."

"Yes. It would be for my brother, who is blind. We stay in the country—a small-holding called The Adobe; a creative center just outside Las Madres. We are hoping that a guide dog would help him to be less dependent on people to find his way about. It is quite a big place, with paths linking the various houses and outbuildings—and of course the music hall."

"It sounds like a guide dog's idea of heaven. So many of our dogs have to live with their owners in small apartments. Of course we pay regular visits after the training, to make sure the two are getting along without problems—and to make sure the dogs are well cared for."

"Are there people who don't look after them well?"

"You would be surprised. Sometimes we have to remove a dog, and that owner will not easily be allowed to get another. No animal should be neglected or mistreated, and a dog that will serve you faithfully for ten years should be considered one of the family."

"So where do we go from here?" Octavia asked.

"We will come and visit you and your brother—look at the routes; see what the dog will need to do. Then your brother will come to our in-house training course for three weeks and learn, with the dog, all he has to know. He will have his own room, and the dog will sleep in a basket next to the bed. They will do everything together. No one else will be allowed to feed or pat him. It is very important that there is no interference while they bond with each other. During this time we will make sure that the two of them are suited to each other temperamentally."

She nodded at Octavia's look of incredulity.

"And then, if all is well, we bring the dog to you—and he is taught the routes he will need to know. One of our people will come every day at the beginning, and then once a week, in case there are difficulties. And then we do a couple of follow-ups to make sure that you are managing. And that's it. You can call us any time if you are having problems."

"When you say 'learn the routes'—what does that mean?"

Cindy laughed.

"You won't believe this, but so many people think you just lean over and whisper in the dog's ear—'take me to the Pancake House'—and the dog mysteriously knows the way there. The dog has to learn that if your brother faces this way, it signals one particular route; that way means another route. They both have to learn this."

She led them to some kennels around the back.

"We have four golden retrievers who have just finished their six-month training with flying colors: two males and two females. Four more will be coming next week. Our next training course with future owners is due to start in three weeks."

She opened the gate into the first kennel. It had a large run, with a tree in it for shade.

"This is Marco."

The dog, in response to her call, came and sat in front of her. She made a gesture with her hand, and he came to heel, watching her face.

"Your brother would need to learn the commands."

"That is very impressive," said Kristiyan.

"They are impressive animals," said Cindy, "and so are their trainers!"

She laughed.

"We are careful to breed only with dogs that have the correct temperament. Even so, not every dog passes the training."

"May I pat him?" Octavia asked.

"Of course."

Marco wagged his tail as she bent to say hello.

"And look at your beautiful coat!" she said. "And what long, wavy golden hair—just like a film star," she added, pointing to his tail and back legs.

"It will take a bit of grooming to keep it like that. Grooming is also very relaxing for a dog, and a good way of bonding. Will your brother be able to do that?"

"He will love it. How old is Marco?"

"They are all from the same litter; just over a year and a half."

"He's lovely."

They walked down the line.

"How tall is your brother?"

"He is a six-footer."

"Then I would suggest one of the males. They are slightly bigger and stronger than the females."

"Will you have a dog for us?"

"Including your brother, there will be eight people registered for the next course, and we have eight dogs. Hopefully they will all pair up successfully."

They entered the last enclosure. Cindy whistled, and the dog came and sat in front of her, looking up at her face. She gave the same command with her hand, and he ran to sit close to her left knee.

"This is Mister Bojangles," she said.

The Wedding

The small congregation stood when they saw Octavia on Lucien's arm, standing in the doorway of the tiny chapel. Together they walked up the narrow aisle, to where Father Rafael was standing in front of the altar.

Octavia wore a simple, white cotton dress and flowers in her hair. She carried a small bunch of lavender in honor of Sebastián's mother, Magdalena, who had planted it all those years ago. She was barefoot, and walked with a slight limp.

Alejandro, recently back from his honeymoon with Francesca, thought she looked like Magdalena reincarnated. Octavia had the same electric energy—the identical, breath-taking beauty; the same "other" quality that had made Magdalena so remarkable.

Sofia, her matron of honor, walked behind with Caradoc.

As she walked up the aisle, Octavia had eyes only for Kristiyan. He was standing a little to the right of Father Rafael, with Salvador beside him.

The service was brief and simple. Father Rafael gave a reading, chosen by Kristiyan, and added his own blessing. The couple exchanged their self-written, simple vows. Following Father Rafael's lead, they declared their formal promises to each other. The rings, which Salvador produced, were given and received with due ceremony.

Father Rafael, with a smile, pronounced them man and wife.

"You may kiss the bride," he said to Kristiyan.

The destination for the honeymoon was still a secret. They would be away for the three weeks when Lucien did his training with Mister Bojangles.

Kristiyan had told Octavia what to pack—informal clothes, suitable for all temperatures: sandals, boots, jeans, a sheepskin jacket and a bathing costume. Now everything was packed into the car—ready for their departure, straight after the wedding ceremony.

Octavia was intrigued. A bathing costume and a sheepskin jacket?

"Aren't you going to tell me?"

"Not yet," he said with a grin.

ㅁㅁㅁ

Kristiyan's parents were unable to be at the wedding on account of his mother's health, but they were happy to hear the news. They asked Kristiyan to send photographs of the ceremony, and of Octavia's family. They sent all their blessings to the couple, and invited them to come and stay for a month, so that they and Octavia could get to know each other, and she could meet Kristiyan's friends and relations. It would also give them a base from which to visit all the places of interest nearby, and offer Octavia a taste of a culture that was different from the American way of life.

They discussed the idea on their way to Albuquerque Airport.

"How would you like to visit my country? After all, it has played such a large role in the imagination of the American people. You can come and see for yourself what gets left out of that picture."

"Oh, Kristiyan—it would be so amazing! I would love to meet your family; to see where you grew up. And the music! We must go to as many concerts as possible! And the ballet! And I want to spend time seeing all the famous icons—and maybe some contemporary ones being painted. I would love that. And I want to feel into the Russian soul that you speak of so often."

She paused.

"What if your parents don't like me? I'm surely not what they had in mind as a wife for you. And won't they want hundreds of little grandchildren?"

"They already have hundreds of little grandchildren," Kristiyan said with a laugh. "I think they—certainly my mother—will be relieved to be able to sit quietly for a change.

"But we have lots of time to plan it. First we have an amazing project to complete here. Then we can sit down, and I will tell you about all the places I think you would find interesting. Then you can decide what time of year—what season—you would like to choose."

"I want to see the Russian winter. And snow."

San Pedro De Atacama

"I can't believe I am really here!"

Octavia sat in the passenger seat—her bare arm reaching out of the window, her fingers playing with the feel of the warm, dry air; her hair sleek in the wind.

"Oh, Kristiyan, I think you will have to pinch me in case I am just dreaming!"

Like an excited child, she bounced on the seat of the hired Land Rover, and Kristiyan grinned with delight at her enjoyment of the surprise.

"I am so happy that we are heading out, away from crowds of people. I have dreamed of this so often. Will you enjoy it all as much as I will?"

"I can't think of any place I would rather be," he said.

He slowed down for a patch of loose stones on the road.

"After all the comings and goings at The Adobe, I think this desert might be just big enough to allow both of us to relax. And when we get to the hotel, you will be able to read about everything that is on offer if we get tired of relaxing. It is an impressive list."

They drove on in silence, gazing out at the vast, shimmering space all around them.

The boutique hotel was on the outskirts of San Pedro. There were six suites, each with its own private courtyard and seating area—and magnificent views of the desert. There was a pool area with loungers and sun umbrellas. For those who wanted privacy, a path through some tall grasses led to the beach—a strip of white sand, and what was called The Pond: a sizeable lake for swimming. Lunch, or at sunset a private, romantic supper—a gourmet's heaven—could be served there on a table for two.

It would be their first night together. Octavia felt nervous just thinking about it. Throughout all the hours on the plane, it was constantly on her mind. Would she know what to do? How was she going to explain her sexual anxiety to Kristiyan? If Georgia had been at home when they married, she might have asked her. But she could not ask Sister Piadosa, and there was no way that she would ask Sofia.

They had supper brought to their room. It came with a complimentary bottle of wine, and some hand-made chocolates for after dessert. A fire was lit for them.

"'The significant drop in night temperature is always a surprise to visitors. It can get to below freezing. If you decide to go stargazing with our guide, make sure you are prepared for it.'"

The supper-dishes had been removed, and now they sat on the couch in front of the fire, sipping their wine and reading through the booklet on Things to Do. They decided to take the first day slowly; to go to the beach, and just feel the landscape around them. They would make a booking to go out that night with the guide, an astronomer who always took a range of powerful telescopes. He would, they read, take visitors deep into the desert, where there was no light pollution.

"I have dreamed of this so many times. I wonder how the reality will compare with my dreams."

"See what it says here," said Kristiyan, reading from the brochure. "'When you look at the stars you are looking into the past, the same way an archaeologist uncovers the past through excavation. There is no way we can really conceive of those vast wastes of time. It is beyond anything we will ever experience in our lives. Much of what you will look at no longer exists.'"

"I know. It is unthinkable—such reaches of time."

"Yet, even time is another of our constructs."

Octavia finished her wine, and said she would take a shower. Kristiyan poured himself another glass, and put a log on the fire.

Octavia stepped out of the shower, and wrapped herself in a warm towel. She took a seat on the chair, and considered the night ahead. Here it was! Was she truly prepared for this—?

Oh, shit! Prepared? Of course you aren't prepared. How could you be quite so naïve?

It had never entered her head to think of contraceptives.

After her accident it was made very clear to her that she should not have children, but at the time it seemed so irrelevant, and she had never given it a thought since then.

How would she tell Kristiyan what an idiot he had for a bride?

In the bedroom she slipped into her soft cotton night-dress, and was brushing her hair when Kristiyan entered.

"You look so beautiful," he said, and took her in his arms. "How did I get to be such a lucky fellow?"

Octavia muttered something.

Kristiyan stood back, and looked into her eyes.

"Is something the matter?"

"Yes."

"Are you going to tell me what it is?"

"Yes."

He waited.

"I don't know how to begin. It is—no, I am—so stupid."

He waited. Octavia blushed, and looked down at her fingers.

Still he waited.

"I never gave contraceptives a thought," she blurted out, and burst into tears.

"But I did," he said gently.

Stars

Afterwards they lay in each other's arms without speaking.

Octavia knew that her life had changed. Something, asleep since her accident, had been reawakened. And that it should have happened here, of all places; that it was between her and Kristiyan, and that the stars had witnessed it, filled her with wonder.

I am a woman, she thought. A woman! How strange to think that this act of love has transformed me forever. I feel like a butterfly, free of the space that held me until I was ready to be born. No one can ever take this away. It is mine; all mine.

She wondered if Kristiyan felt the same way. Was it different for men? How patient he had been with her.

"I can hear you thinking." Kristiyan leaned over to kiss her. "Not sleepy?"

"Not sleepy—no; but so happy, so full of all that this means. How it changes everything for me. I think I am feeling through all the layers of how nothing will ever be the same again." She kissed his hand. "I am so in love with you!" she whispered. "And so full of gratitude for all your patience with me."

She leaned forward on one elbow, so that she could see his face.

"I feel as if I have been burning with such a small light—barely more than a spark; so small that it had to protect itself. And you have turned it into a flame."

Kristiyan laughed.

"I thought you were burning like a forest fire already."

"Not like this."

"Say more."

"I feel as if every cell in my body must surely look different; be different! Like the difference between someone standing still—and a whirling dervish!"

Kristiyan laughed again. "I promise I won't repeat this. No one will ever believe it possible of you; or if they do, it will scare the daylights out of them."

"I remember," Octavia continued, "Sebastián telling me about something Father Octavio said to him. It comes back to me now. He told him to read a passage from Ezekiel—I looked it up at the time, so I know how it goes. It reads—'A new heart also will I give you; and a new spirit will I put within you; and I will take away the stony heart out of your flesh; and I will give you a heart of flesh.' I memorized it then. Now I can feel it. Sebastián said he didn't pay any attention to it at the time. He was too angry. Only after Father Octavio died, and he found the passage, he understood what the priest was telling him. By then it was too late to thank him."

"Did he find it helpful then?"

"I suppose he did."

"You sound doubtful."

"Well, it is only my perspective, I know, and maybe he was right to carry on his mother's work. But it has demanded such a price."

"What else could he have done?"

"Perhaps he could have done what he is doing now. Leave home, and find the life that is waiting for him."

"Don't you think he had to earn that permission in his own eyes, before he could leave?"

"I guess so."

"And what do you make of it personally—this new heart?"

"I think it is something that comes after a profound loss. It is as if you found an abandoned child, and gave her a home—and love. For me, it means that I will truly feel; not just my own feelings, but other people's pain and joy—yours! You! I feel as if a hand has touched me. Not like any touch I have ever known."

"I love the way you think in pictures. You make images with words. No wonder you are an artist. But it wasn't exactly a hand, was it?" he added wickedly.

"Oh, you!" she said, laughing.

"Oh, and by the way," he added, "I feel exactly the same."

Kristiyan was sleeping when Octavia quietly slipped out of bed. She climbed into her warm clothing, boots and a sheepskin coat, grabbed a blanket and went to lie on one of the loungers, out in the courtyard.

She had never seen a sky like this—such a vast sky. It had no end. In all her years in New Mexico, she had never seen such clouds of stars. So many that they looked like a mist of soft brilliance.

She felt the tears, warm on her cold cheeks.

"I am sorry it has taken me so long to get here. Thank you for waiting."

She fell asleep beneath their silence.

□□□

"No moon, no wind—and a clear sky," he pronounced. "It will be cold. Ideal conditions for studying the stars."

They were being driven far out into the desert. Their guide, known only by his nickname, Ojos, because of his keen eyesight, was an astronomer linked to the hotel. Packed behind the back seat of the jeep there were ground-sheets and blankets, fold-up canvas chairs, four powerful telescopes with tripods, and a thermos of coffee to ward off the cold.

"When we get there, I will explain to you what stars and constellations we will be looking at. We will begin by looking at these with the naked eye. That is what people see when they look up at the stars: little sparks of light, some brighter than others. Of course the stars are much clearer here than in most places in the world. That is because of the high altitude and the clean, dry air. But nevertheless, they are still very distant."

He lit a cigarette.

"Then we will take a closer look at what is there; learn the names given to them."

"Will they just be bigger, or will we see more stars?"

"They will look bigger—and you will see many more. As our telescopes become ever more sophisticated—not these ones, of course—and capable of seeing beyond millions of light years, we are able to see stars that no longer exist—think of that!"

Ojos stopped the jeep on a slight rise, and cut the engine. He went to the back of the vehicle, poured two mugs of coffee for them, and then set about placing the telescopes and chairs. He spread out two ground-sheets, and made pillows for their heads with the rolled-up blankets.

"You get yourselves comfortable, and then we will identify some of the bigger stars."

Octavia lay back, and gazed at the starry heavens above her. In an involuntary gesture, her arms reached out on either side of her. Her hands, palms open to receive the light, rested on the cold sand.

She could hear Ojos' voice; a faraway drone. She deliberately tuned it out. She did not want to hear—anything! She would not listen to this list of names, pinned onto each star like butterflies pinned to a collector's board.

How did he dare to do this? To name the stars? Did he not know the blasphemy of such speech? Did he not know that here above them, all around them, they were gazing at the holy mystery—the utterly unknowable?

How could he not know this?

She had been aware of it since she was an infant, and all through her childhood. She had known it then, without knowing that she knew it.

She lay now in silent wonder.

There, beyond time, lay the origins of the wind. The first breath.

There—beyond any attempt to name, measure or understand it—the unknowable breathed a first breath out into the heavens.

There, hidden in the ancient mists of time—before ever time was—the beginnings of all history: stardust flying through space, like seeds blowing in the wind.

The Desert

They stood on a look-out, arms around each other, gazing down over a white salt plain—the Salar de Atacama. They wore hats, sunglasses against the glare that came from the reflected sunlight, and special sun screen because of the high radiation levels and the dryness. Even so, Octavia could feel her skin growing tight.

The sheer vastness of it, reaching out from where they stood and disappearing into the haze, was overwhelming.

"I have imagined what it would be like to stand here," Octavia said softly. "But who could ever truly imagine such a place?"

They stood for a long while in silence.

As they were walking back to the vehicle, Kristiyan spoke.

"I am trying to hear what kind of music—if any— would make sense of this silence; this endless whiteness. It would have to allow so much space between the notes. Tavener comes closest to it, for me. This is such an unearthly landscape. So terrifyingly pure and beautiful. So unforgiving."

They ate their lunch, and drank deeply from the bottled water that had been provided.

"Shall we drive down, and feel what it is like to walk there—see if you will be able to manage it? From here it looks like a smooth beach, but I am sure that is misleading."

They read that the sixty-two mile, mineralized lake had no outlet, and was almost completely covered by saline minerals and dust; that the plain extended for thousands of square miles; that they should wear strong footwear, and carry water.

Up close the surface was indeed very uneven, with both large and smaller lumps of salt. Even with her cane, it would be too much for Octavia.

"You go, Kristiyan. I will wait in the car. I would much rather sit here. I need to have it printed in my brain."

"Well, I'm not exactly the intrepid hiker type who needs to conquer all terrain either," he said with feeling. "I would much rather be with you, and enjoy the silence."

They sat at the breakfast table, discussing their plans for the week.

"I know there are so many places that all the guide books say are a must, but I don't want to be in a crowd of people, all taking photos of each other in front of—whatever."

Kristiyan nodded agreement. "Neither do I. I want to have you all to myself!" She laughed.

"Yes—that too! But I do want you to say what you would like to do, or see."

"Is that a wide open invitation?" he asked innocently.

"Kristiyan! Be serious."

"You think I am not serious? Try me!"

"I am talking about daytime."

"So am I!"

She laughed again. "Oh, you are incorrigible!"

She leaned over the table and kissed him.

"More! More!"

Octavia passed him a large bread-roll.

"You must still be hungry," she said with a straight face. He grinned.

"Now then," she said firmly, "I will begin—"

She caught the look in his eye, and burst out laughing.

"So! I don't want to rush around, seeing things; doing things, however wonderful," she said, trying not to catch his eye. "I want to spend time with you; hear the music you hear—in this empty space. And that is just it. I want the space to remain empty. I don't want what the guide books call the holiday of a lifetime—meaning a dizzying round of filling every minute with a new high."

"I do agree with you," he said, suddenly serious. "I can feel something in my head expanding in all this space. A sense of relief! Almost as if it was safe to just be."

"Yes," she said. "Safe to be."

Memory

They parked the jeep at the top of a pass that overlooked all the shades of emptiness. Behind them, high up on a rock-face, two engraved faces stared out over the land; two rectangular faces with little definition—stylized eyes and mouths—etched high up on the cliff.

"How did they manage to reach so high to carve these, I wonder?"

"Would they have had some kind of ladder?"

"Perhaps."

"Can you feel their presence? Even now?"

"Yes."

"Someone stood here, just as we are standing; gazed out in the same way that we are gazing. Someone who wanted to carry this beauty in his eyes—his memory—for all time."

They stood, not speaking, feeling the silence; feeling the pull of memory that left, as its imprint, two ancient faces on a rock.

"This is what I want to hear in my music. This sense of awe that is just as present now as it was thousands of years ago. This awareness of how small we are in relation to time and history, while the experience of wonder remains immeasurable."

Octavia nodded.

"It is this imperative, this overwhelming sense of awe out of which we create gods. The sudden knowing that there is an invisible something—or perhaps a no-thing—perhaps a verb like 'becoming'—which is always and everywhere—here before us; before anything. And will always be."

"Yes," she said. "And so we leave our small mark in praise of it."

She paused.

"This mark has lasted thousands of years. Maybe it will endure for thousands more. But even that is a blink of an eye in the face of time."

She felt tears prick her eyes.

"And yet this person lives! I know him in me. I feel the same desire to respond to beauty—as I know you do too."

"Yes," he said. "Even a thousand years—two, three thousand—cannot erase that."

They ate their picnic lunch in silence.

A Day in San Pedro

It was toward the end of their stay that they decided to spend a day in San Pedro—buying gifts for everyone at home, and visiting some of the museums and places of interest. Octavia desperately wanted to find a book of desert photographs. It amazed her that the light and colors of the desert—the sunrises and sunsets—were never the same. All of these were constantly shifting, even as the land remained the same.

They had lunch in a small restaurant that served the local food. They resisted the temptation to sample the local alcoholic beverage, having heard that it was deceptively potent.

"I would like to see if I can find a bookshop. Maybe one of the museums will stock a few books."

They paid for their meal, and left.

The Meteorite Museum was cool, and empty of people.

After they had marveled at the different sizes and textures of the meteors in the collection, an attendant led them to some smaller stones that were in an open case.

"You may handle these," he informed them.

Kristiyan held in his hands a rock that was about four and a half billion years old.

"Four and a half billion years!" He ran his fingers over its surface. How could anything come through such a birth, and feel so smooth?

Such vast wastes of time. It was beyond imagination—just like the elemental power of that birth. A hundred thousand orchestras, playing The Rite of Spring out of sync, would be as nothing if set against it.

And all of this, sleeping in the silence of stone.

Octavia held a rock, and closed her eyes. It was beyond memory—even while it was present in her hands. And yet, standing here in the twentieth century—how ridiculous, she thought, to put a name on time—I know that I am a part of it. I am holding in my two hands something that was once part of a star, she thought in wonder.

She opened her eyes, and leaned toward Kristiyan.

"Tell me what you see," she whispered.

"I am listening," he said softly, "to an unholy music."

They found several books in the museum shop. Octavia bought three. Two were photographic, and the third contained a series of essays written by astronomers, archaeologists and geologists.

She read the inscription in the front of the book:

"Our roots are up beyond the light."

They spent their last evening there having a picnic supper overlooking the Valley of the Moon, a sobering lunar landscape surrounded by a desert canyon and red sand dunes.

"The silence here has a foreboding quality," said Kristiyan. "How lifeless it looks."

"But Kristiyan, look at the light that is just touching it! The sunset light! How it transforms everything."

She pointed to the salt-encrusted hills.

"And the jagged hills look as if snow has just fallen on them. And look at how the peak of that distant mountain, rising up out of its indigo shadow, has been stained pink."

"You really do see colors," he said, marveling at her description. "I know now what you mean when you say that you think in images."

Octavia took his hand.

"And you think in sounds—in music," she said.

"The canyon is full of shadows," she said. "Is it really dead, do you think? Or just sleeping?"

"Maybe it's not dead; just grieving a time when it was a fertile valley."

"So what music do you hear?"

"Perhaps Tavener, again. Something from The Protecting Veil—no, Thrinos."
He smiled at her.

They finished their wine, watching the colors shift and change—growing ever darker until the night cold set in.

They packed everything away, and drove back to the hotel.

They made love on a rug by the flickering light of the fire.

Kristiyan ran his hands down the smooth, slender length of her.

His hand paused when it reached the place of trauma from her accident.

"I will always love this wounded hip," he said as he kissed it. "Here—where you wrestled with your angel!"

Octavia lay still, feeling her body come alive under the touch of his hand. She rolled over to face him.

"I never dreamed my life could be like—like this—"

She caught her breath as his hand lightly touched her breast; brushed over her nipple.

She closed her eyes, feeling the hot tide rise up within her in waves that filled her entire body, till it trembled with longing to be taken.

"Oh, Kristiyan," was all she said as he entered her.

"Oh—yes!

"Yes!

"Yes!"

Journal Entry 29

How amazing to be back home. Everything looks different. I think that I have never truly seen The Adobe.

I have an image of the desert silence, printed in my brain. It is no wonder that the desert has always been a place of vision. It is the light. And in that vast salt plain, the feeling that the land is insubstantial; floating in the reflections. Will I ever manage to capture this in beads?

And the emptiness!

And those haunting shifts in the light and the colors. The harsh contrasts, and the sudden surprises: the emerald lagoon—Laguna Sejar; the red earth tones; purple and deep blue shadows—and then the soft fusion of earth and sky. Oh, and all the textures.

316

I am so glad we bought the books—not that I will ever forget this.

How has this changed my work on the animal icons? I will have to find out. I know it has changed me—profoundly.

I know that I still have to do battle with the serpent and the black wave. Why am I nervous about this? And what is that red sun doing?

And Kristiyan. Why was I ever afraid of being married—to him? I can't imagine my life now without him. How much I have learned from him, all these years—and not known it. Where have you been, Octavia?

Lucien comes back tomorrow with Mister Bojangles. I can't wait to see them together. A person from Guide Dogs will come along to start teaching them both the routes. How humbling to know that a dog of less than two years can, and is so willing to do all this! This is going to make such a difference to Lucien's life.

When he feels more settled, we will have another meeting about the music.

And then, this new decision! I have been sensing something for a long time. Now it is time! I am going to paint my studio again. Red! Tuscanny Red!

And now I must go and make supper for my husband!

PART FOUR
THE RED ROOM

Early Sunrise

Octavia sat in her studio, watching the first rays of sunlight strike the wall in front of her, bringing a warm glow to Alejandro's red angel. She found herself repeating out loud the first four lines from the Rubiyat of Omar Khayyám.

I wonder what kind of stone it was, she thought, that put the stars to flight?

The question caused her to get up in a kind of panic.

Where did I put my stones?

She rose, and went to search for the tin in her desk; then in the set of small drawers where she kept her art materials. With sudden urgency she riffled through the boxes of charcoal, brushes, paint-bottles and pencils. Finally, at the back of one drawer, she found the small tin. It bore rust marks where some paint had been scratched away. Octavia felt her pulse quicken at the sight of it.

She carried it back to her chair, and sat down.

Octavia's Stones
Do Not Open

By now the sky had stained the newly painted walls, making them blaze like fire.

In the tin she found the folded note that she had written so long ago. She opened it, noticing the faded paper, and how the creases had yellowed. She read the funny, little-girl handwriting.

These are my four stones. They called to me to come and find them. They will show me my way back to the stars. I found the white one and the black one and the yellow one in the arroyo. But not the red one. I found the red one in the courtyard. The red one comes from a different star.
Signed by Octavia Chavez 1984

She picked up the four stones, one by one, studying each one intently.

A memory of the day she found them came back to her: the hot sun burning in the dry arroyo; the glinting specks of quartz in the stones. She wanted round stones; four colors. The white one was easy to find; and the black one. She discarded the grey stones. They had no appeal for her young eyes. She found a bright yellow stone—not quite round and with a thread running through it, as if it might break open. For some reason this lack of perfection pleased her.

The last stone eluded her. She wanted a red stone.

It was some weeks later, while drawing pictures in the dirt outside the house, that she unearthed the fourth stone: red as blood.

Now, just like the child she was then, she cleared a space on her work-table for the four stones. Outside her door, from the collection of treasures she had gathered over the years, she found a flat stone, a few inches in height. She placed this at the center of the four stones, and put a candle in a small bead-bottle on top of it.

She crossed the room, and turned on the CD player. The rich sounds of Mstislav Rostropovich's haunting cello filled the air.

Octavia sat with her eyes closed, her hands clasped; a smile of utter joy on her face.

□□□

In front of me I see a bush; a thorn bush. I recognize it as the crucifixion thorn. There is no other vegetation. Everything else has been burnt up in a fire. The desert is just sand and stones.

Now I see flames leaping from the thorn bush, but it does not seem to burn. Just more and more flames leap from the thorny branches.

And now, from the center of the bush, a different flame rises. I recognize the Virgin of Emptiness with her aura of fire, standing in the bush—standing in the fire, and reaching out as if in supplication.

She is weeping, but even all her tears cannot subdue the flames.

I know I will soon make the beadwork icon of the white wolf. I can feel his presence, calling to me.

Perhaps, this time, I must go to him.

A Table and Four Stones

Octavia sat in Gregorio's wood-work room, watching him plane the top of what would be a small table for her stones. She loved the way his hands caressed the wood from time to time, as if coaxing it to bring out its hidden grain. It was a piece of Oregon pine that he'd had for years—too small for most things, but perfect for Octavia's small, circular table.

"It's the first time I have made a table for four stones. Still, something new

322

every day," he said with a chuckle. "Would you like me to put a bevel on the edge, or leave it straight?"

"Straight would be perfect. I don't want the table to look like a piece of furniture."

Gregorio raised an eyebrow.

"I mean, it is more like a base for something sacred. It needs to be simple."

Gregorio stood up straight to rest his back.

"You always did have a different take on life, Octavia, but this is something else. Strange—even for you! What does the sacred something look like, or would you rather not say?"

"You already know. The four stones, of course."

"Ah! Of course. The four stones. How silly of me not to remember that."

"Oh, come on, Gregorio! You know you love the idea. I can see it in your eyes. You are just teasing me."

"Indeed I am, Octavia. But I'll tell you this: if I ever make a catalogue of all the items I have made during my lifetime, I will be sure to put a photograph of this table—with the four stones—on the cover!"

He grinned at her.

"Where did they come from, anyway?"

"Oh, round and about. I have had them since I was a young child."

"And you have kept these same four stones all that time?"

"Yes."

A New Heart Also Will I Give You

Sofia was having a three-week break from her singing instruction.

She sat on the bench outside their casita with Erin on her lap, and watched Lucien and Beau, a little distance away, pause at the fork in the path. He was going to have lunch with Kristiyan and Octavia, and the three of them would spend the afternoon discussing the music for the exhibition concert.

She watched him turn his body slightly to the left, and make a swift gesture with his hand; and then the two moved forward again. How quickly they had become a team.

Sofia got up, and hitched Erin onto her hip. It was time to fetch Caradoc from play-school.

Why do I feel so left out—alone?

Stop it, Sofia. You are not ready for them yet. And they are not ready for you.

She stood, looking up at the pink hill until Erin began to kick her legs impatiently and struggle to be put down. Sofia gave her a hug, and Erin gurgled.

"Let's go and fetch Caradoc," she said, and they walked in the opposite direction—toward the small clinic and the young children's play-school.

Sofia was making supper when Lucien arrived home with Beau. Erin was in a high chair, and Caradoc was bringing her an endless array of small dolls and stuffed animals which, with infinite concentration, she dropped over the edge of her feeding-tray. As each one fell to the ground, she clapped her hands with delight.

"Mo', Ca'doc! Mo'! Mo'! Mo'!"

Sofia wiped her hands on a dish-cloth, and went to give Lucien a hug.

"How did it go with the music?"

"It's getting clearer. Octavia is calling the work Lament, which gives us a lead. She wants to do what we did at the concert for the horses—have stills of wilderness in its pristine state, fading slowly into desert. That sort of thing. And of course the animals, somehow disappearing."

"Where do the animal voices come in?"

"As I understand things, at the beginning of the first movement there is just landscape, and the music must reflect this. And then the animals arrive—slowly at first. This is where you will come in. This is the idyllic time—full of the fierceness of wilderness, but with none of the violence that came later. That is a human condition."

"How do you know all this?" Sofia asked in wonder.

"I have been listening to a number of programs recently. There are some excellent documentaries."

"And what comes next?"

"Well, it will build slowly, and then we will introduce the arrival of the early humans."

"How will you do that?"

He laughed. "I haven't the faintest idea!"

He paused for a moment.

"But now that you ask, maybe with the sound of splitting flints; tools being made; stones chipping, pounding and grinding; the sound of an arrow loosed from the bow—that sort of thing. Perhaps some form of early music—clapping, stamping; voices."

"And where would the animals be in this scenario?"

"They would still be a part of it. There was a balance—for a long time. I can't see the photographs of rock art, but from what I hear the animals must have played a large part in the awe and wonder of people's early spirituality.

"I think Reuben's bandoneon and your voice will work so well together here. Somehow we also need to evoke the sounds of the hunt; the silent stealth of following a wild animal—and then the sudden kill."

"How do you put that together with the awe and wonder story?"

"I don't think they had the kind of sentimentality about animals that we have today—or the brutality. They would have given thanks to the animal that had given its life to them."

"A bit of a raw deal for the animal!"

"It is the way wilderness works, as I see it."

"Okay. And then what?"

"The turning-point comes with the arrival of gun-powder and the gun. This will mean a major key change in the music. This will be the second movement. It will build—slowly at first, and then with increasing intensity. There will be the sounds of industry—not the ancient tools, but chain-saws and great trees falling. And then the sounds of strife: battle, gunfire, automatic rifles—all building up to the first atomic bomb.

"In the midst of this—the sounds of animals being hunted; shot. Sudden silence. Just moments of stillness—the vanishing of one species after another; the growing pace of a silent migration into extinction."

"Listening to you talk like this is scary. I don't know how well I will manage my part in all of this." Sofia looked at him wonderingly. "I almost don't know you when you speak like this."

Lucien reached out to her, and she put out a hand. He took her into his arms, and hugged her.

"I'm still me," he said. "But I do feel a new energy growing in me—a voice that is longing to be heard. This music is one way in which I will be able to show it. Actually, this project of Octavia's is like an awakening for me. Like an electric charge from somewhere deep inside me."

"Yes?"

"There is something else she said, which is profoundly disturbing. She has had a phrase going through her mind, for months now—'the mercy of wild things.'"

"And?"

"She wondered what that mercy was. She said she thought it meant that if we are looking at a mass extinction, then the animals, in their mercy, will take us with them."

The children were finally asleep. Beau had been fed, and was stretched out close to Lucien's feet. Now the two of them sat, talking over an after-dinner coffee.

"I can't believe what you are telling me. Is this considered to be a possibility?"

"I think scientists and environmental activists are taking it very seriously, in spite of so much denial. We have to change the way we live. If we don't make radical changes, they believe it is very possible."

Sofia stared at him.

"So what is the final movement?"

"Octavia is some kind of visionary. I don't know where she gets these images from. She has a true gift. This is where the lament becomes most poignant.

"For this, she visualizes a very high peak that casts a long, black shadow. She calls it the edge of the world. The lament is very soft; music with a lot of space in it. One by one the animals appear on the peak—single animals, with no mate. One by one they fall; some large, some very small. From the largest mammals—elephants and whales—to insects, reptiles, fish, birds—all come to the edge and leap, step, fly or fall over it. One species after another disappears for all time. As they fall, they become dark angels. Very dark angels, falling into night. As the last one falls, the music stops in mid-bar.

"Of course, she thinks in images. It will be our job to convey all of this in sound." He smiled. "This will be your challenge. To capture all this in your voice. I know you will be magnificent."

Sofia took the path that led to Octavia's studio. It was the first time she had ever been there. She walked the spiral that brought her to the door, and knocked quietly.

"One minute. I'm coming."

The door opened.

"Sofia! Hello! Would you like to come in?"

"If you aren't busy. I could come another time—"

"Now is perfect. I need to take a break."

She stepped aside, and Sofia entered the room.

The first thing to catch her eye was a rough sketch, tacked to the wall, of the peak Lucien had told her about—animals becoming angels. Falling. Falling.

"Lucien has been telling me some of the ideas for the concert. It sounds very challenging. I am amazed to see what is being drawn out of him."

"Here—take a seat," Octavia said, pulling up a chair. "Would you like something to drink?"

"That would be good, thanks."

She sat, and waited till Octavia returned with the glasses.

"The reason I am here is to ask you a bit more about how you hear the animal voices. Lucien told me about the mercy of wild things. It adds such a devastating dimension. I will soon be back at my singing lessons, and I thought I would ask Madame Jolie if we could begin to work on this. So now, more than ever, I need to hear everything you are seeing and feeling about all of this; not only the project itself, but about where we should all become aware of what is happening."

They talked for over an hour.

"But you will probably hear best," Octavia concluded, "from listening to Lucien's music—the emotional tone of the work. That is where you will get the clearest ideas for the animals. Perhaps you can find one of those recordings that feature animal cries and calls. And then you have to give them the emotional intensity—somehow!" She shrugged. "But I have no idea how you do that!"

Octavia grew serious.

"On another note altogether, I am so glad we are all going to be working together on this project."

"Me too."

On an impulse, Sofia went over to Octavia and hugged her.

It was the first time, since Octavia's earliest childhood, that they had embraced.

A Challenge

Alejandro and Raho sat a few rows from the back of the music hall. They were listening to the musicians, together with Octavia and Sofia, discussing ideas for the challenging composition of Lament.

The two men had been asked to attend the meeting, to offer any suggestions they might have. They had both read the proposal for the composition.

Lucien had written a short musical sketch for each of the three movements, and a melody for the theme that would develop into the full and passionate lament in the final movement. These he now played, interspersing comments on how they might be expanded. It was, he said, just a starting-point; a mark on the page.

Octavia listened with flushed cheeks. This is exactly what I hear in my head, she thought. How perfectly he has grasped the mood of each movement.

She closed her eyes, visualizing the images behind the music. So perfect. Perhaps it would be distracting to have the visuals as well. Yes, take them out. The music said it all.

Alejandro listened intently, but super-imposed onto the music he saw a thousand images of Octavia: her infancy; all her troubled years, fighting like a caged, wild animal—until the accident. Her fight to be herself—to be free to make all the decisions for the future she so passionately wanted. And then all those painful lessons, endured with such courage.

And now, this extraordinary undertaking.

She has come through, he mused, and been deepened by all of it. Only the willingness to look her fate in the eye, and accept it without complaint, could have led to this profound depth. She is the true artist. Nothing will stop her.

Raho sat upright and inscrutable, his eyes closed.

"And this is the idea for the final lament, for which Sofia will sing the voices of the animals as they start to disappear."

The beginning of the movement was understated, as if what was happening could still be ignored. Only the echoes of the leitmotif, appearing and fading—only to reappear with greater emphasis—gradually created a sense of unease in the listener.

Octavia felt such love for Lucien break open her heart. How extraordinary, the human spirit! All that it can endure, and still make this kind of music; still have this deep knowing, in spite of everything.

She made notes throughout the lively discussion that followed. Everyone had something to offer; to suggest. There were also many questions about the animals—how to make them recognizable to a listening audience. Would Sofia's voice be able to carry that?

"Is it necessary for the listeners to understand what they are hearing? Will they not get a sense of it from the atmosphere?"

"Well, they will have to realize that Sofia's voice is the voice of every creature. Otherwise they will be confused by her strange sounds."

"Is that a bad thing?"

"Do you think, perhaps, that the title should be Lament for the Animals?"

"Definitely not!"

"Your reason—?"

"I don't want to spell things out. Besides, when they walk into the exhibition they will know."

The discussion moved from person to person, with Octavia scribbling to keep up.

Finally there was a lull, as people considered everything that had been said. It was into this lull that Raho spoke.

"I was interested to notice traces of anger in the second movement. Could that be explained to me, please?"

Everyone turned to look at him. Surely he, of all people, couldn't have missed what this was all about?

Raho turned to face Octavia.

"Did you intend to have this in the music, or has it crept in uninvited?"

"No. It is intentional."

"To what purpose?"

"Well, it is there to make people aware of the violence that is being done to our world; to every living plant and animal. We are facing a mass extinction—of what proportion, we can only guess. But it all happens out of sight of most people. As long as they have water coming out of their taps and food in the supermarket, they don't ask how it gets there—or at what cost to the environment."

"So, why did you choose anger?" he asked.

"Doesn't it make you angry?"

"No."

Octavia stared at him.

"No?"

"Of course I feel deeply about it. And I look at all of it with a profound sense of loss. I love the lament that Lucien has written—presumably based on your conversations. I think the first movement is very lovely."

He paused.

"The middle movement is powerful, but it loses much of its power through the introduction of anger. Tell me something. In this context, who is angry?"

"I don't follow you," said Octavia. "I am just telling it like it is."

The room was very quiet, listening to this—was it an interrogation? They felt compassion for Octavia. What on earth had got into Raho? He always seemed to be so accepting of everything.

"Are you not telling us about your anger at how it is? There is a difference."

"Are you suggesting that everyone must just sit back and do nothing? This is just the way it is? Is that what you are saying?"

Raho gave Octavia a smile.

"Of course not. Everyone must do what he or she decides to do by way of response—even if it doesn't change anything. We must do everything in our power. With our last breath we must offer this. Not necessarily because it will make a difference to the end result—to what is happening; but out of the conviction that the one thing that cannot be taken from us is how we choose to respond at any given moment to what is."

"And if my response is anger? What then?"

"I would suggest that you unpack that anger. What lies beneath it? But the real question here is: why do you bring it into the music?" He thought for a bit. "And then I would ask—is this anger effective?"

The listeners were beginning to fidget. Alejandro looked around at all the faces in the room. On each face he read the same look of bewilderment and discomfort.

"Perhaps we should leave you two to work through this," he said. "We can meet again when it has been resolved. What does everyone else feel?"

With a unanimous sigh of relief, they all elected to leave the two of them at it.

Octavia did not look at Raho. She sat, reviewing everything that had happened, everything that had been said at the meeting. What was she not seeing? Or what did Raho not understand? Even as the thought surfaced, she dismissed it.

What was wrong with feeling angry?

As if he heard her question, Raho spoke.

"There is nothing wrong with feeling anger. Where would it go if you attempted to repress it—deny it?"

An image of the serpent rising out of the depths, and the black wave covering the sun, flashed in front of her eyes.

"I am not trying to—"

"I agree. But you are projecting your fear and anger onto the very group you are so busy judging for their anger; their violence. What do you hope to achieve?"

"You know what this is about. Why do you ask that?"

"I am asking you to look at a very human, but destructive reaction."

"And that is—?"

"It is what happens when we react. We get another reaction, right back."

"So?"

"Is that what you intend?"

Octavia sat in silence. At last she said: "I want to make people think—to make them look at what they are doing; to make them see. Make them care! Make them stop!"

"I see," he said. "And you think this will achieve that. But answer me this: if someone knocks on your door—a stranger, or perhaps a guest—and you want them to come in, do you open the door? Or do you slam it in their face? Just a thought." He smiled. "Well, I think it is time for lunch."

He rose, and picked up her cane from the floor.

"I think the whole concept is very powerful: not explaining anything. Allowing people to do their own work. Very good. And Lucien's music is inspired."

Octavia stood up, and took the cane.

"Thank you, Raho," she said.

"Think about this, Octavia," he said as he was about to leave. "The potter makes the tea-bowl because he makes the tea-bowl."

"So?"

"It is a form of prayer."

"Prayer?"

"Exactly."

Journal Entry 30

"The world wants to be deceived."
"All life is a dialogue."
"Everyone must come out of his exile in his own way."—Martin Buber
"Have you noticed that if you push a horse, he will push back against you?"

Found this note pinned to my door. Can only be Raho. What on earth is he trying to tell me?

Yes, I saw—when Gregorio groomed the pony, and gave him a push to move over—that he did indeed push back. So what!

Is he playing a game?

No. He does not play games. So, come on, Octavia—use your head.

Who is Martin Buber?

This must be connected to the anger he heard in the music.

But what am I not seeing? I wonder if Father Rafael has any books by Martin Buber. I will ask him when he comes on Sunday. Or maybe Collected Works or Borders will have something.

Another note!

"The answer is, and always has been, within you."

Sunday evening.

Father Rafael knows who Martin Buber is. He inherited many books from Father Octavio, and he thinks there may be some Buber among them. He will have a look.

And another note!

"Not being but becoming is man's task."—Buber.

"True compassion is ruthless."

What on earth does that mean? The man is incorrigible!

I have begun work on the black wave, the red sun and the serpent. Fortunately I have not worked a large area. I thought it would be simple to do—only three main elements. But they seem to have a life of their own. What works in the small painting doesn't want to work in beads. I have made some changes for the beadwork. I have designed the serpent's tail to look as if it is uncoiling after a long sleep; as if the serpent has, after countless centuries, been awakened.

What has happened to disturb it, so that it has risen in such fury?

Now, in turn, it has caused the deeps to form into this mighty, black wave that will destroy all life.

And the sun? This red sun—what has it seen with that hot eye?

What set this rage in motion?

What might contain it? Transform it?

I will sit with it for a bit, and see what it tells me.

Is all life really a dialogue?

How do I engage this serpent?

A Question of Music

Octavia found Lucien in the music-room—bent over the piano, playing three notes over and over, and trying different bass chords with his left hand.

"Hi there, Lucien. Is this a good or a bad time to talk about the music for Lament?"

"A very good time—I need a break. Have you had some new thoughts?"

"Some vague notions, yes. I had a session—that's all I can call it—with Raho. I know that he is hoping I will have some insight into the anger in the music—in me, I should say. I feel as if I am circling around something—you know, like having a name or a word on the tip of your tongue, and you just can't get it. I keep thinking—there it is—and then it isn't. It is particularly infuriating, because I know that I know it."

"So, tell me some of the conversation—or tell me about some of the circling you are doing."

"Well, take the anger, for instance. Raho says two things. First, that I must unpack it—I think you were still in the room at that point."

Lucien nodded.

"By this I think he means that I must ask myself what is beneath the anger—"

"But surely that is obvious."

"And then to ask what is beneath that, and keep asking the question."

Lucien listened carefully.

"And then he went on to say that reacting with anger was a very human, but nevertheless a destructive act."

"Sounds like you had a lot of fun!"

"Like hell I did!"

"Anything else?"

"He asked me whether I thought that using anger was effective in bringing about real change."

"And do you?"

"I used to. Now I am questioning it. I now recognize what a manipulative tool anger can be; that it will probably call forth an equally powerful anger." She gave him a rueful smile.

"I have only to examine my own life to see how that works."

"Okay. Let the self-flagellation begin," he said with a grin.

She laughed.

"But seriously, I think Raho's question about effectiveness is the only question to ask here. And not only for a short-term result that will lead to more difficulty in the end. What would it mean to be truly effective? What would that look like? Certainly, everyone must benefit in some way."

"What about people whose vested interests will not be served?"

"That's the burning question. I am trying to hear what Raho is saying. When I arrived at my studio a few days ago, I found a note pinned to the door with three quotes by a man called Martin Buber—Father Rafael is going to lend me a book of his—and it said: 'The world wants to be deceived', 'All life is a dialogue', and 'Everyone must come out of his exile in his own way.' And underneath that was written—'Have you noticed that if you push against a horse, he will push back against you?'"

"So what?"

"That's what I thought. But I also know that Raho is not just playing—or if he is, it is a very serious game, and he wants me to understand the rules."

She paused.

"And something else comes to me about all life is a dialogue. To me this would suggest a mutual respect, each for the other. This is not an ordinary kind of conversation. This is a rare thing, I suspect. It may even be a dialogue without words."

"I think you just lost me there."

"Let me put it this way. I think life is serious—serious in the way a young child is deeply serious when she is playing alone in a make-believe world; a world that is totally real to her. People think that is cute. It isn't cute at all. I think such a child is more profound in her thinking than most jaded adults, who talk about the real world. They have lost that knowing innocence; that sense of wonder. But she is free of all their concepts and beliefs. Hers is a deep inquiry into how things work in her world."

"Where on earth did you come from? I thought I knew you."

"So let's ask this: what could we introduce into the music that would be effective? That is, what would be most likely to call forth a human response to what we are saying? If Raho is suggesting that using anger is like pushing a horse—which I think is what he is getting at—then I must look at myself. Perhaps I am confusing anger with passion."

"What is the difference?"

"Good question. Because you could have a passionate expression of anger. But the kind of passion I am talking about is the passion I feel when I am working on a beadwork—the wolf, for example. I feel as if I am suffering with him. The suffering unites us. Anger does the opposite. I think that beneath my anger is fear. Maybe that is why I am so angry. I feel powerless."

"Say a bit more."

"I am afraid that all the people who seem to be exploiting the natural world will win in the end. I am afraid that all the animals will slowly disappear; it is happening, even now. I am afraid that this planet, and everything on it, will die. Not today, not tomorrow, but probably less than a hundred years from today you will have to go to a game park or a zoo to see animals that were once wild."

"And underneath the fear is the grief; the loss; the suffering," he said gently. "Isn't that what this is all about?"

333

"I guess so."

"I'm sorry, 'Tavia. I can feel your pain. I know how frightening it is. With my blindness, at least there never was any possibility that I would ever see. It was so hard to accept. At first, when I came to realize what it meant, I was angry. Angry, so that I wouldn't have to grieve. Perhaps, in the end, it was easier to accept precisely because there wasn't any hope. Sounds crazy, I know—and of course I have not escaped the grieving. Almost every day I experience some new challenge that brings me face to face with my blindness. Yet, I have had to accept that this is the way it is."

"Oh, Lucien—"

"But with this project, there is always the possibility that much can still be saved. That is what makes it particularly painful. You can't put it down; not while there is some aspect of wilderness that calls out to you. Maybe we cannot truly grieve until we have some kind of a death experience; something that has that same absolute finality to it."

They sat in silence for some time, both busy with their own thoughts.

"Do you know what I almost dare not say?"

"Say it," he replied.

"What if we cannot change things? What if we cannot change the way people think? What if nothing we do will ever make people see things in a different way?"

Lucien listened.

"What if no one is in control of what happens—to anyone; to anything?"

She was almost in tears.

"What if all that we have is how we, individually, choose to respond to life as it is? Only that? And maybe not even that."

"Well, what then do we have?" Lucien asked. "What are we left with?"

"Questions. We have questions."

Lucien stared at her. He was recalling his three notes, and the different chords he had played. In his own way, he too was asking a question; trying to hear something that wouldn't speak to him.

"Maybe that is all we need," he said. "It sounds too simple, but what if that were true?"

"Is it possible to make music sound like a question?" Octavia asked suddenly.

"Funny," he said in wonder. "That is exactly what I was asking myself when you came in. Why do you ask?"

"Why were you thinking of a question?"

They both laughed.

"I thought," he said, "that maybe the music could ask a question. I think that in the lament there could be some repetitive refrain that keeps asking a question."

"A musical question? Will people be able to understand?"

"They won't have to. They will feel it. What they do with it, as you have just suggested, is out of our hands."

"Lucien!" Octavia went over to him, and gave him a fierce hug.

"Of course," said Lucien with a grin, "there is still the small, and rather annoying little detail of how to write it!"

Journal Entry 31

I and Thou

I am reading Martin Buber. What a homecoming. At the same time, this is one of the most confronting writers I have read.

I get! I get it! I get it!—and I am shattered to see something that I didn't know about myself.

True dialogue takes place when "I" stands in the presence of "Thou."

In this context, I have always addressed stars as Thou; and animals and landscape—particularly desert places.

Something in me resonates with what feels like a sadness in the soul of animals—an ancient sadness. And even in landscape. Is this just my projection? I'm not sure. Do we ever really see what is out there, or do we just project our ideas and feelings onto it?

I see wilderness and its animals as so fierce and pure; and so vulnerable to the violence of the human animal. They have no defense against us. We are the misfits. I feel I need to apologize to the rest of creation for our arrogance; for the plague that we have become.

And when all the animals are banished, where will they go?

"Maybe the only place they will be able to survive is in our dreams, not because they want to be there, but because we need them." That is a quote from someone called Hillman—there is so much I need to read.

I cannot begin to know how I would feel, if I were to walk out into a world where there were no animals. I would not wish to live in such a world. I think my soul is animal! And it is grieving so deeply.

"This is the eternal origin of art that a human being confronts a form that wants to become a work through him."—How I love this! I found it a few days ago. It was written in the back of a second-hand book I bought about rock engravings.

But what about people, Octavia? Where is the Thou in the way you relate to others? How often have you experienced this "I"—"Thou" in your whole life? Ever?

Perhaps you don't let people get that close to you. Have you ever allowed people to see your vulnerability?

Well, maybe Alejandro—and certainly Kristiyan. My parents? Not really.

Why do I feel that I am losing—have lost something that is so precious to me? My aloneness. It has been with me since the day I was born. I have always been aware of it. Perhaps I mean the aloneness of my soul.

Was I born knowing that I would die? And has my anger been a way of not allowing myself to feel what this means?

Is this what sets us apart from the animals—that we know we will die?

It is some comfort to consider that animals are spared this; yet how can we be certain about this?

Martin Buber says that the dialogue is between the one who calls and the one who answers; the one who responds to the call.

Have I been called? By whom?—I cannot say.

How have I responded?

The best of me has responded with passion. But so often I have felt the crippling, downward pull of the world; that I must fight not to be made small too, just to keep everyone else comfortable.

So what are you, Octavia?

I suppose I am a work in progress.

But for the music of Lament we must invite a dialogue between what the music calls forth, and what the listeners will give back through their attention; a mutual vulnerability.

And, as of today, I am calling as loudly as I can! Can you hear me, world?

Please hear me.

This is where I stand—now.

And I am coming!

And—what does lie behind the serpent's rage?

The Banishment of Beau

It was the day of the first full rehearsal.

There was a buzz of activity and conversation in the concert hall as the musicians settled into their seats. Sofia, carrying the full score, arrived with Lucien and Beau. Lucien alone carried all the music for each player in his head.

Santiago had written down the arrangements—an undertaking involving copious notes for Sofia and for the other musicians. It was his task to envisage the work as a whole, and to make sure that it was fully realized. He would conduct the Lament concert.

The air of serious attention was almost palpable as the musicians took up their instruments. Santiago counted them in, and they began playing the quiet introduction.

As soon as they started playing, they encountered the first snag. They made a valiant attempt to play through this, but eventually they collectively had to admit defeat, and collapsed in tears of laughter.

This snag was the loud offering from Mister Bojangles. His soul aroused by the tremulous keening of the strings and the bandoneon's sad lament, he sat up, threw back his head and howled. For all her attempts to contain this canine outpouring of the heart, Octavia could do nothing to silence it. Beau's soul—in spite of many long hours, weeks and months of careful handling and obedience training, to say nothing of decades of selective breeding—burst through all such constraints. It had been awakened. Something ancient and utterly primal had been stirred, and he was responding as only a full-blooded, pedigree golden retriever with his heart on fire could respond.

Martin Buber, Octavia thought, would have been proud of him.

Lucien sat back and grinned.

"It's not the piano," he said sternly. "He has been with me every day for months, and not a single sound. It's the two of you: Reuben—and you, Salvador, with that fiddle—"

"It's a violin," Salvador said with mock severity.

"You and your violin, and that unholy bandoneon—what could you expect from a sensitive hound?"

He called the dog to come to him, and Beau, with an air of triumph, went across the room and sat down next to him.

"Perhaps he will settle down if he stays close to me." Lucien pointed to a space under the piano. "Lie down! Stay!"

When the room was quiet, Santiago stepped forward once more.

"All right. Once again! From the top."

He raised the baton, counted a bar so that Lucien would know when to come in, and the musicians began to play.

It was no good. Beau won the day.

Thereafter, during every rehearsal, Beau spent the morning or the afternoon with Gregorio—doing the rounds, learning how to behave with the farm animals and generally having a break from his duties.

"But what will you do with him on the night of the concert?" Sofia asked Lucien after one rehearsal. "He goes everywhere with you."

"We will have to get a dog-sitter. I know this is a lament for the animals, but it was never intended to be a lament by them!"

Sofia chuckled.

"Do you think we could play some music here—bandoneon and violin, and so on—and desensitize him?" she suggested.

"You could try, but not at bedtime," Lucien said with feeling. "Three howling voices would be a bit much! But maybe he could join you when you are singing the animals' voices."

"Oh, you!" Sofia said with a laugh.

For the Love of Stars

The sun was low in the western sky. Santiago had called a late afternoon meeting with all the musicians in the concert hall. It was not necessary for Octavia to be there. They were going to discuss how to introduce the haunting lament theme in a way that would catch the listeners' attention without pre-empting what was to come. All the musicians, including Sofia, were invited to put forward their ideas.

The late sun was slanting through the skylight when Octavia placed the small Oregon table in a central position underneath it. She stood there, her fingers tracing the lines in the grain, her thoughts on its long journey—how long? Years—decades; perhaps even a century. This small piece of wood was once part of a great tree. And then the felling of it; and a long river journey—not unlike the whorls, streams and eddies in the grain of the wood itself.

A tree with its head in the mist.

"I see you," she whispered.

She crossed the room, and fetched the large stone that would be the base for the candle and candle-holder. She had found the holder in the saddle-room down at the stables; an old tin one, now rusted and dented. Could it be the one she had used as a child? She couldn't remember. It was perfect. Into it she put a plain candle, bought from the trading store in Las Madres.

Octavia stepped outside, and scooped up a handful of reddish dirt and gravel. This would symbolize for her the gravel on which she lay as a child. With it she made a circle around the stone.

Finally she fetched the tin containing the four small stones. These she placed carefully within the circle of earth—the red stone in the north, the black stone in the south, and the white and the yellow stones in the east and the west respectively. She left the tin, with its folded note, open on the table.

Twilight was settling over the valley. Soon it would be dark.

Octavia sat, waiting.

Night had fallen. She stood under the skylight, and gazed up at the stars. Countless millions of them. So bright.

338

She lit the candle with a match, and returned to her chair; selected a new disc, and pressed the "on" button of the player. The sound of a cello filled the room.

Kol Nidrei—All vows and promises...

She sat, watching the flickering shadows play on the rough adobe walls; saw how the candle-light cast its glow onto the red angel, high up on the east-facing wall. And above everything, the silence of the night sky.

She sat listening, hearing a note of sadness in the music, and holding in her heart the memory of the small, passionate child she had been.

Journal Entry 32

How do we ever know where a thing begins? Are we born with some sense—or perhaps an absence—of something vital? Is this what people talk about when they say they were called? But who or what is it that calls?

I have always felt that there was something I could not find; couldn't even say what it was. Only that it had something to do with stars.

And I still do not even understand what that means.

Do we follow a path? Or do we make it?

And what does all of this have to do with the raging serpent?

Journal Entry 33

A different kind of music.

I have discovered something so exciting! I can hear the music in the beads!

Why have I only heard this now? Could it have anything to do with the four stones, or perhaps with remembering the child I was, for whom anything was possible? If I could hear the stars then, why not beads now? After all, beads are prayers.

People would say I am mad!

I know that there is no room for intellect in this work. I must dare to welcome each strange notion—though some might call this a touch of madness. Or perhaps a gift? Don't try to work it out, Octavia! It is not supposed to be reasonable.

Is it because these adobe walls have heard so much music over the past years, while I have been hard at work, that the beads are now resonating in their own way?

It is not the Bach that I hear now. It is more like the early choral music of the Byzantine Empire—the many voices making one tapestry of sound—the way the colors and textures of the beads, although so different, blend together to make one dramatic and harmonious whole.

I can also hear in the music the sadness of creatures who present themselves for the counting. Are they aware, in some way that we cannot comprehend, that the vast swathes of time—which were for them an eternal present—are falling to an unholy scythe?

Is this music—this invisible connection to the creatures I have stitched, using thousands of beads—more powerful than the visible images themselves?

Where does a soul go when it leaves us?

Is it true that we all, in our own way, will be crucified? And is it the animal soul in us that will suffer and die?

I feel this wounding so deeply in my body.

Everything is breath—and once it leaves us, we are no more. Is it this breath, the one breath that we all share, that is slowly dying? Little by little?

I like the notion that there is only one breath.

How is it that there is such beauty in this apocalyptic vision?

I made a copy of the Russian poem Kristiyan marked for me so long ago, and pinned it to the wall near all the bead-shelves. Today I read it again. I had almost forgotten it was there. I think it is only now that I truly hear and feel the poet's voice. I remember, as if it was yesterday, listening to Kristiyan's voice reading it to me.

"Did you ever read the poem I marked—the one by Marina Tsvetaeva?"

"Not yet, I'm afraid to say."

"Would you like to hear it now?"

"I would love to."

Kristiyan opened the book at the mark, and was about to begin reading when he looked up at her.

"There is one line I would like to read first. I am taking it out of context, but it speaks to me so powerfully about everything that you are reaching for; everything that you are saying in your work."

"I am intrigued!"

"The line is—'The storm of stars in the sky will turn to quiet.'"

He waited for her to hear the depth of it.

Octavia was looking down. When she looked up again, he saw the tears on her cheeks.

"It is beautiful," she said. "It is like a prayer; or maybe a powerful prophecy."

"Yes."

"The storm of stars in the sky will turn to quiet." She repeated the line softly. "How does the poem begin?"

Kristiyan bent to read.

"'I know the truth—give up all other truths...'

"Isn't that a powerful statement? One that will surely invite much criticism."

"I can just hear what Raho would be saying!"

"And yet, I think," said Kristiyan, "we have to hear it from her at a deeper level. I think she may be suggesting that if we can endure the storm, and the profound disillusionment that often follows, we may arrive at the acceptance of things just as they are."

"Did she do that? I know nothing about her life."

"She lived at a time of profound upheaval. I think in all the tumult that surrounded her, in the end it became a weary resignation for her rather than acceptance.

"And yet, in spite of this, there is her powerful challenge: 'What do you speak of, poets, lovers, generals?'"

"Why on earth—generals?" she asked.

"What does it say to you?"

She thought for a while. "Maybe it is not only poets and lovers who need to be a voice for the people. Perhaps she is asking: where do you stand, generals, when you are finally pushed against the wall?"

It was a question.

"Perhaps the last two lines give us a clue."

He read the lines slowly.

"'And soon all of us will sleep under the earth, we who never let each other sleep above it.'"

"What happened to her?"

"In the end she took her own life."

Listening to an Image

Kristiyan stood very still in front of the beadwork of a huge condor, flying over an empty landscape.

No life; no vegetation; dark rocks, standing black against bare sand.

Octavia had asked him to come and "listen" to her bead tapestries, and to discuss with her how well the music echoed what she was saying in the images.

He stood, transfixed, allowing the energy to penetrate him. Every minute detail of the bird was impeccably worked. It radiated an intense, fierce rage. Set against this was the dead landscape, and a blood-sky.

"The condor is on the endangered list," Octavia said.

He moved on to consider the next image: a bison. The tapestry was bordered by a stylized representation of the barrier that surrounds a bullring. The bison was standing in the center of it—standing on the line where the blinding light meets a wall of shadow; the danger point.

For Kristiyan the image evoked the atmosphere of a fiesta: the dowels and pics with their gay, fluttering ribbons; the blood-red roses, lying on the bright sand. Even the gaunt, sway-back Picasso horses ridden by the picadors looked festive in their protective trappings. But the face of the matador dispelled all notions of celebration. It was a grinning, yellow skull—grotesque above the rich brocade of his jacket.

"What are you saying in this one?" Kristiyan asked.

"I suppose I am inviting people to take a second look—beyond what appears to be, to what is actually happening. So many people do not question the ethics of this ancient ritual in today's world. They argue that this is part of the culture. I think that every culture needs to reinvent the ways in which it expresses its rituals. People think that a man fighting a bull is a fair fight, but it isn't; not even that. Why the deliberate wounding of the huge neck muscle, if not to make the bull's head come down? There is something so sinister in that. How else will the matador be able to make his kill?

"I am asking questions. I am introducing an element—the grinning skull—to oblige people to think again. Of course some—probably many people—will still defend bullfighting. I am making images that are disturbing. I want to confuse the viewer—to make him think; to feel. I want these works to be contradictory. With this one, I want the viewer to ask the question: why did the artist give the matador a yellow skull?"

She grimaced. Kristiyan heard the pain in her voice. He moved to the next tapestry.

He stared at the image of the Virgin, standing in the flames of the crucifixion thorn bush.

"Now this one reminds me of the Russian icons. It is very different from the others."

"In what way does it differ?"

"It is the formal composition—the round mandala of the bush and the Virgin, set inside a square with the bear, the wolf, the condor and the elk in the four corners. This is what gives it a traditional effect. This one is truly beautiful. And in spite of the formal treatment, I can feel the sadness in it. Something primal. What is the story behind it? And what is a crucifixion thorn?"

"It is the name of a bush we have around here—the crucifixion thorn. About the image: I had a dream—a daydream, really—and this is what I saw. Well, not exactly. In the dream I knew that a fire had destroyed an entire landscape. Those blackened stumps are all that is left of a forest. Everything is gone except this one bush, which burns but is not consumed—like the burning bush that appeared to Moses. In my dream I saw the weeping Virgin in the flames—yet the flames did not destroy her. I wondered at her presence there. And then I wondered why she wept. So I added the four animals. She weeps for them—for a world without that animal breath. I knew that I wanted to elevate the image—to make it sacred—so I gave it the formal appearance of a traditional icon. I can't say more about it—not yet, anyway."

"Where on earth does all this thinking come from? I know you never studied art; chose not to go to university."

"Maybe that is why I feel free to do what I like."

He moved on, spending time in front of image after image. He marveled at the exquisite detail—the contrasts of color, size and texture in each work.

"How many tapestries are you contemplating in total?"

"Well, these ones have taken most of this year. Perhaps another six or eight. I suppose I will stop when I have said what I want to. Not before. There is something else—"

She paused.

"Yes?"

"There is one beadwork I want to make, but I don't want to have it in the same room as all the others. Would that seem strange?"

"Depends what it is."

"I'll tell you more about it when I come to it. It is a very new experience for me—I would call it sacred in a way."

"I suppose you do know that you are fascinating," he said.

He moved on to stand in front of the crucified wolf, and the surreal wolf-head floating in the sky.

"A crucified wolf? A cross! I think you can expect to get some fairly confronting reviews. This is not an exhibition that you stroll through, and then meet someone for lunch."

"I sincerely hope not!"

Kristiyan paused in front of the almost completed serpent-work.

"And what is this about?"

Octavia told him about her strange experience—the image in the round water-jug.

"Are you telling me that you saw this in a jug of water?"

"It was more like a vision. It happened when I was thirteen. It was strange; totally unexpected. I was just sitting, daydreaming—and quite suddenly there it was."

"And what does Raho say?"

"He has only seen the sketch. No doubt he will have something pithy to say about it."

A Postcard from Mexico

Sister Piadosa, accompanied by Catherine, brought the card down to the concert hall. All the musicians were busy rehearsing a difficult part of the composition. It involved the transition from the innocence of the natural world to the arrival of gun-powder and guns. It evoked increasing levels of violence, and the changes that these wrought in the animal voices.

"We thought you wouldn't mind taking a short break. We have a card from Sebastián and Georgia. Sister Ana has gone to call Octavia."

Salvador fetched chairs for the two women, while the other musicians positioned themselves on the edge of the stage.

"How exciting! A card!" said Sofia.

"What is the picture on it?" Lucien asked.

"A dancing skeleton in a large hat, with bright flowers," said Sister Piadosa with a straight face. "I only hope it is not significant."

Octavia, who had arrived just in time to hear this, gave a chuckle and went to sit next to Sofia and Lucien.

"Who would like to read it? It is addressed to all of us."

"You read it, sister—to save any discussion. We have had more than enough of that for one day."

"I will do my best; the writing is very small."

Mexico. March 28 1998
Dear one and all of you—where has the year gone? We seem to be living in an eternal now, and are having the most incredibly rich time. There is just so much here to stimulate all the senses. I am happy to report that Georgia is back, with a new vision: such beautiful, fresh canvases—and all the rich colors of Mexico. And I am writing well, I think. It feels so good to be back in the company of poetry, pen and paper—and not admin! We have decided to store all our things here at the hotel, and then to hitch or walk or train our way further south, following our noses. There is just so much here to see, touch, taste and feel. Yes! We feel like teenagers again, bunking school. This is just to let you know that we are well. We aim to be back in about June or July, but we will let you know dates closer to the time. How is the great opus coming along? Don't you dare have the concert and exhibition before we get back! We send so much love to all of you, and big hugs to Caradoc and Erin. Sebastián and Georgia

"Well, I for one am glad about the extra time," said Octavia. "How does everyone else feel?"

"July is rather late," said Salvador. "But as long as they are back before the summer gets really hot, we should be fine. And we certainly don't want to wait till fall."

"Why not then?" asked Reuben.

"I don't know—just feels like the wrong energy somehow."

"How early do we have to make the booking for the gallery and the concert hall in Santa Fe?" asked Kristiyan. "Maybe we should go ahead and do that, just to make sure we get them."

"And if they decide to stay away for longer?"

"Then," said Salvador, "when they phone to tell us that they won't be back until next year, we can tell them that if they don't get their butts home—pronto—they will miss the whole exhibition! You have to set the parameters for teenagers!"

"And I," said Catherine, "would like to be able to walk, unaided, into the concert hall to hear Sofia sing. I have waited almost my entire life for this moment to come, and I do not intend to be wheeled or carried in!"

Sofia went to sit beside her grandmother, and squeezed her hand. "So that's settled, then," she said firmly. "There is nothing more to say."

"Hear, hear," said Sister Piadosa with mock severity. "Not all of us feel like teenagers!"

During the general laughter that followed this, Santiago said that if they gave him the dates, he would make the bookings for both venues.

"So! Back to work," he said, tapping the music-stand with his baton. "Thank you, sister—Catherine. Carried unanimously!"

Raho's Gift

A light tap on the door.

"Just a minute—I'm coming."

Octavia moved the small dishes of beads away from the table-edge, to keep them safe.

"Oh—Raho! What a lovely surprise. Come in."

"Good morning, Octavia," said Raho, taking a seat in the old cane chair. "I have something for you. I would like you to keep it in this room. I will be away for a few months, so I thought I would bring it to you now."

345

"Oh. Will you be back before...?"

"Yes, I certainly will. There are just a few things I need to attend to where I live, to make sure that I am not entirely forgotten by the brothers."

It was the first time that Raho had mentioned anything to do with his life. He always just appeared, stayed a while—and then, when he had managed to ruffle a few feathers, left again. Where he came from, how he lived, had never been discussed. Only Father Octavio knew something about his circumstances. The two had studied for the priesthood together until, almost overnight, Raho announced that he was leaving to join a brotherhood of Zen Buddhist monks. Now Father Octavio was dead, but Raho still unsettled The Adobe from time to time with his quirky sense of humor and uncomfortable questions.

"Who are the brothers?"

"Oh, just some people I hang out with," Raho said vaguely, and they both left it at that.

"But I brought this for you." He held out a small gift, wrapped simply in crumpled tissue-paper.

"For me?"

"For you."

Octavia carefully removed the paper, and stared at what was inside. It was a very plain, hand-made porcelain bowl. It was undecorated; its beauty lay in its utter simplicity—its exquisite proportions.

"Raho—it is beautiful!"

There was a small envelope inside the bowl. On it was written, in Raho's bold writing: "To be opened later."

Octavia searched his face.

"Just something I enjoy," he said.

"I will look inside later. Raho, I really thank you for this, but why—?"

"I want it to be in this room while you are working."

"And then?"

"Then nothing. However," he added nonchalantly, "you might like to look among Sebastián's books for one with poetry by Kabir. I think he wrote something about a clay jug."

"Oh—you think!" said Octavia with a laugh. "You know you never do anything that innocently."

Raho gave her a look of mock surprise.

"I am shocked that you should say that, Octavia. We have spoken about this before. I do things because I do things. What you or others do with this is not my concern."

"Then I will thank you because I thank you. I think I will put this on my Oregon table, with the stones."

"I noticed them when I came in. What is the story behind the stones?"

Octavia told him about her childhood ritual.

"This bowl feels as if it belongs with them."

Raho nodded. "Good. Then I will be off. See you around, Octavia," he said.

It was as he turned to leave that he saw the new work on the frame.

"Ah!"

He walked across the room, and stood in front of it.

"You have wrestled with this one, haven't you?"

"Yes—but how can you tell?"

"There are three elements, and they all want to dominate."

"Does that invalidate the work for you?"

"Not the work, no. It will certainly make people think. But I am thinking of you. Where do you see yourself in this?"

"I hadn't exactly thought of myself as—in it."

He gave a smile. "This is very different from the other works. It does not seem to relate to your Lament theme. Tell me more about it."

"You know about it; I told you about the vision in the water-jug. You saw the painted sketch."

"Just remind me."

"Oh—it was long ago, when I was thirteen. I made the small painting at the time, and then sort of forgot about it. But *you* don't forget things, Raho! So what are you really asking?"

"What made you decide to pick it up now?"

"Maybe something you said about anger."

"Yes—you did say you were angry at the time you saw the image. Does that anger speak through what you are saying here?"

"I have thought a lot, but I can't say that I have had any radical insights. I do know that it disturbs me."

"Well, just to please an old man, ask the serpent why it is so angry—I see you have put a flash of green into the eye. And ask the wave what it wants to achieve. And the sun—what is it doing inside the black wave?"

"Are you kidding?"

"Do I ever?"

He gave a small bow and left her standing there, bemused.

After he left, Octavia sat down with the bowl in her lap; opened the envelope, and read the short inscription:

"What you are looking for is what is looking."

She pinned it onto her work-frame.

And just why are you telling me this now, Raho?

Octavia stood in Sebastián's office, a small book in her hand. She had indeed found the poem—This Clay Jug, by Kabir. The translation was by Robert Bly.

"Inside this clay jug there are canyons
and pine mountains..."

Octavia read the whole poem several times.
It is utterly beautiful, she thought; this vision in an empty jug.

"...the music from the strings that no one touches..."

She could feel this resonate so deeply within her. But it was the last line that moved her the most:

"...the God whom I love is inside."

Journal Entry 34

I didn't want to come into my studio today.
This bloody serpent story—I have been in tears the whole night.
The great eye of the sun, unable to see—drowning in the black wave; the black wave caused by the awakened serpent with the yellow-green eye.
The sun didn't want to see!
There it was. I remembered the day I saw Lucien kiss Sofia.
There, Octavia. The truth is out at last.
Raho knew there was something like this behind the image.
The vision in the glass jug was for me, so that I would see myself!
This almighty fight for power and control! What is behind it? What was always behind it?
Rage that I couldn't get my own way. Rage that I was powerless—and under that? Fear! The bottom line is fear. Fear of uncertainty. Fear of not knowing how things will turn out. Anything is better than having to live with uncertainty.
And the only certainty is death.
And this is me. The big deal. Calling all the shots!
Everyone must know—must have always known this about me; must have put up with so many hurts, and so much thoughtlessness. And still they love me.

I am so ashamed.

Thank heaven they don't know about this.

I feel as if I have been flayed to the bone.

I spent the whole night awake, seeing how time and time again I have wanted to stay in control—of everything and everyone.

Octavia, you have a dark secret. If you were a true, observant Catholic, you would be in the confessional right now. But I think that would be too easy for you.

So, how do I ever forgive myself?

I need to know and remember that I am capable of this.

I am going for a long walk.

Thank God for the sanity of the desert. I could feel it holding me; could hear a voice from the roots of the earth, saying: "Let everything be the way it is."

Now I know exactly what Martin Buber meant: "Everyone must come out of his exile in his own way."

It is going to take me a long time to learn the depths of my own self-deception.

I am not going to confess this, or tell anyone about it just to make myself feel better. This is a wound I gave to myself. I need to hold it, and remember it—like a precious gift.

It will always be there.

Oh, Octavia, you were flying so high. Weren't you?

Journal Entry 35

As I sit here, focused on the beads, my mind turns up thoughts the way a plough turns the soil, and whatever is in it is revealed.

I need to re-think everything.

I feel safe with animals and landscape. Completely at home in their company.

I have always been afraid of letting people get too close—afraid that they will want me to conform; try to control me.

And yet, here I am—involving a whole community in this project of mine. And it has supported me so willingly!

The Serpent, Black Wave and Red Sun story is mercifully finished. It is both powerful and disturbing. I wonder how many people will relate to it—and if so, in what way.

I am working on a mountain lion. My reference is D. H. Lawrence's poem.

I have placed the mountain lion in the red-orange canyon. I am making her the same color as the rocks, but I will use a slightly different bead for her. You will only be able to see her if you look closely. I want to suggest that this is a species that will soon disappear forever; is already disappearing.

I am so aware of the red angel, watching over this whole process. Why is that?

I have looked again at the sketch I made for the elk beadwork. A trophy-wall: the proud heads of many elk, arranged in a circle; beautiful, noble heads; magnificent racks of antlers. In the center, with blood on his hands, the hunter.

Raho would ask whether I see myself in this. Am I the elk, or am I the hunter? Or am I the judge?

Raho—you have ruined me.

"What you are looking for is what is looking."

What am I looking for?

I am searching, in this threat of possible extinction, for meaning.

I can hear you, Raho! "Do you think the meaning is out there, waiting for you? Wake up, Octavia!"

I want to make more images like the almost absent mountain lion. It is all the more powerful because it does not hit you in the eye.

Sofia is going to Santa Fe tomorrow. I must ask her to take a Lament invitation, and post it to Louise at the Bead Shop in Albuquerque.

Catherine Meets Madame Jolie

"This is my grandmother. Madame Jolie, Catherine de la Cruz."

"Please call me Collette."

The two women shook hands.

"There is no need to tell me that, my dear. The likeness is unmistakable." She stepped aside to allow them to enter. "And it is from you, Sofia tells me, that this extraordinary voice has been passed down. What a legacy! What a gift!"

They moved into the practice-room, and Catherine and Sofia sat in the comfortable armchairs while Madame Jolie poured them some tea.

"Do you take sugar?"

Catherine shook her head. "No, thank you."

"Do you still sing, Catherine?" Madame Jolie asked, taking a seat close to them.

"Yes—at least I did until I returned to New Mexico. I have been living in Mexico for many years. I used to sing in a private club there. Members only. I had reasons for not wanting to go public."

"Will you sing for us today?"

"Oh, please say yes, Catherine," Sofia pleaded. "I have only heard about your voice. I would so love to truly hear you sing."

"I will accompany you, if I know the song," Madame Jolie added.

"Are you familiar with Richard Strauss' Four Last Songs?"

"Of course."

"Well, then I will choose Beim Schlafengehen—Going to Sleep. It is my favorite—Hesse's words: 'And the soul, unwatched, would soar in free flight...' It always makes me think of María. It is how I hold her now."

They finished their tea, and Catherine moved to stand by the piano. Sofia took a seat a little way back in the room.

Although she had heard all about her grandmother's legendary voice, Sofia was unprepared for its soaring strength and clarity, and its surprisingly dark, throaty quality. She sat, transfixed, unable to take her eyes off Catherine's face. She could feel the hairs on her arms and the back of her neck rise, and a shudder move through her like a dark flame.

Madame Jolie, it appeared, was not similarly distracted. She played a piano accompaniment, matching Catherine's pauses perfectly.

There was a long silence after the last notes died away.

Sofia couldn't move. She could feel an ache in her throat; could feel the tears gather behind her eyes. Although she knew the story of her grandfather's refusal to allow his wife to sing in public—and María, his daughter, after her—it was not until now that the full extent of their loss struck at her heart. To deny the expression of such a gift was akin to murder—an attempt to so destroy a soul that the individual would lose all sense of her true identity. She thought of the extreme cruelty they had both suffered at his hands. He had robbed María of a career; of a life with the man she loved, and of the child she would never see. And he has robbed me of a mother; and Salvador of a wife. Sofia felt her heart break for all of them.

She came back to the room at the sound of voices.

"Extraordinary! Magnificent!"

Collette stood up to acknowledge a rare experience.

"You sing with duende! How magnificent! But of course you know that. A rare gift."

She shook her head. "A rare gift indeed."

She smiled at Catherine.

"Sofia has told me a little bit about the family history; that your husband would not allow you or your daughter to sing. But you cannot bury a gift such as this. It will always reappear. It will survive all things, until it is heard."

She shook her head again.

"Ah, if only we were both young again, we would take the world by storm!"

351

Catherine walked over to where Sofia was sitting, and put a hand on her shoulder.

"This is why I am so thrilled that Sofia is studying—with you. And although it has been a very strange journey, I can only thank God that I will finally sit in a concert hall and hear Sofia sing for all three of us."

"And make no mistake. Your granddaughter has inherited your gift. And it is the very suffering you have endured that qualifies you for the duende's touch. Only a brush with death, literal or otherwise, can produce that sound of blood in the throat."

She turned to Sofia.

"This is the gift your mother gave to you," she said quietly.

At this remark Sofia burst into tears.

The Orphan's Lament

"I'm not going to say anything about why I asked you to come here this evening," Kristiyan said to the group of musicians gathered in Octavia's studio. "I just want you to listen to something; and I want you to listen to it in this particular space. We can talk later."

He arranged the extra chairs that had been brought in by Gregorio for the occasion.

"Is everyone comfortable?"

There were nods all round.

"You don't have to do this, of course, but I would like to suggest that you close your eyes."

He turned off the ceiling lights and the work-lamps. The last light of evening, from the high windows and the skylight, cast a blue shade onto the walls, making them recede into the shadows.

Kristiyan placed a disc into the CD player.

The room was filled with the sound of vast, wind-swept, empty spaces—the sound of strange instruments, weaving together to keen into the wind; and a haunting voice, chanting a guttural lament that floated over the land to blow away into the emptiness. The listeners were drawn into a timeless landscape by the chanting; drawn into a primitive sense of belonging; into a time when the land and its creatures, and the people who dwelt among them, were one.

No one moved. No one opened their eyes.

Kristiyan selected another track.

352

Again the listeners heard the sound of voices and instruments calling out into vast, open spaces. But these were almost overwhelmed by the drumbeat of mountain thunder, echoed back by other mountain ranges—a primeval sound, like the breath of the gods of forest, river, earth and sky. It was an invocation, as if to call up the spirits of the natural world, and to mediate between them and the humans crossing their wild terrain.

The musicians could feel the resonant vibrations rise up through their chairs—up into their bodies; could feel the dark echoes fill their skulls.

Kristiyan, watching their response to the ancient music, thought he had never seen such stillness; such surrender to a musical experience.

He waited for several minutes before switching on one of the small work-lamps.

He waited in silence for everyone to return.

He is ahead of me. We are heading toward a vast forest, blanketed by thick snow.
Overhead, a black sky and swirling mountain mist.
Two dark birds float on the thermals.
I cannot see where it comes from, but a strange chanting moves with us over the icy ground. I am not sure if these are human voices, or voices being drawn out of the land by the wind and the yawning emptiness; only that this is the call I have waited for my whole life. And I still don't know what it is.
He has not turned to look at me. His pace never slackens. We have a long way to go.

For a long time no one spoke.

Kristiyan broke the silence. "I think we should sleep on this, and meet again tomorrow for some discussion. Does anyone have anything to say now?"

No one had anything to add.

"Thank you all for coming. See you tomorrow."

Everyone said goodnight, and made their way along the spiral path, back to their respective houses.

Octavia waited until everyone had left.

"What in heaven—?"

Kristiyan closed the door, and came to sit down next to her.

"It is the music of the Tuvan people. The first track is called The Orphan's Lament: you can feel it so deeply. The second is the song of a reindeer-herder, singing about his love for the Siberian taiga—the great forest."

"I've never heard of them. What is their country called?"

"The country is called Tuva. It is a vast basin of plains and hills, surrounded by towering mountains. It is in central Asia, close to the Siberian forest. Mongolia lies to the south."

"And this incredible music—?"

"It is haunting, isn't it? The Tuvans make the same instruments today that have been used there for centuries; and they learn what is known as throat-singing. That is what makes such a distinctive sound. They can sing two, sometimes three or even four different notes simultaneously. But I think it is the grandeur of the high mountains, and the yawning emptiness, that draws out of them this sacred response—a song of praise, humility and awe."

"Why don't more people know about them—their music?"

"There are many people who know the music well. It is, however, not every-one's taste in music today."

"And the people themselves?"

"The Tuvans are unique in that they are perhaps the only people today who are living almost the identical lives that their ancestors lived. Simple lives. They practice shamanism to communicate with the spirits. They are a deeply spiritual people. They see all of nature as one. They have a fierce reverence for all things in the universe."

"I could hear that so clearly."

"That is why I thought we should all listen to their music. You can hear the space in it: wide, open space. They have no fixed buildings, no roads to speak of; no fences. Their animals are free to roam, but they seem to stay close to home never-theless. However, the Tuvans live very close to the edge. Winters can freeze all their grazing; in a hard winter their herds die of starvation; that kind of thing. They are utterly dependent on the animals for everything."

"And how do you know all this?"

"There are many Russians who live in Tuva to this day. I suppose I know some-thing about it, the way you know about countries in South America."

"Have you been there?"

"No. But I would like to, some day."

"Can we listen again? Now?"

"Of course. Would you like the light off?"

"Yes—please."

The Lament of the Animals

It was the first rehearsal of the third movement.

There had been much discussion about how to incorporate something of the Tuvan sound into the work—perhaps into the Lament theme.

"How can we get that deep, guttural sound they have in their voices?"

"Sofia—do you think Madame Jolie could teach you throat-singing in time for the concert?"

"Ha, ha, ha!"

"But it will be quite a challenge to get that edge that makes their voices so strong, and at the same time so tenuous. You need defiance to stand before the ruthless gods of earth and sky that they encounter. How dare a mere mortal stand before them—and sing?"

"And yet it is a form of prayer."

"Yes."

"Kristiyan, would it be possible to tune the cello very low—very, very low—and then play an octave below Sofia's voice?"

"We can try. It might sound rather weird. But bringing the cello down is a good idea. It will bring in a more mysterious, earthy quality."

"What about that deep, booming drum sound? That was amazing."

"I think," Santiago said, "we should have an experimental workshop about some of these ideas. What about tomorrow? Ten o'clock?"

"Good idea."

"Right. Let's get back to work."

The musicians listened to what Lucien had to say about how they could interpret the score, and made notes in the margins of their sheet music. Santiago reminded them again that the various instruments should be guided by Sofia's vocals, some of which would be improvised. After consulting with Lucien, he had brought her part down to a lower register, where it would have the sound of earth and darkness in it.

It was here that the keening of the animals would be most haunting. The lament theme, which had previously been heard like a lost song trying to find its way, now made itself heard in all its pain and beauty.

It was against this background that Sofia had to capture the raw sound of the animals' mating calls; their calling out to another of their kind—a call that would never again be answered.

□□□

Catherine and Madame Jolie sat in the front row of the concert hall. Madame Jolie had come to hear what would be required of Sofia for the animal voices.

Catherine, it was decided, would attend all the rehearsals, to support Sofia and to offer suggestions if they were needed.

The lament was introduced by the violin—a story without words. Kristiyan's cello played long, slow notes several octaves below it; notes so low that they were little more than a deep vibration. Reuben's bandoneon added a note of loss and nostalgia for what had been, and was gone forever.

Santiago tapped the music-stand with his baton, and the musicians stopped playing.

"Much too sentimental! We want to keep the deep sense of loss, but it must have a sharp edge to it. Wilderness is fierce. It doesn't complain. Don't bring in human values here. They don't work. And nothing pretty. If it had the choice, I think wilderness, and all its creatures, would rather die than be tamed. This is not about leaving the beloved house of your childhood, and moving to an apartment in the city. That is change. What we have here is extinction. Get that into the music. Once again, from the top."

Octavia sat a few rows back in rapt attention, astonished to hear a new note sound in the same score—a note so removed from human experience, it would be impossible, she thought, to describe it.

They have heard me completely, she thought.

It was time to introduce Sofia's part. She had done a lot of work on the animal voices with Madame Jolie, who had coaxed her voice down to new depths.

"You have an extraordinary range, my dear, and we can develop it further. Have you never thought to sing this low?"

"Most of my singing has been happy. I think I am only now beginning to see life in a deeper, and perhaps more complex way."

"I want you to feel the death in your soul, and to bring it into the lament. Allow yourself to feel what it is to lose a part of yourself with each animal that steps over the edge of the world. Yes," she said in response to Sofia's inquiring look. "I have read Octavia and Lucien's proposals for the visual exhibition, and for the concert. I can't wait to see the artworks.

"From today, I want you to come five days a week—until the concert. Can you manage that? There is a lot of work we must do so that you will not strain your voice in any way. This is a demanding role for any singer. I will see you tomorrow at ten."

Blood

Sofia stood on the concert hall stage, facing the small audience: Catherine, Sisters Piadosa and Ana, and all the nuns; Father Rafael, Alejandro and Francesca, and Gregorio.

She stood close to Santiago, so that she would be able to see him clearly when he nodded to her, and come in on time. The musicians sat a little way behind them, and to the side.

Catherine sat very upright in her chair. Two bright spots of color lit her cheeks. Her hands were tightly clasped.

She looked at Sofia, standing there so petite and composed—her startling red hair emitting blue sparks beneath the stage lights; her face, with its porcelain complexion, glowing.

ooo

She looked at Sofia, but what she saw was another image which stepped into the picture: the image of María. Then the two images fused into one, so that Catherine could not be sure who was standing in front of her. She recalled vividly the night when María, at sixteen, was the soloist singing with the church choir in the small chapel in Santa Fe. Salvador, who was head over heels in love with her, had composed the music and written the words for a love duet that the two would sing as a finale.

De la Cruz did not know that María had been singing with the church choir for some time. On hearing that she was to be the only soloist in a church concert, he immediately claimed the whole evening as his own creation. He invited influential acquaintances, organized an ostentatious spread of snacks and champagne, and moved among the guests—larger than life, greeting people on the far side of the room over the heads of others.

"Ah! Luis! Good to see you!" he called out—so loudly that heads turned to look at him. "Enjoy our little show."

He gave a thumbs-up to some imaginary greeting from across the room, and a wave in response to another, while acknowledging all those around him with a nod or a pat on the shoulder.

"Great! Great! Glad you could make it!"

Catherine, who did not want to be included in this grandiose display, moved to the edge of the room, where she met Father Octavio. He had come with the beautiful Magdalena Chavez, whom she had met only once before. They had just begun a conversation when de la Cruz appeared, and after a brief hello to Octavio and Magdalena, literally dragged her away.

"Don't you know she is that dreadfully common woman who runs some kind of a salon in Las Madres?"

Even now, she could feel his rage in her body; could feel her joy in the evening being overridden by it. But it was when he saw María, standing close to Salvador in front of the choir—her long, white dress with its low-cut neckline emphasizing her budding womanhood—that his anger erupted. He grabbed Catherine's arm, and shook it.

"Her hair!" he hissed. "That dress!"

"This is a concert, Lorenzo," Catherine whispered. "Be quiet."

And then she put him out of her mind. Her whole attention was for her lovely daughter, who would fulfill the dream she'd had of a singing career. This was the beginning of a rich future for María, and Catherine was not going to allow Lorenzo to spoil it for her.

It was at the end of the romantic duet, when the two lovers fell into each other's arms, that Lorenzo's utterances became too loud to be ignored. Fortunately the

357

standing ovation soon drowned out his protestations. And then the lights came on, and people came up to congratulate him on his daughter's voice—and her beauty.

"That hair!"

That was the beginning and the end of María's singing.

And now it was as if María stood here, in the form of her daughter Sofia, about to step into her destiny.

□□□

Catherine was brought back to the room by the sound of Santiago's baton, asking for quiet.

They were to perform the final movement.

Everyone present had heard Sofia sing before. Everyone knew she had an exceptional voice. But no one had ever heard the likes of what came from her now.

Raw notes, like skin torn from a wound; dark notes—the sound of blood in a snarl, and the disembodied howls of a wolf.

And now, in her voice, the sound of a vast emptiness—a high, thin note; a note that sounded more like a last breath taken by the wind than a human voice—floated over the lament played by the musicians. Waves and waves of emptiness, and then in mid-bar: total silence.

The effect was devastating.

Design for Beadwork #12

"What do you think? Or rather, does it make you think?"

They were looking at Octavia's sketch for the largest of all the beadworks. This was to be the first image that people would see on entering the gallery.

"I like it very much," said Kristiyan.

They were considering the image of what appeared to be a constructed landscape. No part of it showed any evidence of organic weathering. It was clearly manmade. There was no vegetation.

The dominant feature is a very high mountain, almost like a tower, rising up out of a featureless plain. Above it the sky is red. A black coil of smoke rises, and turns into a pair of human hands, reaching across the sky. One shaft of blood-red sun strikes the mountain, and casts a long shadow that spreads over the empty land. The shadow, in turn, falls away over a cliff-edge. On the mountain-top there is a line of creatures, large and small, waiting to fall over the edge into darkness. Many have already fallen: mammals, birds, fish, whales—all falling; some with their bodies twisted, others

358

upside-down or head first. For each species there is only a single creature—the last of its kind. Below the falling bodies, silhouetted against the surreal sky, are black angels. Surrounding the entire image is a border of eyes—animal eyes; some pairs, some single, but all staring directly at the viewer.

"I call it The Edge of the World—of course I will not show any titles at the exhibition. I wasn't quite sure how it worked with the other images. I wanted to make an image that would show the slow and silent migration into extinction; how it happens without a sound. That is what is so sinister. We don't see or hear it happening.

"Does it make sense to you?" Octavia asked.

"And how it does! That sky! It is not only the hunting and deliberate killing of certain species. It is the felling of vast miles of rain forest, the pollution of rivers, and the silent stain of industry that is slowly poisoning all of us. Those hands! Did you intend a reference to the image from the Sistine Chapel—Adam reaching up his hand to receive God's touch?"

"I must say I hadn't thought of it—and I still don't. Those are most certainly not God's hands."

He moved closer to examine a detail.

"What are the black angels?" he asked.

"I'm not sure. They just wanted to be there. Perhaps they remember a debt that will demand payment some time in the future; a moment of reckoning. Or because they will not abandon the animals in this hour. Maybe they are the dark animal souls that refuse to die; that bear witness, so that this will never be forgotten—or forgiven."

Octavia was close to tears.

"That kind of thing. But maybe they have something else in mind. I don't know yet."

"You don't know?"

"No. They may tell me later."

"They will tell you?"

"Perhaps."

Kristiyan gave her a smile. "I can't wait to see how the beads will transform this image. What an incredible medium you have chosen. The brilliance of the beads seems to transfigure even the darkest of your images. At the same time, it is precisely this juxtaposition of the dark image against their glowing brilliance that makes the work so haunting. So powerful. I am always reminded of the Russian icons I have seen."

He considered for a moment.

"One suggestion—would you like to hear it?"

"Of course."

"This looks like the end result of ignoring all the warnings. I would perhaps make it the final image that people see at the exhibition. I would suggest that the crucifixion thorn icon should be the first image they see."

Octavia nodded agreement.

"I like the idea."

"The image of the Virgin in the lit bush really asks a question; and all that bright gold catches the eye."

"Good. We'll do it that way." Octavia stood up, and moved the easel back against the wall.

"I just wanted to show you this before I began the beading. It will be a lot of work; just the size of it is a little overwhelming. I wanted to be quite sure that it was effective as an image before I spent months working on it. I have done the measurements, and this size will just transpose onto the work-frame."

"You don't do things by halves, do you?"

"I still have to learn that!"

The Truth Is Not Somewhere Else

It was evening.

Octavia sat at her work-frame, a bright light trained on the tapestry and the small dishes of beads. The Bach was playing softly in the background.

The work was not going well.

Why now, she thought, so near the end? Why am I feeling so restless; so disconnected, so—she struggled to find the word—so abandoned?

She brought her attention back to the beads. The work was so near completion.

Just do the work, she told herself.

She worked for another hour, feeling her irritation grow and grow inside her until, in something close to panic she got up, crossed the room and stopped the music. She stood still, listening to the silence.

Looking up, she saw the stars through the skylight—bright, detached and silent as always. They appeared to be entirely indifferent to her mood. Why did she suddenly feel so distant from them?

Her stars!

She pulled the cane chair to where she could sit comfortably, and assessed this latest work. What was wrong with it? It was a powerful image; an image you could not lightly dismiss—if at all. Its composition? No, that worked for her. What was the question it asked of her? Perhaps that might tell her something.

She sat still, allowing the power of the work to draw it out of her. But no question appeared. What did come to her was a question—a question that had no words.

She got up, went to turn on the Rostropovich again—and changed her mind. She returned to her chair.

Raho would no doubt ask her some infuriating question. She tried to imagine what it might be. But he too was keeping silent.

"Oh, bloody hell!" she yelled out loud.

Octavia got up, switched on the overhead lights and walked slowly around the room, looking at each finished tapestry in turn. They were indeed very fine works—impeccably wrought. Beautiful, dramatic and confronting. She couldn't fault them. But—

Perhaps it was time to call it a day. She was tired. She would feel better in the morning: clear, and ready to continue.

Still she lingered—feeling that there was something unfinished; something her mind was deliberately preventing her from seeing; something that was right in front of her.

A strange notion came to her: to lock the door, and throw the key out of the window.

That way you won't be able to escape this!

Escape what?

She cast her mind back over the past eighteen months, to the time when she first had the idea for the exhibition and the music concert. How exciting it had been, drawing everyone together; being part of a large project; sharing her thoughts and dreams.

The image of Raho's face drifted past her eyes.

The truth is not somewhere else.

"Damn you!"

She went to sit down, and instantly got up again. She decided to tidy her work-table. She had finished with many of the beads. These bottles could go back onto the shelf.

"Oh, what's the point? You'd better admit it. You're cornered, and you don't even know what has put you there!"

Hearing her voice was some kind of relief.

She turned her thoughts back to Raho; to his last visit to her studio. What had they talked about? Nothing much, apart from his vague remarks about the brother-hood. Then there was the gift, of course. And the note. And the serpent.

She went across to the small Oregon pine table; stood looking at the four stones, the ring of gravel and the large stone supporting the candle in its funny, rusted holder. Even to these objects she could feel no connection.

She lit the candle.

What was happening to her? Am I going completely mad? This can't be me.

One thing Raho had said came to mind. It was about the small bowl. "I want it to be in this room while you are working." He had not offered anything else.

Of course, there was the note—*what you are looking for is what is looking.*

But I am not looking for anything.

"If that is true, then you have found it."

Her own voice startled her again. What had she found? Nothing.

Face it, Octavia. You have come to the end of something, and you have no idea what it is.

On an impulse, she picked up the small porcelain bowl, and gazed into its emptiness. Instantly she felt a profound sense of peace within her.

She stood quite still—holding the small bowl, listening to the huge silence of the night.

And Know the Place for the First Time

"They're here!"

There was the sound of running feet as the musicians hurried up the path to Sebastián and Georgia's house. Gregorio, who had summoned them, went to Octavia's studio to give her the news.

"Oh, my word! Already!" she said as she switched off the work-lamp. "I'll be down in half a minute."

The small group stood outside the house, watching the travel-stained car bump up the last part of the track. Next to them, on a small table, stood three bottles of champagne and several glasses.

The car came to a halt. Santiago stepped forward to open Georgia's door. Sebastián was already out of the car, being hugged by Caradoc and Erin.

"Have you brought a present for me?" Caradoc asked Georgia.

"We have brought presents for everyone," said Georgia with a laugh, as she tried to hug everyone at once. "Oh, but it is so good to be home!"

She stood with her arms open—embracing the entire valley, the cottonwoods and the pink hill.

"I don't think I have ever seen it so clearly," she said.

Turning to Gregorio, she asked: "Have the white doves had their evening flight yet?"

"Not yet. They have been waiting for you. I'll go and open for them now."

Georgia turned to put her arms around Octavia.

"Have you been well? No problems with your back and your hip? Is the work finished yet?"

Octavia laughed.

"Yes. No. Almost," she said, "in that order. I do have some news; but it can wait a bit. It is so good to have you back, mama."

"Lucien!" Sebastián put a hand on his shoulder, and gave it a shake. "We have missed you; and we have missed out on the whole creative process. We can't wait to hear the music. Are you happy with it? Does it tell the story?"

"I will let you decide that once you have heard it," he said.

Kristiyan shook Sebastián's hand, and gave Georgia a hug.

"So good to have you back. The place hasn't been the same without you."

"Indeed," said Sister Piadosa as she poured the champagne. "All that admin, for a start."

When the initial greetings were over, and the champagne had been drunk, Sebastián announced that they would unpack the car, and put everything in Georgia's studio except their clothes and personal things.

"There will be time for all our news after the concert and the exhibition," he said, "but right now we are available to help with anything you care to throw at us. Just say the word."

Sister Piadosa raised an eyebrow.

"Anything—except admin," he added with a wicked grin.

At that moment there was the sound of flapping wings. They all stood, looking up as the white doves made their timeless circles over the valley—rising up and up, the colors of sunset staining their wings. Georgia's eyes filled with tears of joy.

"Now we are really home," she said.

They were sitting around the kitchen table, enjoying a glass of wine: Sebastián and Georgia; Lucien, Sofia with the two little ones; Octavia and Kristiyan.

"So what is the surprise news that could wait a bit?" asked Georgia.

Octavia blushed—suddenly shy. She took Kristiyan's hand.

"We got married," she said. "We got married, and went to the Atacama Desert for our honeymoon while Lucien was away, training with Beau."

"I hope it is all right with both of you. I mean, I haven't asked your permission, and I most certainly would have if you had been—"

He didn't finish, because Georgia jumped up and hugged her daughter; hugged Kristiyan, laughing and crying at the same time.

"But we are so thrilled for both of you! Oh—what a wonderful homecoming gift."

"Yes, indeed," Sebastián said, putting an arm around Kristiyan's shoulders. "Now you and I can go off for an evening out, and not get back till the sun is rising, and—you know, do that man thing where you get a bit drunk and sing out of tune, neither of us mentioning the topic; but when we come back it is all settled."

"Oh, Sebastián!" Octavia gave him a hug.

"And as for you, my constantly and consistently surprising daughter, I wish you all the happiness in the world. And make sure you look after this man very well. I doubt that there is anyone else with his patience and determination on the planet."

They all drank a toast.

Sebastián went to sit next to Lucien.

"And I see that there is a new member who has come to join the Adobe community. Lucien, perhaps you would like to introduce us. He must think we are very rude not to have asked sooner."

Lucien stood up, and at once Beau came to stand next to him.

"I would like to introduce you," he said formally. "Mister Bojangles—my father, Sebastián, and my mother, Georgia.

"He is opening up the world for me," he added.

"We call him Mister Beau, or just Beau for short."

Whereof One Cannot Speak

"Raho! Come in! I am so glad you are back."

Raho pulled up the familiar cane chair and sat, looking at Octavia.

"I see you have been very busy while I was away. Have you finished everything that you wanted to do? What about the one you were wrestling with when I left?"

"It is over here."

She led him to where all the finished works were displayed.

"You have changed the serpent's eyes. What a difference it makes."

"What do you see in them?"

"When I left, they were filled with rage and venom. The body still shows that; but the eyes are uncertain. What did you discover?"

Octavia recounted the process, leaving out any reference to Lucien and Sofia.

"And I must thank you, Raho, for your patience with me—and all those infuriating questions. You have taught me so much."

"I have not taught you anything."

She chuckled.

"Raho to the end! Well, because of your presence I have learned a lot."

"That's a different matter."

He stood back. "So you have finished. Are you happy with it?"

"I suppose so."

"You don't sound very excited. Not what you intended, perhaps?"

"Well—it's not exactly what I thought it would be."

"And so—"

"It's a bit like climbing a steep mountain for years and years; and when you get to the top, you realize it is the wrong mountain."

"There are no wrong mountains."

Octavia looked to see if he was joking.

"I mean it. Sometimes we have to climb a mountain—it might take our whole life—just to know that it is not what we are searching for. How else would we find out? Paradoxically, it is exactly what we need."

"I am not following you."

"As long as we are seeking something, we will of course find everything else! How could it be otherwise?"

Octavia said nothing.

"Are you not happy with the work itself—its composition, its technical aspects?"

"Oh, technically I cannot fault it."

"So?"

"Something happened. I can't say what it was; just a huge frustration. The music I was listening to suddenly got on my nerves. I turned it off. I walked around the room, looking at each work. My feeling that something was very wrong grew and grew. Even the stars grew distant. I felt abandoned. Silly, I know."

"And then?"

"I thought about what you said: what you are looking for is what is looking. And I found myself holding the porcelain bowl you gave me; looking into its emptiness."

"And?"

"Instantly, such a sense of peace filled me. Against that, the beadworks seemed to signify nothing. That is what I mean by the wrong mountain." She ran a hand through her hair, and twisted it into a knot.

"Oh, we'll have the concert and the exhibition. It might even be a success. But somehow that is beside the point. If only one person sees it as a failure, it will be me."

"You have done very well, Octavia," Raho said.

"Are you telling me that you like all these works?"

"That is not what I said. I said that you have done very well."

"Well, I can't say that. When I look at them, I see that I have lost respect for them, and for who or what I am—thought I was. What a terrible thing to say. I haven't told this to anyone—not even Kristiyan. I think the frustration has been growing for a long time, but I never gave it space before. Looking at all of these works now, I can see why they don't satisfy me."

"And why is that?"

"They have no voice—most of them. And if some do perhaps have a small voice, it is complaining. I can't put a finger on what I mean. You know, there are some people who don't seem to be present. They talk, but they have no voice. It's something like that."

"And your voice?" he asked. "Where is that?" He pointed to the beadwork of the tall mountain, the long shadow and the falling animals.

"The idols must topple again and again, but the voice is never silenced."

Octavia frowned. Her fingers fiddled with a loose shirt-button, which eventually fell into her lap. Raho appeared not to notice.

"So tell me about the porcelain bowl."

"It just is," she said. Her fingers became still. "Raho, I will never tire of it—its emptiness; its silence. And yet—it speaks! What is that voice?"

Raho shrugged and said nothing.

"I read the Kabir poem, by the way; how he says that all those things—canyons and pine mountains, the music from the strings no one touches and hundreds of millions of stars—can be found in its emptiness. What an extraordinary vision!"

"Anything else?"

"The statement: 'the God whom I love is inside.' It moves me so. Did he mean inside the clay jug?"

"I didn't write it. I can only know what comes to me."

"And that is—?"

"Yes and no. But that is only what I get. Another person will get something else—or possibly the same as me. Who knows?"

They were both quiet.

"As this work seems to be such a failure in your eyes, what is it that you would like to see?"

"An empty room—with the porcelain bowl on the floor, in the center of it."

"And where would you be?"

"Somewhere else."

"Ah!"

Raho bowed, and left her sitting there.

Octavia got up, and moved all the works to one side of the room. She pulled her work-bench and the frame to the other side. The chairs, the easel and the table with the four stones she placed near the door.

When the space was clear, she took the porcelain bowl and placed it underneath the skylight. In front of it she put a cushion; sat down on it, listening.

How does one address such a silence? Or does it listen to my silence?

She made a rueful face.

But you are not silent, Octavia, are you? You are one big noise!

She sat, willing her mind to be quiet. But the room was soon full of her jabbering. It made her think of someone or something drowning; grabbing frantically at anything in reach—to save her? To blame? Her childhood; the unsympathetic secretary

366

at the university enrollment office; that she didn't have a wise grandmother to guide her as a young child; that she had never had any friends; that she never seemed to fit in anywhere. She was the odd one—and on and on and on!

At last she came to the end of it. She was almost in tears.

And then, in the silence, she heard a new voice.

"It isn't the beadworks, Octavia—or Raho, or the stars, or anything or anyone else.

"It is you!"

She almost laughed.

"It has always been me," she said out loud.

Octavia sat still, her attention on the small bowl. It seemed to be asking a question. But the question had no words. She remembered taking out the small note, and reading it.

"What you are looking for is what is looking."

But I am the one who is looking.

Still it eluded her.

What did meaning really mean? What was underneath the concept? What was the image for this?

She knew it was right in front of her.

"Stop hiding! I know you are there!"

In rage, frustration, excitement, and something—or nothing—else, she gave a yell—

"What you are looking for is what is looking!"

The silence that followed shouted back at her.

Octavia leaned forward, and gazed into the porcelain bowl—at nothing; at its emptiness; its silence.

Perhaps its sole purpose is to give shape to the emptiness.

She repeated the phrase. She knew she was tiptoeing around some profound insight.

What does it mean, to give shape to emptiness?

She went and sat in her chair; gazed up through the skylight at the clear New Mexico sky; gazed in wonder at the aching, blue emptiness above her. She knew the stars were there. In their vast and unknowable wastes of time—or timelessness—she knew they held the secrets to her origins. Since childhood—since infancy—she had listened to their bright silence, not knowing what it was she heard. It was impossible to speak about this, but that she heard them—that was what mattered; that, and the realization that she had never been alone.

Raho, those blue eyes of yours are not as innocent as they look! You have set me up.

So what did it matter that the beadworks were or weren't—whatever? Or whether they asked a question, or didn't?

What did anything matter? She was a part of it, and she was all of it. And this now—this fleeting, indefinable and utterly immeasurable now—was everything.

One by one, all the people she loved passed before her eyes: Kristiyan, her parents, Lucien and Sofia, Sister Piadosa and all the nuns, Raho, Alejandro; all the musicians—Santiago, Salvador and Reuben; and dear, patient Gregorio. Everyone who had been a part of her life—they had all been there for her.

How have I been there for them?

I suppose I have been me—whatever that is.

Even as she thought this, the image of the white wolf appeared to her.

She would begin the new work tomorrow.

The Other Room

Octavia was at the O'Keeffe Gallery in Santa Fe, hanging her beadworks with the help of the gallery staff. The lighting technician would be arriving soon. He had found a way to have each work lit from two angles—one light fading out as the other faded in. The viewer would not be particularly aware of the lights, but would notice the shifts in the reflection of the beads.

She wanted to finish all the setting up before Kristiyan arrived, so that they could walk around together, and discuss what changes, if any, needed to be made. The gallery men would still be available to do this.

The last images to be hung were the miniature icons. Octavia decided to put them on a long screen wall, just inside the entrance to the main gallery. She hoped that they would lead people to expect beautiful images, and that the dramatic contrast between the miniatures and beadworks would create a feeling of displacement.

"Where have you been keeping these exquisite icons?" Kristiyan asked in wonder. He stood in front of each image, marveling at the precision of each minute detail. "They are utterly beautiful!"

He turned to smile at her.

"I must say, you are a dark horse. Not a word about them. When did you make these? They are so—so exquisite."

Octavia described her ritual.

"It all looks very professional. Excellent! Impeccable," Kristiyan said to the gallery assistants. "The lighting is extraordinary. I never understood before what Octavia meant when she said that light was one of the key elements of her beadwork tapestries. Thank you all so much."

He shook hands all round. The men picked up their tools, and left.

"And now, Kristiyan," said Octavia, "I have a surprise for you."

"Another one?"

"Yes."

She walked down the length of the main room, toward a closed double door-way.

"Do you remember that I mentioned having something separate from the main exhibition?"

"Yes. Of course."

Octavia opened both the doors, revealing what Kristiyan took to be an empty room; empty, apart from a white screen that stood at the far end, which held a single frame. He could not make out any details.

"Go in," she said.

"Now walk down to the screen."

Kristiyan stood in front of the single beadwork. It followed very faithfully in the tradition of many Russian icons he had seen.

From the center of the formal composition, the extraordinary blue gaze of the white wolf met his eyes. Behind him was a vast, snow-covered forest.

All around the wolf was white snow. The wolf too was white, so that he was almost invisible, and you had to search for him in the whiteness. Only the startling blue eyes led you to his form.

The texture of his coat and that of the snow differed slightly. Octavia had used a tiny, silver bead to give an electric sheen to the thick, white fur. The snow had the faintest of blue shadows.

Kristiyan stood, transfixed. He had never seen such eyes before. Never. They held his gaze in their blue light.

What was it that it evoked for him? A vivid memory: an image called up from his childhood. A troika, passing in the snow: the sound of bells; the utter purity of it—and his gratitude for the endurance of beauty, even in the midst of troubled times.

Octavia waited.

She could not know all that he was feeling; experiencing. She did not need to know.

What she did know was that she was offering him the most precious of all gifts. She was showing him all that she was—had ever been.

The authority of the wolf's presence was palpable.

She had placed him and his landscape at the center of the work, contained by a circular border of gold beads. This, in turn, was surrounded by an ornate square border. In each corner she had placed a Russian minaret. She had given them the same colors as her four stones. They rose up into a cold, low sky.

Above everything, one star shone its cold brilliance.

Kristiyan stood in silence.
"It is my wedding gift to you," Octavia said.
He leaned forward to read the title on the small card. It read—
"One Breath..."

Duende

"...and their footprints blow
over the plain—
they'll not be back—
no—never again..."

Catherine was wearing the dress she had worn to María's first and only concert. She had not worn it since that evening. It had been kept in tissue, aired from time to time, and then put back in its cedar-wood chest. It was blue—a beautiful shade of blue that matched her eyes. Her husband, Don Lorenzo, had ordered the raw silk fabric from France. But it was what she wore on María's big night, and that overruled any other association it might have had to anything or anyone else. The simple elegance of its design accentuated her regal posture. The years that had passed since María's concert had not diminished her looks in any way. She was still a woman who turned the heads of men, both young and old.

She sat in the front row of the Santa Fe concert hall, half-reading the program, although she knew it by heart—in truth because she did not want to be recognized. How would she explain her disappearance?

She was grateful to be surrounded by so many people who either lived at The Adobe, or who, like Raho, Alejandro and Francesca, were very much a part of it. Sofia's foster-parents were there with their son, Pedro—excited to be at such a popular function—as well as many of the parents of children who went to Caradoc's play-school.

And, of course, Madame Jolie—and next to her, Louise from the bead shop with her husband.

"Are you all right, Catherine?"

Octavia, sitting next to her, could sense the older woman's tension.

"I will be fine, dear. I am just excited and nervous for Sofia."

But it was far more than that. Images from María's concert came flooding back to her. She remembered telling her to take the blue cloak with a hood, even though it was not cold. She knew that if Lorenzo saw her flaming red hair flying loose, he would forbid her to leave the house. She recalled his rage at seeing her like that on stage, knowing that all his influential guests would see her as well—not that they would see anything amiss, she thought grimly.

Stop it, Catherine, she told herself. You are here, now. This is Sofia's evening. Be happy for her, and know that María would be so proud to have such a daughter.

The house lights dimmed. The musicians came on stage to the sound of applause, and took their seats. Santiago followed, bowed to the audience, and beckoned to Sofia in the wings.

There was a fresh burst of applause at her entrance. Many in the audience had heard her sing in small concerts before, and gave her an enthusiastic welcome. She was wearing a long, red dress, cut low and very plain. No jewelry. None was needed, for her hair formed a halo of red fire about her head that was dazzling under the stage lights. Catherine thought she looked like a pagan earth goddess with the face of an angel.

There was no introduction. The program stated that there would be none.

Octavia would never forget that first performance—for two reasons. First, because of the thrill of hearing this extraordinary work played in public. But she had anticipated that.

What she was not prepared for—what had not so much as entered her head— was the profound impact it would have on Catherine.

When Sofia stepped forward to sing the introduction of the animals—their early calls, accompanied by the sounds of wind and open spaces from the musicians— she saw Catherine lean forward, as if to draw in every nuance of Sofia's ethereal voice. At times it was impossible to tell the instruments from her voice, so perfectly did they blend into one.

Octavia, watching Catherine's face, felt her heart break open.

How much—how many images—must be passing through her mind? How many dreams she must have had for herself, and then for María? And all the cruelty they had suffered, without anyone ever seeing it—that was what made it so terrifying; that in this day and age such violence could continue, hidden, for so long.

Octavia, unnoticed by Catherine, watched her face mirror the emotional landscape of the music; saw her nod in recognition of the haunting lament theme as it reappeared again and again.

What did it matter, Octavia thought, who said what about this whole concert and exhibition? This—this moment, watching one woman's entire life being validated—this is what it is all about; this one person, receiving it so deeply. If we have done all of this for Catherine alone, we have not failed.

Can one person be the whole world? Could that be true?

The first faint introduction of the lament theme perhaps already prophesied a future holocaust for wild animals, and the slow death of the even more ancient land-scape. But as the work progressed, there was no mistaking the violence that was being done.

Catherine had a hand up to her face. Tears were falling down her cheeks. She saw images of María, bullied into submission; María being punished for daring to defy her father; María in her wedding-dress, brought back home by an enraged de la Cruz and thrown to the floor, just lying there like a crushed water-lily; the image of María sitting on the floor, cutting all her dresses into long ribbons.

And she remembered the last day she ever saw her daughter—her head shaved by her own hand, her long, red hair hammered into the hated silver comb her father had given her; her final act of rebellion. De la Cruz had found it later, hanging up in his gun-room with the elk trophies.

Octavia reached out, and took Catherine's hand in hers. Their eyes met briefly.

The final movement evoked the utter emptiness of a world that had lost its soul.

Sofia's voice, led by the chthonic vibrations of Kristiyan's cello, grew down into the depths of dark silence, far beyond the world of beginnings and endings. It was an unholy sound—the last breath of the wind.

Octavia felt the hairs on her neck rise and prickle.

This—this is *Sofia?*

She listened with awe to the sounds of haunting that were coming from this small person, who was engaging her entire body in the extreme grief of this final ex-odus.

Octavia wondered from what depths of memory she had drawn this energy up into her voice. She was like one possessed—taken over by dark sounds; the fading cries of creatures falling into night.

And now Sofia's voice embraced something between animal cries and her own sobs, which seemed to be torn out of her, and which moved in and out of the notes of the lament. The music grew in intensity, and Sofia's voice with it.

Octavia started at a sudden recognition—Sofia was the red angel!

Sofia!

Here was Alejandro's vision, which had defied all interpretation; an angel of earth and fire and blood. How silently it had spoken to her—for her whole life.

What an extraordinary connection—she and Sofia! And Lucien!

And here was the Virgin in the burning bush! The Virgin, not consumed by the fire. What did that mean?

The last sounds of life faded. And then it was over. From the musicians came the echoes of the lament—and Sofia's voice floating over vast, empty spaces where nothing moved; a disembodied voice, floating on the wind.

And then, silence.

A long silence.

Catherine was the first to stand.

And then, like a roar from behind her, came the applause—almost drowning out the shouts of "Viva!—Duende!"

As wave after wave of applause sounded and resounded, and more and more voices could be heard shouting the highest praise for singer and musicians, Catherine turned to Octavia. Tears streamed down her cheeks.

"However will I thank you for this—this...?"

The applause continued.

"I have no words...No words..."

Octavia stood surveying the audience. Did anyone know what the concert was addressing? Or was it just a damn good little show?

"That is for them to decide," she said, not quite under her breath.

A tall figure came walking toward her. He gave a little bow. Raho!

"Ah! Octavia. You are to be congratulated. You and all the others have done magnificently. Are you happy with the result?"

"I think so. I just wonder what everyone made of it."

"Just listen to the applause. Doesn't that tell you?"

"No."

Raho raised an eyebrow.

"Perhaps there is further work for you, then. It will be interesting to see what that might be. But meanwhile, you have done very well."

He gave another bow, and was about to go, but paused for a moment and turned back to face her.

"Ah, yes," he said, almost as an afterthought. "You might like to ask yourself a question."

She stared at him.

"A question? What question?"

"You might like to ask yourself this: what is the face of the coming guest?"

"What is the what—?" she asked.

But he had gone.

The White Doves

"There is something I want to give you."

Sebastián found Octavia in her studio, working on designs for her new project. Of all the works she had made for Lament, it was the subtle, hidden quality of the mountain lion that most intrigued her.

Now she wanted to make a body of work containing similar hidden shapes that meant nothing; that had no message other than their visual impact. She wanted people to have an experience—the way music is experienced—not an understanding. Above all, she wanted to achieve something like the emptiness of the small bowl Raho had given her. She wanted the light, the brilliance of the beads to re-awaken the memory of a childhood reverence.

"And I want to give it to you next to Magdalena's cross, on the pink hill where the yuccas grow. Do you think you can make it up there?"

"I'm sure I can. But why there?"

"Well, she is my mother and your grandmother, so the three of us have something in common. Not just ancestry, although that as well."

He smiled at her bewilderment.

"It has something—no, everything—to do with other."

"Other?"

"Yes."

"Yes?"

"It has to do with knowing something."

"Knowing what?"

"That's just it. I can't tell you. But I want to give you this instead. It is the closest I have ever come to it."

"Okay. All very mysterious. When would you like to go?"

"Now?"

"I'll just get my stick."

They sat together below the white cross, on the black basalt rock. The late afternoon sun was just beginning to put some pink into the sky.

"Your grandmother would have loved you so much. I only wish the two of you could have met. You would both be so surprised."

"Why surprised?"

"Because you are alike in so many ways—and you look just like her. When she drove into Las Madres, the woman who worked at the rectory for Father Octavio—Elena was her name—told him that a new blessing had come into the community. And she added: 'Mark my words, father; she is other.'"

"And did Magdalena ever find out what it was—this other thing?"

"Perhaps. But I don't think she ever thought about it. Or rather it was so close to her, so much a part of her that it would not have occurred to her to name it. Maybe, in the end, it cannot be named. It was as natural to her as breathing. But everyone else felt it. They might not have named it that. Quite possibly they never even associated it with her."

"So what did it look like?"

"It was like a magnetic field—an electric energy that surrounded her; almost as if she was a transformer. Wherever she went, things happened."

"Like what?"

"Well, her plants grew out of season—thrived. People came together around her, and suddenly their lives were enriched. Things that hadn't worked before began to work. And it was irresistible. People who tried to resist found their lives becoming increasingly uncomfortable. Things just happened around her."

"And what does this have to do with me?"

"Everything. You are just like her. Look what has happened here over the past years! So much; so many changes. Comfortable? Uncomfortable? The question is irrelevant. But were they resistible? Not even a chance. There are some who say that the duende speaks through such people."

Octavia looked at him.

"You mean that blood in the throat thing that Madame Jolie speaks about?"

"That is one way it shows up. But another day for that," he said.

He handed her a small book. "I'm going to leave this with you. Open it at the bookmark once I have gone."

Octavia sat, watching him make his way down the zigzag path until it turned a corner, and he was gone. Only then did she read the title page: The Book of Hours by Rainer Maria Rilke.

She opened it at the mark, and read the poem. It had been translated by Robert Bly.

"I live my life in growing orbits..."

When she came to the closing lines, she repeated them out loud:

"...and I still do not know if I am a falcon, a storm
or a great song."

Octavia heard the sudden rush of wings. The white doves had been released, and were taking to the sky for their evening flight. She watched them circle the small valley as they had done for so many years, ever since they arrived with María; watched how, for an instant, they disappeared as they turned, only to reappear with the light full on their wings again.

And they will still be here long after we have gone, she thought. They are María's song—a song you can see! She smiled at the notion.

Octavia sat, taking in the beauty of the ever-changing, ever-the-same flight patterns as the white doves rose to clear the tall cottonwoods. She watched them turn and fly low over the fields, and rise up toward the window where María used to stand and watch them.

Nothing ever dies, she thought. The one breath is everywhere. Only the form changes.

She read the closing lines again, and then put the book down; looked out over the valley at the cottonwoods, and the hills beyond; up at the sky, which was now on fire with red and purple and gold.

She remembered the day she laid the black stones for the spiral path that led to her studio; and how, before that, Alejandro had shown her Magdalena's labyrinth herb garden. Her father had laid those stones.

Is everything a pattern that repeats and repeats—never quite the same—until something manages to break free from the grooves of habit or control? And yet, even that is part of an even greater pattern. It is all one. How could you take any one thing out of it?

But of course! Why had it taken her such a long time to see this?

One breath!

She recalled, as vividly as if it was yesterday, her conversation with Kristiyan about fado.

It speaks to me with such compassion. With all the yearning, the joy and the utter grief that life can bring.

But it goes far, far deeper even than that. I feel something move in me like a strong, deep ocean current that is unperturbed by transitory things.

It is as if these songs hold all that is best and worst in us. But they make no judgment. Something like that. They know all the terrible things that happen to us, and still there is no complaint.

I hear how the past is somehow always with us in the present. It is part of us. It makes us who we are. Perhaps it is only we who make that separation. In those voices I hear what perhaps only those who have suffered much and survived can know: that the acceptance of fate is always now!

I hear the pain we feel when bad things happen; the questions that cannot be answered. And yet it is both wild and mysterious, and it brings with it such a strong sense of celebration; in spite of everything.

And then she began to laugh.

She laughed till the tears streamed down her cheeks—laughed till her body ached with it; great streams of laughter that welled up out of her, wave after wave of it. It floated out, till the whole valley was filled with it.

From somewhere below, where the light was beginning to turn indigo with the approach of night, she fancied she heard an answering echo—the sound of a woman's laughter, which rose up out of the past like a fragrance on the breath of the wind; a trace of lavender.

And then it was all one: the laughter, the fragrance, the purple sunset and the blue light; and through all of it, the white doves flying those timeless spirals, carved out of the sky by their flight.

Had she imagined it?

She didn't think so.

But she couldn't be sure.

EPILOGUE

What Is the Call?

He was looking directly at her.

His eyes were unmistakable.

He stood in the light of his own clear, blue gaze—surrounded by the silence of a vast, white emptiness.

How long had he been there? A thousand years? Two thousand? Less than a heartbeat?

He turned, as he had turned once before, and began to lope off effortlessly over the pristine whiteness, into the measureless reaches of unknowing.

She knew she would follow him.

She knew at once that this was her country—this unknowable, and at the same time instantly familiar otherness; this space that might be anything you allowed it to be, if you dared to let it be—nothing.

There was no thought of turning back. This was far more than the end of one thing, and the beginning of another. She had no words for it. No words for herself. She had never been here before, and she had always been here—unseeing and unseen.

This was not a new step. And it had nothing to do with time or distance.

And then she heard it: a strange, keening call that floated over the white emptiness. It was a voice that carried earth and sky in it; a voice that was not separate from the land. It was in a language she did not know, but she knew instantly that the call was for her.

"I am coming," she said softly.

Some distance ahead of her, the white wolf stopped and turned. She could feel the pull of that blue gaze.

"I am coming," she whispered again.

He turned once more, and set off with the same effortless lope. He was heading for the forest.

378

And now she heard the raw music of earth and sky once more; the high, keening sound of ancient chanting, carried by the wind.

Octavia looked up at the leaden sky, at the swirling mists; at the two dark birds floating above her.

"I am coming," she said—

And then the emptiness embraced her.

The white wolf disappeared.

And she with it.

READER'S GUIDE

1. The novel is divided into four parts, corresponding to four different colors. In three cases, these colors are linked to the color of Octavia's work-room at a particular time. In what way are these color choices reflected in the themes and concerns that are raised in each part? Is it significant that these colors also correspond to the colors of the four stones Octavia later remembers choosing as a child? Finally, how do you understand the significance of Alejandro giving Octavia a red angel when she is a baby?

2. The morning and evening flight of the white doves is a recurring theme throughout the novel. It is represented as a source of both pleasure and reflection for most of the main characters. In what ways are these flight patterns significant? You could refer specifically to Octavia's remarks about patterns toward the end of the novel.

3. Throughout Part 1, there are short chapters—called Images—that interrupt the main narrative. These sections feature variations on ritual acts that are often not immediately comprehensible to the reader. What are the different kinds of ritual that are explored in the novel, and how does their purpose change? For instance, how do the early rituals described in the Image sections differ from Octavia's ritual for the four stones in Part 4?

4. At the end of Part 1, Octavia laments: "Why do we make everything so small—so safe?" At about the same time, Alejandro becomes fascinated with the beauty and wildness of a black mare, and begins to have recurring dreams about her. What is the understanding of wildness that these two characters share, and how is it explored in the novel? Octavia's commitment to conserving wilderness offers an obvious starting-point for this discussion. Also comment on the ways in which different characters experience their own wildness as under threat, and how they seek to protect and nurture it.

5. Early in her development as an artist, Octavia reads the following piece of advice from a manual about working with beads: "Remember to step back from time to time. It is a good idea to have a moveable light to see the effect of the brilliance and the shadow in the overall work." How is this advice relevant to the relationship of Octavia and Alejandro to their respective disciplines? You could refer to Alejandro's response to the call he received as a boy, and how he comes to understand his calling as a much older man.

6. In a chapter called The Cornerstone, Sister Piadosa has a conversation with Octavia about

the meaning and importance of discipline. If one thinks of discipline in terms of the broad context suggested here, it is significant that most of the novel's main characters are engaged in one discipline or another, whether associated with art, service or both. Is it possible to identify a general direction in which these relationships between the characters and their work ultimately develop? You could refer to Alejandro's response to Frank's letter, and also to Raho's remarks about the Japanese tea ceremony and the makers of tea-bowls.

7. In one of his conversations with Alejandro, Raho asks him: "Has it ever struck you that you have spent your entire life looking up—up at the stars; up at the light? And what might you discover if you allowed yourself to grow down; down into the earth?" How do you understand the term "growing down," and what is its significance in terms of Alejandro's development at this point?

8. Toward the end of Part 3, while walking the labyrinth herb garden designed by his mother, Sebastián remembers her saying that "there is only one path." How does he understand this statement differently now, as opposed to when he first heard it as a young man? You could refer to the shape of the labyrinth itself, and also to its importance as a metaphor throughout the novel.

9. Octavia's first powerful encounter with fado prompts her to comment that "the acceptance of fate is always now..." This statement has an obvious resonance in terms of her specific circumstances at the time, but how do you understand it in the context of the entire novel? You could use Alejandro's definition of a true artist as someone who is willing to be deepened by experience as a starting-point.

10. At a particular point of crisis in Octavia's work toward her exhibition, Raho pins a note to her door which reads: "Have you noticed that if you push against a horse, it will push back?" Why do you consider this to be a significant question in terms of Octavia's changing perspective? More specifically, how does it relate to the conversation she is having with Raho about anger at the time? You could also refer to the importance of questions as opposed to statements in the music Lucien comes to write toward the end of the novel.

11. There are many references to silence throughout the novel, beginning with the sentence from Wittgenstein from which it derives its title. Using the porcelain bowl Raho gives to Octavia as a starting-point, what do you think the novel is suggesting about the importance of silence and emptiness? Why do the characters find it so particularly challenging to learn about these things?

12. In one of her later journal entries, Octavia writes: "I know that there is no room for intellect in this work." She refers to the images that appear to her as "strangers with gifts." What do you think she means by these statements, and why are they important in understanding her approach to her work? Using Octavia and Alejandro's dreams as a point of reference, what do you think the role of such dreams and images might be?

13. Toward the end of the novel, Octavia writes: "Naming anything makes it smaller." Her refusal to listen to Ojos as he names the stars is a powerful demonstration of this attitude. How do you understand Octavia's particular relationship toward naming? You could refer to the way in which she is identified as "other." Why is it so important that "other" can only be experienced, but remains unexplained?

14. At several crucial points throughout the novel, Octavia finds herself in the presence of a white wolf that only she can see. The novel deliberately does not explain his sudden appearance. Rather, it is interested in the ways in which Octavia feels called by his presence, and how she responds to this call. Using the open question at the beginning of the epilogue as a starting-point, how do you understand this encounter? What does Octavia learn from it, and why is this learning so important to her? You could use the phrase "the mercy of wild things" as a point of entry when answering this question.

www.ingramcontent.com/pod-product-compliance
Lightning Source LLC
Chambersburg PA
CBHW030630020726
47493CB00006B/1641